Windrush: Jayanti's Pawns

Windrush: Jayanti's Pawns

Jack Windrush Series – Book V

Malcolm Archibald

Prelude

'Welcome to Lucknow!' Lieutenant Elliot ducked behind the embankment as an enemy cannon ball screamed overhead. 'When I'm an old man, I'll bore my grandchildren with tales of this campaign.'

'If we live to have grandchildren.' Jack leaned against the trunk of a *gul-mohur* tree beside the sunken track. 'These mutineers are giving us harder fighting than the Ruskies did at Inkerman.'

'Aye, that's for sure.' Elliot cautiously peered over the embankment. 'They never give up, do they? We beat them again and again, and still they come back.'

'Sir Colin will sort them out,' Jack said. 'We have thirty-one thousand men now, and over a hundred guns, ten times the number we had with Havelock last year. This time we'll capture Lucknow and hold it against all comers.'

The mutineers' artillery opened up in a frenzy of flame and smoke, hammering at the British positions. Jack glanced at his men. He didn't need to order them to keep their heads down; they were veterans of a score of battles and skirmishes from the earlier campaigns of Lucknow and Cawnpore, while some had been with him through the nightmare of Crimea. Two or three had even fought in Burma, six years ago. They looked back at him with steady eyes in nut-brown faces, tobacco-chewing professionals in this vicious game of war.

'Bloody pandies,' Private Thorpe muttered as a roundshot landed among the Sikh infantry to their right. 'Why don't they give up now? They know they haven't a hope with old Campbell against them.'

'It's because they're scared, Thorpey.' Coleman ejected a stream of tobacco juice onto the ground, narrowly missing a column of ants. 'Remember how General Neill treated them, even before Cawnpore?'

'He hanged the bastards,' Thorpe said. 'He hanged every one he caught.'

'That's why they're still in the field.' Coleman lifted his Enfield rifle and sighted at the walls of the Little Imambarra. 'They know what will happen if they surrender.'

'We'll hang them all.' Thorpe spoke with savage satisfaction. 'We'll hang all the murdering, backstabbing women-raping bastards.'

Jack listened without emotion. He understood the men's venom. His veterans had witnessed the well at Cawnpore where the mutineers had thrown the mutilated bodies of the British women and children they had murdered. Men such as Coleman, Riley and Thorpe had ensured the replacements were aware of the full horror of that atrocity, adding as many embellishments as they felt suitable. At a time when British men often treated their women with veneration, the Cawnpore murders created intense hatred.

'The boys are still angry,' Jack said.

Elliot nodded. 'They haven't forgotten.'

Jack checked his revolver, chamber by chamber. 'Nor have you.'

'I never will.' Elliot touched the hilt of his sword. 'I never will. The Lord tells us to forgive us our enemies, but I'll never forgive what the pandies did at Cawnpore.'

'I doubt any of us will fully trust them again.' Jack inched to the lip of the embankment, lifted his binoculars and scanned the enemy positions. He could see the heads and smoking cannon-muzzles of the defenders. Despite the British numbers, their impending attack would be a bloody experience.

'Can I take the Colours now, please, sir?' Ensign Green looked as if he should still be sitting at a school desk, rather than commanding men in battle. His face was too smooth to have felt the kiss of a razor while his long eyelashes would undoubtedly endear him to a plethora of girls.

'Not yet, Green. Wait until Sir Colin orders us forward,' Jack said.

'Yes, sir.' Green hesitated. 'This is my first battle, sir.'

'I know, ensign.' Jack forced a smile he didn't feel. 'I'm sure you'll be a credit to your family. Follow orders and do your duty.' He tapped Green's sword. 'You might have the opportunity to use that.'

'Yes, sir!' Green looked eager.

'Good luck, ensign,' Jack said. 'Now get back to your men. They need your leadership.' He watched as Green's slim figure darted back to the men. 'Sometimes, Arthur, I feel very old.'

'You are very old, respected captain, sir,' Elliot said. 'You must be all of twenty-four now.'

'I was twenty-five last month,' Jack said. 'I feel like eighty-five when I see children like Green all keen to go to war.'

'We were like that once,' Elliot said.

'It seems a long time ago.' Jack lifted his binoculars again and studied the triple row of earthworks that protected their objective, and the mutineers that waited for them.

The Little Imambarra loomed ahead, another palace within a walled garden. If the British took the Little Imambarra, there would be nothing between them and the palace of the Kaisarbagh. Beyond the Kaisarbagh lay Lucknow, with its army of mutineers and rebels that defied the right of the British to own India.

Elliot lifted a battered silver hip flask to his lips, swallowed, and offered Jack a drink.

'No, thank you.' Jack concentrated on the Kaisarbagh. In common with nearly all the palaces that adorned the ancient city of Lucknow, a massive wall surrounded a rectangular enclosure in which was a series of gardens and once-beautiful buildings of marble. Although the elite had built the compounds for their pleasure, each made a natural defensive position that the British had to assault on their slow advance. The mutineers had added earthworks and ranks of cannon.

'Thirty thousand trained mutineers are inside Lucknow, they say,' Elliot murmured, 'with another fifty thousand volunteers.'

Jack didn't ask where Elliot obtained his figures. 'It's the volunteers that bother me,' he said. 'We can beat the mutineers; after all, we trained and armed them, so we know how they fight. These matchlock-men and warriors, the Indian soldiers loyal to a native Rajah, or to Oudh.' He shook his head. 'They're not fighting for some fancied grievance over greased cartridges or some such. They're fighting for their monarchs, much as we are fighting for the queen. They're patriots, and that makes them more dangerous.'

'As long as our men are even more dangerous,' Elliot said, 'I won't worry too much about the pandies.'

A trio of British rockets whooshed off, each leaving a trail of red sparks. One veered off course and soared straight into the sky, while the others exploded before they reached their target, leaving a smudge of white powder smoke drifting in the air.

'That'll scare the birds,' Elliot said. 'It certainly won't do anything else.'

'I hope Sir Colin gives the order to attack soon.' Jack slid back onto the track and bit the tip of a cheroot. 'The longer we wait, the less daylight we'll have to fight in.'

'He's not the fastest of commanders.' Elliot scratched a Lucifer and lit Jack's cheroot. 'He is the most thorough, though. He won't attack until he's certain of victory.'

'Windrush!' Colonel Grey strode along the 113th's position, not deigning to duck when the mutineers fired a salvo of grapeshot.

'Yes, sir.' Jack hid his irritation. He needed to concentrate on the impending attack; he did not wish his commanding officer to distract him.

'I want you to take Number Two Company to the left flank.' Grey stroked his whiskers as the enemy musketeers fired a volley. One musket ball raised a tiny puff of dust as it hit the embankment between Jack and the colonel.

'Yes, sir.'

'You'll know that Nana Sahib led the uprising at Cawnpore,' Grey said.

'Yes, sir.' *Why do senior officers state the obvious?*

'Nana Sahib's bodyguard is said to be in the Little Imambarra.' Grey said. 'If you see them, destroy them.'

'Yes, sir,' Jack said. 'How will I recognise them?'

'You'll know them when you see them.' Grey nodded and strode away.

'He's a queer beggar,' Elliot said. 'We've to destroy Nana Sahib's bodyguard. So what do we do?'

'We take the left flank and destroy everything that opposes us,' Jack said. 'As we always do.'

Jack lifted his head as a bugle blared in the rear. 'That's it! We're going in.' He raised his voice. 'Ready, Number Two Company of the 113th!'

The bugle sounded again, its brassy notes clear against the batter of artillery. There was no hesitation as the British and Sikhs rose to the attack.

'Oh Lord, I shall be very busy this day,' Elliot whispered. 'I may forget thee, but do not forget me, a sinner.' Taking another quick pull at his silver hip flask, he stood up and drew his sword. 'Follow me, lads!'

'Cry Havelock!' Coleman gave the battle cry that Elliot had created the previous year when they formed part of Havelock's small army that battered its way to Cawnpore. 'And let loose the dogs of war!'

'Let loose the dogs,' Thorpe echoed and looked at Coleman for approval.

Ensign Green held the Colours high, the yellow-buff fly with the number 113 faded by sun and damp, torn by musket balls but still proud. Two yards away, rangy Sergeant Greaves held the Queen's Colours. The multi-crosses of the Union Flag announced that Queen Victoria's fighting men were returning to reclaim the city.

After days when the British artillery had thundered to breach the defences, and the mutineers' guns had responded with a will, now the bayonets of the British and Sikhs and the kukris of the Nepalese would contest the issue with the matchlocks and tulwars of the defenders.

Mutineers and warriors lined the wall of the Little Imambarra, firing muskets at the advancing British lines. White powder smoke jetted out to lie thick in the dense air, so the British seemed to be moving towards a fog that partially concealed the first defensive wall. Orange muzzle flares flashed through the smoke and men began to fall. The Sikhs forged forward, with the 10th Foot – the Lincolnshires, matching them step for step.

'Keep moving!' Jack yelled. 'Leave the wounded for the doolie-bearers.' He spoke for the benefit of the replacements. The veterans didn't need instructions. Jack flinched as a musket ball whizzed past his head, swore and increased the pace. His men followed, cursing and stumbling, with Riley singing a soft song.

'Wait there, you bastards,' Logan muttered. 'Wee Donnie's coming for you. Don't run away, you pandy buggers.'

'They won't run,' Riley said. 'They'll still be there.'

'I hate crossing open ground under fire.' Thorpe ducked as something flicked at his shako. 'Bloody hell!'

'Think of it as penance for all those sins and crimes you've committed,' Coleman said. 'And the reward will be killing these murdering buggers.'

Twenty yards now, with the mutineers' musketry increasing. A six-pounder cannon roared, spreading grapeshot among the Sikhs, who raised their pace, stepped over the dead and writhing wounded and yelled their war cry.

Jack grunted as he heard '*Jai Khalsa Ji*' – "Victory to the Khalsa", the old battle cry when the Sikhs had been an independent nation.

'Follow me, lads or the Sikhs will beat us to it!' Jack broke into a run, tripped over a loose rock, staggered, recovered and swore as Elliot overtook him.

'Come on, sir!' Riley hesitated. 'Are you hit?'

Shaking his head, Jack ran on.

Logan, the smallest man in the regiment, was first to the wall. 'I cannae get up!' Logan glared upwards jabbing uselessly with his bayonet, until Riley threw himself up the wall, lay along the top and extended a hand downward.

'Come on Logie and watch you don't stick your bayonet in me!'

Scrambling up, Logan slashed at the defenders, using his bayonet as a sabre to clear a space. 'Come on you bastards; wee Donnie's here!'

In front of Jack, the artillery had done its job and tumbled in a section of wall, with sword-wielding warriors waiting in the breach. They looked like something from the Middle Ages – lithe, dark-skinned men with turbans and round shields.

Jack shot one, staggered as another slammed at him with a shield, fired again and missed. A warrior lifted his sword, screaming his hatred, and doubled over as Ensign Green thrust the staff of the Regimental Colour into his stomach.

'Good man, Green.' Jack rolled away, aimed and fired. The bullet smashed into the warrior's chest, knocking him backwards.

'Thank you, sir.' Green looked shocked at the carnage around him.

'Come on, ensign!' Jack saw Elliot exchanging sword strokes with a long-bearded Rajput as the Sikhs surged onward to his right and the 10th Foot charged at a second defensive line.

'To me, 113th!' Jack ran on. 'Don't let the Poachers get in front of us!'

Mutineer infantry clustered around a small battery of artillery, firing muskets in support of the six-pounders. A sudden roar from the rear alerted Jack, and he saw the Sikhs burst open an arched gate and charge into the enclosure. A slender, active man rallied the defenders with shouts in a high, if muffled, voice. Rough grey cloth covered the lower half of his face, while he had pulled a black turban low over his forehead, emphasising the intensity of his eyes.

'That man looks dangerous,' Elliot gasped. 'He might be Nana Sahib's bodyguard that Colonel Grey told us to look for.'

'In that case, he should be with Nana Sahib.' Jack levelled his revolver, fired and missed. 'Damn the man.'

The man in the black turban lifted his tulwar high and shouted something Jack couldn't understand. The mutineers gathered around him, facing the advancing British, panting, some yelling, bayonets and swords held ready.

Something plucked at Jack's sleeve as he looked around for his men. They followed Ensign Green with the Colours, khaki-clothed, sweat-stained and swearing.

'Come to me and keep your discipline, lads!' Jack roared. 'We'll hit them together, not as a mob of individuals.'

The 113th stopped for a moment to dress their lines and pushed on, bayonets levelled.

The man in the black turban brandished his tulwar. *'Maro Firinghi Soor'* – "kill the foreign pigs", and his followers repeated his words.

'Maro Firinghi Soor!'

'Remember Cawnpore!' the British replied.

'Bole so nihal Sat siri Akaal' – "The one who believes in the truth of God is immortal" the Sikhs shouted as they rushed forward.

The defenders were fighting hard, with warriors clashing swords against the bayonets of the 10th and 113th Foot, firing their clumsy matchlocks while the mutineers, the men who had recently been sepoys in the Honourable East India Company's Bengal Army, fired and withdrew in sullen discipline. Jack saw the man in the black turban lead a counter-attack to check the advance of the 10th Foot.

Jack lunged forward, only for a surge of desperate warriors to halt him. 'Get that fellow!' He pointed to Black Turban. 'He's rallying the enemy.'

'Yes, sir!' Green shouted.

'Logan! Riley – go with the ensign!' Jack motioned two of his veterans forward.

The fighting intensified as the mutineers once more rallied behind the man with the black turban. Jack levelled his revolver and fired, missing again. 'Damn this thing!' Running closer, he saw Logan shoot at a mutineer and then lunge forward with the bayonet as Riley knelt and aimed at a desperate farmer armed with a crude hoe.

The man in the black turban man swapped his tulwar from his right hand to his left and slashed sideways. One of the British replacements fell, staring as his intestines tumbled out in a pink and white coil. He opened his mouth in a silent scream, trying to replace his insides as the man in the black turban parried the swing of a Sikh sword, disarmed his adversary with a twist of the wrist and decapitated the man. The Sikh's head lifted on a jet of blood and landed on the ground.

'Jesus, that fellow is good,' Jack said.

'I'll get him, sir!' Holding the Colours as a lance, Green charged forward.

'No, Green!' Jack knew the youngster would have little chance against a man who was so expert. Aiming his revolver, Jack fired again, to see his target immediately duck. *Who the devil are you?*

'Green! Come back!'

The man in the black turban man straightened up, saw Green with the Colours and stepped forward. As if in slow motion, Jack saw Green swing the staff, miss, and Black Turban slice forward with his tulwar. The blade took Green across the face. He screamed shrilly as a child and fell, dropping the Colours.

'Save the Colours!' Jack yelled, jumping forward. The Colours were the soul of the regiment and to lose them was a major disgrace. He felt sympathy for Green, but the lad had signed on as a soldier and had to take his chance.

Black Turban shouted something, and a rush of mixed warriors and mutineers charged between the 113th and the Colours. One lifted the staff and held it high, with the yellow-buff fly crushed and stained with Green's blood. A surge of mutineers came to help, cheering at their psychological triumph.

'Come on, lads!' Logan led the counter-charge, sliding under a mutineer's bayonet to gut him, roll across the ground and rise in the middle of the enemy ranks. When Riley followed, with Coleman and Thorpe at his back, all the fight left the mutineers, and they fled in disorder. The warriors remained, standing around their leader, clashing their tulwars on round shields and flaunting their prize. The man in the black turban stepped to their front, lithe, slim and undoubtedly in command.

Jack aimed at Black Turban and fired his final round, cursed as he hit a retreating mutineer, holstered his pistol and drew his sword. 'You and me, Black-hat!'

Black Turban waited for him, tossing his tulwar from hand-to-hand, his eyes focused on Jack. The sun glinted blood red on a ruby ring on the index finger of his left hand.

Sergeant Greaves was at the forefront of the charge that smashed into the warriors' flank, and a melee began, bayonet and rifle butt against sword and shield. The force of the 113th pushed the enemy back, and the wiry man holding the Colours staggered as Logan smashed his rifle butt into his face.

'Sir!' Jack didn't see who shouted, he remained intent on facing Black-Turban. 'The Sikhs are in the Kaisarbagh!'

The man in the black turban glanced down at the writhing Green and slid his tulwar into the ensign's groin, twisted and stepped back into the mass of the warriors as a corporal lifted the Colours.

'You monster!' Jack roared as Green's screams redoubled. 'I'll find you!'

A bank of powder smoke momentarily obscured the enemy as Jack knelt beside the writhing ensign.

'Let's have a look at you,' Jack said and flinched. The tulwar had destroyed Green's face, splitting one eye, cutting off his nose and leaving a bleeding gash across his mouth. No girl would look at him again. Jack only glanced at the bloody horror of Green's groin and looked away quickly. 'It's not too bad,' he said. 'The surgeons will soon put you right.'

Patting Green's shoulder, Jack stood up. In the few seconds he'd spent with Green, the battle had moved on. The 113th was roaring over the walls of the Kaisarbagh, in company with the 10th and the Sikhs.

Without time to reload his revolver, Jack drew his sword and ran, jumping over the dead and wounded of both sides. He had two objectives in his head: lead his men to victory and find the man in the black turban.

Once over the Kaisarbagh wall, he found himself in a series of magnificent gardens with fruit trees and marble arbours, sparkling canals and tinkling fountains.

'We're in paradise.' The sheer beauty of his surroundings forced Elliot to stop in admiration. The whine of a bullet passing close by brought him back to reality.

'Keep after the pandies,' Jack ordered, 'there will be time for sightseeing later.' He ran into a sequence of courtyards overlooked by Venetian windows and with mutineers appearing on the roof above to fire and then disappear.

'Stand and fight!' Jack yelled.

'*Maro Firinghi Soor*! somebody shouted with another voice adding,'*Allah Akbar! Angrez kaffirs!*'

Jack stepped sideways as a tall, shaven-headed Pathan appeared in a doorway and fired a *jezzail*. The Pathan shouted something, half drew the long cleaver known as a Khyber knife, held Jack's gaze for an instant and then slid away.

'Stand and fight!' Jack slashed uselessly with his sword and ran on, with a press of the 113th and Sikhs at his back. The Pathan vanished into the maze of courtyards and gardens, and Jack tried to follow, brandishing his sword as he burst into the palace itself. Men of the 113th were behind him, exclaiming at the treasures that surrounded them. There was more wealth in one room than they would ever see in ten lifetimes.

'This is more like it!' Private Armstrong, saturnine and predatory, said. 'Bugger the pandies.'

'Leave the loot!' Jack warned. 'There are still mutineers around!'

Soft carpets deadened the sound of their feet; silk hangings decorated the walls, mirrors reflected their images so for a second Jack prepared to strike at a wild-eyed swordsman before he realised it was himself.

'They're running!' Elliot sounded amazed. He stood with his pistol in his left hand and his sword in his right, panting as the mutineers and warriors began a fighting withdrawal from the Kaisarbagh.

'Stand and fight, you pandy bastards!' Logan waved his rifle at them; blood dripped from the bayonet. 'Remember Cawnpore!'

After the massacres at Cawnpore and Meerut, the British had no mercy. They killed anybody who did not immediately surrender. Jack watched without emotion. The penalty for mutiny and treason had always been death, and the mutineers had murdered British women and children. In this war, there was little mercy on either side.

'Loot!' somebody else shouted, and the cry spread among the British and Sikhs. As the enemy fled, the attackers realised that they were safe and within a selection of buildings that held immense wealth. 'Loot, boys, gold and jewels for us all!'

With those words, the drive eased from the attack as men turned their attention to rapaciousness rather than soldiering. What they couldn't steal, they destroyed, so in minutes the Kaisarbagh became an orgy of pointless vandalism and theft.

'Stick together, 113th!'

Men ignored Jack's shout as they delved into rooms to see what loot they could find.

'113th! To me!' Jack roared. He didn't want his men scattered around the Kaisarbagh where they could be vulnerable to enemy ambush. Capturing a town or palace was the most testing time for any military unit. Regiments held together in battle or on the parade ground, but British soldiers were prone to the temptations of loot or drink.

'Sir!' Riley ran up with small, ugly Logan at his side.

'I thought you'd be first at the looting, Riley.' Jack knew that Riley had been a cracksman, a professional thief before he joined the army.

Riley shrugged. 'There's as much smashing as stealing, sir. These lads have got no idea.'

Jack glanced around. Most of the veterans were with him, together with some of the replacements, the Johnny Raws who hadn't yet recovered from their first sunburn. Armstrong was missing, which didn't surprise him. 'Well done, lads.'

The black-turbaned leader appeared from behind a fountain. He looked directly at Jack, raised his tulwar in salute and vanished. Jack did not see where.

'Who was that sir?' Logan was on one knee, aiming his rifle. 'I cannae see the bastard.'

'I don't know who he was,' Jack said, 'but I think we will see him again.' He replaced his sword in its scabbard. *And when we do, I will kill him.*

Chapter One

'We have trouble, sir.' Sergeant Greaves came to attention and saluted.

'What sort of trouble, sergeant?' Jack asked.

'We have two men missing, sir.'

Jack sighed. Sergeant O'Neill would have sorted such a thing out himself without recourse to an officer. 'Let me guess – Thorpe and Coleman.' Two old soldiers with a liking for drink and women, Thorpe and Coleman were nothing but trouble when the 113th was in cantonments and worth their weight in gold when the bayonets were out.

'No, sir,' Greaves said. 'Riley and Logan.'

'That's unusual,' Jack responded. 'Have you asked Mrs. Riley where her husband might be?' Charlotte Riley was a sensible woman who usually kept her husband out of trouble.

'No, sir.'

'Come on then, sergeant.'

Charlotte Riley was washing clothes in a wooden tub. She looked up when Jack arrived, drew the back of her hand across her forehead and nodded acknowledgement. Behind her, a group of women similarly engaged stopped work to listen. Three children, dressed in clothes inappropriate to the weather, scampered back inside the native huts the 113th had appropriated for temporary married quarters.

'Good morning, Captain Windrush.' Charlotte Riley spoke guardedly, with her eyes bright and wary.

'Good morning, Mrs. Riley. We seem to have mislaid your husband.'

'Have you?' Charlotte's eyes widened.

'We have, and that other reprobate, Donald Logan.'

'Wee Donnie?' Charlotte Riley smiled. 'Now there's a surprise.' She eyed Jack. 'It must be important for you to be involved, captain. How long have they been gone for?'

'Two hours, Mrs. Riley.' Sergeant Greaves replied at once.

'Oh, is that all?' Charlotte sounded relieved. 'Don't concern yourselves, gentlemen, they'll be back.'

'How do you know?' Sergeant Greaves asked.

'Riley wouldn't leave me behind.' Charlotte returned to her washing. 'He's not deserted.'

'That is true.' Jack knew that Riley was close to Charlotte. 'Do you have any idea where they might be, Mrs. Riley? I'd like to find them before they end in serious trouble.'

Charlotte pondered for a moment. 'Well, Captain Windrush, Riley is not interested in other women, so don't think of brothels. Neither he nor Wee Donnie drinks much, so it's not that.' She shrugged. 'They'll turn up. I can't think what else interests them.'

I can. Jack remembered that neither Riley nor Logan looted the Kaisarbagh. *Why not? Riley had been a professional cracksman, a high-class thief, and Logan was a street Arab from Glasgow, always on the lookout for what he could take for nothing. The only reason they would not join in the general orgy was if they had something else in mind.* 'They haven't deserted,' Jack agreed. 'Thank you, Mrs. Riley. Sergeant Greaves, go and find Thorpe. He can help us.'

'Thorpe, sir? Yes, sir.' Greaves was too much of an old soldier to reveal his surprise.

Thorpe was on guard duty, standing outside the regimental lines with his rifle in his hands. He slipped a stubby clay pipe inside his mouth as Jack and Greaves approached.

'Stand at attention when an officer is present, Thorpe!' Greaves roared.

'I am, sir,' Thorpe mumbled.

'It's all right, Thorpe, you're in no trouble,' Jack said. 'And you'd better take the pipe out of your mouth before you burn your tongue.'

'Yes, sir. Thank you, sir.' Thorpe looked uneasily from Greaves to Jack.

'We have come to you,' Jack said, 'because you are an old soldier, a veteran of battle and siege.' He could feel Greaves staring at him, wondering what he was doing. Officers didn't normally speak to private soldiers in such a friendly manner.

'Yes, sir,' Thorpe was equally suspicious.

'You know all that's going on,' Jack continued. 'Where everybody is and who has secrets.'

'Yes, sir.' Thorpe gave a little smile.

'I thought I could rely on you, Thorpey.' Jack clapped him on the shoulder. 'We fought together in Burma, remember?'

'Yes, sir,' Thorpe said.

'Now, I need your help. I have to tell Riley something, and I can't find him. Do you know where he is?'

'Yes, sir.' Thorpe didn't remove the pipe from his lips, so a puff of foul smoke accompanied every word. 'He's down by the River Goomtee for a little swim. Remember when we evacuated Lucknow last year, sir? They were the days, eh?'

'They were, Thorpey, they were indeed. Whereabouts by the river is Riley?'

'He's where we evacuated the city, sir, last time we was here.' Thorpe frowned, evidently thinking he had made that plain. 'Do you want a smoke, sir?' He produced a sweaty handful of something vaguely resembling tobacco. 'Me and Coley make it with cow dung and weeds, sir and a bit of real baccy when we can find any.'

'No thank you, Thorpe. You might need it.' Jack hastily withdrew before Thorpe began patting his shoulder and calling him Jack.

'Down by the river Goomtee.' Greaves repeated. 'Why the devil would he be down by the river? And it's not for a swim.'

'I agree with you, sergeant, and we'll soon find out. Come on.'

'I'll bring a picket, sir.'

'No need, sergeant.' Jack shook his head. 'I know these men.'

'That's what I mean, sir. So do I.' Greaves grimaced. 'Riley is a smooth-tongued blackguard, and I can feel Logan watching me every time I turn my back. He's gallows bait, that one, sir.'

Jack smiled. 'You'll get used to them, Greaves. You only joined us a few months ago, didn't you?'

'Yes, sir. Three months ago. I was in Number Three Company in Malta when this mutiny blew up.'

'You'll get to know the men. Come on, sergeant.'

Jack saw the flash of white skin in the water as he marched along the muddy bank of the Goomtee. 'Riley!' He roared the name.

Riley started, and Logan appeared from behind a ruined building, rifle in hand.

'What are you doing, Riley?'

'Swimming sir.' Riley was the picture of innocence as he stood stark naked and thigh deep in water. 'It's hot.'

'Swimming!' Greaves raised his voice to a roar. 'You should be on duty, Riley! By God, I'll have you two at the triangle before I'm through.'

Jack saw Riley's expression alter. Once before, Major Snodgrass had ordered Riley flogged and neither he nor Charlotte had ever forgiven the major. Now his eyes narrowed at the threat.

'Aye, would you?' Logan shifted his rifle enough to cover Greaves.

'There won't be any of that if you're back on duty within the hour.' Jack hardened his voice. 'And you'll remain under Sergeant Greaves direct supervision until I say otherwise. Logan!' Jack turned around. 'Your tunic is not buttoned properly, and your rifle is loaded. You're on extra guard duty tonight once the sergeant finishes with you! Now get back to camp, the pair of you!'

Jack watched as Greaves force-marched both men away. He looked back at the river where sad trees dipped their branches into the slow-swirling waters, and colourful birds hunted for insects. If he had Sergeant O'Neill with him, rather than Greaves, he would have found out more, but Greaves didn't know his men. Now it was unlikely he would ever discover what Riley and Logan had been doing at this river.

Lighting a cheroot, Jack sauntered back to the 113th's lines, glad that the campaign was nearly over. He had been fighting since the previous summer, battle after battle and march after toiling march. He had lost count of the number of actions he'd survived and only knew that he needed rest, a period of peace. Surely now that Lucknow had fallen, the pandies would throw in the towel.

Please God, let this nightmare end soon. I have had enough of killing and death for a while.

'Soldiers? You're not soldiers! You're babes just out of the crib! You ain't a pukka soldier until you've had a nap hand.' Sergeant Greaves paced slowly along the line of replacements, meeting the gaze of each man and saying nothing until he reached the end. 'Soldiers? I've seen Sawnies fresh from the heather who knew more about soldiering, Paddies straight from the bogs who could march better and Cockneys from the stews who had more brains.'

'He's not bad.' Watching from the side-lines, Coleman gave his professional opinion as he sucked on the stem of his pipe. 'Not as good as O'Neill, but not bad.'

'I wonder if he can fight as well as he can talk.' Thorpe dealt out the greasy playing cards.

'He did no' bad at the Kaisarbagh,' Logan said. 'He never ran away, anyway.'

'Let's see how he is when we're not winning,' Coleman grunted at his cards.

Riley examined his hand. 'Did you shuffle the pack, Thorpey? You've given me five aces.'

Logan grunted. 'Aye, me too. You're a cheating bastard Thorpey.'

'No I'm not,' Thorpe looked up, 'I'm not a cheating bastard, sir.'

'They're pulling your leg, Thorpe. Ignore them and get on with the game.' Jack eased the sudden tension.

'He's right, Thorpey. Concentrate on the cards.' Coleman said. 'That blustering sergeant will pull the beer trick soon. See if he doesn't.'

'All right,' Sergeant Greaves returned to the centre of the line. 'Step forward two paces, all those who drink beer.'

The replacements glanced at each other in wonderment, deciding what trick the sergeant was playing. Greaves waited, with the sun drawing the sweat from his face and evaporating it nearly simultaneously. Two men took a deep breath, and one stepped forward.

'They always fall for it,' Coleman said.

Logan glanced at Riley. 'Aye. Bloody fools.'

'So you drink beer, do you?' Sergeant Greaves thrust his face close to that of the lone volunteer.

'Yes, sergeant.' The man looked about twenty, with neatly shaped black whiskers and red skin peeling from his nose. Jack couldn't place which part of Scotland his accent was from, although it was vastly different from the harsh gutter Glasgow of Logan.

'Do you eat bread and cheese?' Greaves asked.

'Sometimes, sergeant,' the private said.

'Well, that's nice. You eat bread and cheese and drink beer. You'll need that for you are about to become a soldier. Now, what's your name?'

'MacKinnon, sergeant. Alexander Mackinnon from the Island of—'

'Well MacKinnon, we have a Sergeant's Mess here. I want you to trot along and tell them that nice Sergeant Greaves has sent you to have one bottle of beer with his compliments.' Greaves watched as MacKinnon hurried away.

'The rest of you,' Greaves spoke in a conversational tone, 'are lying dogs. You lied to your friendly sergeant about not drinking beer, and for that, you will double around the square with your *bundooks* above your head, until I tell you to stop. Now move, you lying bastards! Don't drink beer eh? By the living Christ! If you're the army, thank God we've got a navy.'

'Stupid buggers,' Thorpe said with neither malice nor sympathy. 'I'm having three cards.'

'An officer is coming,' Riley warned.

The officer was tall and slender, with black hair slicked back and lapping his neck and a moustache that drooped past the ends of his mouth. He wore the insignia of a lieutenant colonel.

'Stand up, lads,' Jack said quietly as Sergeant Greaves called his section to attention and slammed an immaculate salute.

'Oh, don't bother with that nonsense,' the officer spoke to Greaves. 'I'm looking for Captain Windrush. Captain Jack Windrush.'

'That's me, sir,' Jack stepped forward.

The colonel subjected Jack to prolonged scrutiny. 'You're Captain Jack Windrush?'

'I am, sir.' Jack knew it was highly unusual for an officer to associate so closely with the men and wondered if the colonel would comment.

'I am Charles Hook, Lieutenant-Colonel Charles Hook.'

Jack nodded. 'Yes, sir.'

'You knew my brother, Lieutenant Hook. You served together in Burma.' Hook held Jack's gaze. 'He mentioned you in the last letter he ever wrote to me.'

'He was a good man.' Jack couldn't think what else to say. He'd been a very young and inexperienced griffin when he fought beside Lieutenant Hook.

'Come with me, Windrush. Your men will be all right without you for a few moments.' Hook nodded to the Dilkusha palace which was still magnificent, despite the battering it had received during this final assault on Lucknow. 'I've found a modest apartment in the Dilky.'

Hook's idea of modest differed from Jack's. Two burly Sikhs stiffened to attention as Hook approached the studded doorway to his requisitioned apartment. He entered with a nod, and Jack followed him into a room lit by pointed latticed windows and cooled by an invisible *punkah-wallah*.

'Some minor prince or other lived here,' Hook said casually. 'I sent in my lads to ensure it was untouched during the general looting.'

'They did a good job.' Jack looked around him. He had been in half a dozen Indian palaces and forts during the present conflict, but only during the attack, or after the British had captured them from their previous owners. This room had the furnishings undamaged and the drapery intact. Jack stared at the silks and satins, the inlaid furniture and the exquisite wall hangings, with carpets from Afghanistan and Bokhara and a display of jewelled weapons on the wall. The two chairs appeared like thrones, broad and semi-circular with deeply padded seats and arm-rests carved into the likeness of snarling tigers.

'It will do for now.' Hook sounded nonchalant. 'Take a seat, Windrush.'

Jack sat on the smaller of the two thrones, sinking into the luxurious cushion.

'Now, Windrush,' Hook remained on his feet, pacing back and forth from one of the windows to the door, 'I believe that you've seen quite a bit of action in India.'

'A bit, sir. I was with General Havelock's column in the relief of Cawnpore and Lucknow, and then with Sir Colin Campbell.'

'You participated in both of Campbell's campaigns against Lucknow,' Hook said. 'And before the Mutiny, you were in the Crimea and Burma.'

'That's correct, sir.' Jack wondered how Hook knew so much about him.

'Colonel Maxwell told me you were a useful man.' Hook answered Jack's unspoken question. 'He suggested that you were a little unorthodox and less regimental than most officers. When I saw you playing cards with your men, I knew that to be correct.'

Jack was unsure how to reply.

'Would you agree with our assessment, Windrush?' Hook didn't halt his pacing, yet his gaze never strayed from Jack's face.

'Colonel Maxwell knew me well, sir,' Jack said.

'I heard you were involved in some interesting escapades against the Plastun Cossacks around Sevastopol,' Hook said.

'Yes, sir.' Jack remembered the biting cold and nervous strain when he had led his men against the best irregular infantry in the Russian army.

Hook's sudden stop took Jack by surprise. 'You were successful.'

'Some we won and some we lost, sir, like the campaign itself.'

'You killed your adversary,' Hook said. 'The object of war is to out-manoeuvre and destroy the enemy, which is what you did. You are a soldier, Windrush.' His smile was genuine. 'And I am looking for a soldier who is not hide-bound by tradition and regulations.'

'There are many more experienced soldiers than me in the army.' Jack avoided Hook's last statement. 'Lieutenant Elliot was with me most of the time, and he is a fine officer and a gentleman.'

'I am fully aware of Lieutenant Arthur Elliot's abilities,' Hook said. 'As I am aware you have acted the spy on occasion.'

'I had no choice, sir.' Jack knew that most officers thought spying was dishonourable. He decided to end the colonel's game. 'What do you wish me to do, sir?'

'Good man. Take the direct approach and hang the consequences, eh?' Hook sat on the larger throne. 'I want you to work for me.'

Jack felt the increased patter of his heart. 'Doing what, sir?'

'Whatever I wish you to do.' Hook's gaze was level. 'Well? I could make it an order, captain Windrush.'

'You'll have to, sir. My duty is with the 113th, beside my men.' Jack knew it was foolish to argue with a superior officer.

'Maxwell was right about you. He said that as well as being un-orthodox and less regimental than most officers, you have loyalty to your men.'

'We've been through a lot together,' Jack said.

Hook's smile faded slightly. 'I suspect that you have more to go through before this war is over.' He sat on the larger throne. 'You saw the well at Cawnpore.'

'Yes, sir.' Jack would never forget the horror of the well at Cawnpore. Heads, torsos, arms and legs of women and children had filled the well in a sickening scene that still haunted him. The massacre at Cawnpore had put new savagery to an already terrible war, with atrocities and retaliation on both sides.

'Do you know who was responsible?'

'I heard it was Nana Sahib, sir, or his lover, Hussaini Khanum.'

'Hussaini Khanum is a fascinating woman.' Hook took a long cheroot from an inside pocket and tapped the end on the arm of his chair. 'Do you think that women can be as ruthless in war as men?'

Not expecting the question, Jack had no ready answer. 'I haven't thought about it, sir. I suppose I always think of women as the gentler sex.'

Hook lit the cheroot, leaned back in his throne and exhaled blue smoke. 'That is what most people seem to think,' he said. 'Have you heard of Uda Devi?'

'No, sir.' Jack shook his head, wondering where Hook was leading him with these seemingly disassociated questions.

'No? That surprises me, considering you were involved in the battle where we killed her.' Hook drew on his cheroot. 'You must remember the affair at Sikandrabagh when the Highlanders shot a female in a papal tree?'

'I do, sir,' Jack said. 'The woman had killed some of our men.'

'That woman was Uda Devi.' Hook paused for effect. 'She was not the only woman warrior, but allegedly the leader of a company of female fighters, many of whom died in the battle for Lucknow.'

'I see, sir. She was a brave woman, whoever she was.'

'Our intelligence informs us that she was trained in guerrilla tactics, martial arts and espionage. She was much more than an angry woman killing British soldiers but... we don't know what she was.'

Jack waited. It was not politic to rush a senior officer.

'You are wondering what the connection is between Uda Devi and you.' A slow smile spread across Hook's face.

'I am, sir,' Jack said.

'We believe that another woman has taken Uda Devi's place,' Hook said. 'Our informants are very vague. They tell us that they have heard the name "Jayanti".'

'Jayanti.' Jack ran the name around his mouth. 'That's evocative.'

'The name is interesting,' Hook said. 'It means "victorious".'

'Victorious?' Jack raised his eyebrows. 'We have defeated the muti-neers wherever they have made a stand.'

'Orientals don't view time as we do,' Hook said. 'They may view this war as only the first round in a prolonged struggle.' He shrugged. 'Now that they've given us fair warning, we'll take the appropriate action. More important for the present, this Jayanti may be planning to raise another army of women.' He exhaled blue smoke. 'If they are as skilled as Uda Devi, or as ruthless as Hussaini, then they could cause us a devil of a lot of trouble.'

'The Mutiny is all but over now, sir, is it not?' Jack suffered a prickle of unease. 'We've recaptured Delhi, defeated every army they raised and taken Cawnpore and Lucknow. There is only Central India to pacify and the ragtag and bobtail to mop up.'

'If only it were that easy.' Hook's laughter lacked any mirth. 'This is India, Windrush. We are sitting on the lid of a cauldron while the devil stokes the fire. You know what happens when a boiler has no outlet, don't you? It explodes. This mutiny was an outlet, and now we must ensure any future outbreaks are small and quickly subdued. We might not find Jayanti easy to control if we don't stop her soon.'

'By we, do you mean me, sir?'

Hook nodded. 'Why else would I be telling you all this? I want you to find Jayanti, and either capture her and bring her to trial, or kill her.' He stretched out on his chair. 'If she even exists. All we have is rumour and speculation.'

Nausea rose in Jack's gut. The army was once again using him for the unorthodox. 'I'm sure other officers know India better than I do, sir. Perhaps somebody from John Company with a more intimate knowl-edge of the native peoples would be more suitable.'

'Maxwell told me you were an argumentative sort of fellow, Win-drush.' Hook examined the end of his cheroot. 'In case you have for-gotten, John Company's sepoys have just mutinied. How can I trust one of their officers after that? You are Indian-born and have more experience than most in irregular warfare.'

Jack knew there was no point in arguing further. 'How many men can I have, sir?'

'I leave that up to you, Windrush. You know what is best. Remember that too many men will make you conspicuous and too few and you'll be vulnerable to every band of badmashes and broken pandy unit in India.'

'Yes, sir,' Jack said.

Hook's grin was as reassuring as a tiger stalking its prey. 'Here is what you are going to do, Windrush. Have you heard of the Rohilkhand Field Force?'

'I've heard the name included in a hundred shaves, sir.'

'Well, here is what is happening. Rohilkhand, as you know, is a large province northeast of Delhi, and near Meerut, where this entire horrible business began.'

'Yes, sir.'

'It appears that Rohilkhand is a rallying place. The survivors from Delhi have fled there, and the local Rohillas joined them. The Rohillas are a tough crowd, descended from Afghans. Their leader, Khan Bahadur Khan is a formidable presence. As if that was not sufficient, the Nawab of Farukhabad has raised the standard of rebellion as has the Maulvi of Faizabad.'

'All the disaffected clans,' Jack murmured. 'All we need is Bonny Prince Charlie.'

'Or Bonnie Princess Jayanti,' Hook said. 'I think you are beginning to understand. The Mutiny is not yet over; it has assumed a new form, that's all.'

'Yes, sir.' Jack resigned himself to another summer's campaigning in the heat of India.

'Sir Colin is sending four columns against Rohilkhand. General Penny is marching from Meerut; Brigadier Coke is leading a division from Rurki, Seaton will advance from Fatehgarh and Brigadier-General Robert Walpole from Lucknow.'

'Yes, sir.'

'You will join Walpole's column until you hear news of Jayanti. After that, you either strike out on your own or report your intelligence to me, if I am available.'

'Yes, sir.'

'Oh, and Windrush; keep an ear and eye open for Nana Sahib and Major Snodgrass, would you? You know that Snodgrass and his entire command vanished.'

'I'll do that, sir.' The senior major of the 113th, Snodgrass had been in charge of an escort for the regiment's women and children when the Mutiny began the previous year. He and the escort had disappeared one night, leaving the women to find their own way to safety.

'I know you didn't always see eye-to-eye with Major Snodgrass,' Hook again revealed his thorough knowledge of Jack, 'but he is a British officer.'

'Yes, sir.'

'After all this time, I doubt you'll find him alive,' Hook said. 'The mutineers probably ambushed the poor fellow.' Hook finished his cheroot and immediately lit another. 'However, I'm telling all the searching columns to look out for him, and I'll tell you too.'

'Is there anything else, sir?'

'Yes, Windrush. At present, we don't know much about Jayanti, and we don't want any false rumours to spread across the army. God knows there are sufficient lies and exaggerations already. Keep the object of your search between yourself and Elliot.'

'Yes, sir.'

'I think that's all, Windrush. You have your orders. Find this Jayanti woman and look out for poor Major Snodgrass. Good luck.' He held out his hand.

'Thank you, sir.'

Hook's hand was as hard and cool as his eyes.

Chapter Two

'You know Jack', Elliot uncorked his silver hip flask. 'We've been in India for centuries, yet we're less part of it now than we ever were. We exist in a regimental cocoon while India lives outside us.'

'We're not in a regimental cocoon for much longer, Arthur, we're on the road again.' Jack leaned against the wall of their shared quarters.

Elliot held out the flask. 'I guessed that when Hooky wanted you.'

'Do you know him?'

Elliot shook the flask to attract Jack's attention. 'I know that he's a man best avoided. Where is he sending us?'

Jack took the flask and sipped at the contents. 'God that's rough! What's it meant to be?'

'Whisky. Campbell's 79th make their own.'

'What do they make it from? Dead horses?' Jack choked down the fiery liquid. 'Thanks Arthur, I needed that, and you'll need the rest when you hear what Colonel Hook wants us to do.' He looked around their bare chamber, comparing it to Hook's luxurious quarters and sighed. 'We're after a woman named Jayanti. She's said to be the head of a regiment of female warriors.'

'Amazons by Jove.' Elliot swallowed more of his whisky, coughed and wiped a hand across his mouth. 'And where does Jayanti live when she's at home?'

'That's the interesting part,' Jack retrieved the flask for another swallow. 'We don't know.' He explained the situation.

'I had thought the 113th had redeemed its reputation after Inkerman and Lucknow,' Elliot said. 'Apparently not. It seems that the powers-that-be still use us for the dirty jobs that other units don't want.' He shook his head. 'A British regiment hunting down a woman. What would Wellington have said?'

'He would have said, "do your duty".'

'Probably.' Elliot downed some more whisky. 'So we wander about India knocking on doors and enquiring politely if a woman named Jayanti is inside?'

'We are part of a large column,' Jack said. 'We march and fight, gather intelligence and listen.'

'You'll have to say your goodbyes to Mary.' Elliot eyed Jack over the mouth of his flask. 'What are your intentions with that woman, Jack?'

'Honourable.' Jack kept his voice neutral. He'd met Mary when the mutineers attacked the 113th cantonment at Gondabad the previous year. They'd forged a close friendship despite the fact that Mary was Anglo-Indian, with a British father and an Indian mother, and therefore not a woman that a respectable British officer should know.

'How honourable?' Elliot didn't allow Jack to wriggle off his hook.

'I will not dishonour her,' Jack said. 'I'm not my father.'

Elliot passed across the flask. 'I remember that your father had a friendship with a Eurasian woman.'

'He fathered me to a native of the country,' Jack said. 'I'm a half-breed.'

'Your mother was only half-Indian,' Elliot said, 'making you three-quarters white and anyway, you are a British officer.' He kept his voice quiet.

'If the queen learned of my antecedents, she would revoke my commission.' Jack held Elliot's gaze.

'Not our Victoria.' Elliot said. '*If* the queen did such a thing, and it's a big if, Her Majesty would be losing one of her finest officers. However, that is not likely to happen, and you are avoiding my question. What are your intentions with the delightful Mary?'

'I don't know,' Jack said. 'I like her.'

'The whole regiment knows that you *like* her.' Elliot couldn't hide his smile. 'And also, that she likes you. The question is, how *much* do you like her?'

'I don't know,' Jack said again.

'For your sake, Jack, find out,' Elliot said. 'I'm your friend, I hope, so when I speak, I'm only thinking of your happiness. Keep Mary as a friend, by all means, but no more than that. Don't, for God's sake, contemplate matrimony.'

Until that moment, Jack hadn't seriously considered marrying Mary. However, as soon as Elliot gave his advice, Jack frowned. 'I'll do as I damn well please, Arthur.'

'Will you?' Elliot said. 'Best consider the future, Jack. Jack!' He raised his voice as Jack rose from the chair and stormed away.

'Damned cheek,' Jack grumbled to himself as he lit a cheroot. 'Telling me what I can and can't do and who I can and can't marry. Bloody cheek of the man.'

Mary had found lodgings in a small chamber near the Dilkusha palace. She looked up from her small charpoy when Jack tapped on the door.

'Come in.'

'You look tired.' Jack stepped inside the bleak chamber.

'I'm a lot better than most in here.' Mary sat up and ran her hands through her thick black hair.

'You're acting as a nurse, aren't you?' Jack sat on the woven *mooda* stool that was one of the few pieces of furniture in the room.

'No.' Mary shook her head. 'I'm not *acting* as anything. I *am* a nurse. There are a lot of badly injured men who need help.'

'I've heard,' Jack said. 'The pandies have left powder stores all over the city, and our men light their pipes and throw away the Lucifers.'

'Exactly so.' Mary reached for the chapatti that lay on the small table beside her charpoy. Tearing it in half, she passed one piece to Jack and bit into the other. 'Some of the poor devils lie there and pray for death, and no wonder with most of their bodies burned to a crisp. All we can do is try to soothe their pain.'

'You're a good woman, Mary Lambert,' Jack said.

Mary washed down the chapatti with a drink of water from a brass bowl. 'No, Jack, I'm only a woman.'

'You're one of the best,' Jack told her.

'What can I do for you?' Mary's smile only highlighted the tired lines around her eyes.

'I've come to tell you that I'll be leaving Lucknow shortly,' Jack said.

'Are you allowed to tell me where you are heading?'

'Into Rohilkhand,' Jack said.

'Rebel territory.' Mary put out a hand. 'Be careful, Jack, please be careful.'

'I will,' Jack said.

'No.' Mary shook her head. 'I know you. You will charge into whatever danger there is and end up with more wounds and more scars, or worse.'

'That's part of the soldier's bargain,' Jack said.

'It's a poor bargain,' Mary responded. She waved her hand to fend off a circling fly. 'I'll be thinking of you.'

Jack nodded. He tried to think of something reassuring to say. 'I'll be thinking of you, too.'

'You know where liars go,' Mary said with her mouth full of half-masticated chapatti. 'You won't think of me at all, only of your beloved regiment.'

'I will think of you,' Jack said quietly. He wanted to touch her.

Mary held his gaze for a long minute before she replied. 'I know you will.' Her voice was equally quiet. 'I do.'

Jack knew that she was still watching as he left the chamber. He wished he could have said more as he stalked away with his temper growing fouler by the minute. *What am I going to do about that woman?*

'We are joining Walpole's column with orders to remove any rebels from the left bank of the Ganges and bring British rule and justice into the districts through which we pass.' Jack addressed his junior officers. 'Our goal is Bareilly, one hundred and fifty or so miles away.'

'Another long march.' Elliot glanced upwards. 'And the hot season is reaching its zenith.'

'Check the boys fill their water bottles,' Jack said, 'and ensure the bullock waggons have extra water. I don't trust these *bullock-wallahs* any more than I would trust a pandy.'

'Sergeant Greaves has already checked,' Elliot said.

'Well, do it again,' Jack ordered. 'I'm not going to depend on the word of a sergeant to look after my men.' He knew he was bad-tempered this morning and Elliot was doing his best. However, junior officers were there to assuage the wrath of their superiors. Jack looked at his men, some marching, others riding six-a-piece on bullock-daks. They were relaxed, jesting and fit. He had no real worries with them. He glanced back toward Lucknow, hoping to see Mary.

Damn the woman. She could at least spare a few moments to wave goodbye. So much for her protestations of thinking about me. Bloody woman.

'We have a decent little army here,' Jack forced his mind onto other things. 'A Highland Brigade, two battalions of the Rifle Brigade, the Company's 1st Bengal Europeans, two sepoy regiments, two regiments of Queen's cavalry, three Punjab cavalry regiments, seamen from HMS *Shannon* and a gaggle of engineers and artillery.'

'And us,' Elliot said, 'two companies of the 113th Foot. The pandies won't stand against this lot so it will be a wasted expedition.'

'They might not have to stand,' Jack said. 'All they have to do is keep mobile and let us chase them across India. They can live on rice, water and burned corn and they ignore the sun while we'll lose men by the score with heat exhaustion.'

'It's better being on the move than waiting in Lucknow,' Elliot said. 'The quicker we beat the rebels, the sooner this war will be over. Any-way,' he shrugged, 'I've had more than enough of Lucknow with its dead bodies putrefying in the streets, mines waiting to explode and murderers hiding in the alleys.'

'The men are still keen,' Jack said.

'They want to kill pandies,' Elliot agreed. 'They won't forget Cawnpore.'

Jack took a last look at Lucknow, the city of palaces where he had met Mary and lost his mother. There was no familiar, friendly face waiting to wave him off.

'Come on Arthur, let's find this Jayanti woman and finish this blasted war.'

* * *

The searing wind raised a mist of dust that hid the sun, coated every surface and scoured every face. The column marched through waist-high dust, spat out dust-filled phlegm and narrowed their eyes to protect sensitive pupils. When the men drank, they swallowed dust-tasting water, and they tried not to scratch at the dust that seeped inside their clothes and made walking a chafing nightmare. India had indirect methods of fending off invaders.

'Tell me again, Coley, why do we want India?' Thorpe took off his hat, shook off the dust and replaced it, as dusty as before.

'India,' Coleman said, 'is the jewel in the Empire's crown, the glory of the nation and a money-spinning gem for the Honourable East India Company.'

'Oh.' Thorpe thought about Coleman's words for a few moments. 'That might be right, Coley, but why do *we* want it. It's a cesspit.'

Coleman sighed. 'It brings money to the East India Company,' he said. 'It's all about money for the nobs.'

'So how come we're fighting here and the nobs aren't?' Thorpe asked. 'We don't want the bloody place.'

'I don't want it either,' Parker said.

'Can we not just tell the East India Company that we don't want their country and give it back to the Indians?' Thorpe said.

'That's what we'll do!' Hutton said. 'We'll all go to the East India Company and tell them that. You go first Thorpey, as it's your idea.'

'Will you come with me?' Thorpe asked.

'We'll all come with you,' Hutton said. 'You lead us Thorpey, and we'll follow.'

'Thanks lads,' Thorpe said. 'Where is this East India Company?'

'In London,' Coleman said. 'We can go after the war.'

Thorpe grinned and straightened up. 'All of us?'

'All of us, Thorpey. The whole regiment, band, Colours, colonel and all.'

'Thanks, lads,' Thorpe said. 'You're real mates, you are.'

Jack watched them as they marched on into the dust, weary men with no future except fighting, disease and poverty, living on false hopes and the prospect of a few hours oblivion through alcohol and cheap prostitutes. 'It's strange, Arthur, that ultimately the Empire depends on these men. Without them, there would be nothing.'

'Aye,' Elliot nodded. 'They're the base of the pyramid and the directors of John Company are at the top.'

'Surely the Queen is at the top,' Jack said.

'Is she?' Elliot looked away. 'I wonder if money is not more important than monarchy now.'

After Havelock's lightning marches of the previous year, Walpole's advance seemed interminably slow. There were few roads in this part of India, so they had to move in the full heat of the day, sheltering in *topes* of trees at night. With the cavalry scouting ahead, there was little for the infantry to do except march and curse or sit in the dusty wagons and curse.

'I hope the pandies stand and fight,' Logan muttered. 'If they fight, we can smash them.'

Jack peered through the curtain of dust that screened the surrounding countryside. 'When I lived in England, I thought India was a land of romance and jungles, with tigers and princes and fabled cities. Now I see it as a land where anybody can be an enemy.' He preferred being in charge of his own destiny, rather than obeying the orders of a superior officer he didn't know.

The British moved slowly, dragging the guns through the dust, frequently stopping to allow the column to keep together, tormented by flies and heat. The bullocks proved more trouble than expected, lying down at their leisure and refusing to move until their drivers taught the soldiers a simple trick. While one man held the tail out straight, another placed a stick on each side and rubbed vigorously up and down.

'That makes the bugger jump,' Thorpe said.

'It's cruel sore on the animals,' Parker said in his broad Liverpool accent.

'I'll be cruel sore on you, unless you shut up and march on,' Sergeant Greaves snarled.

Soldiers and syces, horses and camels, elephants that smelled of pigs, servants of every variety, doolie bearers and warriors marched, cursed, swore, and laughed as they crawled across the vast Indian countryside. Some villages were deserted, others were full of huge-eyed, scared people. There were empty fields and the occasional temple or mosque. Cavalry cantered to check every copse of mango or peepul trees, infantry scouted every village for a sight of the enemy, and Walpole's column advanced to reclaim India for the Honourable Company and its shareholders in London's Leadenhall.

On the 14th April, only fifty miles from Lucknow, Walpole ordered a halt, and the long, straggling column stopped.

'What's happening?' Jack asked. Elliot seemed to have some hidden power, which enabled him to garner intelligence from unknown sources.

Elliot didn't let him down. 'There's a fort in that patch of jungle.'

'How the deuce do you know that?' The heat was making Jack irritable.

Elliot shrugged. 'You'll know more than me, soon, the general's runner is coming for you.'

'I'm sure you're psychic,' Jack said.

'Captain Windrush.' The cornet of the 7th Hussars had a peeling red face and the enthusiasm of youth. 'General Walpole sends his regards and requests—'

'I'm coming.' Jack pulled his reins aside and kicked in his heels.

As the most junior officer in the group which formed around Walpole, Jack stood at the back and listened without giving any comment. Dust had rendered the kilts of the Highlanders as khaki as most of the uniforms, while there was a grim determination among the whiskered, bearded faces that listened to the general.

'We cannot yet see it, gentlemen,' Walpole said, 'but inside that patch of jungle is Fort Ruhya. We have to take it before we continue.'

The circle of officers nodded. Most had seen action before and knew what to expect. A naval officer caught a fly and flicked the dead body onto the ground.

Walpole continued, his voice more hesitant than Jack had expected from a general. 'Nirpat Singh holds the fort, with some fifteen hundred men. He is an adherent of Nana Sahib, so we can expect a resolute defence.'

'How are the approaches, sir?' a major of the 42nd asked.

'There is a belt of jungle around the fort,' Walpole replied.

'On all four sides, sir?' Brigadier Adrian Hope of the 93rd Highlanders asked. 'That is unusual. The garrison must have some method of entry – I suggest we send in a party to have a look. It will certainly be hard to drag the guns through the jungle.'

Jack decided to keep silent. It must have been difficult for Walpole to command men with so much more experience, for Hope had fought in the Kaffir Wars in Africa, as well as the Crimea.

'Then we go without artillery,' Walpole decided. 'It's only a small fort. It won't present any difficulties.'

Hope looked at the officers of the 42nd, raised his eyebrows and tried again. 'I believe that a trooper of Hodson's Horse was a prisoner in the fort, sir and escaped. He said that Nirpat Singh would put up token resistance and then surrender.'

'That's the story, sir,' a deeply tanned Company major agreed. 'If we roll up to the gate with artillery and infantry, Nirpat Singh will fire a few shots for honour's sake and run. We'll take the fort without any casualties.'

'Nonsense,' Walpole dismissed the idea. 'The infantry go in on the north.'

'Sir Colin's instructions are clear, sir,' one of the Highland officers said. 'We are to bombard any fort with artillery and then send in the infantry to storm the breach. The commander-in-chief has ordered that we should not attack any fort without at least two heavy pieces of artillery.'

Jack nodded. Although some of the more fire-eating officers of the army termed Sir Colin Campbell "Old Khabardar" or "Old Be-Careful" for his caution and lack of speed, he had far fewer casualties than most commanders in this war. Havelock's final advance to Lucknow had been prolific in British lives compared to Sir Colin's approach.

'We don't need to do that,' Walpole said. 'We will advance immediately. Brigadier Hope, take four companies of the 42nd, with the 4th Punjab Infantry. Windrush, your company of the 113th will be in support. Once the 42nd and the Sikhs are in, you follow up.'

'Yes, sir,' Jack said as the Highlanders glanced at each other.

Brigadier Hope was a Scottish peer and a typical leader of Highlanders. Once Walpole had issued the orders, he did his best to follow them to a conclusion. 'Follow me Windrush,' he was laughing, 'and we'll have the British flag flying over this fort within the hour, with or without the artillery.'

'We're going in,' Jack said on his return to the 113th. 'Extended order, boys, fixed bayonets and keep your heads down.'

'Where are the guns, sir?' Greaves asked.

'No guns this time, Sergeant. We're doing this the old-fashioned way, straight through the jungle and over the walls.'

'Hugh Gough style, eh?' Greaves had been in the army longer than Jack had and remembered the battle of Chillianwala, where the 113th had first seen action. To the shame of the regiment, they had turned and run before the Sikh artillery.

'We're a better regiment now than we were under General Gough,' Jack said.

Greaves nodded. 'Yes, sir.'

Jack raised his voice. 'Make sure you have ammunition in your pouches, boys, and water in your canteens. 'Thorpe, you stay close to Coleman. You Johnny Raws, do as the sergeants and officers tell you and don't mind the shine. It will be noisier than anything you've ever heard before, and you will see things that will make you sick. That's all part of the soldier's bargain. Don't linger and if you're hit, lie quiet and wait for the doolie bearers to pick you up.'

The veterans had heard it all before. The replacements, pale under their tan, listened. Some tried bravado in an attempt to impress their new comrades, who said nothing.

'Do your duty, boys,' Elliot said quietly, 'that's all that the regiment expects.'

They moved forward in extended order, Highlanders and Sikhs and a company of the 113th, walking toward an unknown number of rebels in a fort they could not yet see. Jack's 113th was in the second line, with the kilts of the Black Watch rustling in front.

'The scouts say it's only a small fort, with a high mud wall and bastions at each angle,' Jack instructed as they began the advance. 'There are two gates; we'll go for the one on the left unless the 42nd or the Sikhs force an entrance elsewhere.'

'I don't like this,' Elliot said. 'We've no skirmishers out in front, no flank guards and no artillery. This Walpole fellow is a bit casual, is he not?'

Jack grunted. Although he agreed, it was unprofessional to croak about superior officers.

'How many defenders are there, sir?' Young Ensign Wilden asked.

'The general thinks there are fifteen hundred,' Jack said.

'I heard there were only a couple of hundred.' Elliot's information was usually accurate.

''We'll gut the bastards, however many there are,' Logan said.

With their feet trampling the dry grass and snapping stray twigs, the British and Sikhs moved into the thorny undergrowth of the jungle. A flight of birds exploded from above them and insects buzzed around their faces, probing into ears and eyes, biting the sweat-softened skin of necks and wrists, distracting them from the job at hand.

'I hate bloody India,' Thorpe said. 'There are too many flies.'

'Face your front,' Greaves snapped. 'Don't worry about the insects. You'll have enough to occupy you when we attack the fort.'

'Which bloody fort?' Hutton complained. 'There's no bloody fort here.'

'Shut your mouth.' Armstrong made a rare contribution to the conversation. 'You know nothing, you.'

The jungle grew thicker, with thorns hindering their advance and tree branches cutting the view of the sky. The 113th advanced through a dense green dimness, silent now as they expected to see the fort, holding their Enfield rifles in brown, calloused hands and careful of every footfall. Jack gripped his revolver, called encouragement and watched the Black Watch, ten yards in front, vanish into an even denser patch of woodland.

'Remember Burma?' Coleman grumbled. 'They dacoits would love this. They would have a hundred ambushes waiting for us here. These pandy bastards don't know how to fight.'

'They know how to run though,' Logan said. 'Cry Havelock!' He raised the 113th battle cry, extending the final vowel of Havelock's name.

'Let loose the dogs of war!' the 113th responded.

'There it is!' Thorpe pointed ahead. 'There's the fort!'

The first line pushed through the jungle fringe to a clearing, a *maidan*, in the centre of which stood the khaki-coloured walls of Fort Ruhya. Compared to the splendid palaces of Lucknow it wasn't impressive, a low walled, mundane-looking building with irregular bastions – the lair of a robber baron rather than the abode of a rajah.

Although Jack had expected the rebels to defend the fort, the volume of musketry took him by surprise. Muzzle-flares lit up the loop-holed walls, the bastions, the tops of the gate and the bushes on either flank.

'That's not a token defence,' Elliot said.

'Steady, 113th!' Jack shouted. Firm leadership was required as men dropped from all three regiments. The first volley could test even the staunchest of troops.

'With me, Highlanders!' Brigadier Hope pushed himself forward, tall, urbane, distinguished and as brave as any regiment would expect. 'Follow me, the Black Watch.' For one minute, he strode in front of the army, a smiling Scottish aristocrat and a veteran commander and then he staggered, threw up his hands and crumpled to the ground.

'Jesus, they've shot the brigadier!'

'They'll shoot you too, Hutton, if you don't get under cover!' Greaves said. 'Find a tree, boys and wait for orders!'

The musketry continued, sweeping the open ground in front of the fort and felling everybody who tried to advance. Crumpled bodies littered the *maidan*, some lying still, others writhing and moaning in pain.

'It's the Redan, all over again,' Elliot said.

'We can take them, sir,' Logan said.

'Get down!' Jack didn't see who gave the order. Officers and men slumped to the ground, to seek whatever cover they could find. One replacement hesitated, looking forward at the fort until Riley hauled him unceremoniously to the ground.

'Get your bloody head down, you stupid bastard!'

The rebel musketry continued, joined by artillery that swept iron grapeshot across the *maidan*.

'That's a killing ground.' Greaves gave his professional opinion. 'Who's in charge of the fort, sir?'

'Nirpat Singh,' Elliot said. 'He's one of Nana Sahib's merry men.'

'Fire at them!' Ensign Wilden lifted his revolver and loosed three shots.

'Hold your fire!' Jack countermanded. 'Men lying on the ground can't reload and if the enemy sally, I don't want our boys to face them with empty rifles.'

As the British slid under whatever shelter they could find, the firing from the fort eased. Unable to find any targets, Nirpat Singh's musketeers waited behind the walls, ready for movement.

The rising sun scorched the British while busy insects feasted on their sweat. Every so often, the rebels fired a volley that cut through the branches above the attackers' heads and dropped leaves and twigs on their prone bodies. Between the gunfire, there was birdsong and the occasional scream of a monkey. Always, there was the buzz of flies and the moaning of the wounded.

A few yards from Jack a man yelled and grabbed his leg. 'Snake!' He half rose, there came the sharp crack of a rifle, and he fell without another sound.

'Shot right through the head,' Armstrong said. 'Good shooting by the pandies.'

'That came from above,' Riley said. 'They've got sharpshooters in the treetops.'

Jack frowned. Uda Devi, the woman who had killed so many men in the second relief of Lucknow, had sheltered in the top of a tree. Perhaps the mysterious Jayanti woman used the same technique.

'Don't stand up,' Jack ordered, 'try and scan the trees.' He shifted slightly, heard the crack of a rifle and flinched as a shot thumped into the tree at his side. *That was too close.*

'I see him, sir,' Whitelam, the ex-poacher whispered. 'Don't move an inch.'

'Where is he?'

'About sixty yards to your right, halfway up a tall peepul tree. For God's sake, don't move sir, he's watching you.' Whitelam's words brought cold sweat to Jack's forehead despite the baking heat. To know that an expert sharpshooter was waiting for him was unnerving.

'I'm going after him,' Jack decided. *Better moving than lying as a target.*

'He's pointing his rifle right at you, sir.' Whitelam spoke in broad Lincolnshire as the strain worked on his nerves. 'You won't be able to move fast enough before he fires.'

'I'll catch the bastard's eye, sir,' Logan said. 'I'm no' lying here all bloody day just to keep some pandy bugger happy.'

'You keep your head down, Logan!'

'Aye, right sir. So I will.' Logan was moving on the last word. Rolling from his cover, he ran back to distract the sharpshooter. Jack was on his feet before the rifle's echo reached him. He had to run the sixty yards to the rebel's tree before he or she could reload, and then climb up the bole without either the sharpshooter or the defenders of the fort shooting him. It was a tall order.

Another shot sounded, followed by Logan's voice. 'Missed the bugger! He moved.'

Jack glanced up and saw a drift of white gun smoke from a peepul tree. That must be the one. He hurried towards it, unfastening his sword belt as he did. The sabre was long and would be cumbersome as he climbed. He felt a bullet whiz past him as somebody fired from the fort, but hitting a moving figure at over a hundred yards amidst waist-deep scrub was nearly impossible.

The lower few feet of the peepul's trunk was smooth, without handholds, so Jack had to throw himself upward to grasp the lowest protruding bough. He climbed quickly, hoping the sharpshooter had not yet reloaded.

There was more shooting from the fort, and another bullet knocked splinters from the bole of the tree. Jack looked upwards, gasping. He could see only a tracery of branches and foliage; there was no sign of the sniper. Grabbing for the next handhold, he hauled himself up. As a boy, Jack had enjoyed birds nesting in the woodland around the Malvern Hills and the grounds of his school. He had never expected to use his tree-climbing skills hunting rebels in Rohilkhand.

'He's searching for you, sir!' Whitelam's voice floated to him. 'I'll try a shot.'

'No! You can't reload!' Jack shouted.

Something dropped from above, rustling through the leaves and missing Jack's shoulder by a few inches. He looked down and saw a spear quivering in the ground, swore, pointed his revolver upwards and fired a single shot. He didn't expect the bullet to take effect but hoped to unsettle the sharpshooter. This situation was unnerving, playing hide-and-seek with a sniper while climbing a peepul tree.

Jack knew that after he'd fired the six chambers in his revolver, he had no weapon. Without time to reload, he had to hit the sharpshooter or rely on his strength and experience to defeat him. That could be interesting, as many rebels were veteran warriors with more skill in close-quarter fighting than he had.

Jack cursed as a dense clump of branches blocked his view up the tree. 'Can anybody see him?'

'Twenty feet, sir!' Whitelam shouted. 'He's twenty feet above you!'

The musketeer fired as Whitelam spoke, with a puff of white smoke giving his position away. Jack dragged himself upward into the thick foliage, hoping to catch his quarry while he reloaded.

Thrusting his head between two branches and uncaring of the scrapes and scratches, Jack saw a small timber platform above him. The sharpshooter squatted on top, wearing a black turban, with a grey cloth covering the lower half of his face. *Is that the same man who mutilated Ensign Green?*

The man looked down, and for a moment, Jack stared straight into his eyes. They were brown and strangely gentle, without any of the viciousness he had expected. Jack lifted his revolver, took quick aim and swore as the sharpshooter moved to the side.

Inching higher, Jack tried to climb onto the platform, pulling back as the sharpshooter kicked at his head. Firing involuntarily, Jack had no idea where his shot went. The sharpshooter vanished.

He must be somewhere on the platform. Jack crouched immediately beneath the rough timber. He wondered if a bullet from his revolver had the power to bore through the platform and hit the man, and if so, would it be able to inflict a telling wound? He had four shots left, should he try, and maybe waste a bullet?

The spear point crashed through a gap between the planks, grazing Jack's shoulder. He flinched and yelled, and the spear withdrew, to plunge down again, harder than before. Simultaneously, a bullet thudded into the tree a few inches from Jack's leg.

Jack jerked his leg aside, swearing. *Jesus! There's more than one sniper!* There was another somewhere, firing at him. Jack glanced around, saw only the tops of trees and launched himself upward. If he remained where he was, he would be a target for the second sharp-shooter. If he kept moving, he would be harder to hit.

Dragging himself over the edge of the platform, Jack rolled on the timber as the sharpshooter lunged at him with a spear. He was a lithe man, clothed in baggy green. As the spear thudded into the platform, an inch from his groin, Jack pointed his revolver at the sharpshooter and squeezed the trigger. The shot sent the man staggering backwards. Jack fired again, and again, seeing the bullets smack into the sharp-shooter's body, seeing the flower of blood as each shot pushed the man further back. Jack squeezed the trigger again, realised that the hammer was falling on empty chambers and rose to a crouch.

The sharpshooter tottered on the edge of the platform, stared at Jack, made a last ineffectual lunge with the spear and fell backwards. Jack watched him bounce through the branches and land on the ground far below.

'You were a brave man,' Jack said. 'You were worthy of a far better cause than rebellion and mutiny.'

Sitting on the platform and hoping that he was out of the vision of any more snipers, Jack began the laborious process of reloading his revolver. He had to place each round down the muzzle and into the chamber and then fit the percussion cap. As he worked, he looked around. A jezzail lay on the platform, the old-fashioned but accurate musket used by Afghan tribesmen. There was also Minié rifle with a quantity of ammunition. Four spears, a long steel dagger and a tulwar, completed the weapons. His erstwhile opponent had prepared well for the fight.

'Captain Windrush!' Riley's voice floated from below. 'Are you all right, sir?'

'All right, Riley,' Jack called down. 'Keep under cover. There are other sharpshooters.' Replacing his revolver in its holster, Jack lifted the Minié, remembering using the weapon in the desperate action at Inkerman where the 113th rediscovered their soul. He loaded it quickly and scanned the trees for movement.

The jets of smoke from the fort attracted Jack's eye an instant before he heard the reports, and a dozen musket balls hummed around his tree, flicking off leaves and crashing through the branches. None came close. Jack knew that the mutineers would be lucky to hit him with the weapons they had, yet with so many men firing it would only be a matter of time before one found its mark. He moved to the northern side of the tree, so the bole afforded some protection. Even from here, the forest concealed most of the British and Sikh force although Jack could see men and officers cowering on the ground, under bushes and behind trees. The rebels had stalled the British advance and held the upper hand. Jack grunted; Sir Colin had been right about the use of cannon.

Ignoring the fort, Jack studied the trees, spotting an occasional spurt of white smoke where other sharpshooters fired at the British lines. Distance or foliage concealed the majority of the snipers, so only one was visible. Jack steadied himself and aimed the Minié. The rebel wore the same baggy green clothing, black turban and drab veil as the man Jack had killed.

Jack's shot splintered the timber at the man's feet, making him leap aside but doing no further damage. Jack grunted and rolled away as the sniper scanned the trees to see who had shot at him. Knowing his gun smoke would reveal his position, Jack lay prone for a few moments as flies explored his face. As soon as a bullet sprayed chips from the bole of the tree, Jack stood to reload.

Looking towards his adversary, Jack saw him doing the same, and it became a race between the two as they hammered bullets down the rifle muzzle and placed the caps on with nervous, desperate fingers. Jack was a fraction slower and saw the enemy's Minié rise. He flinched as the muzzle flared orange and he felt the passage of the bullet, and then he steadied himself, took a deep breath and fired.

The bullet took the sharpshooter high in the chest. He staggered, fell and dragged himself to his feet, looking for his adversary. Jack reloaded with desperate haste, fired again and missed. Despite his wound, the sharpshooter began to load a jezzail. The superbly balanced weapon was lighter than the British rifles and had a more extended range. Jack threw himself down, rolled away and lifted the jezzail that lay beside him. He'd never fired one before, hoped it was loaded, aimed and fired in a single movement. The kick was less than he expected, and he didn't see where the shot went.

For a moment, Jack stared at his opponent across the intervening foliage, and then both moved together, scrabbling to load. Jack chose the rifle, the enemy lifting the jezzail and both concentrating on their weapon and oblivious to anything else. Jack knew that he was faster than most at loading, yet his wounded enemy was first and was aiming the jezzail while Jack lifted his Minié.

Both shots merged in a double crack. Jack felt the tug on his right sleeve even as he saw the opponent stiffen and fall. He took a deep breath to still the hammer of his heart. That had been close. These black-turbaned musket men were expert. Now he should leave his perch before another targeted him. *I've been lucky twice; if luck deserts me, I'll be dead.*

Kicking the weapons to the ground, Jack swung over the edge of the platform and slithered down the tree, swearing as he hit half a dozen branches on his descent.

'Welcome back, sir,' Whitelam said, 'and keep your head down. The pandies are angry at you.'

Jack agreed as a cannon fired from the fort, spraying grapeshot all around. Throwing himself to the ground, he rolled to the back of the tree and lay still as the enemy used him as a target. *How old am I? Twenty-five? If I was a cat, I'd already have used up all my lives.*

'We've to withdraw, sir,' Elliot reported. 'The general's ordered in the artillery.'

'Bloody General Walpole!' Jack heard one of the 42nd shouting. 'He cannae organise a simple assault. Look at the dead – Walpole's a murdering sot, so he is.'

Others seemed to agree, to judge by the comments. With their unblemished record of victories now spoiled, the Highlanders were incensed, blaming Walpole for their defeat.

'The Sawnies are right,' Thorpe said. 'Walpole's a murdering sot.'

'Enough of that!' Jack shouted. 'Get back to the camp and leave the moaning to others.' Jack knew that he should nip any criticism of the higher command in the bud, for criticism led to disobedience and then mutiny, and this war started with mutinous soldiers. The 113th trudged back with their heads down and murder in their hearts, and as they withdrew, artillerymen pushed forward two eighteen-pounders and a pair of mortars.

'Leave it to the artillery.' Jack looked at the dead and wounded that the abortive attack had cost. *Ordinary soldiers always pay the price of a bad commander's folly.*

'People laugh at Sir Colin for his caution,' Elliot said. 'He's a far better commander than Walpole or a hundred Walpole's will ever be.'

Jack didn't respond directly. 'Take command of the men.'

'Where are you going, sir?'

'To look at those sharpshooters I killed,' Jack said. 'Do you remember Uda Devi, the woman the Highlanders shot outside Lucknow?'

'I do,' Elliot said.

'She fought the same way, shooting from the top of a tree. I wonder if either of those snipers were women.' Jack realised he was shaking. 'I hope one was Jayanti. It was only good fortune that they didn't kill me.'

'Good luck, sir.' Elliot handed over his hip flask.

Not caring if Elliot saw him trembling or not, Jack took a deep draft. The taste no longer mattered; he needed the alcohol to settle his nerves. 'Thank you, Arthur. Get the men safely back.' He returned to the jungle.

The eighteen-pounders began their bombardment, shaking the ground and pouring acrid smoke through the trees. There were no birdcalls now, and even the insects seemed subdued as Jack searched for the peepul where the first sniper had been. There were so many trees, and all looked so similar that it was ten minutes before he located the peepul and another five before he found the body. It lay a few yards from the foot of the peepul, face down and already furred by flies.

'Sorry, my brave enemy.' Bending over the crumpled, bloody mess, Jack turned him on his face and pulled off the veil.

'Oh, dear God, I was right.'

The face of a young woman stared sightlessly up at him. She was darker skinned than most indigenous people of the area, lithe and wiry. Jack guessed her to be around twenty years old.

'Why?' Jack asked, 'why must a girl like you die?' He sighed. 'Rest easy, warrior woman. You fought bravely for what you believed.'

The second markswoman had fallen into a tangle of vegetation. Jack eventually saw a leg sticking up and cleared the undergrowth until he found the body. Kneeling down, Jack gently unrolled the veil that covered the lower face. Again, young features stared at him, twisted in death.

'Go with your God,' Jack said, 'or rather, your Gods.' He unfolded the veil and replaced it over the woman's face to protect her from the questing flies.

'So now we know,' Elliot said when Jack passed on his information. 'Colonel Hook was correct, and we're on the right track.'

'I wish we had some spies we could trust.' Jack lit a cheroot. 'General Walpole doesn't seem to favour our normal information gathering techniques. We can't plan anything based on two dead women.'

'Could we not ask the trooper who escaped from Ruhya Fort?' Elliot asked. 'He seems like a handy sort of fellow.'

'I think he's gone back to Hodson's Horse.' Jack was pleased that for once he knew more than Elliot did.

'That's a shame.' Elliot passed across his hip flask. 'We must carry on blind then, and hope for a break.'

'At least we know a little more.' Jack sipped at the flask. 'We know that female warriors are fighting for the rebels and the fact that they all dress the same indicates they're in the same unit. I wish we knew how many of them we have to face.'

Elliot retrieved his flask. 'Could you imagine a whole army of Uda Devis? The women here are every bit as dedicated as the men.'

Jack thought of his stepmother's calculating years-long wait to unleash her vengeance on him. 'That could be true for women in general. We place them on a glass pedestal, we call them weak and emotional, we claim they lack common sense, and we say we have to look after them.' He shook his head. 'Except for a couple of fleeting encounters in Hereford and on the boat to India back in '51, I had never spoken to a woman until I met Myat in Burma. I knew nothing of them.'

Elliot grinned. 'I know what you mean. Public schools aren't the best preparation for mixing with women. Some of the officers I've met seem genuinely afraid of them.' He laughed.

'You never talk about women,' Jack said.

'I've got four sisters.' Elliot sipped at his flask. 'I know they are neither angels nor demons.' He grinned. 'Some days they are a mixture of both! Now your Mary—'

'She's not *my* Mary,' Jack denied at once.

'Methinks you doth protest too much.' Elliot's grin returned. 'Your Mary has more of the angel than the demon in her.' His expression became serious. 'Be careful there, Jack, my lad. While your old *amour* Helen may have enhanced your career, what with her being a colonel's daughter and all, Mary will not, however delightful a woman she might be.'

'We are not here to discuss Mary Lambert,' Jack said.

'Of course not.' Elliot switched the subject with ease. 'Did you hear about poor Colonel Grey?'

'Colonel Grey? What about him?' Jack asked.

'He's dead. Dysentery.' Elliot grunted. 'That's another colonel the 113th has lost.'

'This regiment is hard on colonels,' Jack said. 'We hardly get to know them and then they're gone.'

'That is so.' Elliot shrugged. 'Death is common out here.'

'Too common,' Jack said. 'And it comes too young. That woman I shot was about twenty years old, and a Dalit, I think. That's an untouchable, the lowest caste in India.

'I know what a Dalit is, Jack, damn it!' Elliot said.

'One in every six people in India is untouchable.' Elliot shook his head. 'I can understand why the Rajahs fight us. They want control over their lands again. I can also see the sepoys' point in mutinying if they believed that we were interfering with their religion. But I don't understand why the untouchables fight. Every other caste despises them and condemns the untouchables to the lowest and most menial jobs. One would think they would welcome British help, and maybe wish us to end Hinduism and the caste system.'

'One would think that,' Jack agreed cautiously. 'Religion is a strange thing.'

Elliot sighed. 'I once believed that the Indians liked us because we bring fair justice and some security. If even the untouchables don't want us, perhaps I was wrong.'

Jack nodded. 'I thought that we belonged here. I was born here, after all. People always say that as India was never a single nation, there are no foreigners and we, the British, are viewed as just another caste by the Hindus.' He shrugged. 'Now, with this rebellion, I'm not sure.'

'I don't know anymore,' Elliot said. 'Then you think of our Indian allies, Gurkhas, Sikhs and the camp followers, and you remember the loyal sepoys of the Madras and Bombay Presidencies. These men fight beside us and share all the danger we face. If they ever combined against us, they would so vastly outnumber us that we couldn't hope to stand against them.'

'Let's pray that doesn't happen,' Jack said.

They sat in silence for a moment as the heat built up and the regular batter of the eighteen-pounders reminded them that the battle for Fort Ruhya continued on the other side of the belt of jungle.

'I used to think that we had more morality than the native peoples,' Jack said at last. 'After we hanged hundreds or thousands of people on our rampages through the countryside, I'm not sure that we are superior.'

Elliot grunted. 'I wonder how things will be after this war.' He looked sideways at Jack. 'I don't know if I should ask this again, Jack.'

'Ask,' Jack said. 'We've been friends long enough.'

'Mary,' Elliot said. 'And Jane. How do you feel about things?'

Jack took Elliot's hip flask without asking and drank deeply. 'If you ever send in your papers, Arthur, don't consider a career in the diplomatic corps.'

'Sorry, Jack.'

'How do I feel about being a quarter Indian, my father having an affair with a Eurasian woman and my liking for another Eurasian?' Jack handed back the flask. 'That's a lot to ask in one sentence, Arthur.'

'I know,' Elliot said.

'I am glad to have friends who are still my friends despite my mixed blood,' Jack admitted. 'And that is not to say that I'm ashamed of my mother and her line.'

'Jane was a fine woman,' Elliot agreed, 'a true Christian and one of the best.'

Jack thrust an unlit cheroot into his mouth. He could talk to Elliot about such matters. There was nobody else on Earth, except perhaps Mary, in whom he would confide. 'As soon as I arrived in India, I felt as if I belonged,' he said. 'That feeling hasn't disappeared. The pandies, the massacres and the battles haven't altered anything. Sometimes I hate the heat and the poverty, the flies and the disease, and other times I love the colour and the friendliness, the generosity and the beauty, but I never feel like a stranger here, as I did in Burma or the Crimea, or Malta even.'

'I hate the place,' Elliot admitted. 'I hate the cruelty and the poverty and the heathen gods. I'm counting the days until I leave.' He nursed his flask. 'And now the big question, Jack. Again: what about Mary?'

'I wish I knew the answer to that,' Jack decided to light his cheroot. His hand was still shaking. *I don't want to go into battle again.*

Chapter Three

When the 42nd Highlanders, the Black Watch, learned that some of their wounded remained in front of Fort Ruhya, Quarter-Master Sergeant John Simpson led a patrol of four volunteers who returned carrying severely injured men. Simpson won the Victoria Cross for rescuing men under heavy fire. The eighteen-pounders continued their pounding as the infantry wondered why Walpole had so casually put these men's lives at risk.

With his memories unsettling him, Jack patrolled the lines, speaking quietly to those men who acknowledged him and allowing the others to relax.

'Good lads, the Sawnies,' Riley said. 'They'll hate being stopped by the pandies.'

Logan gave a sour grin. 'Dinnae worry about the Forty-Twa. They'll get their ain' back, and God help any pandy that gets in their way. There'll be bloody bayonets before this campaign is over.'Leaning back on the ground, he pushed a short pipe into his mouth. 'You and me though, Riles, we've got plans, eh?'

Riley saw Jack passing. 'So we have, Logie, and we'll keep them to ourselves.'

'That we will,' Logan said. He unsheathed his bayonet and began to sharpen it. 'Nae bastard will stop us, eh?'

Did Logan intend that last phrase as a threat to me? Jack wondered. Although he and Logan had fought through two wars together, he knew that the little Glaswegian had his own unique code of morality. If Logan took a dislike to him, Jack knew he would have to watch his back, officer or not. The threat of hanging wouldn't deter Logan if he believed somebody had wronged him.

That night's camp was dismal with dispirited men slumped in the heat.

'I heard why the pandies beat us,' Elliot said.

'Why was that?' Jack was still wondering what Logan and Riley had been discussing.

'We were meant to have supports,' Elliot said. 'They never came, and the reserves went to the wrong place completely.' He shook his head. 'We took Havelock and old Sir Colin for granted. If either of them had been here, we would be inside that fort now.'

'The Sawnies are cursing,' Lieutenant Bryce said. 'They're calling Walpole for everything under the sun. It's the first defeat they've experienced since Culloden. What a blasted shambles.' Bryce was in his thirties and had transferred to the 113th in the hope of action and promotion.

'Enough of that croaking,' Jack said. 'Even Wellington had the occasional reverse. We dust ourselves down and carry on.'

'Defeated by the pandies over a blasted mud-walled fort.' Lieutenant Bryce ignored Jack. 'And the 113th was involved again. It's like Chillianwala, all over again.'

'Nobody will even notice we were there.' Elliot calmed Bryce down. 'The Highland Brigade will get all the attention.'

'As you choose not to take my orders, Lieutenant Bryce, you can take a patrol out to the fort.' Jack kept his voice level. 'See what's happening and report back.'

'Sir.' Bryce gave a formal salute to show his displeasure.

Jack watched him march stiffly away. 'He'll learn,' he said. 'I just hope he learns quickly and doesn't lose any of my men in the process.'

'I remember hearing about a keen young ensign disobeying orders to attack a Burmese stockade,' Elliot said.

'He was a bloody fool.' Jack looked back at his younger self without pleasure.

When Bryce reported that the rebels had abandoned the fort, the column marched on in sullen anger, stamping their feet on the hard ground and glowering forward. At that moment, Jack thought, the infantry hated General Walpole more than they hated the enemy.

'I hope the pandies make a stand,' Logan said. 'Then we can smash them.'

'I hope they don't,' Armstrong grumbled. 'Bloody Walpole will get us all killed for nothing again.'

On the 22nd April, Logan had his wish as the rebels' halted their retreat at a small village called Sirsa.

Jack scanned the enemy positions with his binoculars. 'Cavalry, infantry and artillery,' he reported. 'Nirpat Singh is going to fight.'

'Come on, boys!' Logan hefted his rifle.

'Not this time,' Riley said. 'Walpole's discovered he has guns. He won't need us.'

'Does Walpole even know what infantry are for?' Logan asked as the British artillery pounded the enemy camp.

'If he doesn't use us, Logie, then we've more chance of surviving,' Riley said. 'And we've something to live for, remember?'

'Aye.' Logan sounded surly. 'I still wanted to fight them.'

Jack noted snatches of the conversations between the crashes as Walpole's artillery pounded the enemy. Only when the guns had weakened the defences did Walpole send in the cavalry. After a brief, if bloody skirmish, the rebels ran, abandoning their artillery and, more important, leaving the bridge over the River Rāmgangā intact.

'Well,' Jack said, 'Walpole won that battle efficiently enough.'

'There's no glory for us in this campaign,' Lieutenant Bryce said.

'If you're looking for glory, Lieutenant, you've come to the wrong regiment. In the 113th, we don't look for glory. We do our duty. Now check your men.' Jack turned away, aware he sounded pompous.

Walpole's column marched on, until twelve days after the affair at Fort Ruhya, they merged with Sir Colin Campbell's main army and continued towards Bareilly. With elephants and camels, hordes of camp followers and thousands of men in the reinforced column, Jack guessed that only a significant rebel army would face them and any possibility of gathering intelligence was limited.

'I wish I spoke the language better,' Jack said after a fruitless day asking the pickets if they had any sign of men or women in black turbans and dropped the name Jayanti among the scurrying servants with no success at all.

'Yes.' Elliot pulled at a cheroot. 'I think all officers in India should learn at least one of the languages. Especially us, with the strange assignments we get.' He gave a twisted grin. 'Or at least Hooky could have provided us with a translator. Mary, perhaps.'

'That's enough,' Jack said. 'We're not discussing Mary again, and I'm not putting her in any danger. We had enough of that in the last campaign.'

'Yes, sir,' Elliot said. 'I won't mention Mary again.'

'Best not, Lieutenant Elliot.' Jack adopted his captain's tone.

At the beginning of May, Brigadier Penny's column reinforced Campbell's force. They marched relentlessly onward along a raised roadway with the ground on either side flat and featureless, dotted with *topes* of trees and the occasional village. As they neared the old British cantonments at Bareilly, the terrain altered, with a small river hiding within a deep bed and a hundred *nullahs* in which the rebels could hide, to pounce on any part of the unwieldy British column.

As always, Sir Colin Campbell made detailed preparations, so the army was ready for the final march and the capture of Bareilly. With unknown numbers of rebel cavalry on the prowl, Sir Colin ordered a strong guard for the straggling supplies and ensured the sick in their doolies were on the right side of the column, where the enemy was least likely to attack.

'Sir Colin's doing his best,' Elliot said.

'He's very slow,' Bryce complained. 'He should leave the sick and supplies behind and attack with the fighting men.'

'If he did,' Elliot murmured, 'the rebels would have a soft target, and then the army would lack food, tents and ammunition.'

On the 5th May, they left camp as dawn splintered the horizon and the heat of the day was already mounting.

'When do the rains come?' A replacement asked as he staggered under the force of the sun.

'Not yet,' Coleman said. 'It's maybe a month until the monsoon. You'll notice when the rain starts.'

'I hope they come before that.' The man wiped a hand across his forehead.

'I don't care about the heat,' Logan said. 'I wish we could march without all these bloody halts to allow the artillery and baggage to catch us. Havelock didn't need all that rubbish.'

'Havelock lost more men through heat exhaustion,' Coleman said. 'I'll have old Sir Colin any time.'

'I'd have old Sir Colin any time,' Thorpe echoed.

Riley gave Coleman a searching look. 'You're not as stupid as you look, Coley. Bonaparte had the right idea planting trees for shade. We've nothing here except some scrub.'

The British moved on in a jolting procession, half-blinded by the dust and with uncountable flies tormenting them, seeking moisture in eyes and mouths and nostrils. The sound of boots on the road was a monotonous drumbeat, augmenting the thunder of elephants and occasional snort of camels.

'It's like travelling with a circus,' Riley said.

'You would know about that.' Armstrong said and spat a mouthful of dust-filled phlegm on the ground. 'You and that actress woman you call a wife.'

Jack intervened before Logan retaliated for Charlotte's honour.

The landscape altered as they came closer to Bareilly. The open country gave way to small but thick woods of peepul and mango trees, with the occasional straggling village or lonely house, mostly abandoned in the face of the squabbling armies.

A sweating cornet reined in his horse beside Jack. '113th to go to the front!'

'Give me a proper report, Cornet!' Jack snapped.

The cornet took a deep breath. 'Sorry, sir. Sir Colin sends his respects, sir, and could the 113th take up a position at the front of the infantry.'

'That's better, Cornet. Please convey my respects to Sir Colin and inform him that we will be there directly.'

It was good to have the men stretch their legs and march past the other regiments, good to hear the shouted insults and catcalls of the Black Watch as they gave ribald encouragement.

'Go on, the 113th; soften them up for the real soldiers!'

'Away, you teuchter bastards,' Logan replied in uncompromising Glaswegian. 'Make way for the 113th.' He grinned. 'That told them, eh, Riley?'

'Aye, Logie, you told them,' Riley said. 'Remember to keep your head down.'

There was marginally less dust at the front of the column, with only the cavalry screen between the 113th and any possible enemy. Jack revelled in the relative freedom. *Here we are, the once-despised 113th, leading Sir Colin Campbell's army against the rebels. Much as I hate the bloodshed and agony of war, this is the reason I became a soldier, and for the minute there is nowhere in the world I would rather be. Here our peers accept us as soldiers and men; here we matter.*

The cannon broke Jack's reverie, and the solid iron shot bounded past the cavalry screen to roll along the pukka road.

'Ready boys.' Jack knew that his veterans would be alert. The replacements might need some encouragement.

'It's mid-day,' Riley said. 'That's the pandy's dinner gong.'

'Is that what it was?' Thorpe said. 'I thought they were firing at us.'

'Nah, they wouldn't do that, Thorpey,' Coleman said. 'They're going to welcome us with beer and cheese.'

'Are they?' Thorpe thought for a moment. 'I don't think they will, Coley. I think they were firing at us.'

Whitelam pointed ahead. 'You're right, Thorpe. There's a pandy gun on the road, and it's firing at us.'

Jack lifted his binoculars. The rebels had built a small earthwork beside the road, with the muzzle of a single cannon protruding through an embrasure. 'One cannon won't halt the army,' Jack said. 'The best it can do is delay us a little.'

'Here's Sir Colin's reply.' Elliot brushed a questing fly from his eyebrow.

Two pieces of artillery galloped past with the gunners whipping the horses and laughing at the prospect of action. 'Make way for the guns, 113th!' They unlimbered two hundred yards in front and fired a few rounds at the enemy emplacement.

When the British cannonballs bounced around them, the rebels abandoned their cannon and fled in apparent panic.

'They didn't stand for long,' Elliot said. 'What are they planning, I wonder?'

'They weren't in sufficient force to halt us,' Jack said. 'I think they fell out with Nana Sahib and he ordered them here as punishment. I can't think of any other reason.' *Unless they're trying to entice us into a trap.* Jack scanned the surroundings with the binoculars, searching for anything that might indicate an enemy ambush. He saw nothing except drifting dust and a heat haze.

Jack lowered the binoculars. 'The pandies have to make a stand at Bareilly, or they're admitting defeat. Their little victory at Fort Ruhra will have heartened them, and they'll think they have our measure.'

'Thank God that Sir Colin's in command again and not that fool, Walpole,' Elliot said. 'I hear that Khan Bahadar Khan is in charge at Bareilly.'

Jack looked at his men. It didn't matter to them who led the enemy. They were marching through the dust, staggering under the heat and cursing fluently. *Good.* If British soldiers ever stopped swearing, he would know something was seriously wrong. 'Who is this Khan Bahadur Khan fellow, Arthur?'

'The descendant of a long line of Rajput rulers,' Elliot said. 'He's the grandson of Hafiz Rahmat Khan if that helps.'

'Not in the slightest,' Jack confessed.

Elliot smiled. 'Well, I only know the name. Khan Bahadur Khan took over Bareilly when the Mutiny began. He is about thirty-five, a bearded, dignified fellow. I don't know how good he is as a soldier.'

'We'll find out soon enough,' Jack said.

As they marched, Jack surveyed his surroundings. Bareilly was not as exotic as Lucknow, as evocative as Cawnpore or as politically vital as Delhi, yet it was significant in its own right as the capital of Rohilkhand. The city sat on the level, with a gentle slope toward the south, from where Campbell led the British army. Bareilly was straggling rather than compact, with groves of trees scattered over a plain intersected by gulleys and a few defensible streams. Jack lifted his binoculars again, searching for enemy cavalry.

'Bareilly's rather beautiful,' Elliot said. 'Why do we have to destroy it?'

'Ask this Khan Bahadur Khan fellow.' Jack continued to eye the terrain. The atmosphere was tense, as if the land was waiting for something. 'Or ask Jayanti and her young warriors. All the pandies have to do is stop fighting, and we can all have peace again.'

Elliot nodded. 'The rebels might view it differently. They might say that all we have to do is leave India and they can live without us. They might prefer their heathen gods, their wife-burning suttee, their thugee, their castes and all the rest.'

'Once we've defeated them, we can ask.' Jack lifted his binoculars. 'There go the cavalry.' He watched as the Company sowars cantered forward to investigate the plain.

'The shave says Khan Bahadur has 30,000 infantry in Bareilly,' Elliot said, 'with 6,000 cavalry and forty guns.'

'Is that what the shave says?' Jack watched the Company cavalry spread out across the plain. 'Where did he get that many men? We've smashed the main rebel armies and broken the mutineers. Cut the figures in half, and we'd be more accurate.'

Elliot grunted. 'There'll still be plenty of them.'

'We won't argue with that,' Jack said. He saw the Company sowars congregate around a ford of one of the rivers. There was a jet of white smoke and sowars reined back. 'It looks as if we've made contact with the enemy. That was cannon fire.'

'Here we go again,' Elliot said.

'Captain Windrush!' Jack recognised the sun-reddened cornet that approached him. 'I have a message from Sir Colin for you, sir.'

'Thank you, Cornet.' Jack read the note the cornet handed him. 'Please convey my respects to Sir Colin and inform him that I will act immediately.'

Elliot watched as the cornet galloped away. 'That young Griff needs his bottom kicked. What does Sir Colin say?'

'We've to patrol ahead of the column and see if there are any enemy in the *topes.*'

'Is that not what the cavalry are meant to do?' Elliot asked.

'Aye, but we do it better,' Jack said. 'Right Elliot, take the right flank, Bryce, take the left. I have the centre with Ensigns Wilden and Peake.' Jack gave unhurried orders. 'Advance in extended order lads, loaded rifles and bayonets fixed. If in doubt, shoot.'

'What if they're civilians, sir?' Elliot asked.

'Do you think any civilians will still be here, with two armies about to do battle?' Jack paused. Elliot had made a valid point. 'Don't shoot any civilians and look out for Jayanti and her women.' By now, everybody in the 113th knew the real purpose of their mission. 'If you kill any of them, mark the spot. I want to see the bodies later.' *I want that woman who mutilated Ensign Green.*

The 113th moved forward slowly, probing every *tope* for signs of the enemy and stopping to drink at the streams. The heat was punishing, pounding them into the Indian soil, making every movement torture while each man moved with a circlet of flies around his head, and dust in his boots.

The first *tope* was of bamboo, crackling in the heat, tall and serene. Logan swore as a colourful snake slithered away. 'It's bad enough with the bloody pandies, let alone the buggering wildlife.' He stepped back to allow the creature to escape.

The 113th moved on, checking the treetops, probing the undergrowth, wary of an ambush.

'Sir,' Greaves spoke quietly. 'Something is moving in front. I don't know what.'

Jack nodded. Too experienced to show any alarm, he peered to his left. 'Whereabout, Sergeant?'

'There's a dip in the ground sir, and I swear I saw a shadow move. There's no wind.'

'I'll have a look. Be ready to support me.'

'Yes, sir.'

Patrolling alone was unprofessional. Leaving his men was wrong. Jack didn't care. He could not send a man to do a job he would not do himself; no proper officer would. With the dry grass brittle under his boots, he stepped forward, one hand on the butt of his revolver. Every yard took him further from his men and closer to the enemy. The notion came that at that moment he may well be the most advanced infantry soldier in the British Army.

A single bird rose from a *tope* two hundred yards to his left, and then another. The second bird called, the sound harsh in the oppressive air. Jack shook away the memory of the melancholic beauty of the blackbirds calling around the Malvern Hills. The ground dipped, as Greaves had said, and Jack felt the handle of his revolver slippery with sweat.

One moment Jack was walking over an empty landscape and the next the woman in the black turban was in front of him, watching. She was medium height with the bottom half of her face veiled and she had the most intense eyes Jack had ever seen.

Jack loosened his revolver in its holster. The woman wore similar clothing to the other female warriors, with green baggy clothes, black turban and the khaki veil over the lower part of her face. She also wore a studded leather glove on each hand and didn't carry any weapons.

'Who are you?' Her voice had the musical intonation of most Indians. To Jack, raised in Herefordshire, it sounded nearly Welsh.

'I am Captain Jack Windrush of Her Majesty's 113th Foot.' The woman seemed unconcerned by either the heat that hammered down on them or the circling flies. 'Who are you?' He'd already guessed the answer.

'I am Jayanti,' the woman said. She held Jack's gaze as if challenging him.

The rumours are correct, Jayanti exists. 'I've heard of you.' Jack felt the butt of his revolver slip a little in his hand. He contemplated lifting it, firing and ending this quest here and now.

'I would not try.' Jayanti seemed to read his mind. 'At this moment I have five rifles pointed directly at you. All I have to do is raise my hand, and they will fire.'

'I could still kill you,' Jack pointed out. 'A life for a life and your life is more important to your cause than mine is to Her Majesty.'

Gauging Jayanti's feelings was hard. Her eyes remained as intense as ever. 'I am unarmed,' Jayanti said. 'You are a British gentleman. Your code prevents you from killing me.'

'You're a clever woman, Jayanti,' Jack said. 'Sufficiently clever to realise that you cannot win this war. My Queen can send out many more regiments of professional fighting men with the most modern equipment.'

'You are a clever man, Captain Windrush,' Jayanti echoed his words. 'Sufficiently clever to realise that although you may win this campaign, you ultimately cannot win this war. India will wait until the time is right and then overwhelm you. Britain is many thousands of miles away. India is here.'

'Why are you telling me this?'

'Because you are different from the others,' Jayanti said.

'I am no different from any other British officer.' *What does she mean?*

Jayanti stepped back. 'Think about what I said, Jack Baird Windrush. You are different. And look out for your men. There are others very close by who do not wish to merely talk.'

'Come back!' Jack shouted, just as the rifle cracked and a spurt of dust rose a yard in front of him.

'Five rifles, Captain,' Jayanti reminded. She took another step back and vanished as suddenly as she had appeared.

'Sir!' Sergeant Greaves shouted. 'Cavalry!'

They erupted from the riverside, a horde of irregular cavalry with flowing robes and flashing swords. Jack swore. Spread out in the open, his men would be easy prey to these superb Indian horsemen.

'Form square!' He shouted as he ran back, all thought of Jayanti forgotten in his sudden concern for his men. 'Form a square!'

The 113th ran toward him, with the officers and NCOs hectoring the men, pushing the few laggards and watching the fast-approaching cavalry through nervous eyes.

'By platoon!' Jack ordered. 'Remember your training!'

The cavalry advanced at a canter, their hooves kicking up a curtain of dust through which only their heads, shoulders and waving swords were visible. A walnut-faced private, limping from an old Crimean wound, stumbled as he ran for the square, and sprawled in the dust. As if in slow motion, Jack saw the veteran rise and stare at his fellows, now fifty yards away. The veteran's rear-rank-man hesitated and ran to help, arm outstretched. Three rebel cavalrymen galloped free from the press toward the lone private. With one leg injured, the veteran fell to one knee and levelled his rifle. Then the cavalry was on him, a sword flashed in the sunlight, and the private's head rose in the air. His comrade turned and ran toward the rapidly-forming square.

One minute the injured private was alive and the next he was dead. He had been some mother's son, reared in the hell's kitchen of an English industrial slum, or in an Irish cabin or Scottish clachan. Some months from now the private's family would learn of his death and would mourn him for a day or a month or perhaps dismiss his memory with a shrug. He would have been born with hope and love only to die in a pointless skirmish many thousands of miles from home.

Rule Britannia. The poorest always paid the price of Empire to ensure profit for the richest.

Jack's men formed around him, taking their positions as automatically as they had done on a score of training exercises and field days.

'Front rank, kneel!' Jack ordered. There were no more stragglers out on the *maidan*, and already the charging cavalry was past the private's decapitated body.

'Second rank, cap!'

The men fitted their percussion caps, the replacements with shaking hands, the veterans with studied calmness.

'Ready!' The rifles came to the present on all sides of the square, a hundred British Enfield rifles ready to blast the approaching cavalry. It was the same formation that Wellington had used at Waterloo and not much different from the schiltrons that King Robert the First had used at Bannockburn over five centuries previously.

The cavalry increased their pace from a trot to a canter, half-seen in the dust, hundreds of fierce warriors, some of the best horsemen in the world, veterans of battle and skirmish.

The 113th faced them, the old soldiers' expressionless and the replacements white under their sunburn, wide-eyed, scared. Tongues licked dry lips; hands shook on the stocks of Enfields.

'Steady, lads,' Jack said. 'It's only men sitting on horses.'

'Come on you bastards.' Logan gave his ubiquitous invitation. 'Wee Donnie's waiting for you!'

'Cry Havelock!' somebody shouted, prolonging the final vowel so the others could join in. 'Let loose the dogs of war!'

'Ready!' Jack glanced to his right and left. His men were holding, the replacements drawing strength from the veterans. 'Second rank, on my word, fire a volley… Ready… Fire!' The Enfields cracked; the bullets sped toward the advancing cavalry. Unable to see for the dust, Jack could only imagine the chaos, the fallen horses, the injured men, the blood and agony and death.

'Second rank, cap and load! First rank, present!'

The cavalry emerged from the dust, wild men from the plains wielding curved swords, professional warriors ready to savage these northern invaders from across the *kala pani*, the black water.

'First rank, fire! Second rank, present!'

The rifles hammered again, and this time the cavalry were so close that Jack could see the havoc. Horses fell, screaming, torn by lead bullets. The riders immediately following trying to get past them, leaping over the kicking legs and writhing bodies. Men shouted, struggling to control their mounts.

'First rank, cap and load. Second rank, fire a volley!'

The bullets hammered in, remorseless, maiming, killing, wounding. The leading horses turned away, nostrils flaring, terrified, some falling under the hooves of the cavalry immediately behind.

'Second rank, cap and load! First rank, fire a volley!'

The 113th acted like a machine, firing and loading, aiming into the mass, professional soldiers doing their job, the cutting edge of Empire, the ultimate tool in Queen Victoria's arsenal, the little men at the sharp end who enforced the politicians' snake-tongued words.

'They're breaking, sir!' Greaves shouted.

'First rank, cap and load. Second rank, fire a volley!'

The 113th was unsupported. Cavalry could have charged into the enemy's flanks and completed the rout or artillery could have fired grapeshot into the retreating enemy horse. As it was, the 113th could only stand in their square and watch their enemy ride away.

'Come back and try again!' Logan roared.

Only a few yards in front of the square, thirty men and horses lay in a tangle, some dead, others writhing or groaning. The rebels had paid the price for attacking the 113th.

'Keep in formation,' Jack ordered. 'March back to camp.' The incident was over, and it would be foolish to remain out on the *maidan* in case more cavalry appeared, this time backed by musket-carrying infantry or artillery to blast his small square to bloody fragments.

Only when Jack returned to camp did he realise the full implications of what had occurred.

'Jayanti called me Jack *Baird* Windrush. How the devil did she know that? How does she know my full name?'

Elliot shrugged. 'I'm blessed if I know, Jack. These Indian fellows have spies everywhere. I wouldn't be surprised if half the bearers and doolie carriers in the column were giving information to the enemy. Why, they'd cut their granny's throat for a rupee and hand back the change.'

Jack nodded and tried to shake off the feeling that something was very wrong. How would a leader of irregular Indian low-caste warriors know his full name? Why would she approach him and, if she had five rifles aimed at him, why did she not kill him where he stood? There was more to Jayanti than he knew.

What sort of pickle has Colonel Hook landed me in?

The 113th didn't have much time to recover. That evening, 4th May 1858, Khan Bahadur Khan prepared to defend Bareilly. The British Army buckled its collective belt, checked its powder was dry and sharpened its bayonets for the test ahead.

'Here we go again.' Elliot loaded his revolver, tamping each bullet down the barrel and checking his percussion caps. 'Lord, I shall be very busy this day. I may forget thee, but do not forget me.' He looked up. 'And may God have mercy on us all.'

Jack couldn't muster a smile. 'I hope He has, Arthur, I do hope He has sufficient mercy for us all.'

The senior officers gathered around Sir Colin Campbell with the heat bouncing from the ground and the smell of men's sweat potent in the air. Jack glanced around the stern, bearded faces and the uniforms that spoke of glory and triumph, and wondered what the public back home would think if they ever experienced the reality of war.

'Windrush.' Campbell always muted his Glasgow growl when he explained his plans for a forthcoming battle. 'I know your men are expert in skirmishes and ambushes, scouting and picket work. It's time they made their name in a major encounter.' Campbell's dour, moustached face glared at Jack.

'My boys were at Inkerman, sir, and with General Havelock's advance on Cawnpore and Lucknow.'

'I am aware of that, Windrush.' Campbell gave what he probably believed was a smile. 'That's why I'm putting your 113th on the front line.'

'Thank you, sir.'

'Khan Bahadur Khan means to fight,' Campbell said. 'He has positioned his artillery on a range of sand hills directly on our line of advance. He also has cavalry on the flanks, so we have to keep formation, or he'll ravage our infantry.'

Jack wondered if he had thanked Campbell too soon. Glory and honour were all very well for the officers and the reputation of the regiment, but all too often it came at the price of maimed and broken men.

'We will advance in two lines,' Campbell informed the gathered officers. 'In the front line will be the Highland Brigade, the 113th, the 4th Punjab Rifles and the Baluch battalion. I will place a heavy field battery in the centre to counter the enemy artillery, and we'll have horse artillery and cavalry on the flanks. If Khan Bahadur Khan unleashes his horse, our guns will shatter them from a distance, and our cavalry will destroy what remains.'

There was nothing original about Sir Colin's plan. It was methodical, practical and sound.

'The second line will include everybody else,' Sir Colin said. 'Nobody will be left behind. The siege train, the baggage and the camp followers, the wounded and the sick will follow the fighting men.'

Elliot checked that his hip flask was full, pulled his sword from his scabbard to ensure it didn't stick and gave a weak smile. 'Good luck, Jack.'

'Good luck, Arthur.' They shook hands, and Elliot lifted his flask in salute.

'Here's to the next to die.'

'The next to die,' Jack echoed. He couldn't think of life without Elliot. After years of bloody campaigning, they were closer than brothers. 'Try to stay alive, Arthur. If you fell, I would have to tell your father what a rotten soldier you are and how little chance you ever had of becoming a captain, let alone a general.'

'And I want to see Helen again and tell her she married the better brother.'

During the Crimean War, Helen had left Jack for his half-brother, William, an officer in the far more prestigious Royal Malvern regiment and heir to the family house and fortune.

The men were also making their preparations for the forthcoming battle.

'If I die, Thorpie, make sure you see me buried, eh? Don't leave me for the wild beasts to eat.'

Thorpe shook his head. 'I won't Coley. I'll see you buried decent. You do the same for me, too.'

'I will.' Coleman sharpened his bayonet on a stone. 'Don't leave me, Thorpey, not out here. Swear that by the Book will you?' He produced a very battered Bible. 'Swear it, Thorpey.'

Thorpe recoiled slightly. 'I can't read, Coley.'

'That doesn't matter. Just swear. God won't mind that you can't read.'

Putting his hand on the Bible, Thorpe mumbled, 'I swear not to leave your body for the beasts to eat.'

Coleman did the same. 'Thanks, Thorpey. You're all right.' He returned to sharpening his bayonet.

Jack saw Thorpe look away to hide the tears in his eyes. Men such as Thorpe, orphaned at a young age and deprived of familial affection, prized any sort of relationship.

'That's the way, lad.' Sergeant Greaves marched up to them. 'Use that bayonet properly mind, Coleman, and you too, Thorpe. I don't want you poking like an old woman with a knitting needle. When you see an angry pandy, you think of me, yell *bastard*, stick it right in him, twist and withdraw.'

'Yes, Sergeant,' Thorpe said. 'I always say bastard when I think of you.'

'Good lad, Thorpe. I knew you weren't as stupid as Coleman looks.' Greaves marched away to spread his words of encouragement.

At seven in the morning, the advance began, a slow march across the stream-seamed plain with the sun already hammering at the men. Within a few minutes, Khan Bahadur Khan's artillery opened up.

'Maybe if we kick up enough dust, they won't see us,' Thorpe began to shuffle his feet.

'Good idea, Thorpey,' Coleman said. 'The pandies will think the dust is a mist and all the noise is the monsoon starting. They'll all go home and let us win.'

'Do you think so, Coley?' Thorpe shuffled harder.

'Try and see,' Coleman said as a roundshot crashed into the ground in front of them, bounced once and rolled toward the extended khaki line.

'Jump over that ball! Don't try and block it!' Although the iron ball looked slow and cumbersome as it growled along the ground, it had tremendous momentum. In previous battles, Jack had seen raw soldiers try to stop a rolling roundshot with their feet, only to lose their entire leg. Somewhere to their right, the Highland pipes sounded, high and wild in the Eastern air.

'There are the pipes,' Logan said. 'Come on the tartan!'

The British advance continued, the slow, purposeful, remorseless march of professional infantry with a tradition of near-unbroken victory behind them. British, Sikhs and Baluchis marching side by side, bayonets and Enfields, turbans and the feather bonnets of the Highlanders mere specks on the dusty Indian plain.

'The pandies are moving.' Elliot peered through the screen of dust and powder smoke. 'I think they're coming out to attack us!'

Jack took a deep breath. The rebel infantry liked little better than a face-to-face battle with swords and shields against the British bayonets. They were ferocious fighting men, skilled and brave. Jack drew his sword. He didn't relish the massive, bloody melee that would occur if thousands of rebel warriors met the British in the open.

'Come on, you bastards!' Logan had his own opinion. 'Wee Donnie's waiting for you!'

'They're not coming out,' Greaves said. 'They're withdrawing.'

'They're on the run!' Thorpe said. 'You were right, Coley, the pandies thought we were mist!'

'That's what it was, Thorpey, that's just what it was.' Coleman spat a mouthful of dust and phlegm onto the ground. 'Your kicking up dust won us the battle. You'll get another Victoria Cross for that!'

As the British advanced, most of Khan Bahadur Khan's forward defensive line withdrew inside the city. Always careful with his men, Campbell ordered a halt when the British reached the stream that coursed between the advance and the suburbs of Bareilly. Those units of the rebels that had not retreated stood on the far side of the river, waiting in silence with the sun glinting on the steel of swords and the long barrels of jezzails. A thin wisp of smoke drifted from the muzzle of their cannons, positioned on the British side of the bridge.

'We'll have to get over the river.' Jack eyed the single bridge and the rebels who crowded on the far side.

'That's the Nukutte Bridge,' Elliot said. 'If the pandies decide to stand here they can do us damage. Their positions are a bit amateur though, with their guns at this side of the bridge and that *nullah* behind them.'

'Maybe not. The pandy artillery can fire without damaging the bridge.' Jack swept his binoculars across the enemy position. 'If they had decent leadership, they could have made a fine stand there. It's like the Alma, and on their day the Indians are as doughty fighters as any Russian.'

The rebel cannon opened up as soon as the British came within range, orange spurts of flame splitting the smoke.

'For what we are about to receive,' Elliot murmured, 'may the Lord make us truly thankful.'

'Bloody pandy bastards.' Logan was less philosophical.

Before the first enemy cannonball landed, Campbell sent forward the British artillery, and a gun duel began. The infantry watched in interested impotence as British and rebel artillery exchanged shots across the sun-hot *maidan*. After less than an hour, the rebel guns stopped firing.

'They're running,' Bryce said as the enemy fired a few final shots and then pulled out, toward Bareilly.

'Not all of them.' Elliot pointed towards the nearest *tope*. 'See over there?'

Jack focused his binoculars on the trees. Sunlight flashed on the helmets and swords of cavalry. He couldn't tell how many. 'Aye, they're waiting for the infantry to advance. Once we break formation to cross the river, they will pounce.'

'What's happening?' Lieutenant Bryce asked.

'Khan Bahadur Khan has placed his cavalry in the *topes*. Sir Colin will bring up the guns to scatter them,' Jack said. 'Here we go! We're moving again. Keep together, 113th!'

As the wary British crossed the bridge and forded the stream, Campbell sent the artillery forward to bombard the enemy cavalry. The steady hammer of the guns and the black streaks of cannon balls arcing overhead punctuated the advance.

Elliot thrust a cheroot into his mouth. 'Bahadur's taken over the old cantonments, where the Company sepoys were stationed before they mutinied.' *Trust Elliot to know what is happening.* 'Thank God Sir Colin's using the artillery. Old Havelock would have us rushing straight down their throat.'

Jack surveyed the British lines, with the kilted Highlanders, the turbaned Sikhs and his 113th in faded khaki. 'Sir Colin is a bit more careful of his men's lives, thank goodness.'

'There's no glory in that,' Bryce said.

Jack marshalled his men over the bridge and checked they were ready to repel any attack, but Campbell's caution ensured the rebel cavalry didn't have the opportunity to mass and charge. When the second British line was over the stream, Campbell's methodical advance began again, with the artillery bombarding every *tope* and every building.

'We're just crawling along.' Bryce removed his hat to wipe the sweat from his forehead.

'We're making progress.' Jack focused his binoculars on the left. 'Something's happening over there.' He watched as the 4th Punjab Rifles doubled forward to the old sepoy cantonments, turbans bobbing and rifles held ready.

'That's our Sikhs,' Elliot said.

'Beyond them,' Jack pointed to a mass of white-and-green clothed men waiting in and around the outer suburbs of Bareilly. 'Those men are not ours. It looks like they're going to try and turn our left flank.' He raised his voice. 'Ensign Peake! Convey my compliments to Sir Colin and inform him that there is a large force of rebels about to threaten our left flank. Have you got that?'

'Yes, sir!' Peake looked eager as he began to move away. Jack grabbed the sleeve of his jacket. 'Say it back to me, Peake.'

'Captain Windrush sends his compliments, and there is a large force of rebels about to threaten our left flank.'

'Off you go and be quick about it!' Jack watched Peake jink through the British lines to Campbell. The ensign returned a few moments later, red-faced and eyes bright with excitement.

'He sends his—'

'Who sends his? Report properly, Ensign Peake!' Jack fixed the boy with a hard glare.

'Sorry, sir! Sir Colin sends his compliments and could the 113th please support the 42nd in helping the Punjabi Rifles in repelling the enemy.'

'That's better, Peake.' Jack spared the boy a few moments of his time. 'Always repeat a message exactly, Ensign. You could miss out some small word that alters the meaning and causes disaster.'

'Yes, sir.' Peake looked crestfallen. 'Sorry, sir.'

'You'll know next time, Peake. Now off you go to your men and do your duty.'

Jack watched Peake for a moment, thinking that it was only a year or so ago that the youngster's greatest worry was his headmaster's cane. Now he was responsible for the lives of grown men.

Jack raised his voice. 'Form two lines, boys! Lieutenant Bryce, take the left flank, Lieutenant Elliot, command the second line!' Jack gave them time to form up and then strode forward, revolver in hand. As always, he felt the mixed surge of elation and fear, with the excitement of knowing he was doing what generations of his forbears had been born to do, leading men into battle.

On his right, he saw the 42nd Foot marching forward with the élan and confidence for which all Highland regiments were famous. The officers walked or rode in front, kilts swinging as the men's bayonets gleamed wickedly in the sun. In the middle, grizzled face as calm as if he was strolling through his native Glasgow, Sir Colin Campbell encouraged his men.

'Come on 113th!' Jack roared. 'Don't let the Sawnies beat us to the enemy!'

A bank of powder smoke rolled ahead, punctured by orange and yellow muzzle flashes and the rattle of musketry.

'The rebels are in those houses.' Bryce pointed to a clump of single-storey buildings in the Bareilly suburbs. White smoke spurted as the enemy fired into the Punjabi Rifles, the moment they moved into the old sepoy cantonments. Taken by surprise, the Punjabis recoiled and began to retreat toward the advancing 113th and 42nd.

'Prepare to open ranks and allow the Punjabis through,' Jack said. He didn't want his men to remain in a close formation when a mob of retreating Sikhs crashed into them. Jack remembered the opening phase of the battle of the Alma in the Crimean War, when one unit had fallen back, disorganising the regiments immediately to their rear. The 113th would have to maintain their discipline as the Punjabis withdrew through them.

'Jesus!' Parker blasphemed. 'The barrel of my rifle is red hot!'

Other men were having the same experience as the sun heated anything metal until it was too hot to the touch.

'India is fighting back,' Elliot said. 'The Russians may talk about General Winter; over here India has General Summer, Colonel Monsoon and Major Disease.'

'What the devil?' Bryce drew his sabre as hundreds of sword-wielding men burst from the half-ruined houses and ran at the with-drawing Punjabis, screaming '*deen, deen!*'

'Ghazis!' These were the men Jack had seen gathering on the flank. Muslim fanatics, they wore white robes with green cummerbunds and charged with their heads down, protected by small, circular shields. As they ran, they slashed and hacked with their wickedly sharp tulwars, turning the Punjabi's withdrawal into a rout.

'Stand, the 4th Rifles,' Jack shouted, knowing the tumult of battle drowned his voice. 'Don't let them see your backs! Steady, the 113th!'

'Sir!' Bryce looked at Jack. 'What are your orders, sir?'

Jack swore. If his men fired, they could as easily hit the Punjabis as the Ghazis. If they held their fire, the Ghazis would chase the Punjabis into the 113th, disorganising them so they would be in no position to face the enemy. It was the sort of quandary that no officer liked.

'*Deen! Deen!*' The yells of the Ghazis were clear above the screams of the wounded and the fear of the now-panicking Punjabi Rifles. '*Bis-millah! Allah Akbar!*'

Sir Colin Campbell, vastly experienced, solved the dilemma. 'Fire away, men! Shoot them down. Shoot every man jack of them!' The gruff Scottish voice gave confidence to all who heard. 'Bayonet them as they come on!'

The 42nd fired at once, the kilted Highlanders trying to avoid the Punjabis and aimed for the charging Ghazis.

'Come on 113th! You heard Sir Colin! Fire!'

Jack had expected some hesitation, but he'd been mistaken. The 113th fired the second he gave the order, with some of the replace-ments stepping forward in their eagerness to be involved. The situa-tion had altered now. If the 113th retained their open formation, the Ghazis would break in and cause havoc. 'Close ranks!'

'Steady there, men!' Greaves' voice sounded above the crackle of musketry. 'Keep in line! Close up the ranks!'

'Close up, men!' Bryce added his orders. 'Don't leave gaps for the pandies to get through!'

'First rank, cap and load. Second rank, fire a volley!' Jack used the old, familiar phrases, knowing that hours of training on the parade ground now proved their worth as the men worked by instinct, following orders as if by numbers and the whole company working together on the word of command.

The Enfield rifles crashed out, the bullets hammering into the charging Ghazis and hitting some Punjabis.

'Stupid buggers!' Logan gave his philosophical thoughts. 'They should have fought, then we wouldn't be shooting them. Stand and fight you bastards!'

'The Ghazis are getting close!' Bryce balanced his sabre against his right shoulder. 'It'll be hand to hand in a minute.'

Bent almost double to make themselves as small a target as possible, the Ghazis sheltered behind the illusive protection of their shields, raised their tulwars high and circled them in the air, yelling as they raced on. For a second Jack wondered if his great-grandfather had seen something similar as he stood with the Royal Malverns at Killiecrankie, when Bonny Dundee's Highlanders had poured down the hillside to smash the redcoats. That was the only battle where the Royal Malverns had ever broken and fled, he remembered, and vowed that his 113th would not follow that example.

As they neared the British lines, the Ghazis bent even lower, ducking under the jabbing bayonets and slashing at the legs of the 113th and 42nd.

'Aye, would you, you bastard!' Logan blocked a swinging sword with the barrel of his rifle.

'I've got him,' Riley sidestepped and jabbed his bayonet into the neck of the Ghazi. The man tried to straighten up, and Logan finished him with a thrust through the heart.

'Close up!'

While the sustained, regular volley fire had been the result of hundreds of hours of drill on the parade ground, the clash of steel on steel as the Ghazis closed with the 113th and 42nd proved something more primeval. The British Army taught basic techniques of bayonet fighting to its men, but there was something instinctive about the way the 113th and 42nd faced the tulwars of the Ghazis. The men parried and thrust as their training dictated, while adding boots and fists, rifle butts and knees in a more primitive manner that the men had learned on the back streets of Dundee and Newcastle, Cardiff and Dublin. Gaelic slogans combated the Ghazis calls of '*Din, din!*' and '*Allah Akbar!*'

'They've outflanked us!' Elliot shouted.

A body of Ghazis had come from the left, having hidden in one of the *topis* of trees. Ignoring the 113th, the Ghazis charged at Colonel Cameron of the 42nd. Cameron dragged free his sword and fought a snarling Ghazi on the right side when another two on the left grabbed his tunic and pulled him from his horse.

'They've got the colonel!' Colour-sergeant William Gardener of the 42nd shouted and ran forward, kilt flying. He bayonetted two of Ghazis as they prepared to hack Cameron to death while a private swivelled and shot the third.

'We're holding them!' Greaves said, and then it was over. The Punjabis streamed through the British lines to reform. Rifle fire and bayonets of the 42nd and 113th ensured that no Ghazis got through the line, while cold-eyed privates from both regiments stepped forward and plunged their bayonets into any of the fanatics who showed signs of life.

'That's not right,' Bryce objected. 'We don't murder the wounded.'

'Would you rather they waited until you stepped over their prone bodies and they slashed at your privates with their tulwars?' Jack asked. 'Any Indian veteran has seen that. This is not European warfare, Lieutenant. There are no civilised conventions here.'

Bryce glowered, shook his head and said nothing.

'Forward!' Sir Colin ordered, and the line advanced over the carpet of dead Ghazis, staggering under the heat as the sun reached its zenith.

'Jesus, but it's hot,' Hutton said.

'This is the killing time.' Greaves looked upwards. 'I've seen it so often out East; men survive a bloody battle and then die of heat exhaustion when we chase the retreating enemy. If India doesn't get you one way, it'll get you another.'

Sir Colin was equally aware of the perils of the Indian summer. As soon as the British reached the outskirts of Bareilly, he ordered a halt.

'We should pursue the pandies,' Bryce said. 'Harass and push them until they have to stand and fight. We can break them and win this war.'

Jack nodded to the 113th, as they staggered with exhaustion after their day's exertions. 'I am sure all the breakfast table strategists back in Britain would agree with you, but India is a place where practicalities outweigh theories, and the laws of European warfare do not apply. An Indian Army will move faster across India than any British Army, especially in hot weather and Khan Bahadur Khan will not stop to fight unless he has overwhelming force. A rapid pursuit will cost us many casualties even without any fighting.'

'It would be worth the risk,' Bryce insisted.

'The longer we march,' Jack said, 'the more men we'll lose to the sun, and therefore the weaker our army will be. The rebels could gather forces at any time, so when Khan Bahadur Khan thinks that the balance has tipped sufficiently in his favour, he would turn and rend us. No, Lieutenant Bryce, Sir Colin is correct.'

A rising tumult from the rear disrupted the conversation. Jack focused his binoculars. 'Pandy cavalry!' He swore. 'They're attacking the baggage train.'

'We have to do something.' Elliot looked suddenly agitated. He checked his revolver. 'Could I take out a platoon, sir?'

'They've got an escort,' Bryce frowned. 'We're not here to babysit grooms and syces and camel drivers.'

'We'd best help them, sir.' Elliot ignored Bryce.

'What's to do, Elliot?' Jack knew by Elliot's tone of voice that something was wrong.

Elliot hesitated, glanced at Bryce and made a formal request. 'May I have your permission to take a party to help the baggage train, sir?'

'Yes, if you think it necessary,' Jack said.

'Thank you, sir.' Elliot ran at once, shouting: 'Greaves, bring the Lucknow veterans. *Jildi!*'

'What the devil?' Jack watched as Elliot led a file of fifteen men at the double, bayonets fixed. 'Oh, damn it to hell. Bryce, take over here. Corporal Hunter, select ten more men and come with me.' He followed Elliot, ignored a gaggle of bearers who ran in the opposite direction yelling 'Sowar! Sowar!' and examined the baggage train.

Chaos, he thought. There was no other word to describe it other than chaos. A mob of animals and camp followers covered the road and the surrounding fields, all dashing for the security of the British encampment, with a few score rebel cavalrymen slashing and hacking at them. Defeated or not, the rebels had proved yet again that they could strike back.

Ignoring a panicking, splay-legged camel and the fleeing camp followers, Elliot led his men straight through the middle of the confusion and around a trio of rebel cavalry that circled a terrified elephant. The cavalry sliced at the tendons at the back of its legs until the beast trumpeted in agony.

Without waiting for orders, Private Parker dropped to one knee, aimed and fired in a single fluid movement. One of the horsemen staggered, and Parker immediately reloaded. 'Look at them,' he said. 'Torturing that poor elephant.'

'Oh, for God's sake,' Elliot said. 'Help Parker, somebody, and then join us.'

Elliot led his men to a bullock cart labouring at the rear of the scattered column. 'Guard this wagon with your lives, men. The cargo is invaluable.'

'Yes, sir.' The men spread out around the cart.

What is that man doing? Jack asked himself. 'Come on Greaves!' he increased his speed.

A group of sowars galloped toward the wagon, saw the determined men of the 113th and reined away. They were there to kill and spread panic, not to fight professional soldiers.

'What's happening, Elliot?' Jack left Greaves and Corporal Hunter to arrange the wagon's defence.

'We're just protecting the convoy, sir,' Elliot said.

'Why this particular wagon? What are you hiding, Lieutenant?' Without waiting for a reply, Jack vaulted onto the back of the vehicle and pulled back the canvas cover. 'Oh, dear God in heaven.'

'Hello, Jack.' Mary looked up at him.

Chapter Four

'Do you mean you knew that Mary was travelling with the column?' Jack stared at Elliot.

'Yes, sir.' Elliot stood at attention inside the tent. Sweat glistened on his face.

'Why the devil did you not tell me?'

'I thought you had enough worries,' Elliot said. 'I kept an eye on her.'

'Dear God, man – she could have been killed!'

'Yes. That's why I kept an eye on her.' Elliot remained stubbornly unrepentant.

'Go and find her and bring her here,' Jack ordered.

'No need for that, Captain. I'm already here.' Mary pushed back the flap and entered the tent. 'Arthur is not to blame, Jack. I made him swear not to tell you.'

About to blast her, Jack took a deep breath to control his temper. *This woman drives me to distraction.* 'Why are you here?'

'Sir Colin needed an interpreter,' Mary said.

'Did he ask for you?' Jack asked.

'I volunteered my services.' Mary held Jack's glare with impressive composure.

'Have you any idea how dangerous that could be?'

'Why no, Captain Windrush,' Mary said. 'I thought it would be as safe as strolling in the cantonment at Gondabad.'

Jack opened his mouth and closed it again. The previous year, he had helped rescued Mary from the mutineers at Gondabad. 'You should have told me.'

'Lieutenant Elliot was correct in what he said. If you'd known, you would have worried about me. That might have impaired your ability to do your duty, and I do not wish that on my conscience.'

'Leave us, Elliot,' Jack said.

'Yes, sir,' Elliot said. 'Sir—'

'Leave us!' Jack glowered at Elliot until he hurried out of the tent.

'Now, Miss Lambert,' Jack said, and realised that Mary was laughing at him. Although her face was immobile, her eyes were alive with bright mischief.

'Before you shout at me, Captain Jack,' Mary said. 'I have one thing to say.'

'And what is that, pray?'

'This.' Leaning forward, Mary gave him a single kiss on the forehead. 'I'm glad that we are both still alive, Jack.'

Jack touched her arm, his anger completely gone. 'I wish you would keep yourself out of danger, Mary. Battlefields are no place for a woman.'

'Battlefields are no place for *anybody*,' Mary said. 'Every night I pray to the Lord that there are no more battles, and every day I learn that the Lord has desires contrary to my wishes.'

'There will be another battle tomorrow,' Jack said. 'Khan Bahadur Khan will fight to defend Bareilly, and that will be ugly. I saw street fighting in Lucknow, and we lost far too many men.'

'Let's hope that the Lord helps him see sense and surrender.'

'Khan Bahadur Khan will not surrender,' Jack said. 'We hang our prisoners or blow the poor fellows from a cannon. They have nothing to gain from surrender.'

'I have never found Sir Colin to be particularly bloodthirsty,' Mary said. 'He is a good soldier and a humane man.'

Jack shook his head. 'He's the most humane commander I've ever known.' He frowned as a sudden thought struck him. 'Have you been here ever since we left Lucknow?'

Mary shook her head. 'No. I watched you march away with Walpole, and I felt sick, frankly.'

Jack frowned again. British gentlewomen should not be so forthcoming about their emotions.

'Thank you,' Jack said, aware how inadequate his words sounded. 'I didn't like leaving you behind. I would have liked it less to have you come with us.'

'Oh?' Mary's eyebrows rose. 'Don't you like my company?'

Jack frowned. 'I do like your company. I don't like to think of you being in danger.'

Mary couldn't hide her smile as she looked away. 'In India, Captain Jack, we are in danger all the time. Until this war is over, nowhere is safe.'

'I'll do my best to finish it quickly for you.' It was not hard for Jack to alter his frown into a smile.

'Take care, Jack,' Mary said seriously. 'I also like *your* company.' She deliberately repeated Jack's words. 'I don't like to think of you being in danger.'

'Danger is part of the soldier's bargain,' Jack said. 'We know that when we accept the Queen's shilling or the Queen's commission. You have done neither. It's my job to try and protect the civilian population.' He lowered his voice. 'On the other hand, I *want* to protect you.'

Mary nodded, once. Her eyes didn't stray from Jack's face. 'I know,' she said.

'Captain Windrush!' The educated voice came from outside the tent.

Jack sighed. 'Somebody wants me.'

'So it seems.' Mary rose from her seat. 'We never have time together. I'll leave you to your duty.' Her hand lingered on his arm for longer than was necessary.

'Thank you.' Jack watched her leave the tent before he raised his voice. 'I'm Captain Windrush!'

The ensign was red-faced, as they all seemed to be this season, and fair-haired. 'Colonel Hook sends his compliments, sir and requests your presence in his tent at your earliest convenience.'

Colonel Hook? How did he get here?

'That means now,' Jack said with a wry smile. 'Thank you, ensign. Pray convey my respects to Colonel Hook and inform him that I will be along directly.' He hesitated. 'Or I will when you tell me where his tent might be.'

Hook's tent was in the centre of the British encampment, with two heavily bearded Sikhs on guard at the flap. They moved aside when Jack announced himself.

'Ah, Windrush. What have you to report?' Hook sat at an ornately carved bureau, half hidden behind a pile of paperwork.

'I met Jayanti,' Jack said and described what had happened. Hook listened, nodding where necessary.

'Interesting woman,' Hook said. 'I wonder why she didn't kill you. Indeed, I wonder why she spoke to you at all.'

'I wonder how she knew who I was, sir,' Jack reminded. 'She even knew my middle name.'

'That's even more interesting.' Hook selected a long cheroot from a silver case. 'There's a lot more here than we know about.'

'Yes, sir.'

'You have done better than I expected, Windrush. I thought you might find some intelligence about Jayanti and here you have succeeded in contacting her.'

'She contacted me, sir and I would like to know why,' Jack said. *There are two women in my life now, and both are trouble.*

'I'll have to check with my colleagues and see if they can enlighten us.' Hook gave a sudden smile. 'As you're part of the organisation now, Windrush, you should know who they are. We have William Muir, the magistrate fellow in Agra, and Major Herbert Bruce. Have you heard of Bruce?'

'No, sir,'

'He used to work in the Punjab police and served under General Neill and Havelock as well as Sir Colin. He's a good man.'

'I see, sir.' Jack realised that there were layers of British rule about which he knew nothing.

Hook tapped his cheroot on his bureau, his gaze never straying from Jack's face. 'You'll know about Raja Nahr Singh, of course.'

'No, sir. I've never heard of that gentleman.'

Hook lit the cheroot, allowing smoke to spiral around the tent. 'He was our spymaster in Delhi. He kept William Muir informed of everything that happened inside Delhi.'

'He is a loyal man, sir.'

'No.' Hook shook his head. 'Or rather, not loyal to the Queen, if that's what you mean.'

Jack frowned. 'Do you mean he was loyal to John Company?'

Hook's smile was as intriguing as anything Jack had ever seen. 'Not exactly, Windrush. He and John Company were both loyal to the same thing.'

'The Empire?'

Hook laughed. 'Not quite.' Reaching into a small bureau that stood behind his chair, Hook unlocked the top drawer and pulled out a small leather draw-bag. 'They are both loyal to this.' Opening the bag, he poured out a golden cascade of guineas, sovereigns and mohurs. 'Money, Windrush. Wealth. This country runs on two things, information and wealth. It is a venal society with professional intelligence gatherers such as Mukhdum Baksh. Poor Mukhdum worked for us in Delhi and latterly was my agent in Bareilly.'

Jack wished he had never asked. He didn't recognise this India. 'You say that Mukhdum *was* your agent?'

'Correct. Nana Sahib found him and had him executed.' Hook waved his cheroot around his head. 'You don't wish to know the details.'

Jack shook his head. 'No, sir.' Indian executions could be gruesome.

Hook scooped all the golden coins back into the bag and lifted it in the air. 'This,' he jingled the bag, 'is what India is all about. Money. The Company wants to increase its profits, and the rajahs and princes want the wealth that comes from power. The mutineers buy recruits, the rebel princes pay their followers, and we give our sepoys regular pay. If we stop paying the sepoys, they have no reason to be loyal to us. The British, as John Company, are in here for profit, while Britain needs the revenue, and the prestige.'

'I thought this mutiny was about religion, sir.' Jack thought of the fanatical Ghazis, sacrificing themselves against the bayonets of the 42nd and 113th.

'It is, in part,' Hook said. 'The men who run it manipulate the sepoys with stories of threats, real or fanciful, to their religion, and the Ghazis and so on are genuine in their hatred of our missionaries and their fear that we are trying to Christianise the whole country.' He shrugged. 'But the men – and women – at the top want their positions back, and the wealth that goes along with it.' Hook threw the leather bag in the air and caught it one-handed. 'Wealth and power, Windrush; that's what everything comes down to, here and elsewhere.'

'The love of money is the root of all evil.' Jack gave one of the few Biblical quotes he remembered.

'Timothy, chapter six, verse ten. Simplistic but true to an extent,' Hook said. 'Add the love of power to that, and I would agree.' He examined the tip of his cheroot, flicked off the excess ash and replaced it in his mouth. 'Now, you have made some progress with Jayanti, Windrush – continue with the search.'

'Yes, sir.' Jack paused. 'Do you wish me to take out my company and search the Terai to the north?'

'No, you can start in Bareilly,' Hook said. 'We'll have some rebel prisoners who may wish to help in exchange for their lives.'

'We have to capture it first,' Jack reminded.

'The rebels will run,' Hook said casually. 'They won't fight.'

'Are you sure, sir?'

'Quite sure.' Hook smiled. 'Information and wealth, Windrush. Trust me, we'll have Bareilly in two days with the minimum of fuss, and then you will have some prisoners to interview.'

'Yes, sir,' Jack said. An order was an order.

Chapter Five

On the 6th May, British artillery started bombarding suspected insurgent strongpoints in Bareilly. Next day, with the dust and smoke still drifting across the city, Campbell drove in his column without resistance. The enemy had fled.

'We're still chasing Jayanti.' Jack lit another cheroot, coughed, and sat on the chair next to Elliot. A servant salaamed and brought a brass bowl, brimming with water.

'Do we know where she is?'

'Not yet, Arthur. Colonel Hook suggests that we ask the prisoners.'

Elliot snorted. 'I'm sure they will willingly tell all before we hang them.' He looked up. 'How's your Pushtu? Alternatively, will they speak Hindustani? I can speak about a dozen words in total.'

'I know a few words, and I know good translator,' Jack said.

'Do you mean Mary?' Elliot lifted the flask again.

'I do,' Jack said.

Elliot swallowed. 'It could be difficult for her.'

'I won't force her,' Jack said. 'I'll give her a choice.'

'I know your choices.' Elliot took another pull at his silver flask. 'Take it or take something worse.'

'I won't be like that with Mary.' Jack smiled. 'I like her.' Jack waited for Elliot's reaction.

'Only *like* the woman, or do you more than like the woman? Do you like her as much as you liked Helen?'

Jack considered. 'I think Mary is a better person than Helen.'

'That is not what I asked, my verbally elusive Captain Windrush,' Elliot said.

Jack smiled. 'I know it's not. I will tell you the answer when I know it myself.'

Elliot nodded. 'Be careful, Jack, that is all I ask.'

'At present, I need Mary as a translator,' Jack said.

'You could ask one of the Company wallahs. They work with the natives; they have to speak their languages.'

'The sepoys mutinied against the Company,' Jack said. 'I doubt they would talk to a Company officer.'

Elliot nodded. 'Will they be any more willing to talk to a woman? How will you convince your prisoners to talk?'

Jack shrugged. 'I've seen the Sikhs burning their prisoners alive. I could offer to hand the sepoys over to them.'

'Others might do that, Jack. You wouldn't.' Elliot leaned back in his cane chair. 'We're supposed to be officers and gentlemen, representatives of the most civilised nation on earth, and here we are condoning murder and torture. Thank God that Sir Colin is against such slaughter. Our men want blood though. To them, any native could be a pandy, and the only good pandy is a dead pandy.'

Jack nodded. 'You're right there. We may pay for this brutality later.' He thought of the black-turbaned woman slicing at the injured Green. 'The trouble is, the enemy can be every bit as barbaric, so atrocity leads to retaliation.'

'They are very like us, and we are very like them,' Elliot said. 'That's what worries me. We announce our progressive civilisation and Christianity and then act as badly as the enemy.' He shrugged and poured more whisky down his throat. 'It's enough to drive a man away from drink.'

'I've allocated a permanent sentry for Mary and placed her in a tent in the centre of the camp, between our lines and the 42nd. No pandy will dare try attacking her.' Jack stood up. 'I'll see if she agrees to translate.'

'Be careful, Jack.' Elliot raised his flask in salute. 'Don't get too at-tached to her. A girl like Mary will only ruin your career.'

Jack nodded. He knew Elliot was correct.

Hutton saluted as Jack approached the tent. 'Good afternoon, sir.' He kept his face immobile.

'Good afternoon, Hutton. Is the lady at home?' Jack scratched on the canvas and waited for Mary to invite him in.

'Of course, I'm at home!' Mary answered. 'Come in, Captain Jack.'

'I need your help,' Jack said as he entered.

Mary smiled. 'You should never try to be a diplomat, Jack. You're too blunt for that.' She stood up from her charpoy and stretched her arms. 'What can I do for you?'

'I need your language skills.' Jack explained the situation.

'These prisoners you want me to question.' Mary was frowning. 'When you've questioned them, what will happen to them?'

'Oh, they'll be hanged.'

'I thought so.' Mary sat back down. 'I've seen enough suffering in this war, Jack.'

'I'm not asking you to torture them.'

'No, you're asking me to help interrogate people who know we're going to hang them.'

'They're traitors and rebels.' Jack fell back on traditional beliefs.

'Or patriots and men whom our actions forced to rebel.' Mary coun-tered him without losing her patience. 'Do you think they will help you, knowing their death is inevitable whatever they say?'

'You have something up your sleeve, Mary,' Jack said. 'Come on now, out with it!'

'Freedom,' Mary said. 'Offer them their freedom if they co-operate.'

'They might lie to save themselves.' Jack sat cross-legged on the floor, not caring how undignified a position it was.

Mary's smile always took him by surprise. 'They might lie anyway, knowing it doesn't matter what they say.'

'Yes.' Jack tried to retain his patience. 'But how can we trust them? They'll tell us anything for freedom.'

Mary's smile broadened. 'If any of them know where Jayanti is, make him guide you there, and you will only free him when you know he's not lying.'

'You are a cunning lady.' Jack sighed. 'You have all the answers.'

'Why, thank you, kind sir.' Mary sunk into a graceful curtsey. Jack was unsure if her eyes were friendly or mocking.

Even with the offer of freedom, few of the prisoners were willing to be helpful. Most sat in silence as Mary asked questions, with some replying with shouted slogans and threats. Only three responded to Jack's request; one was a Pathan from the Khyber, and the other two had been sowars in the Company's cavalry, high-class Hindus with land and families.

'We'll speak to these three,' Jack decided, 'and ignore the others.'

The sowar mutineers were proud men, defiant despite their capture. They answered Jack's questions with short, sharp answers and glared at him.

'Of course, I know of Jayanti,' the first sowar said.

'Everybody knows about the devil woman,' the second replied, 'except the proud sahibs.'

'Only Shiva can catch her,' the first sowar said. 'The sahibs will need my help.'

'I can lead you to her lair,' the second offered, 'for a thousand rupees and a fast horse.'

'Why are you helping?' Jack asked the final question.

'To get back to my family,' the first mutineer said.

'To get back to my family,' the second sowar gave an identical answer.

Jack sent both away. 'I don't trust them,' he said.

'Would you prefer to see the Pathan?' Mary sounded amused. 'Pathans kill for fun and rob as a matter of course.'

'Bring him in,' Jack said. 'The mutineers have already broken their faith and now say they are willing to betray one of their own. I would trust them as far as a wooden threepenny bit.'

The Pathan was tall and lean, with a face that would give Satan nightmares and even in chains, he looked as if he would murder his brother for a handful of gold mohurs.

'Your name?' Jack had sufficient experience with the men of the 113th to recognise a rogue.

'Batoor.' The Pathan held Jack's gaze without fear. Jack had heard that if a Pathan met Queen Victoria, he would look her in the eye and shake hands as if to say, "I'm as good a person as you are". People also reckoned Pathans as faithless, thieving and predatory, while their mothers prayed that their sons became famed robbers. With this fellow Batoor, all these stereotypes appeared to be correct.

'So you claim to know the whereabouts of Jayanti, even though she is a Hindu and you are a Pathan?'

Batoor grunted. 'I know where she may be,' he said.

That's the most honest answer so far. One point for the Pathan.

'You were captured fighting against us; why would you help us now?'

'I was fighting for money,' Batoor said. 'I have reasons for being here, and if I help you, I will be free again.'

Jack glanced at Mary, who nodded. 'That makes sense,' she said. 'I would love to know what his reasons were.' She gave a half smile. 'Being a Pathan, it will be something to do with money or *Pashtunwali*.'

'What in God's name is *Pashtunwali*?'

Mary smiled. 'Aren't you glad I'm here to educate you, Captain Jack? *Pukhtunwali* is the Pathan code of honour. They must give fugitives refuge and protection, they must give hospitality, even to an enemy, and they have to avenge any insult to the family or the tribe.'

Jack eyed Batoor and nodded. The Pathan held his gaze. With his shaven head and long beard, he looked every inch a warrior. 'I've seen you before,' Jack said. 'You fired a jezzail at me at the Kaisarbagh!' He waited for Mary to translate.

Batoor smiled. 'I was at the Kaisarbagh, and I fired at many British soldiers. You might have been one of them.'

'Good God, man!' Jack shook his head. 'Why are you at Bareilly now? Do you hate us so much?'

Batoor's smile didn't waver. 'As the woman says, it has something to do with *Pashtunwali.*'

Jack was beginning to respect this man. In a different world, he would have fitted into the 113th without difficulty. 'If you are free, would you fight against us again?'

Batoor rattled his chains. 'I might. I might not.'

'He's honest by his own lights,' Mary added after she translated.

'You're a lying, treacherous murdering blackguard, Batoor,' Jack stood up, 'and I can't think of any reason why I should trust you.'

Batoor rattled his chains again. 'You don't trust me, but you need me. Who else can lead you to the devil woman who plans to destroy your Company?'

'Nobody, damn you.'

'Will you keep your word, Captain Windrush?' Batoor turned the conversation around, with Mary hiding her smile as she translated.

'Of course, I will, I'm a British officer!' Jack had to control his temper.

Batoor's laugh was high pitched, and as cynical as anything Jack had ever heard. 'Only the British believe their own lies. I am asking you, Captain Windrush, man to man – will you keep your word?'

Mary raised her eyebrows as she translated. 'He's not wrong, Jack, Lord Dalhousie is not the only British official to distort the truth to the native peoples of India.'

Jack frowned. Brought up to believe that a British gentleman always honoured his word, he still found it hard to believe that some broke that code.

Batoor spoke again, and Mary translated. 'Batoor is asking the same question, Jack. Will you keep your word? Will you free him if he leads you to this woman?'

'Of course I will, damn it!' Jack felt his anger rise again. Taking a deep breath, he faced Batoor. 'Yes, Batoor, I will keep my promise. You have my word on it as a British officer and...' Jack extended his hand.

'I do not know what crimes you have committed in the past or who you have killed or why, but if you take my hand, we will shake on it, man to man.'

Batoor looked to Mary for the translation before he slid his hand hesitantly into Jack's. They shook, and Jack knew that whatever happened, he would keep his word to Batoor.

'One more thing.' Jack had come prepared. Taking a small packet from his pocket, he drew his sword and emptied the contents onto the blade. The white powder formed a little pyramid on the steel.

'Take the salt, warrior, and swear your loyalty to me.'

Batoor's grin was white behind his beard. He put his hand on the blade, lifted a pinch of salt and placed it on his lips. Mary translated his words. 'I am your man, Captain Windrush.'

'If you let me down,' Jack said, 'I will hunt you down and kill you.'

Batoor grinned. 'Yes, Captain Windrush. And if you let me down, I will kill the woman and then you.'

Mary's expression didn't alter as she translated Batoor's words. 'Accept that Jack,' Mary added. 'I'm in no danger as long as you are true.'

Jack fought down his recurring anger. 'We understand each other,' he said to Batoor. Raising his voice, he called in the guards and had the Pathan taken back to confinement.

'When are we leaving?' Mary asked.

'We?' Jack said. 'You are not coming.'

'You took me last time,' Mary said. 'When you were searching for the regiment's missing women.'

'This is different,' Jack said. 'This is a military operation, and there are still pandies around.'

'There were more pandies around last time,' Mary reminded. 'And you'll need a translator if you are wandering around the countryside, or have your language skills improved in the last few minutes?' Her smile was as sweet as a hunting cobra.

'We'll manage,' Jack growled at her. He sighed and admitted the truth. 'You know that I'd prefer to have you along, Mary, but it's too dangerous.'

She stood up. 'It will be a lot more dangerous for you to blunder around not able to talk to anybody. Is Lieutenant Elliot able to speak Urdu or Pushtu? No! How about Sergeant Greaves or any of your men? Goodness, Jack, most of them can hardly speak English.'

Jack matched her temper with the anger he had been trying to control all day 'It's too damned dangerous, Mary!'

'My, my.' Mary's sudden smile took Jack by surprise. 'Is that how British officers and gentlemen talk to women?'

Jack stopped in mid-tirade. About to say "only when they care for them", he stopped and stood erect. 'You are correct,' he said. 'I should not have shouted at you. I do apologise, madam.' He gave a stiff, formal bow, turned around and marched out of the room. He knew that he was retreating from a conflict that he couldn't possibly win. He hoped that Mary didn't realise the same but knew she would. *Damn that woman. One thing is sure; she's not coming with my column.*

Chapter Six

'O'Neill's back!' Riley was first with the news, and soon the words spread around the company. Jack looked up as Sergeant O'Neill marched in, gaunt-faced but as erect as ever, with his uniform clean and his rifle in his hand.

'Sergeant O'Neill reporting for duty, sir!' O'Neill gave a smart salute.

'Good to have you back, Sergeant,' Jack said. 'How's the wound?' O'Neill had been injured during the fighting in the tunnels underneath Lucknow, when Campbell had relieved the siege earlier in the war.

'The medical men saved my arm, thank you.'

Jack nodded. 'Are you fit for a long march? Don't say you are, if you're not.'

'I'm fit, sir. I could outmarch any Johnny Raw.'

'Aye, you probably could, O'Neill. Sheer bloody determination would see you through.' Jack looked around. He had moved his company of the 113th outside the walls of Bareilly, away from the temptation of looting and the dangers of women and drink. The men had grumbled at first and, being British soldiers, many had tried to sneak back into the city. Now they were panting in the heat, or under fatigues, or cleaning their rifles. 'I hope so, O'Neill because we're on the march soon.'

'Where are we going, sir?'

'I'm not sure, sergeant,' Jack said. 'Have you ever heard of a woman called Jayanti?'

'I can't say that I have, sir.' O'Neill looked suddenly defensive. 'Has she been asking for me, sir?'

'No.' Jack had no desire to ask about O'Neill's amorous adventures. 'She is the leader of a band of fighting women, like Uda Devi.'

'I remember that name, sir. That's the bint that hid up a tree and shot some of our lads.' O'Neill stamped his feet. 'I hoped we didn't meet others like her.'

'There are others, sergeant, and this Jayanti woman is their leader. We've been ordered to find her.'

'And kill her, sir?'

'If we can, sergeant.' Jack waited for O'Neill's reaction. 'What do you think of that?'

'I don't normally hold with killing women, sir.' O'Neill gave the reply Jack would expect from any British soldier. 'But if this Jayanti is anything like Uda Devi, well, she killed some of ours, sir, so she's fair game.'

Jack asked O'Neill a question he would never have asked Greaves. 'How will the men react to being ordered to kill or capture a woman?'

O'Neill screwed up his face as he considered the question. 'I'm not sure, sir. Our lads won't be too happy about it, sir. They won't want to kill a woman, even that one. Some of the others, though,' he shrugged, 'they'd kill their grannies for the price of a drink.'

Jack nodded. He understood what O'Neill meant. By "our lads", O'Neill meant the Burma and Crimea veterans that bloody battles had bonded together. Jack shared O'Neill's opinion of others that the Army had recruited from the criminal class, the lowest of the low, men rejected by other regiments to end up in the 113th.

'When do we leave, sir?'

'In two days, sergeant,' Jack said. 'I'm taking fifty men and a Pathan prisoner who claims to know where Jayanti may be based.'

'Oh, does he claim that, sir?' O'Neill looked sceptical. 'And who told him? Some fellow down the public, or maybe his granny heard it when she was washing her clothes in the river?'

Jack smiled. 'I share your disbelief, sergeant. That's why he'll be under close guard all the time, and if he tries to bolt, we'll shoot him like a dog.'

O'Neill grunted. 'He's a Pathan, you say? They are the most devious devils under the sun, sir. He'll cut a few of our throats at night, steal half a dozen rifles and slip back to the Khyber.'

'He won't' Jack said. 'Not with you watching him.'

'Yes, sir.' There was a hint of a smile on O'Neill's face. 'I thought you were coming to that.'

Both men stopped to watch a regiment of Gurkhas march past, small, stocky men resplendent in red coats and blue pantaloons, very much like the Zouaves the 113th had known in the Crimea.

'Cocky little buggers,' O'Neill said. 'I'm told there are 16,000 of them with us now.'

'They fight well, I've heard,' Jack said.

O'Neill eyed them sourly. 'Aye; we'll see. Since the sepoys turned traitor, I have little time for native troops. I won't trust them again, and that's the truth.'

'There's a lot of people think like that,' Jack murmured. 'Nothing will be quite the same in India after the Mutiny.'

An hour before dawn they marched out of Bareilly, heading north and east. Jack led with Elliot and Lieutenant Bryce behind him, and Ensigns Wilden and Peake at the rear. In between marched fifty men with Sergeants Greaves and O'Neill. All were in khaki, with handkerchiefs to protect their necks from the sun and Enfield rifles at their shoulders.

'You'd better not be leading us into an ambush,' O'Neill warned Batoor. 'If you try any funny stuff, I'll ram six inches of steel up your arse.'

Batoor replied in Pushtu and spread his hands in an expression of innocence that would have made Jack smile in other circumstances.

'Try it once, son, just try it once.' The diminutive Logan was a full head shorter than Batoor. 'I'll gut you.'

Batoor only grinned, with his shaven head bobbing above Logan's hat and his wrists chained together.

Jack stepped aside and watched his men march past. As well as Logan, the truculent Glasgow man, there was Riley, the gentleman-thief, Coleman and Thorpe, forever arguing until the fighting started. There was the ex-poacher Whitelam, Parker from Liverpool with his love of animals, and the Welshman Williams who had done sterling work during the defence of Lucknow the previous year. Hutton was next, a quiet man, steadier than the majority of the 113th, and beside him slouched Armstrong. Jack didn't like Armstrong, the one-time deserter who had been inside the army's detention centre at Greenlaw and harboured resentment against authority, but he was useful in a fight.

Jack kept them marching until the sun grew too hot and then they camped in the shade of a small clump of trees, with the men dropping to the ground and gasping for air.

'There's still pandies around!' O'Neill and Greaves kicked them back to their feet. 'Get this camp in order! Hutton, Armstrong, Smith, Monaghan, you're on picket duty! The rest of you, get the tents up!'

'Leave it to the sergeants,' Jack advised the ensigns. 'They know what they're doing, and the men listen to them.'

'Yes, sir,' Wilden said. 'But I'm an officer, I hold the Queen's commission. I outrank the sergeant.'

Jack stared at the boy while Elliot looked away to hide his smile. 'Sergeant O'Neill fought in Burma against dacoits and faced the Russians at the battle of Inkerman and the Redan. He was in the first relief of Lucknow; he fought at Cawnpore and was wounded defending Lucknow. What have you done?'

Ensign Wilden coloured.

'Exactly,' Jack said. 'Now take two men and patrol back the way we have come. March one mile, check to see if there are any pandies and return. Move!'

'What was that for?' Elliot asked.

'To get the young Griff out of my way,' Jack replied.

'We were young too, once.' Elliot said.

'I'm sure we were never that young,' Jack said with a smile.

The officers had a tent each, while a dozen men had to share. When the heat reached its zenith, officers and men not on duty would lie near naked on their charpoys, struggling for breath in the scorching atmosphere and wishing the monsoon would come. With pickets posted and the men eating and drinking, Jack could relax a little. He checked his half company. A few years ago, the 113th had been the worst regiment in the British Army, and now they were slowly gaining a reputation as a hard-fighting unit able to take care of itself.

'We're still at the bottom of the pile, Jack.' Elliot had known him long enough to gauge what he was thinking.

'Are we, Arthur?'

'We'll never be socially acceptable like the Brigade of Guards or the Royals.' Elliot lit a cheroot and allowed the aromatic smoke to coil around them. 'We'll always be the regiment that generals turn to for the dirty jobs.' He passed over a cheroot to Jack.

'Could you imagine the Guards or the Royal Malverns tracking a woman across India?' Jack shook his head. 'It would be far beneath their dignity. You're right, Arthur. We're here for the tasks nobody else wants.'

'Or the tasks nobody else can do,' Elliot said. 'Our men have skills the Guards or Royals may lack.'

Jack glanced over at Riley and Whitelam. 'We have thieves, housebreakers and poachers. Yes, we have a fine collection of men; they are quite the pick of the country.'

'You're in a bad mood,' Elliot said. 'What's bothering you, Jack?'

'Where are we headed, Arthur? What is all this about? We've broken the back of this mutiny, killed God-only-knows how many pandies and civilians, and lost thousands of our men and women. What then? India carries on, and the Army will send you, the 113th, and me somewhere else to squash another trouble spot, lose more men to disease and the bullet. What's it all about, Arthur?'

'I'm damned if I know,' Elliot said. 'This was the only career open to a duffer like me. I'm the third son, with no money and no prospects.' He shrugged. 'What else can I do? I haven't the head for business or the inclination to follow my father into the church.'

Jack pulled on his cheroot. 'I know your people wish you to be a general,' he said. 'General Sir Arthur Elliot. That sounds good. I was always intended to be a career soldier, as you know.'

'I know,' Elliot said. 'Like your father and your grandfather.'

'And my great grandfather and great-great grandfather and as far back as records go.' Jack blew out a perfect smoke ring and watched as it wavered in the heat. 'I do not doubt that there was a Windrush at the Battle of Hastings, although God knows which side he was on, and when Boadicea faced the Romans, there was probably a Windrush in her army as well.'

'The Romans must have viewed her as we view Jayanti or Hussaini Khanum or the Rani of Jhansi,' Elliot lay back and contemplated a pair of hunting birds high amidst the clouds. 'And now we are the foreigners invading other countries to bring civilisation. How times change.'

'Except India was not a country when we came here, so we are not foreign,' Jack said. 'Or at least, we're no more foreign than the Sikhs or Ghurkhas or Pathans.'

'And we're better rulers.' Elliot watched as one of the birds swooped down on its prey. 'We are benevolent, kindly and honourable.'

'Tell that to all the mutineers we've hanged or blown from guns,' Jack said. 'Or the hundreds of men General Neill executed without trial.'

'I was being sarcastic,' Elliot said. 'Halloa, something's up. Whitelam's all of an agitation there.'

Jack looked up. Whitelam was talking to O'Neill, his arms flapping and his voice raised. 'I'd better go and see before he talks himself into trouble. You stay here and rest, Arthur. All that deep thinking must be very tiring for you.'

'I'm telling you, sergeant, that's what I saw!' Whitelam was shouting, nearly pressing his face against that of O'Neill.

'And I am telling you, Whitelam, that you will not be disturbing Captain Windrush with any of your nonsense. Now go and dig a latrine trench like I told you.'

'What's the trouble, sergeant?' Jack had a final pull on his cheroot and flicked the stub away.

'It's nothing to worry about, sir.' O'Neill gave a smart salute. 'Private Whitelam here is just leaving.'

'What did you see, Whitelam?' Jack asked.

'Somebody is dogging us, sir. I swear there is. I saw him twice on the march, and again ten minutes ago.'

'What was he like?' Jack knew that Whitelam was not a man to speak out of turn. He had been a poacher before he took the Queen's Shilling and after a lifetime spent dodging gamekeepers, he would know if somebody was following him.

'I can't rightly say, sir.' Whitelam screwed up his face with the effort of thought. 'He was a slim fellow, keeping to the shadows and the dead ground.'

'Was he wearing green clothing and a black turban?'

Whitelam refused to be drawn. 'I don't know, sir. As I said, he was in the shadows.'

'Right.' Jack thought quickly. 'Where did you see him last?'

'Over there, sir, past that grove of babul trees. He was walking slowly and ducked into cover, sir.' Whitelam gestured to a small group of acacia trees a few hundred yards to the south.

'Has he moved since?' Jack asked.

'Not that I've seen, sir, and I've been watching for him.'

If Whitelam hadn't seen him – or her – move, then he was still there.

'Sergeant O'Neill,' Jack said. 'I don't want this man or woman alarmed. It might be Jayanti or one of her women. Take a picket out and see if you can round him up. Be careful, if it's Jayanti she is very dangerous.'

'Aye, sir.' O'Neill screwed up his eyes as he peered through the glare of the sun. 'It might be best if I flushed him, sir, drove him towards the camp.'

'Good man, O'Neill. I'll wait for him. I'll give you ten minutes and then form a cordon with a dozen men. We'll catch him, or her, in a net.'

'I'll leave Greaves in charge of the Pathan, sir,' O'Neill said.

'Wilden!' Jack motioned to the ensign. 'You're with me.'

'Where are we going, sir?' Wilden couldn't disguise his smile.

'We're going to catch a mutineer. Do as you're told and don't ask fool questions. Whitelam, take a position a hundred yards out and to the right. Hutton, do the same on the left. Find dead ground and don't be seen.'

Both men were veterans and needed no further orders.

Jack watched as O'Neill led a dozen men well to the right of the babul trees, and then ordered them into an extended line five yards apart. The sergeant headed left for a hundred yards, turned and walked back. At his crisp order, each man fitted and lowered his bayonet, moving behind the viciously pointed blades.

'That should chase him out,' Jack said. His picket waited at the fringe of the camp, with Coleman and Thorpe watching, stony-faced.

'Do you want us to kill him, sir?' Thorpe asked.

'I want to see who he is,' Jack said, 'and why he's following us.' *He might be scouting for a larger body or merely a curious bystander.*

'That means we take him alive, Thorpey,' Coleman explained. 'Dead men can't talk.'

Thorpe nodded. 'Yes, Coley. I won't kill him, sir, unless Captain Windrush wants me to.' He stamped his feet. 'You could have let me go in, sir. I would have set fire to the trees and got him that way.'

'Thank you, Thorpe,' Jack said. 'Maybe next time.'

O'Neill's men were at the fringes of the *tope* now, advancing cautiously in case of an ambush. O'Neill gave a sharp order, and four men remained outside, watching while the others entered.

'Here he comes, flushed like a partridge.' Thorpe raised his rifle.

The lone man emerged at a run, holding a hood over his head as he scurried free of the trees.

No black turban. It's not Jayanti or one of her women.

'With me, lads, and be careful.' Drawing his sword, Jack strode forward, knowing his men would follow.

The fugitive saw the soldiers ahead, turned, saw O'Neill's men behind and stopped.

'He's surrendering, sir,' Coleman said. 'Either that or he's up to something. You've got to watch these pandies, sir. They're tricky devils. Best let me and Thorpey get him.'

Ignoring the advice, Jack broke into a run. 'Drop your weapon and get your hands in the air, you blackguard!' Although the man wouldn't understand the words, the tone and menace would be evident.

The fugitive raised his hands and stood still as the British net closed. He was small and slight, dressed in a hooded cape that extended from his head to the ground.

'Right, you.' Jack sheathed his sword. 'Who the devil are you, and why are you following us?' Grabbing the man's hood, he hauled it off the fugitive's face.

'Why, Jack, don't you recognise me?' Mary smiled at him. 'And do you need all these men to capture a single woman?'

'What?' Jack stared at her. 'What are you doing here?' He signalled with his hand, and the circle of soldiers lowered their bayonets. Some were openly grinning.

'I told you that you needed a translator.' Mary sounded as calm as if she was sitting sewing in the British cantonment.

'I ordered you to stay behind!' Jack felt his temper rising.

'I know you did, Jack, but I'm not one of your soldiers.' Mary smiled serenely. 'You have no power to order me around.'

Jack realised that he had an interested circle of listeners, most of whom were now nudging each other, highly amused at their officer's discomfiture. 'O'Neill, get these men back to camp.'

'Yes, sir! You heard the order, lads!'

Was O'Neill's use of "order" a deliberate echo of Mary's words? Jack glowered at the sergeant until he doubled away with his men.

Mary raised her eyebrows. 'Well, Captain Jack, or should that be Captain Windrush? Now you have me, what are you going to do with me?'

Jack took a deep breath as a sequence of images flashed through his mind. 'I know what I would like to do with you,' he began and shook his head as Mary raised her eyebrows in mocking interest. 'I should send you back to Lucknow under an escort.'

'But then who would translate for you?' Mary asked sweetly. 'And wouldn't you look a bit silly? And you would be depleting your force, just for one weak woman.'

'You're about as weak as Genghis Khan.' Jack's anger was reducing as Mary smiled at him. 'This will be a dangerous mission, you know.'

'I know,' Mary said.

'I don't like to put you in danger.'

'I know that, too,' Mary said. 'You're not putting me in danger. I'm putting myself in danger, and I'm probably safer with you and your *badmashes* than anywhere else in India.' Her smile broadened. 'Come on now, Jack, we both know that you and your men will look after me.'

'You're an irritating woman, Mary,' Jack said.

'So your mother used to say.' Mary deliberately reminded Jack of their family connection.

'You'd best stay with us,' Jack said, grudgingly. 'You might be useful. If any of my men bother you—'

'Your men have never bothered me,' Mary said quickly.

Jack thought of Armstrong and some of the handful of replacements he had brought with him. 'I'll find you a tent and post a sentry at the flap.' *I'll also warn O'Neill and Greaves to keep an extra eye on you, as if they didn't have enough to do.*

'If you think it best.' Mary agreed without a protest.

'All right, Mary, if you're sure, then welcome aboard.' Jack considered for a minute. 'In fact, you can start now.'

'I knew you needed me.' Mary didn't disguise her smug smile.

Batoor was sitting with his back to a tree when they approached.

'Stand up!' Jack ordered, adding *jildi* to prove to Mary that he had mastered at least one word of the native languages.

Logan helped by yanking Batoor to his feet. 'Up you get, you, when the officer tells you.'

'Where are you taking us, Batoor?' Jack asked, with Mary putting his words into Pushtu.

'Northward, Captain Windrush.' Batoor rattled his chains. 'And then westward.'

'How far to the north?'

'If I told you, Captain Windrush, you would not need me, and you may kill me.' Batoor smiled. 'I'm not yet ready to be a martyr. I have things to do.'

'You mean you have throats to cut in the Khyber country,' Jack said.

'A woman betrayed me to the British.' Batoor rattled his chains again. 'Else I would not be wearing these.'

'You gave me your word,' Jack said, 'and I gave you mine so we should trust each other.' He tapped the chains. 'It appears that neither of us trusts the other.'

Batoor smiled and said nothing.

'Well then,' Jack unlocked Batoor's chains and threw them into the darkness. They clattered against something hard. 'There is a sign of my trust.' He was aware of Mary watching him, her eyes quizzical while Logan lifted his bayonet, ready to thrust it into Batoor's belly.

Batoor rubbed the raw marks the manacles had left on his wrists. 'You are a strange man, Captain Windrush.'

'I'm taking a chance on you,' Jack said.

Batoor looked at Logan before he replied. 'I'd like a weapon before this man tries to kill me.'

'He'll only kill you if you try to escape, or attack one of us.'

Batoor spread his arms. 'I've eaten your salt.'

'Where are you taking us?' Jack asked again.

'Gondabad,' Batoor said. Even Jack understood that name without Mary having to translate. Jack took a deep breath. That was where he'd been born and where the Mutiny had started for him.

'I know the way.'

Batoor nodded as Mary translated.

'Are you sure that Jayanti is there?' Jack asked.

'I am not sure she is there. I think she may be there.' Batoor answered before Mary translated. 'Yes, Captain Windrush, I speak English.'

'Well, that is truthful for a Pathan,' Jack said. 'My men will still watch you.'

'I believe you.' Batoor eyed Logan, who ran a calloused thumb up the length of his bayonet.

* * *

Jack heard the gunfire from deep in his sleep. Rolling on his side, he grabbed his revolver and sword and was outside his tent before the echoes of the second shot died away. The third came an instant later, followed by an irregular fusillade.

'What's happening? Jack buckled his sword belt around his naked waist. 'Elliot! Bryce!'

'Somebody fired into the camp, sir!' Bryce was fully dressed and had his revolver in his right hand. 'I had the sentries fire back.'

'Cease fire!' Jack ordered. There was a single shot and then the eerie silence of the night, broken only by the buzz of insects and the chirping of frogs. 'Did anybody see anything?'

'I did, sir.' Parker said. 'I saw a muzzle flash over to the left.'

'Is anybody hit?'

'No, sir,' O'Neill said.

'Elliot, take Sergeant Greaves, Parker and ten men, search in the area from where the shot came.'

'Sir.' Elliot detailed nine veterans and a replacement named Mahoney. He vanished into the night.

'Who was it, sir?' Ensign Peake asked.

'We don't know, Peake,' Jack said. 'We won't know until Lieutenant Elliot returns, and we might not know even then.'

'Shall I go and look, sir?'

'No! Go and attend to your men.' Jack glowered at Peake until he disappeared.

'You were a little harsh on that boy,' Mary said.

'He has to learn his duty,' Jack said. 'If he went out there,' he nodded into the night, 'the pandies would cut him to pieces.'

'I see.'

'And God only knows what they'd do to you. Get back inside the camp, get into your tent and keep your head down.'

Mary opened her mouth to protest, saw the determination in Jack's face and nodded. 'Yes, sir.' She took three steps and turned around. 'You know, it might be better if you put some clothes on next time you gave me an order. It would be more dignified for both of us.'

'What?' Jack realised that he was wearing nothing except his sword belt. 'I was in bed,' he said. 'A real lady would not comment on such things.' His retaliation was too late for Mary was ten paces away, striding for her tent. *Blasted woman. Only Mary can drive me to such irritation.*

'Nothing, sir,' Elliot reported when he returned. 'We found nothing at all, not a sign of anybody.'

'All right, I didn't think you would. It might have been a stray mutineer trying his luck, or just a passing *badmash* causing trouble. Double the sentries.'

'Yes, sir.' Elliot lowered his voice. 'Is Mary all right, Jack? And the Pathan?'

'Mary's in her tent,' Jack said. 'I've posted a sentry, and I want him relieved every two hours.'

'Yes, sir,' Elliot said.

'The Pathan is still here,' Batoor's deep voice sounded. 'He did not take advantage of your confusion to escape.'

Jack gave a small smile. 'I didn't think he would.'

Jack didn't try to sleep again that night. Dressing quickly, he spent the hours until midnight patrolling the camp perimeter, quietly talking to the pickets and peering into the dark. He roused the camp three hours before dawn, supervised breakfast, loaded the camels and had everybody on the march within the hour.

The men stumbled through the dark, swearing quietly, alert for any ambush, holding loaded rifles and wondering if they should have thrown back the shilling they'd accepted from a smooth-tongued recruiting sergeant.

'Sir,' Sergeant Greaves saluted Jack. 'One of my men reports we're being watched.'

'I'm sure most of the men think that, Greaves.'

'Yes, sir. This time it's a bit different,' Greaves said. 'This man is certain, sir.'

Jack sighed. 'Bring him up, sergeant.'

The private gave a hurried salute. 'I know you,' Jack said. 'You were the lad MacKinnon, for whom Sergeant Greaves bought beer.'

'Yes, sir,' Mackinnon said.

'What do you have to say then, MacKinnon?'

'There's somebody out there in the dark, sir.'

'What have you seen?'

'Nothing, sir.' MacKinnon hesitated. 'I can feel them, sir, out there.'

'Do you know where, MacKinnon?'

'No, sir. I do know though, sir.' It was evident that the man couldn't explain further.

'Thank you, MacKinnon.' Jack frowned. 'Where are you from?'

'Skye, sir. It's an island in the Hebrides, off Scotland.'

'I see.' Jack wondered if he had just experienced an example of Hebridean second sight. 'Keep me posted, will you?'

'Yes, sir.' MacKinnon seemed relieved to escape.

'Greaves, send out strong pickets on either flank and double the rear guard, at least until day-break.' Jack saw Wilden watching nervously and called him over.

'Wilden,' Jack spoke quietly. 'How long have you held a commission in the army?'

'Nearly nine months, sir,' Wilden said proudly.

'And how much of that time have you been with the men?'

'One month, sir. The rest of the time I was travelling from England.'

'Well ensign, here is some free advice. These men come from bad backgrounds. Many are orphans, or their parents were drunkards, jail-birds or walked away and left them. Some are petty criminals; others are not so petty. As you see, they are a mixture of old soldiers and young lads very much like you, except without your education.'

'Yes, sir.' Wilden was sensible enough to realise that Jack was speaking from his own experience.

'If you treat the men decently, listen to their problems and help them, they will follow you to the gates of Hell and beyond. All they want is somewhere to belong. The regiment is their family. We, the officers, are surrogate parents. Do your duty, help them to do theirs, guide them and watch over them.'

'Yes, sir,' Wilden nodded eagerly. 'Like us, sir, they joined for queen and country.'

Jack grunted. 'Patriotism is said to be the last refuge of the scoundrel, ensign. For most men, this regiment is the last refuge of the desperate.' He passed over a cheroot, as if to a friend. 'Belonging to the regiment is vital. Officers can transfer or buy their way into other regiments; the men cannot. The 113th is their home. The more pride they have in the regiment, the better their morale and the better they will fight.'

'Yes, sir.'

Jack nodded. 'When it comes to action, lead from the front. It's the only place for a British officer.'

'Of course, sir!' Wilden said.

Jack smiled. 'In plain speaking, Wilden, just do your duty, and you'll be fine.' He patted the boy's shoulder. 'Now off you go and look after your section. Make sure their water bottles are full of water and not gin, make sure their rifles are not rusty, make sure their bayonets slide free from the scabbard and they have ammunition in their pouches and not loot or whisky.'

'Yes, sir.'

'Drink is the sin of the soldier, Wilden. Drink and women. I'm sure you have experience with the latter; your duty is to ensure the men don't cause themselves disease.' Jack winked and walked away, lighting a cheroot. The column trudged on, rifles slung, boots kicking up dust.

'That was kindly,' Mary said.

'I feel like a grandfather,' Jack said.

'How old are you, Jack?' Mary asked.

'Twenty-five,' Jack said. 'I feel about fifty-five.'

Mary smiled. 'How long have you been a soldier?'

'Since 1851 – coming up for seven years.' Jack looked back on himself. 'I was like Wilden then, young, keen and stupid.'

'How many battles have you been in?' Mary walked at Jack's side, matching him stride for stride.

Jack thought of Rangoon and Pegu, Inkerman and the Redan and the battles for Cawnpore and Lucknow. 'I don't know,' he said. 'Too many, Mary, too many.'

'Once this campaign is over the army may give you a rest.'

'Maybe they will,' Jack said. *That won't happen. The army will use the 113th for the dirty jobs, the unpleasant tasks without glamour or glory. My future is one of constant fighting until the grave, a soldier's life and a soldier's death.* He realised that Mary was looking at him with her head slightly to one side and her eyes thoughtful.

'You don't believe that, do you?' Mary asked.

'No.' Jack looked up as a flock of birds exploded from a tamarind tree. 'Wilden, take your men and see what disturbed these birds.'

Mary withdrew. 'I'll leave you to your duty.'

They marched on, more wary, with men gripping their rifles and peering into the fading grey of the early morning. India could be indescribably beautiful, tragically poor or insufferably hot. There was a combination of colour and dust, obscene cruelty and nonstop kindness, loyalty beyond reason and always variety. Jack pulled aside as the men slogged past.

'Did you find anything Wilden?'

'No, sir.'

'Carry on. How about you, Sergeant Greaves?'

'All well, sir. All present.'

The first shot came just as dawn silvered the sky, followed by a screaming charge on the 113th's left flank. One minute the column was marching solidly through a seemingly empty countryside, the next they were under attack by an unknown number of men. Jack had a nightmare vision of glaring eyes and gaping mouths, gleaming blades and flowing robes as the enemy rushed in. The flanking picket took the first shock and withdrew, firing and cursing, as Jack shouted for the central column to form a square around the transport camels.

'Hold your fire until ordered!' Jack glanced at his men, trying to ensure they were all in the square. 'Fire!' White and acrid, powder smoke drifted across the perimeter as the yelling subsided. Men peered into the half-light, sweaty hands slippery on the stocks of their rifles.

'Where are they?' Bryce fingered the trigger of his revolver. 'They've gone. We've beaten them off.'

'Keep quiet!' Jack snarled. 'Can anybody see anything?'

'They're still there, sir,' O'Neill said. 'I can smell them.'

'They're on this side, sir!' MacKinnon gave the warning. 'I know they are.'

Jack nodded. 'Left flank, load and cap. Right flank, aim low, fire a volley, fire!'

The Enfields crashed out with fleeting muzzle flares and spurts of smoke, a scream from the dark and then shocking silence. Powder smoke caught dry throats; a man coughed.

'Right flank, load and cap!' Jack ordered. 'Keep quiet and listen.'

The music began so softly that Jack thought he was hearing things, Indian music, rhythmic and subtly beautiful, with undertones that unsettled him.

'What the devil are they doing?' Bryce asked.

'Serenading us,' Elliot said.

'They're trying to unnerve us,' Jack said.

'They might be trying to mask the sounds of an attack,' Elliot said.

'Good thinking, Elliot. Everybody keep quiet, ignore the music and listen.' Jack glanced over his shoulder. Mary was amidst the camel drivers in the centre of the square, squatting. He lifted a hand, and she acknowledged with a wave. She was as safe there as anywhere in the square.

'It's getting lighter.' Jack was used to the speed of the tropical dawn. 'We can see them now if they come.' He relaxed a little, confident in the ability of his fifty men to defeat an attack by many times their number. After serving with Havelock and Sir Colin Campbell, he knew the fighting prowess of the British soldier. His 113th was as good as any soldiers in the world and better than most.

'They've gone sir,' MacKinnon said.

'The music is still playing,' Bryce pointed out.

'Sir!' O'Neill gave a quick salute. 'Packer's missing.'

Packer was one of the replacements, a thin, undersized youth from London.

'Has he fallen out?' It was common for Johnny Raws to collapse on long marches, from either exhaustion or heat.

'No, sir,' O'Neill said. 'He was with us ten minutes ago. I think the pandies grabbed him in that first rush.'

'Oh, dear God almighty.' Jack took a deep breath. 'We'll have a look. O'Neill, you're with me. I want Coleman, Thorpe, Riley and Logan.'

'Where are you going, sir?' Ensign Wilden asked. 'Can I come?'

'Not this time, Wilden.' Although officers needed to blood Griffs and Johnny Raws, there was a time and place, and this was neither.

'Elliot, take command.'

'Yes, sir,' Elliot said and lowered his voice. 'I'll take care of her, sir.'

'Come on, O'Neill.' Jack slipped through the square and into the growing light outside. They were in an area of extensive fields, small *topes* of trees and abandoned villages. A hanged man swung from the bough of a tree; victim of mutineer, vengeful British or local lawmaker, Jack did not know.

'Sir,' Coleman knelt on one knee. 'Over here. Blood.'

A cluster of flies rose from the bloodstain as Jack examined it. 'We got one of them, then, whoever they were.'

'Yes, sir,' Coleman agreed. 'Unless that's Packer's blood.'

'I hope it was quick.' Riley said what they were all thinking.

'They've gone now.' O'Neill scanned the open terrain. 'There's no sign of anybody.'

'They'll be there, watching us,' Jack led them in a wide circle around the 113th position, searching for Packer and the enemy and finding nothing.

'We'll stay put for a couple of hours,' Jack ordered when he returned. 'Greaves, Elliot, Bryce, take out patrols and look for Packer.' He could only afford a couple of hours. Any more and he would be marching in the afternoon and would lose more men to the heat. In this sort of expedition, they moved from water to water, sought the shade or died.

'Now we wait,' he said to Mary.

'And Packer?' Mary asked.

'We hope.'

Mary nodded, touched his arm and searched for the closest shade. She knew he was worried about his missing man.

One by one, the patrols returned, all with grim faces and a shake of the head. 'The pandies have gone,' they reported.

'And Packer?' Jack asked, already aware what the reply would be.

'There is no sign of Packer.'

Jack swore. He hated leaving a man behind.

'We beat them off, sir!' Wilden put a more optimistic slant on the encounter.

'You did well,' Jack said. 'You stood with your men and did your duty. That's what soldiers are supposed to do.' He turned away, knowing that his few words would have boosted Wilden's morale more than a hundred brass bands or long speeches.

'Forward!' Taking his place in front of the column, Jack waved them on. Already the heat was intolerable. Within fifteen minutes, the men would be sodden with sweat, made prickly by the dust of the road sticking to them. Within another half-hour they would be flagging, some staggering as the heat smote them like a brass fist. He looked ahead, knowing there was a village two miles along the road that would have a well.

'Wilden; take a picket ahead, find water. Take five men, three old soldiers and two Johnny Raws.'

That was an easy enough mission that would improve the lad's confidence and give him and the replacements some experience of acting outside the regimental framework.

'You'll really need to learn some languages.' Mary seemed comfortable sitting inside a pannier, slung at the side of one of the baggage camels. With a scarf shading her head, she looked as if she belonged in this environment.

'Why?' Jack was preoccupied with scanning the surrounding countryside. 'I have you.'

'I won't be here forever,' Mary said. 'You didn't want me here this time.'

Jack frowned, wondering if Mary was hinting at something. 'You'd better teach me, then.'

'Now?'

'Not now! I'm leading a column in hostile territory! Damn it, woman!' He thought of Packer, wondering if he could have done more to find the missing man.

We can start when we camp then.' Mary ignored his irritability.

'Yes,' Jack said, 'when we camp, unless the mutineers attack.'

'Oh?' Mary raised her eyebrows, a habit she seemed to have. 'Surely you would not allow the mutineers to interfere with your education.'

Only the slightest twitch at the corner of her mouth indicated that Mary was pulling his leg. Jack shook his head. 'You'd better get back in the middle of the column in case the pandies come.'

'Yes, Captain Windrush, sir,' Mary gave a mock salute that raised a smile on the faces of the nearest men.

Aware he was watching her rather than concentrating on his duty, Jack looked away abruptly. *Duty, duty, first and last. Duty to the death.*

'Penny for them,' Elliot said.

'What?'

'Penny for your thoughts,' Elliot said.

'I was wondering if the pandies would try to attack us again.'

'You're a lying hound, Jack Windrush,' Elliot said pleasantly. 'You were thinking of Mary Lambert.'

'I was doing nothing of the kind!'

'Another lie!' Elliot said. 'You'd better be careful, Jack, or Saint Peter will bang the pearly gates in your face and kick you downstairs with the thieves, robbers and blackguards.' He grinned. 'And I'll be waiting with the 113th to welcome you.'

'Watch your blasphemy, lieutenant, and you a clergyman's son.'

'She's a good woman, Jack,' Elliot said.

'As good as any other.' Jack tried to sound grudging in his praise.

'You risked your life to save her in the evacuation of Lucknow,' Elliot reminded. 'And she nursed you when you were wounded.'

'She knew my mother,' Jack said.

'There's more than that.' Although he was talking, Elliot never ceased to survey the countryside through which they passed. 'You know there is.'

'She's a useful woman with her language skills, and she's a pleasant companion.' Jack eased off a little.

'Is that all?' Elliot raised his binoculars to study a ruined village on the horizon. He grunted. 'Something is moving over there. Could be pandies.'

'Riley and Logan are on the flank picket. If there's anything out there, they'll pick it up.'

'She likes you, too.' Elliot accepted Jack's opinion on the distant village. 'And more than likes you, or she wouldn't have followed you here. Be careful, Jack.'

'I know what I'm doing.' Jack was becoming used to Elliot's warnings of doom where Mary was concerned.

'She'll be bad for your career,' Elliot said. 'She's Anglo-Indian, or Eurasian or whatever you wish to call it. Could you imagine introducing her into the Mess? What would the officers say? How would the other wives react?'

Jack felt his temper rising. 'Who the hell cares what the officers say, or how the other wives react? Surely any decision would be between Mary and me, and I'm not saying that I have any idea about marriage or anything else.'

'Mary might care,' Elliot said quietly. 'Could you imagine what sort of life she would have, especially if the Army posted us home? The wives would shun her, and the other officers would treat her like dirt. It's not fair on Mary to lead her on, Jack, and as for you...' Elliot shrugged. 'You could whistle for your next step. No matter what heroics you did, a man with a Eurasian wife would never get promotion. You would remain a captain, Jack until you were in your dotage and Horse Guards would find some excuse to put you on half pay so you would rot in Eastbourne or Brighton or some other nowhere.'

'Thank you for your advice, Lieutenant,' Jack said stiffly. 'And now if you could return your attention to your duty, we would all be grateful.' Jack had been watching Ensign Wilden hurry back from his patrol.

'There is a village ahead, sir, with a working well.'

'Good man, Wilden,' Jack encouraged. 'Now take ten men forward and secure the village perimeter until we get there.'

'Yes, sir!' Wilden looked excited as he called together the nearest ten men and rushed forward again.

'Poor lad.' Elliot was not the slightest abashed by Jack's rebuke. 'He'll learn.'

'Let's hope he has time to learn and the pandies don't get him,' Jack said. 'Or the cholera.'

The village centred on a well and a babul tree. In peacetime, elderly men would gather under the tree, exchanging gossip and watching the world go by, but in the present war, the place was deserted.

'Water the camels first,' Jack ordered, 'then the men and the officers last.' There was an order of priority in the army and any officer who drank before his men would soon learn of his mistake.

'This place is eerily quiet.' Mary dismounted with a single fluid movement and stretched her limbs before walking toward Jack.

'It's the war,' Jack said. 'We're marching through a land accursed by God.'

'It's more than that,' Mary said.

'Something's wrong.' MacKinnon held his rifle ready. 'Something's wrong here, sir. There are no birds or anything.'

'He's right,' Mary said. 'There are no birds, not even in the tree.'

Jack frowned. Even if the villagers were absent, the babul tree should be swarming with birds. Where were they?

'That camel, what's wrong with it?'

The camel was swaying from side to side as if drunk. As Jack watched, it fell to one side, spilling its load of tents and water-canteens.

'What the devil?' Jack jumped forward. 'What's happening here?' He grabbed the camel driver. 'What have you done to the beast?'

The man stared at him, terrified.

'He's done nothing,' Mary said. 'You can't blame him! Look at that other camel!'

A second camel was also swaying, staggering from side to side.

'The blasted things were all right a minute ago,' Jack said.

'They were all right until they drank from the well,' Elliot pointed out.

'Bad water!' Jack yelled in near panic. 'The pandies have poisoned the well. Get the animals back! Nobody touch the blasted water!'

'The foul bastards!' Elliot was not normally prone to swearing. 'Get back, lads! Don't touch the water! Get away from the well!' He extended his arms and pushed back thirsty camels and thirsty men. 'Back!' They retreated, swearing.

'That's a new trick,' Jack said. 'It's a dirty thing to do in a hot climate.'

'We need water.' Elliot pushed back a thirsty camel. 'Neither the men nor the animals will last another day without it.'

Unfolding his map, Jack spread it on the ground, weighed down the corners with stones and pored over their position. 'It's the dry season' he said as if speaking to Griffs, 'so there is little standing water in this part of the world. We have to find a well.'

'Yes, sir.' Elliot agreed.

'We passed close by a deserted village a mile or two down the road,' Jack reminded. 'They'll have a well.'

'The pandies could have poisoned that one too,' Lieutenant Bryce said.

'Take out a strong picket out and find out, Bryce,' Jack decided. 'Be careful.'

'Yes, sir.' Bryce selected a dozen men and marched off. Jack posted sentries around the village as the remaining men sought shade, cursing the enemy and the climate.

'What do we do now?' Mary asked.

'You keep away from the sun,' Jack said. 'I'll do my duty.'

'You're worried.' Mary touched his arm.

'The men can't see that. They must think their commander is confident of success at all times.' Jack checked his revolver was loaded and looked around the village once more. Both camels that had drunk at the well were now dead, and Jack gave orders to redistribute their loads among the others.

'What's taking Bryce so long?' Jack scanned the distant village through his binoculars.

The rifle fire was flat and vicious under the pressing sun.

'Ambush,' Jack said. 'The pandies have ambushed Bryce. Form up, men! We're heading out!'

For a moment, Jack wondered if he should leave his camels and Mary behind with an escort, but decided that further splitting his force when facing an unknown number of the enemy would be foolish.

'Keep together. Elliot, take the right flank, Wilden, and O'Neill, take the left, Peake, command the rear guard. Follow me.'

As Jack doubled back toward the village, he saw that Bryce and his men had gone to ground, lying in an extended line to fire at an invisible enemy.

Jack ducked as a bullet flicked his forage hat, and then Bryce was rising beside him.

'They're firing at us, sir,' Bryce reported.

'Get down, man!' Jack ordered. 'There's no sense in making yourself a target. How many of them are there?'

'I don't know, sir,' Bryce said. 'Maybe a hundred or so.'

'Very good, Bryce.' Jack didn't need to ask where the enemy was; he could see powder smoke rising from the village and various points on either side.

The village was no different from a thousand others in India, with a peepul tree near the centre of a straggle of houses of different sizes. Jack knew the rules when ambushed. He could find cover and try to fight it out, knowing that the ambushers held all the advantages of position and surprise, he could withdraw, or he could charge for the throat and hope to unsettle them. In this case, retreat was not an option.

'Hutton, Smith; stay with the translator and don't let her come to harm. The rest of you, follow me! Come on the 113th!' Jack charged forward. Cheering and swearing, his men followed. There was no time to think of tactics. He had to rely on force and speed.

'Cry Havelock!' Elliot used the old battle cry. 'And let loose the dogs of war!'

The dogs were loose.

Smoke jetted from the windows of the nearest house, and Jack felt something flick past his face. Lifting his revolver, he fired back. A mutineer appeared at the upper window, his scarlet jacket now faded with sun and exposure. For a moment, Jack stared right into his face. He was a havildar – a sergeant of native infantry – with greying hair and impressive whiskers, a man who had grown middle-aged in the service of John Company and now had lost his pension and his reputation by turning against his old employers.

Weaving from left to right, Jack ran forward and fired again, knowing he had little chance of hitting the havildar. The door of the house crashed open, and a press of men rushed out, some were mutineers, other warriors in white clothes and twisted red turbans with curved tulwars and round shields. Jack shot the leading man, dropped his revolver as it jammed and drew his sword.

There was no time for hesitation now. For the next few moments, all Jack saw was screaming faces and darting bayonets, slashing tulwars and round metal shields. He thrust, parried and swore, felt the shock of impact as his sword entered a man's chest, and then something heavy crashed on the side of his head, and he staggered, falling to the ground.

He lay there, dazed, seeing only the white trousers of the mutineers and the bare brown legs of a swordsman. A mutineer in a faded scarlet tunic and loincloth straddled him and poised a bayonet.

Here is death, Jack thought. He wasn't scared. He was a soldier, and this was a soldier's death. The mutineer snarled at him and lifted the bayonet, ready to plunge it into his chest. The man's face twisted in hatred, his eyes wide open and his teeth bared. Jack wondered why an NCO had not pulled the sepoy up for having a rusty blade and then a naik pulled the man away. Jack rolled to his feet and grabbed his sword.

'Sir!' O'Neill and a press of men arrived with sweating faces and thundering boots. Logan dispatched the sepoy with a casual thrust of his bayonet. 'Are you all right, sir?'

'I'm all right,' Jack said. 'What happened?'

'You were on the ground sir, and an old naik saved you, sir,' O'Neill said.

'Why?' Still dazed, Jack felt the side of his head. 'Why did the naik save me?'

'Dunno, sir.' O'Neill shook his head. 'Rum fellows, these sepoys. You never know what's going on in their heads.'

'Where is the naik now?'

'He's gone, sir,' O'Neill said. 'He shoved Jack Pandy aside and fled.'

Jack wiped sweat from his forehead and looked around. There was a litter of bodies on the ground, but after the brief skirmish outside the houses, the mutineers had not fought. Only three of the enemy remained, standing in the open with tulwars and round shields.

'They think they're in the middle ages.' Elliot fired two rounds from his revolver, and the tallest of the enemy spun and fell, gasping and holding his shoulder. Armstrong stepped forward and casually bayoneted the wounded man.

'Don't kill them!' Jack shouted. 'I want them for questioning!'

He was almost too late as Logan ducked the swing of a tulwar and thrust his bayonet into the stomach of the next man. 'There's a Cawnpore breakfast, you pandy bastard!'

The third man stood alone, clashing his sword against his shield and shouting what Jack took to be a challenge.

'Come on!' Ensign Peake drew his sabre and dashed forward. 'Single combat, old man!'

'Get back, you stupid boy!' Jack shouted. 'He'll chop you to pieces!'

The rebel parried Peake's slash with his shield and sliced sideways. Peake leapt back, so the tulwar missed him, and then O'Neill arrived with a clubbed musket and battered the rebel to the ground.

'I was winning, sergeant,' Peake said. 'It was a fair fight!'

'This is war, not the school playing fields.' Jack looked at the rebel. 'Well done, O'Neill.'

'Aye. That was too easy, sir.' O'Neill kicked away the tulwar and shield. 'Look at this bugger; look at his scars.'

Dressed in a loincloth that revealed numerous scars on his upper body, the rebel was about thirty-five, with a small beard.

'He's a warrior, that one,' O'Neill said. 'He would have easily killed Ensign Peake, sir.'

'Maybe he wanted to be a martyr,' Jack said. 'More importantly, sergeant, form a defensive perimeter around the village. Keep this man for now; we'll question him later. Greaves, check the well is sweet.'

'It's as sweet as Irish honey, sir!' Greaves reported.

'Thank God for small mercies; get the camels and men watered.'

'That was too easy, sir,' O'Neill said. 'They outnumbered us, and they were in a strong position.'

'I know.' Jack retrieved his pistol and slowly reloaded. 'Make sure the pickets stay alert, sergeant.'

They heard the first scream an hour later, as the men were trying to sleep in the shade of the deserted houses.

'What's that?' Mary asked.

'It could be anything.' Jack tried to concentrate. Ever since the blow to his head, he'd been dizzy, and his thoughts were unclear.

'That's Packer,' Jackson said. 'I know his voice. That's Packer, I tell you.'

Another scream sounded, longer than before, ending in a long, drawn-out howl that raised the small hairs on the back of Jack's neck.

'They're torturing him!' Jackson said. 'We have to do something, sir!'

Jack considered. He could send out a patrol, but the rebels would expect that and would have an ambush waiting. By now, they knew his numbers and disposition; they held all the cards. On the other hand, if he sat and did nothing, the morale of his men would drop, and they would think he had no care for their lives.

'Elliot! Take charge of the camp. O'Neill, I want you, Coleman, Thorpe, Logan and Riley.' He had chosen his veterans, men who had threaded through the Burmese jungles and out-foxed the Plastun Cossacks in their homeland. 'We're looking for Packer. Hutton, you and Smith, guard the translator.' He felt Mary's gaze on him and didn't look around.

The dark closed around them, hot and humid. Jack took a deep breath. A few years ago, he had revelled in these night expeditions as he sought opportunities to make his name, while the excitement had driven him to deeds that now made him shudder. Now, these patrols were routine, something he had to do, although he could not deny the flutter of nervousness in the pit of his stomach and the dryness of his mouth. He closed his eyes for a few seconds, trying to control his bouts of dizziness.

Am I turning into a coward? Or have I already stretched my nerves past their limit?

The ground was hard under his feet. In six weeks or so, the rain would come, and this area would be a morass. That was India, his second home – perhaps his first home.

The screaming subsided into agonised sobbing that lasted for minutes. Jack sensed the anger of the men. They had witnessed more suffering in three years than most men would see in their lifetimes. Experience had added callouses to their skins and taught them to value friendship and loyalty above all. Now a friend was being tortured within their hearing, and they were powerless to help.

'Spread out,' Jack whispered. 'Not too far. Keep within two yards.' He didn't want the enemy to capture any more of his men.

They moved slowly, not putting their boots down until they had checked for dry twigs or loose stones that could rattle and give their position away, controlling their breathing, listening for any sound that did not belong.

O'Neill raised his hand, and they all halted, listening, peering into the dark. Jack felt the sweat slide down his back and loosened his grip on his revolver. He could hear nothing except the expected night sounds. They moved on, step by slow step.

The attack came suddenly, a rush of men from the dark straight for the centre of their line. Logan fired first, with O'Neill and Thorpe half a second later. The muzzle-flares erupted, and then there were a few furious moments of bayonets, rifle butts and boots hammering against semi-visible opponents. Jack felt hands grab him and fired, with the revolver bucking in his hand. One man fell, a second took his place, and somebody dragged him forward, struggling desperately.

Coleman and Riley came in from the flanks, swearing, bayonets plunging.

Something hard and heavy crashed on Jack's right wrist. He gasped and dropped his pistol, kicked out with his right foot, felt a surge of satisfaction as he contacted something soft, and tried to draw his sword. He swore as his numbed fingers failed to grip the hilt.

'Sir!' Coleman fired as he approached with the bullet taking one of Jack's attackers in the chest. The force threw the man back and then

Riley was there, dapper and dangerous. The mutineers melted into the dark, leaving Jack gasping and holding his injured wrist.

'Are you all right, sir?'

'I think so. Nothing is broken anyway.' Jack flexed his wrist. 'What happened there?'

'They tried to kidnap you, sir,' Riley said.

'Why would they do that?' *That was a stupid question. I'm not thinking straight.*

'Information maybe, sir,' Riley said. 'Or a ransom. It is quite common in parts of Europe, kidnapping people for ransom.' Trust Riley to know the criminal practices of other countries.

'This isn't Europe, Riley, and they would get nothing by ransoming me.' Jack shook his head. 'I'm blessed if I know. Thank you for rescuing me, men.'

Riley turned away. Coleman grinned in embarrassment.

Having achieved nothing, Jack led the patrol back. There was no more screaming that night. He didn't try to sleep.

'That's twice something strange has happened,' he said to Elliot. 'First, the naik stopped a man from killing me and then an attempt to capture me.'

Elliot lit a cheroot. 'Your guardian angel is looking after you.' He smiled through the smoke. 'Seriously though, Jack, it's a rum do. I can't think what it is. This entire war has been strange, like a civil war against our friends and with the men running wild. Have you ever seen British soldiers behave in such a manner? Have you ever heard of them wanting to hang and execute like they are now?'

'I haven't,' Jack said. 'And I want to know why that naik saved my life and these pandies tried to capture me.'

'To question you, I guess,' Elliot said.

'I'm only a captain.' Jack shook his head. 'I don't know what's to do at all.'

'Well,' Elliot patted his shoulder. 'You're alive, your wrist is unbroken, and that's all that matters. Don't let the men hear that you're uncertain. They need a confident commander, not a worried one. Now if you'll excuse me, I have my rounds to make.'

'Aye, off you go, Arthur. Thank you.' Jack lit a cheroot and stared at the sweltering countryside. He felt as if India was playing with him, patting his mind and body back and forward like a shuttlecock. He would be glad when this campaign was over, and peace returned to this tortured land.

Jack gasped at the sudden pain in his head. He didn't know what was happening; he only knew that something was wrong. He closed his eyes as another dizzy spell came to him. Grasping the bole of a tree, he held on. He couldn't let anybody see this new weakness. He was the commander, he must always appear strong and confident, or the men would lose faith in him. He must do his duty.

Chapter Seven

'There's something on the road ahead, sir.' Sergeant Greaves reported. 'Shall I go and see what it is?'

'Yes, sergeant.'

Greaves trotted ahead and returned at the double. 'It's a head, sir! A human head!'

Jack sighed. *With how many more horrors will India torture me?*

Somebody had severed the head at the neck and thrust it onto the end of a stake. They had gouged out the eyes and placed something in the mouth.

'That's Packer!' Jackson hurried forward, only to stop as he reached the head. 'No, it's not.'

'No,' Jack said. 'It's not Packer. It's a European, though.'

'It's Keay, sir, of Number One Company,' Greaves said. 'How did he get here?'

'He was with Major Snodgrass,' Jack struggled to remember. 'They were escorting the women to Cawnpore from Gondabad last year.' Colonel Hook asked me to keep an eye out for them.

'I remember, sir,' Greaves said. They all vanished, if I recall.'

'That's right. And now Keay has turned up here, or part of him has.' Jack carefully detached the head and removed the contents of the mouth. 'It's a note.' He read it out.

British soldiers, why fight for a shilling a day when you can earn twenty times that amount fighting for a better cause? Why fight for the shareholders of the Honourable East India Company when you can fight for yourselves and have beautiful Indian women as your companions?

All you have to do is walk away and join us. Welcome bhaiya! Welcome, brother!

Realising that his men were listening to every word, Jack forced a laugh, screwed the paper into a ball and threw it away. 'Well, that's a lot of moonshine. Who would believe the word of a rebel?'

'Somebody might,' Greaves said. 'Not all our men are blessed with strong minds. Some might believe the lies. Others might want the money and women.'

Jack grunted and raised his voice so that everybody could hear. 'Not in this regiment. We are the 113th. Our lads have more sense than to believe that nonsense. Now, let's bury what's left of this poor fellow.'

'Why would they do that?' Elliot asked. 'Why torture the poor soul?'

Jack grunted. 'Why do we blow mutinous sepoys from the mouths of cannon, or make them lick up the blood of our women and children before we hang them?' He hardened his voice. 'Bring the prisoner to me. And fetch Mary.'

Armstrong and Hutton dragged across the man they'd captured at the village. He stood there, erect and semi-naked, unemotional.

'Ask him what's the meaning of this?' Jack demanded. 'Why did they torture and murder poor Private Keay?'

When Mary translated, the prisoner looked at Keay's head, smiled and said nothing.

'Ask him again,' Jack said to Mary. 'Tell him that we'll hang him in pigskin unless he tells us what it's all about.'

Mary shook her head. 'He's a Hindu,' she said. 'Pigskin is no threat to him.'

'Tell him we'll hang him with a cowhide rope then,' Jack said. 'Tell him any damned thing you like as long as it helps us find out why they tortured Private Keay.'

Mary spoke to the prisoner for a few moments, with his answers coming calmly. 'He says that Jayanti ordered it,' Mary said at last. 'Jayanti ordered the foreigner to be put to death to frighten us.'

'Frighten us?' Jack stared at the prisoner. 'Disgust us, maybe. Damn it, we have beaten the rebels and the mutineers; we're not going to be frightened by a rag-tag mob of broken men. Ask him where Jayanti is, Mary.'

A circle had formed around the prisoner, angry men listening to the questioning and offering unwanted advice regarding what to ask and how to treat him.

The prisoner ignored the shouts from the onlookers as he replied.

'He says that Jayanti is going to destroy the British,' Mary reported.

'Is that not what they said last year?' Jack snorted. 'They should try something original, the murdering hounds.' He frowned and took a deep breath. 'Ask him where Jayanti is.' He looked up. 'You men, get about your duty or by God, I'll find you something to do! Bryce! Elliot! Don't you have duties to perform? Check the pickets, send out patrols!' He glowered until the men moved back, giving him more space with the prisoner.

'You're getting out of temper,' Mary told him.

'I have to think,' Jack said. 'Ask him where Jayanti is and how she has so much power over men.'

'He says she is the great woman who is going to blow the British out of India.'

Jack nodded. 'Ask her real name, for by Christ, I don't believe it's Jayanti.' He waited as Mary exchanged words with the prisoner.

'He does not know, and please do not blaspheme, Jack.'

'Or he says that he doesn't know,' Jack said. 'All right. How many men does she have?' *Am I blaspheming?*

'He says ten thousand.'

Jack grunted. 'Ten thousand pandies and they're scared to attack a handful of the 113th? No wonder their mutiny failed.' He gestured to Armstrong. 'Take this liar away and keep him secure until I decide what to do with him.'

The screams of the night and the incident of Keay's head had unsettled Jack, and he was silent as he led the column on the road to Gondabad. Now that he knew his destination, he didn't need Batoor.

He could send the Pathan back to Lucknow under escort, bring him along with the column or release him.

Although he had promised Batoor liberty in exchange for information, Jack was reluctant to release a man who knew his numbers and destination. He grunted; the mutineers' intelligence service was so efficient they probably knew where he was bound before he did himself.

'Bring Batoor to me,' he ordered.

The Pathan stood erect in front of Jack, his eyes level.

'We had a deal,' Jack said. 'If you helped us find Jayanti, you would be released.'

'That is correct, Captain Windrush,' Batoor said.

'I have already released you from your chains, and you have not run, so we trust each other to an extent. If Jayanti is in Gondabad, I will free you entirely and inform the authorities that you are not a rebel.'

'Yes, Captain Windrush.'

'If she is not in Gondabad, I will hang you.'

'Yes, Captain Windrush.' Batoor gave no visible sign of emotion at either his liberty or death.

'Now answer me this, Batoor,' Jack said, 'why are you still here? You could slip past my sentries any time.'

Batoor smiled. 'I have my reasons for helping you find Jayanti, Captain Windrush. I am using you as much as you are using me.'

Jack nodded. 'Thank you, Batoor. That was an honest answer. When we find this woman in Gondabad, I will give you a tulwar and a horse.'

Batoor smiled. 'If we do not find her you will give me a rope. If you can hold me.'

'That is what will happen.'

'Then we understand each other,' Batoor said.

As they marched on, the days grew hotter and the ground dustier. Jack led them off the main roads and onto bullock tracks, the network of paths that bound all the villages and towns of India together. Dust rose as they marched, irritating their eyes, entering their noses and ears, coating their uniforms. They greeted the occasional river like manna, leading in the camels and drinking their fill.

'Avert your eyes,' Jack advised Mary as he allowed the men to bathe, and forty naked men gambolled like children in the water. The remaining ten were on guard duty, cursing their luck and enviously waiting their turn in the river.

'Yes, Captain Jack.' Rather than obeying, Mary turned towards the river and watched, smiling.

'Gentlewomen would not look at such things,' Jack said.

'Then I am thankful to be Anglo-Indian and not included in any gathering of gentlewoman,' Mary said. 'I nursed sick and wounded men, Jack. I have seen everything there is to see, and I have survived.'

'I would prefer that you looked elsewhere,' Jack said.

'There is little to see elsewhere. Watching your men is more amusing.' When she smiled at him, Jack wondered if Mary was genuinely interested, or if she found teasing him more entertaining. 'When your men are finished splashing around,' Mary said, 'you could send one or two to the shallows upstream, near that tamarind tree. There will be shoals of rohu fish at that spot, not great eating perhaps, but they would make a change in diet for everybody.'

'You are an interesting woman, Mary.' Jack decided he couldn't force her away from watching the men bathing. *If I had the opportunity to watch forty naked young women, would I watch? Yes, I would.* 'Indeed,' he said, 'I think you are the most honest woman I have ever met.'

'Why, thank you, Captain Jack.' Mary's mocking curtsey did not match the thoughtful expression in her eyes.

The country gradually changed, so they marched through a vast landscape of ochre-yellow earth, scrub and clumps of dark rock, interspersed with groups of thorn trees and stretches of pampas grass.

'Captain Windrush.' Mary pointed from her pannier. 'Best warn your men to avoid these *datura* plants.' She pointed them out. 'They look pretty, but they are poisonous.'

'Thank you, Mary, I'll pass that on.' Jack lifted his binoculars and scanned an outcrop of rock. He raised his voice. 'Lieutenant Bryce, take a patrol out to those rocks there, I think I saw movement.'

'We haven't seen the pandies for days, sir.'

'We haven't seen God either, but we both know he's there!' Jack snapped.

The days continued one very much like another, with the occasional flurry of activity to investigate a village or *tope* of trees. Twice a musket man fired at them, and each time Jack sent out a patrol. Each time they returned empty-handed.

'These pandies are like smoke,' Elliot smeared sweat across his forehead. 'They vanish into the country.'

They marched past an area of dark ravines where men pointed out mirages that floated above the land like castles from an Arthurian romance, and they stopped at settlements where the inhabitants had never seen a European before, let alone heard about the Mutiny. One village set above a river opposite a small temple was like an Elysian scene, with naked little boys and handsome men bathing, some smacking the water, so it rose in diamond-bright showers. When they left, a score of women took their place, laughing and quarrelling as they beat their saris in the water and spread them around the rocks. A few waded deep into the water to bathe, while the 113th watched, willing the women to undress. The women did not comply and emerged with streaming unbound hair and the saris plastered to their bodies. The barking of pi-dogs and the smell of cooking enhanced the scene.

'That is the real India,' Jack said. 'India without armies and killing and plunder.' He led his men on, leaving the village and temple and the peaceful people behind.

In other villages, watchmen guarded studded doors in the mud walls and stared at them from behind the protection of a large stick while little naked children laughed at these exciting strangers invading their world.

There were stretches of country where the incessant noise of crickets rattled around Jack's head until he wanted to cover his ears, and where the Johnny Raws pointed to snakes on the track.

'Here, you!' Jack pointed to a man who staggered in the heat and dropped his water bottle. 'Pick that up! You'll need it later.' He rationed the water and ensured each man wore his hat and neck-flap. He positioned O'Neill or Greaves at the back of the column to stop anybody falling by the wayside. He made sure his men camped in the shade, and he took every precaution he could to preserve their health.

When Jack accepted the hospitality of isolated villages, he paid generously for chapattis from the hands of wide-eyed women, filled up the men's water bottles from wells, picked ripe tamarind fruit from the trees, and ensured nobody interfered with the local women or killed the village animals. Always, Mary asked for Jayanti and Major Snodgrass.

They heard nothing about Snodgrass, but on three occasions they heard rumours of Jayanti, a woman the locals swore had risen in the ashes of the Mutiny. Each time the intelligence was vague, with only one evident fact resulting.

'The people are certain that Jayanti is powerful,' Mary said.

'Her fame is spreading, with nothing ever definite.' Jack rubbed his head. He had been experiencing headaches ever since the mutineer had cracked him over the skull.

'Are you all right, Jack?' Mary sounded concerned.

'It's just a headache. It will pass.'

'You've had headaches for days now,' Mary said.

'It's nothing, I tell you. It will pass!'

'You've been more irritable since you left Bareilly as well.' Mary placed her hand on Jack's head. 'You have to take better care of yourself.'

'It's more important that I take care of Jayanti.' Jack closed his eyes, as he felt suddenly dizzy. He thought of that strange meeting with Jayanti outside Bareilly. *I should have killed her there and then. I neglected my duty through fear of his life. I failed. Duty should come first, last and always. Duty, duty, duty.*

Only vaguely aware that Mary was watching him, Jack walked away. *I must catch Jayanti. I have to kill her before she murders anybody else. It's my duty. Oh, God, I wish it were cooler.*

Chapter Eight

A full moon glossed the countryside, shining on the *topes* of trees and the patches of jungle. In the distance, the city of Gondabad sat under its protective fort, with the now abandoned British cantonment a mile away.

Jack lit a cheroot and slowly inhaled. He had been born in Gondabad in 1833. Now, in 1858, he was going back with fifty hard-bitten men of the 113th Foot, a Pathan, a prisoner, a rag-tag of camel-drivers and servants and one woman. Of them all, that lone woman concerned him most.

Apart from his stepmother and his mother, there had been two women in his life. Myat had been the first. He had been a very raw ensign, a Griffin, during the Second Burmese War in 1852. Had that only been six years ago? It seemed like a lifetime when he had rushed into every action in his hope to make a name for himself and gain promotion. He had taken a fancy to Myat until he learned that she was the wife of one of his sergeants. It had been a sickening disappointment, alleviated when he met Helen, the daughter of Colonel Maxwell, the then commander of the 113th.

Jack inhaled, watching the tip of his cheroot glow bright red. He tried to ignore the constant thumping of his head.

Jack had harboured high hopes of Helen. She had been everything that a woman should be, beautiful, shapely, intelligent and incredibly courageous. Her family connections helped, of course. If he had married a colonel's daughter, he would have almost guaranteed a smoother passage to promotion. Fate decreed otherwise.

The dirty copper coin clattered onto the stony ground at Jack's feet.

'There's another penny, Jack. Now you have to share your thoughts.' Elliot had his silver flask in his hand.

'I was thinking about Helen.' Jack didn't need to hide his recent past from Elliot.

'Ah, the delectable Helen of dubious intentions,' Elliot said. 'The woman you intended to marry who scrambled off with your esteemed brother.' He sipped from his flask. 'Your best view of Helen was her backside, as she wriggled farewell.'

'Indeed.' Jack said no more.

'You're better without her,' Elliot said. 'And now you have Mary, another woman with no future.' His voice hardened. 'As I have already told you, more than once.'

'Thank you for your advice,' Jack said. 'Which I will completely ignore.'

'I thought you would,' Elliot said. 'You're too fat-headed to listen to the truth. You know the old army maxim about women, don't you? Catch them young, treat them rough, tell them nothing and leave them.'

'Not my style,' Jack smiled.

'I know.' Elliot passed over his flask. 'You're going to talk to Mary, aren't you?'

'I am.' Jack took a swallow and coughed. 'By thunder, Arthur, what is this muck you're forcing me to drink?'

'I've no idea. Riley found it for me. We were much better in the Crimea; Campbell's Highlanders always had a supply of the real Ferintosh.'

'Well, Arthur.' Jack handed back the flask. 'Thank you for the Indian courage. I am off to speak to that woman of whom you disapprove.'

'I don't disapprove of the woman,' Arthur said. 'Only of the effect she might have on your career.'

'To the devil with my career,' Jack said.

Chapter Nine

'I wonder how old that place is.' Elliot sipped at his flask as they surveyed the ancient fort of Gondabad. 'And what sort of terrible things have happened there.'

The fort squatted on top of a hillside, its red walls sprawling along the summit, with circular towers every hundred yards and the sun flashing on the steel points of spears and helmets on the battlements. It looked sinister, a massive place that dominated the sprawling acres of flat-roofed buildings and alleyways at its base.

'I'm less concerned about its age than its security,' Jack said, 'and whether or not Jayanti is inside.'

'The Rajah and Rani of Gondabad live in there,' Elliot continued. 'They are two of the most mysterious rulers in the country.' He borrowed Jack's binoculars to scan the walls. 'They're the most northerly Hindu rulers in this part of India, I think, scions of the Rajputs and nobody knows if they are loyal to the mutineers or us.'

Jack grunted. 'That will depend on who looks like winning.' He signalled to Batoor. 'Right, Batoor, this is where you prove your worth.'

The Pathan grinned through his beard. 'Yes, Captain Windrush.'

'Don't let me down,' Jack said.

'I would not trust him.' Bryce was openly sceptical.

'He's eaten our salt,' Jack wasn't as confident as he tried to sound. 'And he's not betrayed our trust yet.'

Bryce grunted. 'That means nothing.'

'All right Batoor, I want you to go into Gondabad and discover if Jayanti is there,' Jack said. 'Then you return and tell me. We are here on your word.' As Batoor walked away, Jack called him back. 'Batoor!'

'Captain Windrush?'

'Take this.' Jack threw across the tulwar he had taken from the prisoner. 'You might need it.'

The Pathan caught the sword one-handed, smiled and stalked away, his stride long and confident.

'That's the last we'll see of him,' Bryce said.

'You could be right,' Jack said. *I have taken my men to Gondabad on the word of an enemy, and now I have allowed him to walk away. Am I stupid?*

Mary was sitting outside her tent, watching the moon when Jack arrived.

'Good evening Jack,' she said, 'or is it Captain Windrush?'

'It's Jack.' Jack cursed his bluntness.

'What can I do for you, Captain Jack?'

'Just a social call,' Jack said. 'Elliot is looking after the camp.'

'It's in good hands, then,' Mary said.

They looked at each other, with a distant jackal breaking the silence. Moonlight cast quiet shadows across Mary's face as Jack stood under a banyan tree.

'I would offer you tea, but I haven't any,' Mary said at last.

Jack forced a smile. He couldn't think what to say. 'I thought this would be a simple search expedition to find Jayanti. It seems it might be something more, something I don't understand. First, that naik saved my life and then Jayanti knew my name. There was also the attempt to kidnap me.'

'You're an important man, Jack Windrush,' Mary said.

'I think we're putting the lid on a boiler,' Jack said. 'Unless we do something fundamentally different, India will simmer and boil, and we'll sit on top, smiling and smug until it explodes again.' He sat at Mary's side, watching the moon. 'Oh, we'll defeat them this time. With men such as Campbell and Sir Hugh Rose, we'll scatter their armies.

My lads of the 113th won't get beaten by any number of pandies.' He lit a cheroot. 'We were lucky though. If they had a couple of decent leaders, things could have turned out completely differently.'

Mary sat on a small *mooda* stool that somebody had found for her. 'Do you think the sepoys can be trusted any more, Jack?'

Jack considered for a moment as he studied the familiar sky. 'I don't know, Mary and that's worrying. The sepoys are good soldiers. I would say they are equally brave as our lads and careless of dying. They don't have our Christian doubts or humanitarian sentiment, and scenes of slaughter and mutilation don't concern them.'

'In that case, how do we always defeat them? Is it all down to leadership?'

'We don't always defeat them,' Jack said. 'They have inflicted quite a few reverses on us.'

Mary nodded. 'How then are we *usually* successful? Is that only due to our superior generals?'

'Not only better leadership.' Jack said. 'I said that the sepoys, or the pandies, match us in bravery and are less concerned about casualties. We have other qualities.' He pointed to the pickets, where Coleman and Thorpe were walking a few steps outside the perimeter of the camp. 'See these two there?'

'Coleman and Thorpey?' Mary gave a little smile. 'An odd couple, they are always quarrelling.'

'They are, yet when things are tough, they will never let each other down. They use dark humour to get through even the worst of situations. These two things, plus their innate determination never to get beat helps us win. Even after a defeat, our men don't *think* they're the best. They *know* they're the best.'

'That's very arrogant,' Mary said.

'It may be.' Jack pulled at his cheroot. 'If so, then thank God for arrogance. If we lose the humour and the comradeship, we'll be like any other army.' He stopped as he heard somebody shouting.

'Listen.' Mary held up her hand.

'We are the 113th!'

'That's something else we have.' Jack couldn't restrain his smile. 'We have regimental pride.'

'I noticed.' Mary was also smiling, but whether at him or with him, Jack couldn't tell.

Jack realised he was having an intelligent conversation with Mary, unlike the light nonsense he had exchanged with Helen. Had the Mutiny altered him that much, or was Mary a different kind of woman? He looked at her anew, seeing the light lines around her eyes and the determined set of her mouth.

She was a woman, rather than the half-child that Helen had been. Jack took a deep breath. 'Oh, dear God,' he said softly.

'What's the matter, Jack and do you have to blaspheme?'

'It's nothing.' Jack suppressed his sudden desire to reach across and kiss her. 'It does not matter.'

'I see.' Mary said. 'You can tell me when you're ready.'

They sat side-by-side in the now-comfortable silence.

'I'm scared, Jack. If we lose India, where will we – people like me – go?' Mary continued to gaze at the sky.

'We won't lose India. Not this time anyway,' Jack said.

'We will sometime,' Mary spoke quietly. 'And then there is nowhere.'

Jack saw the opening and opened his mouth to speak. Mary was faster of speech and forestalled his words.

'Your mother used to tell me that I could marry an officer. I thought about it, Jack and I looked after their children and spoke to them. Some officers treated me as an equal – nearly. Most treated me as a servant. I found their lives to be excessively boring.'

'Boring?' Jack started. 'Don't you think it would be fun to have female company, with regimental parties, afternoon teas and a change of scenery every time the army posts the regiment elsewhere? You would see the world, with guaranteed accommodation and friends.'

'No.' Mary's headshake was emphatic. 'It's a trivial life centred on the husband's work and sport. All the wives must do is look respectable, dress decently and not say anything outrageous at the endless dinner parties and balls. It would be claustrophobic and confining, wasting one's time and only being an appendage to one's husband. I need more than that, Jack. I want to be useful in my own right.'

'Oh,' Jack felt something sink inside him. He wasn't sure what to say.

'I have two skills that may help.' Mary seemed unaware of Jack's discomfiture. 'I have many languages, and I'm happy with children. I could be a language teacher at a school somewhere, if they would have me.'

'Why would they not have you?'

'Because I'm Anglo-Indian,' Mary said. 'Eurasian, a half-caste, a part blacky, I've a touch of the tar-brush.'

'All right.' Jack stopped her. 'That's enough of that.'

Mary smiled as if all her troubles had suddenly vanished. 'So, I promised I would teach you languages, Jack and there's no time like the present. Come on!'

* * *

'Batoor's not coming back.' Elliot tipped back his hip flask.

Jack nodded. He was disappointed in Batoor, he had thought the Pathan would remain true to his word. It was a full thirty hours since Batoor had entered Gondabad and there was no sign of him. *What should I try next?*

'He probably has some private business in Gondabad.' Elliot passed over the flask, shaking it to encourage Jack to partake. 'He'll have a throat to cut or a horse to steal.'

'That will be it.' Jack was in no mood to argue. Was their entire journey wasted? Had he been following a will-o-the-wisp on no more evidence than the word of an enemy?

'I'm going in myself,' Jack announced. He had no choice, he couldn't return without having achieved anything.

'Don't be a fool, man!' Elliot nearly dropped his hip flask. 'You'll never get away with it.'

'I'm not coming all this way to turn back right at the gates,' Jack said. He would search for Jayanti. Warrior women would inevitably be prominent. When he found her, he would kill her. The decision wasn't hard. A British officer and gentleman would not kill a woman, he knew. He also knew that it would ruin his reputation and his career. That didn't matter if it saved India from more bloodshed and more carnage.

India was as much his home as Britain was. Killing Jayanti might save his homeland much bloodshed. After all, what reason had he to live? He couldn't afford the next step to major, he couldn't afford to leave the army, and with Mary determined not to marry an officer... *There, I've admitted that I had contemplated marriage to that blasted woman.*

'They'll spot you right away,' Elliot said.

'We got away with it in the Crimea,' Jack reminded.

'You could look Russian,' Elliot pointed out. 'You don't look Indian.'

Jack's smile was more ironic that Elliot realised. 'I should,' he said. 'I'm part Indian, remember?'

'I remember,' Elliot said. 'You're also a British officer. Are you certain you wish to act the spy?'

'I've done it before,' Jack said.

Elliot sighed. 'If you want to risk your fool neck, then I'll come with you.'

'No, you won't,' Jack said. 'You'll look after the men until I get back.'

'Yes, sir!' Elliot gave a smart salute. 'You're a blasted fool, sir.'

'Thank you, Lieutenant Elliot.' Jack returned the salute. 'Now you can help me prepare.'

Naturally dark haired and with a complexion that easily tanned, Jack, didn't have to apply blacking. Dressed in a flowing white robe that descended to his ankles and with a dirty white turban on his head, he concealed his revolver next to his skin and thrust a long Khyber knife through the green cummerbund around his waist.

'There you go,' Elliot said. 'You look every inch a bazaar badmash.'

'What's this?' Mary peeped inside the tent. 'What's happening here?'

'Captain Windrush is going into Gondabad,' Elliot said.

Jack could feel Mary's sudden anger.

'Why?' Her voice was like ice.

'To search for Jayanti,' Jack said.

'Is there nobody else who can do that job?' Mary's eyes were smouldering. 'You're meant to command this force, not swan about acting the spy.'

'It's because I am in command that I have to go,' Jack said.

'You can hardly speak a word of any native language,' Mary said.

'I'll grunt a lot,' Jack said.

'I'm coming too,' Mary told him.

'You are not!' Jack said. 'I order you to remain behind.'

Mary's laugh may have been genuine. 'I'm a civilian, Captain Windrush. You can't order me to do anything.'

'By the living Christ, I can!' *This woman can make me angry with only a few words.* 'I can send you back to Lucknow.'

'I wish you would stop blaspheming, Jack! And would you send me back on my own?' Mary asked sweetly. 'With so many pandies around? Oh, Captain Jack Windrush, how could you be so cruel?'

'You little minx!' Jack's glare bounced off Mary without effect as Elliot began to whistle a little song and walked away to study the bark of a tree as if he had never seen such a thing before.

Jack took a long deep breath. *Why do we always argue?* 'If you come,' he conceded inevitable defeat, 'you do as I say and keep out of trouble.'

'Yes, Captain Windrush,' Mary said meekly.

'I don't like the idea.'

'Yes, Captain Windrush,' Mary said again. 'You do forget something. I have been walking through Indian towns all my life, and I grew up around Gondabad. I know the city and the people far better than you do, or anybody in your little army.'

Jack had no answer to that. 'I plan on going into the fort as well.'

'All right,' Mary said. 'I'll talk to the women. They will know more than the men do. Where will you start?'

'In the bazaar,' Jack said.

'That's as good a place as any,' Mary approved.

'We'll leave after dark,' Jack said. He wasn't happy to take Mary into danger once more. 'Maybe you'll be glad to have a boring and claustrophobic cantonment life after this trip.'

He felt Mary's eyes surveying him and wondered what she was thinking.

Chapter Ten

The city of Gondabad had long outgrown its walls, sprawling into the surrounding countryside in an array of slum housing and the more impressive dwellings of merchants. Pi-dogs barked at irregular intervals.

With her head covered and a green and red sari extending to her ankles, Mary walked a few steps behind Jack as he walked boldly toward one of the city's side gates. As a warrior, he adopted a swagger, snarling at anybody who tried to speak to him and spitting betel-nut juice at infrequent intervals. Only when he approached the gate did Jack realise how difficult it might be to get into the city.

Three guards lounged at the gates, two wearing the uniform of Bengal Army sepoys and the third sporting a spiked helmet and a breastplate. The sepoys stepped forward, Brown Bess muskets extended.

'Don't say a word,' Mary gave a quiet order. 'I'll say you're mute.'

Jack nodded, placed a hand on the hilt of his Khyber knife and increased his swagger. He walked right up to the muzzle of the closest sepoy and grunted as Mary spoke in Hindi. Within a few moments, the guards stepped aside, and Jack marched into the city.

Last time he'd been in Gondabad, he had been removing a private from a brothel in the days before the utiny. Now the mutineers and their allies held the city and possibly the vast fort above, with any British expelled or dead. The loyalists in Gondabad would be sitting quietly, waiting for the British to return, while the majority would wait to support whichever side turned out to be stronger.

'This way,' Mary took over, leading Jack through the twisting narrow passageways of the ancient town. Avoiding the sewers that bisected the streets, they passed shuttered windows and walked underneath overhanging balconies. The smell, as always, was strong, a mixture of filth and exotic spices, camels and other animals, and crowded humanity. They passed windowless houses with deeply inset ornate doors, heard evocative Indian music and hurried past the large *havelis* – townhouses – of merchants before they stopped at a wide, pointed gateway.

'The bazaar is through here.' Mary appeared more relaxed than Jack felt. She frowned. 'I'm interested in knowing how you expected to question people when you can hardly speak a word of any Indian language.'

'Remember that we're looking for Jayanti.' Jack ignored her sarcasm. 'She might be conspicuous.'

'I won't forget,' Mary said.

The bazaar was crowded with men and women, all talking and shouting, buying and selling and living their lives. Jack had thought the war would have created poverty, but the shops in the bazaar were full. Wherever he looked, he saw custard apples and mangoes, guavas and vegetables, with the aroma of hot sweets enticing little boys, while little girls sported glass-bead bangles or eating sticks of sugar cane while their parents haggled with goldsmiths who worked on tiny scales. It was a scene of vibrant colour and life, with itinerant merchant and a dancing bear, children darting everywhere and rangy dogs snarling and fighting amongst the crowds. A handful of sepoys merged with the rest, talking and laughing as if they belonged. Jack stilled the anger he felt when he saw the mutineers.

'Your time will come,' he promised himself. 'We'll round you up and have you dancing at the end of a rope.'

'What was that, Jack?' Mary asked.

'I didn't say anything.'

'You were talking to yourself in English. Be careful.'

A wounded warrior limped past, with bloody bandages around his head and leg. Jack nodded in satisfaction. He didn't like human suffering but listening to the pandies torturing and mutilating one of the 113th had killed any lingering sympathy he had held for the mutineers. In some way, it had been worse than the well at Cawnpore.

'I can't see any woman warriors,' Jack said.

'Did you think Jayanti would come to the bazaar to buy her bread and fruit?' Mary's sharp tones revealed her inner strain. 'Now stay with me and keep quiet.'

Walking to a crowd of woman around a stall, Mary began to talk to them, with Jack feeling out of place. A passing sepoy glanced at him, and Jack glared back, hoping to intimidate. The sepoy spat on the ground and walked on.

Mary took hold of his arm. 'It's all right, Jack, they will think I'm your wife, or at least your woman.' She kept her voice low.

'Did you learn anything?'

Mary guided Jack to a corner of the wall, stinking with urine and spices. 'I said that I was glad there were some female warriors and not only men, who seemed to run away every time the British fired their guns.'

'Did it work?'

'Oh, yes,' Mary smiled. 'If one wants to make friends with a woman, all one has to do is insult men. It creates an instant bond that transcends race, religion or nationality. It's an international sisterhood.'

'What did you find out?'

'They are only low caste women, so they're not highly educated,' Mary began. 'They told me that Jayanti is in the fort and will drive the British away without any help from the men.'

'That was quick work,' Jack said. He sighed. 'You did well, Mary.'

'Speaking the language helps,' Mary said. 'Honestly, Jack, I don't know what you were thinking of trying to come here alone.'

Jack grunted, ignoring his blinding headache and the dizzy spells that were becoming more frequent by the hour. He found it hard to do anything, let alone think. 'I was doing my duty,' he said. 'Let's have a look at the fort.'

From the outside, Gondabad Fort was ugly, with granite walls twenty feet thick pierced by ten gates and a deep moat. On the north side, the wall rose perpendicular from its granite base, while on the south the gates opened directly into the city.

'It's strong.' Jack had passed the fort many times when the 113th had garrisoned Gondabad. 'I hadn't realised how big it is.'

'It's fifteen acres in area.' Mary surprised him with her knowledge. 'The Chandela kings were here for centuries, and the Rajputs strengthened it centuries ago, and then the Moghuls captured it. I heard that thousands died in the siege and sack of the city.'

'And then we took it,' Jack said.

'No, we didn't,' Mary said. 'We always had an agreement with the Rajah, so he retained power as an ally or rather a client, of the British.'

'I hadn't realised that.' Jack gave her a little bow to acknowledge her scholarship. 'We were not allowed to approach the fort. The Rajah had an arrangement with the army.' He shrugged. 'It was all very mysterious.'

'I don't know what happened when the mutineers took the city,' Mary said.

'Whatever happened, Sir Colin or Hugh Rose will capture the fort and city.' Jack swayed as another bout of dizziness swept over him.

'Jack? Are you all right?' Mary sounded concerned.

'I'm fine.' Jack tried to concentrate on the fort. With its defended gateways and round towers, even Sir Colin's well-equipped army would have difficulty storming such a place.

'Are we going in?' Mary stared at the imposing walls.

'What is there that a bold man will not dare?' Jack misquoted the Bold Buccleuch. 'I'm going in. You are going back to the camp to tell Lieutenant Elliot what you've discovered.'

'No.' Mary shook her head. 'I'm not leaving you alone here. You're not well.'

'I'm fine,' Jack said.

'Don't lie to me, Jack Baird Windrush,' Mary hissed. 'You're not thinking straight. The best thing for you would be to get back to the camp and let Elliot take over.'

'No!' Shaking his head increased the pain. 'I'm going into the fort.'

'And what will you do when you get there?'

'Kill Jayanti.' The words were out before Jack could stop them.

Mary stared at him. 'Jack! You are not thinking at all! Even if you get in, you'll never get close to her, and the second you kill her they'll kill you!'

Jack shrugged. 'That's all right. Elliot is quite capable of getting you and the men back safely. He's a better officer than I am.'

'And how about me when you are gone?' Mary asked.

'I said that Elliot would get you back safely.' Jack was unsure what point Mary was trying to make.

'How about us, Jack?'

'Us?' Jack hadn't expected that question.

'Us – you and me?'

Jack stared at her. 'I thought you didn't wish to marry a soldier.'

'Oh, for goodness sake, Jack!' Mary visibly controlled her temper. 'All right, we'll discuss this later, not in a bazaar full of mutineers.'

Even Jack saw the sense of that. He winced as his dizziness returned. 'You get back to camp,' he said.

'No, Jack. We will stay together. Somebody has to look after you.' Mary shook her head, muttering about men who wanted to be spies without knowing a single word of the language.

'We'll try up here.' Mary indicated a long narrow street. 'It leads to one of the smaller gates into the fort.' She gave a half smile. 'Come along, Captain Jack.' Turning, Mary smiled over her shoulder and stepped ahead.

Jack saw the hand reach from a doorway to wrap around Mary's mouth. He lunged forward, just as a tall sepoy appeared from an alley and blocked his view. Pushing the man aside, Jack saw another, and then a naik with greying hair and neat whiskers stood in his path.

'No, Windrush sahib,' the naik said.

Momentarily forgetting his role, Jack stared at the naik. 'You saved my life back in that village. How the devil do you know my name? Get out of my way!' Producing his revolver, Jack aimed directly at the man's face. 'Move aside, damn you!'

There were other men around him, sepoys with brown eyes and oiled whiskers, some wounded, others in smart uniforms. Jack struggled to get through. He saw someone drag Mary backwards and swore, squeezed the trigger and heard the shot.

The darkness was sudden and complete as somebody dropped a hood over his head. Jack shouted and felt somebody grab his wrist. He fired again, unable to see anything, aware that he was in the midst of a group of mutineers and only concerned for the safety of Mary.

Not sure what was happening, he kicked out as somebody lifted him. Many hands closed on him, carrying him away from the alley. Jack shouted into the stifling darkness, squeezed the trigger and heard only a frustrating click as the hammer fell on an empty chamber.

The next few minutes were a blur as the mutineers carried him inside some large building. He heard the different sound as their footsteps echoed from stone and felt the jerky movement as they ran up a flight of steps.

'Put me down, damn you!' Jack shouted. The hood muffled his words. He sensed a change in atmosphere and guessed that they were indoors, and then whoever carried him lowered him gently onto a soft surface.

'You are safe, sahib,' the naik's voice sounded and the bag removed from his head.

'What the devil?' Jack looked around him. The naik and his sepoys were withdrawing through an arched door, and he was alone in the most luxurious bedroom he had ever seen in his life.

The bed was lower than Jack was used to, and much larger, with a padded silk coverlet in vibrant red and gold. Persian carpets covered the floor while rich silks covered the walls, except for the four small pointed windows. Scented candles infused the air with a heady perfume that Jack couldn't help but inhale.

Cringing at the pain any movement caused him Jack stood up and moved to the windows. They were too small to allow him to leave and too high up even if he did. He looked out on the city of Gondabad far below.

'What the deuce is going on?' He asked himself. 'I'd expected to be taken to some dungeon or a torture chamber.' *Where is Mary?*

A bottle stood on a small table at the side of the bed, with a single crystal glass and a bowl of fruit. Suspecting poison, Jack ignored both bottle and fruit. He tried the door. It was locked, and his captors had taken away his pistol and Khyber Knife.

What do I do now? More importantly, where is Mary?

The door opened, and a small man with a neat beard, silk robes and a large turban stepped in.

'Who are you?' Jack backed away, searching for a weapon.

'Muhammed Khan,' the man answered at once. 'Who are you?'

'I think you already know that,' Jack said. 'I am Captain Jack Windrush of the 113th Foot.'

Khan's smile would have shamed a hunting tiger. 'Thank you, Captain Windrush. What is your full name?' He had a soft, cultured voice.

'What has that to do with you?' Jack asked. 'You've captured me, a British officer; now do whatever it is you do to prisoners.' He remembered the screams outside the camp and Keane's mutilated head and felt sick.

'If it was up to me,' Khan spoke with hardly a trace of an accent, 'I would hand you to the women to be castrated and burned alive. However, it is not up to me.'

'Who is it up to?' Jack asked.

'What is your full name?' Khan repeated. 'Be careful how you answer for your future depends on your words. If you give the right answer, then your treatment will be kind. If you give the wrong answer, then I will have charge of you. What is your full name?'

Fighting the pain in his head, Jack stood to attention. 'Captain Jack Baird Windrush, 113th Foot.'

Khan smiled again. 'Good. We have the right man. I will send in a doctor in a minute.'

'Wait!' Jack said. 'How about Mary?'

'I don't know a Mary.' Khan closed the door.

'You kidnapped her!' Jack shouted in frustration. He kicked the door, swearing. 'Let me out of here!'

'What's all the noise, Captain Sahib?' The man who entered was young, with almond-shaped eyes and a wispy beard. He carried a small leather bag.

'You have Mary,' Jack said. 'You kidnapped my woman.'

'No,' the young man said. 'Nobody kidnapped your woman. The half-caste who came with you is not in the fort.'

Jack took a deep breath. It seemed that the mutineers knew all about him. 'Who are you?'

'I am Khitab Gul,' the man said. 'Doctor Khitab Gul.'

'You speak excellent English.'

'I know. I also speak French, Spanish and Italian as well as native languages. Call me Doctor Khitab and lie back.'

'Why?'

'You have been wounded twice recently,' Doctor Khitab said. 'Once on your right wrist and once on your head.'

'How the deuce do you know that?' Jack tried to sit up, only for Doctor Khitab to push him back down on the bed.

'We've been watching you, Captain Windrush. Lie still please.' The doctor's hands were gentle as they examined Jack's head. 'Have you experienced any headaches, captain? Dizziness? Lack of concentration?'

'All of those,' Jack said.

'Yes. That was a nasty crack on the head. Your skull is not broken, fortunately. You also suffer from much nervous tension. You need rest and sleep, which you will not find inside the camp of the 113th. It's all right, captain, Lieutenant Elliot is taking good care of your men although Private Carruthers has gone down with dysentery.'

'How…?'

'Oh, we know far more than you realise, captain. Now lie still and drink this.' The doctor poured a small glass of something. 'It's all right, captain. It's just to help you sleep.'

'I don't want to sleep, damn it!'

'I know you don't want to captain, but you do need to.' Doctor Khitab held the glass to Jack's lips. 'It is all right, captain. It will help you and when you wake you will feel much better.'

Jack drank the liquid. He saw the doctor's smile broaden and then fade.

When Jack awoke, his headache was gone. He stretched on the bed, looked around at the room and felt better than he had for weeks. 'I could get used to this,' he told himself as sunlight seeped through the small windows to land on the beautiful carpets.

'You are feeling better.' Doctor Khitab was sitting at the side of the bed. 'Good. You do not rest enough, Captain Windrush. You need weeks of rest and sleep, not merely one day and one night. First, you need a wash, a barber and a change of clothes.

'I'm fine,' Jack said. 'What is all this for? I'm your prisoner, where am I, and where is Mary?'

'Oh, no, Captain Windrush, sahib.' The doctor salaamed. 'So many questions! You are not a prisoner. On the contrary, you are our most honoured guest in the Fort of Gondabad.'

'I'm your enemy, damn it,' Jack said.

The doctor's laugh would have been heart-warming in different circumstances. 'Would you rather we treated you like the British treat their enemies? Do you wish us to hang you, sahib? Or blow you from the muzzle of a cannon, perhaps?'

'I'm no mutineer,' Jack defended what he knew to be the truth. 'I was never disloyal to the Queen.'

The doctor salaamed again. 'That, at least, is correct, Windrush sahib. You are no mutineer, and you were never disloyal to your queen. Now if you will follow me, please?'

'Why? Is Mary there?'

'Please, sahib.' Doctor Khitab's smile didn't waver. 'I assure you we mean you no harm. On the contrary, we can help you find everything your heart desires.'

Jack tensed himself, ready to try and escape. The doctor opened the door wider, to reveal two muscular Rajputs, with long pistols thrust through sashes and tulwars held ready. They looked as if they knew what they were doing.

'Lead on, MacDuff,' Jack said. 'I suppose there's no help for it.'

'There is no help at all, Windrush, sahib,' Doctor Khitab said.

With an armed Rajput warrior a few yards in front and another at his back, Jack knew that escape would be impossible as the doctor led him through a succession of corridors. From his impressions of the exterior, he had expected the fort to be a bare, bleak place of stone walls and austerity. Instead, the interior was more luxurious than anything he had seen in his life. Silk hangings decorated the painted walls, sticks of incense wafted perfume through the air, oil lamps provided light between the ornate windows, and he walked on Afghan and Persian carpets that would cost more than a humble captain earned in five years. There were cushions of Bokhara silk, bed covers of Sind cotton and decorations of the Tree of Life with capering monkeys. All was light, gaiety, and colour.

'In here, Windrush, sahib.'

After the splendour of the corridor, the chamber was surprisingly bare, with a small drain in the middle of a stone-flagged floor and arched glazed windows with little décor. Three wiry old men stood beside three tubs of water.

'What's this?' Jack asked. 'Some form of torture?'

'No, Sahib. It is some form of washing.'

As the Rajput warriors took up positions on either side of the door, the elderly men stepped forward and gently removed Jack's clothes. Smiling, they led him to the centre of the room.

'What's to do?'

'We don't sit in a tub to bathe, Captain Windrush sahib.' The doctor shook his head. 'We think that is strange, having one's dirt splashing all around us. Stand still.'

One by one, the three elderly men dipped beakers of water into the tubs and emptied cool water over Jack. He stood there, determined not to admit that this Indian bathing method was superior to the British.

'Now you are cleansed for the day. Do you wish to pray?' Doctor Khitab asked. 'It is an Indian custom.'

'Maybe later.' Jack looked for his clothes. A white-coated servant presented him with a new set, with white cotton trousers and jacket and a simple yellow turban.

'Put them on, Windrush sahib,' Doctor Khitab said. 'When the *Angrez* first came to this land, they adopted our dress and our customs, and many married our women. We were like one people. Now there is a gulf between us.'

The clothes were soft, clean and very comfortable compared to Jack's habitual stiff uniform.

'Good, Windrush sahib. Now follow me.'

Once more into the corridor with the silent Rajput escort, the doctor led Jack down a flight of marble stairs into a large room. Brought up believing that England was the pinnacle of civilisation and that his family home of Wychwood Manor compared to anywhere in the world, Jack could only stare at the majesty of the room. He had been in a few Indian palaces and forts during this war, but only in the aftermath of cannon fire and siege. The shambles of a palace during wartime could not remotely compare to the splendour of this room.

'This is the minor Durbar room,' the doctor said. 'You may know that the name durbar can mean a state reception, or the hall in which such events take place.'

Jack ignored the lecture as he gazed at the Durbar room. Ornate plasterwork embellished every surface of the walls and ceiling, dominated by symbols of Ganesha, the elephant god that brought good fortune. One wall carried three depictions of peacocks while sticks of incense and masses of flowers sweetened the air. As with the corridor, a carpet covered the floor, so luxurious that Jack felt his slippered feet sinking into it. An ivory screen hid the furthest corner of the room, behind which an orchestra played evocative Indian music.

These details barely distracted from the two people who sat at the head of the room, watching Jack as he walked in. Five marble steps led to their ornate thrones, with their armrests carved into the likeness of leopards, whose snarling faces intimidated those who approached. The seat and back were of padded silk, while on either side sat marble tigers, so realistic that Jack wondered at the skill of the sculptor.

'The Rajah and Rani of Gondabad,' the doctor spoke in hushed tones.

The Rajah sat upright, with long robes from neck to ankles and a sarpech set with diamonds and emeralds in his turban. His fourteen-strand necklace of natural pearls must have weighed ten pounds while his clothes glittered with gold, and rings gleamed on his fingers. His face was serene, with a neat white beard and mobile brown eyes that never strayed from Jack.

Beside him, the Rani was quieter and much plainer in a simple white silk sari, while a plain muslin dupatta covered her head. Jack guessed her age at about twenty-eight, much younger than her husband, and she stared at Windrush without expression. Smoke from the incense created a slight haze around the thrones, so the faces and persons of the Rajah and Rani were blurred, nearly ethereal as if lesser mortals should not view them.

Jack hesitated, feeling very much out of place. If he had been in uniform, he would have known how to act. In his Indian clothes, he was a stranger, a part-Indian foreigner, an interloper in a world about which he knew nothing.

'Approach.' The Rani spoke in a low clear tone.

As Jack walked forward, he became aware of the guards. The opulence of this Durbar room had astonished him, so he had not seen the dozen or so stalwart men in chain mail and steel helmets that stood against the walls.

'I am Captain Jack Windrush of the 113th Foot.' Jack announced. He bowed, straightened up and waited to see what would happen next. If what he had heard of Indian royalty was correct, they could order him trampled by elephants, immured forever in a dungeon or any other sort of horror.

'Why are you here, Captain Windrush?' The Rani spoke in English, with an attractive singsong accent.

'I am searching for a murderer.' Jack decided to speak the truth. These people already knew all about him so it would be foolish to lie. He straightened his back. Whatever clothes he happened to be wearing, he was a British officer and gentleman, and he was damned if any foreign princeling would intimidate him. 'Her name is Jayanti, and she has murdered British soldiers.'

'Why did you not come through official channels?' the Rani asked. 'Why did you choose to come sneaking into our home like a thief?'

'I did not think you would see me,' Jack said. 'India is disturbed at present with the misguided actions of some of our sepoy regiments. I was unsure whether you wished to compromise your security by accepting a message from a junior British officer.'

The Rajah and Rani exchanged a private conversation for a few moments before the Rani spoke again. 'Where should our loyalties lie, Captain Windrush?'

'Your loyalties should lie with the British,' Jack said.

'Why?' Although the Rani's voice was gentle, there was no mistaking the steel behind her question.

'To ensure peace and stability and a fair system of justice.' Jack couldn't think of any other answer. He wished that Elliot were here, with his quick mind and capacity for more profound thought.

'The British have been in India for two hundred and fifty years,' the Rani said. 'During that time there have been wars and conquest and a lack of stability.'

Jack thought quickly. 'There was warfare and conquest and instability before the British arrived,' he said. 'And beyond the British frontier, there is still warfare and conquest and instability. Better to retain British protection than to return to anarchy, where states fought states, Muslim fought Sikh and Hindus and the law depended on bribery rather than legality.'

The Rajah and Rani conferred again, both glancing at Jack from time to time before the Rani spoke again. 'Then why is there war again within the British area of peace, stability and justice?'

'The sepoys, the Indian soldiers of Britain, have broken their oath,' Jack said. 'They have believed lies told against their masters and have attacked the hand that fed them. Others have joined in, the malcontents, evil men and women.' He paused. 'I believe that Jayanti, one of those evil women, a murderess of the worst kind, is within your Majesty's dominions now. I think she is hiding, ready to cause trouble and spread violence among your loyal subjects.'

Are these two playing with me? Jack wondered. *Are they teasing me, before they kill me? Or are these questions genuine?* The scent of the incense was more powerful now, making Jack's head swim so that he saw the Rajah and Rani through a thickening haze, while the Indian music was a distraction.

'If we help the British, how will the British reward us?' the Rani asked.

'You will have done your duty.' Jack gave the answer that would most appeal to a British officer and then paused to consider what an Indian prince most wished. 'The British would ensure that you maintain your position as Rajah and Rani of Gondabad.'

What more can I say?

'If we help the enemies of the British, what will happen?' The Rani's voice was unemotional, as if she was discussing a menu with her servants.

'The British will surely quell this mutiny,' Jack said what he believed. 'The British have already reconquered Delhi and put the rebels to the sword. Sir Colin Campbell has recaptured Lucknow and wreaked vengeance on the mutineers and rebels there. The British know that your majesties are loyal and that the troubles in Gondabad were against your wishes. They will not blame you for what has happened. However, if your majesties join the forces of evil and discontent, Sir Colin Campbell or Hugh Rose will surely capture your city and lay siege to your fort. There will be death and disaster and much slaughter, as there was in Delhi and Lucknow.'

Jack took a deep breath. He hadn't spoken so much in his life. *Am I too forceful with my threats?*

The Rajah and Rani conferred again, and the Rani flicked her finger. 'You may go now, Captain Windrush.'

Doctor Khitab took hold of Jack's arm and ushered him to a side door, with the two Rajputs a few steps behind him. The Rani's voice followed him. 'Take him to the other one.'

'The other one? Who is the other one? Is that Mary? Do you have Mary here?' When Jack tried to ask questions, one of the Rajputs shoved him onward.

'Keep quiet, Captain Windrush, sahib. It is rude to question royalty,' Doctor Khitab said. 'All will be revealed for he who is patient.'

'What is this all about?'

'Have patience, Captain Windrush sahib.' Doctor Khitab patted his shoulder. 'Everything is as it should be; you are a guest among friends.'

Leaving the Durbar room, they marched along what seemed like miles of passages, along which an army of servants hurried without a word or a sound. The luxury gradually faded until Jack's surroundings were merely lavish and there were warriors among the servants. There was no mistaking the two different types of people, with men carrying swords and shields, spears and muskets. One or two were bandaged or scarred, veterans of skirmish, siege or battle.

'In here, Captain Windrush, sahib.' Doctor Khitab stopped before a massive door studded with iron. 'I hope your mind is clear.'

'My mind? What do you mean?'

The doctor didn't respond to Jack's questions as one Rajput opened the door and the other propelled Jack inside the chamber.

Chapter Eleven

While the Durbar room had been about opulence and luxury, only warriors occupied this room. The floor was stone-flagged and the walls bereft of any decoration except an array of spears and fearsome looking daggers. A rack of tulwars sat beneath unglazed windows while another of long jezzails stretched to a plain wooden table around which sat a group of men.

They watched Jack step in.

They were warriors with quick movements and smooth muscles, hard eyes and the direct stare of men who were not afraid to act. Three reached for swords, and another with a spiked helmet lifted a long pistol that he had been loading.

'*Ram ram*,' Jack said and waited for a response. Alone and unarmed, he knew he would not stand a chance if these men attacked him. He also knew that he would fight and neither run nor surrender.

The warriors spoke quietly as the man with the spiked helmet pointed his pistol at Jack. Suspecting that they were discussing his immediate death, Jack marched toward them.

One man stood up. In his early thirties, he was round-faced and black haired, slightly overweight with a small beard and sharp, round eyes. Shaking his head, he pushed the pistol back on the table and turned over a large hourglass. Sand began to trickle from the upper to the lower container. The man's smile was friendlier than Jack had expected as he spoke in perfect English.

'You are welcome, Captain Jack Baird Windrush of Her Majesty's 113th Foot.'

Jack nodded. 'Thank you. You have the advantage of me. I do not know to whom I am speaking.'

'I am Dhondu Pant, a Peshwa of the old Maratha Empire. You may know me better as Nana Sahib.'

'Dear God!' Jack reached for the sword he no longer had. 'Nana Sahib!'

Nana Sahib was the warrior and aristocrat who had fostered and led the rebellion in Cawnpore, the man ultimately responsible for the murder of hundreds of British men, women and children. This smiling, urbane man was the arch-enemy of British rule in India.

The others at the table jumped to their feet, most reaching for swords or pistols.

'Peace, *bhaiyas*, peace, brothers,' Nana Sahib calmed them down in Urdu and English. 'Captain Windrush is no threat to me or you. He has no weapons and has even adopted our way of dress.'

The warriors sat back down, with only the man in the spiked helmet continuing to glare at Jack. '*Barnshoot Firinghi*' – "incestuous foreigner", he said, until Nana Sahib waved him to silence.

'You seem surprised to see me, Captain Windrush, and I do not know why. After all, this is my land, and these are my people.'

'Gondabad is not part of the old Maratha Empire.' Jack forced aside his hatred.

'It was once,' Nana Sahib said.

'You are a traitor, a rebel and a murderer.' Jack wondered if he could jump across and strangle Nana Sahib before his followers chopped him to pieces. *No, these warriors are alert and experienced. I would merely throw away my life.*

Nana Sahib smiled. 'Insults from an enemy are as sweet as compliments from a friend. Are you an enemy, Captain Windrush?'

'You became the enemy of my people the moment you turned against us.' Jack tried to remain calm. He watched the slowly emptying hourglass and wondered what its function might be.

'I could say that your people became my enemy the moment they turned against me,' Nana Sahib countered.

'Why am I here?' Jack asked.

'To learn.' Nana Sahib's smile faded. 'Sit down, captain,' he indicated a chair opposite him at the table.

'Why me?'

'There are reasons,' Nana Sahib said. 'Now listen.'

Jack sat down, acutely aware that the man in the spiked helmet moved the position of his pistol so that the muzzle pointed directly at his chest.

'I'm listening.'

'You think I am a monster,' Nana Sahib said.

'I think you are a treasonous murdering traitor.' Jack guessed that Nana Sahib would shortly order his death. He had nothing to gain by attempting to be pleasant.

'Listen to my story.' Nana Sahib did not appear in the slightest annoyed by Jack's reaction. 'You will know about Badgee Rao, the old Peshwa of the Mahrattas?'

'I know the name,' Jack admitted. 'He was a good man and a loyal friend of the British.'

'And how did the British repay that loyalty?' Nana Sahib's voice remained calm and smooth. 'They repaid it with deceit and robbery. Badgee Rao gave his assistance to the East India Company when they warred with Tippoo Sahib, the Tiger of Serangipatam in 1799. The East India Company won that war, and how did they reward Badgee Rao?'

'I do not know,' Jack admitted.

'Then allow me to educate you.' Nana Sahib's voice remained calm. 'The Company made treaties with Badgee Rao, broke their word on many occasions and in 1817, they grabbed his lands. After fighting against the might of the Company, Badgee Rao eventually led his army to face General Sir John Malcolm's force, with the Deccan as the prize. Malcolm sent in a flag of truce and proposed that Badgee Rao should renounce his sovereignty and surrender with his family and some adherents and attendants.'

'That would save needless slaughter.' Jack defended the British general.

'The British offered to respect Badgee Rao and his people and locate them in Benares or any other holy city. They offered a pension to Badgee Rao and his family and promised to provide for his attached adherents. The pension for Badgee and his family was to be at least eight lacs of rupees a year.'

Jack did a rapid calculation. 'That's about £80,000, a very fair offer.'

'Quite a sizeable sum,' Nana Sahib agreed. 'However, when he was an old man, Badgee Rao was still childless.' He stopped. 'Badgee Rao adopted me as his son and heir. He died in 1851 and immediately the Governor-General, Lord Dalhousie cancelled the pension the Honourable East India Company had guaranteed. My family and I were reduced to poverty.'

'I see.' Jack wondered how a man reduced to poverty could be as plump and sleek as Nana Sahib. 'So your revolt and all the deaths and suffering are due to your desire for more British money.'

For the first time, Nana Sahib showed some emotion. A flicker of anger crossed his face. He continued.

'I asked the Lieutenant Governor of the North West Provinces to reconsider Lord Dalhousie's judgement. In return, the Company granted me a few acres of land for life. The British Commissioner of Bithoor, an honest man, issued an urgent appeal on my behalf and the Company severely reprimanded him. I contacted the Court of Directors in Leadenhall Street. They issued a reply a year later, telling me to try the Indian government. I did that with no response.'

Jack said nothing. Having lost any title to his lands in England through illegitimacy, he could understand some of Nana Sahib's sense of injustice. The lower section of the hourglass was now three-quarters full.

'The lands that Badgee Rao ceded in 1802, 1817 and 1818 gave the East India Company a million pounds a year in revenue.' Nana Sahib continued. 'I have a few paltry rupees.'

'So your rebellion is about money, then,' Jack said. 'It isn't about religion or Indian nationalism or race.'

'I am protesting about British injustice,' Nana Sahib said.

Jack nodded. Do you mean British injustice to those who would like to rule or British injustice to those who the old rulers oppressed? Do you mean the injustice of suppressing suttee and of ending thugee, the injustice of not accepting bribes and of one law for rich and poor?' Jack knew he was playing with fire.

Nana Sahib sat down. 'Your family connections led me to believe there was hope for you, Captain Windrush. I see I was wrong.' He grasped the hourglass just as the top section emptied. 'Take him away!'

What family connections? Jack was about to speak when three Rajput guards entered the room and hustled him away into the corridor outside.

Chapter Twelve

Jack tried to follow their route as the Rajputs dragged him out of the chamber and down a flight of stairs. The walls were bare of decoration, the steps worn by the passage of many feet and the air progressively fouler. They stopped at a long corridor poorly lit by torches, barged through a narrow door and plunged downward again to a vast area with what seemed a score of open arches. One of the guards had taken a torch from the wall, and its flickering light illuminated a series of stone chambers, some large, some small.

The guards moved in silence, not responding to Jack's demands that they release him until they arrived at a weighty, iron-studded door. One Rajput turned the key in the lock, and the others dragged him inside. The guards shoved Jack against a granite wall and fastened manacles around his ankles and wrists. Checking his chains to ensure they were secure, the Rajputs left, slamming the door. Jack heard the key rasp in the lock.

Oh, dear God, what happens now?

Jack lay against the wall, hearing something rustle in his dungeon, a rat or insect maybe, and closed his eyes. A few hours ago, he had woken in a luxurious apartment with a gentle doctor treating his injuries. Since then he had met a Rajah and a Rani and then, one of the deadliest enemies of British India. Now his enemies had entombed him in a filthy dungeon. Had they tested him in some way? If so, he must have failed.

The mysteries remained. Jack wondered how the rebels knew his name and so much about him. Why had they singled out him for attention? There were many far more distinguished officers than him, men who had made their name in half a dozen campaigns, men who were famous far outside the often-claustrophobic confines of the British Army. Why had the rebels not captured one of them? Was he merely more vulnerable because he led a small party? Jack shook his head. By walking into Gondabad he had virtually placed himself into their hands, and now – he rattled the chains in futility – he must pay the price.

I wonder what fate they have in mind for me. Will they have elephants trample me to death? Will I be tortured with tiger-claws and blinded?

Jack took a deep breath. Whatever happened, he had tried to do his duty. That was his only consolation for an abortive campaign to remove Jayanti, and his failure to care for Mary.

The rustling continued, and something ran over his legs. Jack started and jerked aside. The creature fled with sharp claws scraping him. Jack closed his eyes, trying to garner strength through sleep.

He didn't know how much time had elapsed before another three Rajput guards arrived with a torch. While one man held the torch high, another released Jack from his chains. The second Rajput grunted and pointed to Jack, indicating that he should follow them.

'By God,' Jack said. 'Not until you tell me where we are going.'

The Rajputs said nothing, merely prodded at Jack with the point of a tulwar, which was a sufficiently strong hint to follow. 'I am a British officer,' he said. His guards didn't look impressed as they shoved him toward the door, helping him along with repeated jabs with the tulwar.

After what seemed an interminable journey along dark passages and up flights of stone steps, the Rajputs stopped at a heavily studded door, outside which stood one of Jayanti's female warriors. Jack eyed her, noting the black turban and the veil across the lower part of her face. She scrutinised him in return, touching the tulwar she wore at her waist. When Jack saw that she didn't wear a ruby ring on her left hand, he lost interest.

The Rajputs stepped aside, and the female warrior rapped on the door and pushed it open.

Jack stepped inside, into a different world.

He didn't know what he'd expected, either a torture chamber or a military barracks. Instead, he entered a light and airy room where birds flew around a tracery of foliage and sunlight dappled the Persian carpet on the floor. A mirror on one wall enhanced the size of the room, while the crystal chandelier hung like draping diamonds from the high ceiling.

Two more female guards stood against a wall of light bamboo, and directly opposite him, sitting at a beautifully carved ivory table, Jayanti sat on an armed chair, with her veil in place and her turban pulled low over her forehead.

'Welcome, Captain Windrush.' She indicated a chair on the other side of the table. 'Please join me. Would you care for a drink? I can offer you wine, whisky, rum, *nimbu pani, aam pani*, coconut water, *toddy* or water.'

Jack became aware of his thirst, and for some reason, he wished he'd washed and shaved before meeting Jayanti. 'Just water, please.' He watched as Jayanti clapped her hands and gave quiet instructions to a smooth-faced servant, who returned in a few moments with a brass jug and two small brass cups. Jayanti filled both cups with water.

'Take one,' she invited, 'and I will drink the other.'

Jack selected one at random. 'I doubt you have brought me here only to poison me,' he said. 'You could have killed me at any time from the moment you had me kidnapped.'

Jayanti lifted her veil sufficiently to drink.

The water was sweet, cool and very welcome. 'Is Mary safe?' Jack asked.

'I do not know,' Jayanti said. The veil muffled her voice slightly.

'You kidnapped her,' Jack accused.

'I did not,' Jayanti responded.

'Why have you brought me here?'

Jayanti eyed Jack across the table. 'Have you heard of the game of chess, Captain Windrush?'

'I have,' Jack responded.

'Have you ever played chess, Captain Windrush?'

'I played chess when I was at school,' Jack said. *Those days seem so far away.*

'We shall play.' Jayanti clapped her hands, and two female servants carried in a low marble table and a yellow ivory box. As Jack watched, one servant placed the table on the ground. Skilled hands had carved the ivory into the familiar black-and-white squares of a chessboard. The second servant opened the box and set up pieces that resembled the chess with which Jack was familiar, except that a chariot replaced the rook and an elephant the bishop. Small rubies adorned the crown of the king and queen; tiny emeralds shone for the elephant's eyes.

Jayanti walked across with her trousers rustling and a long dagger in a jewelled sheath at her waist. 'Did you know that chess was invented in Northern India, twelve hundred years ago?'

'I didn't know that,' Jack admitted.

'It spread to Persia and then when the Muslims overran the Persian Empire, they carried the game all over the Islamic world and into Europe.' Jayanti nearly whispered the explanation as she lifted the carved ivory pieces, one by one. 'The rules and the names and function of the pieces have altered through time.' She looked up. 'We will play with Indian pieces, but European rules.'

'I have no desire to play chess,' Jack said.

Jayanti lifted the king. 'This piece was known as the rajah; you know him as the king. In chess, captain, the object is to capture the king. He is the figurehead, while the most powerful player is the queen.' She held the queen in her left hand. 'In the original game, there was no queen, and the equivalent piece was called the *mantri*, or minister. In this case, the Europeans may have improved matters. Ministers, like other politicians, cause trouble while a queen will make a better ruler than any rajah.'

'Gondabad has a Rajah and a Rani,' Jack pointed out.

'I know,' Jayanti said. 'You will sit opposite me, captain, and we will play. Chess is like war, a contest of manoeuvre, nerve and skill, with casualties when one player makes a mistake or a successful gambit.' She sat down gracefully. 'We called chess *chaturanga*, which means four divisions, infantry, cavalry, elephantry, and chariotry.'

Jack eyed the pieces. Despite the Indian shapes, he could recognise their function. 'Thank you for the history lesson. I have not played for a long time.'

'Think of it as a battlefield, Captain Windrush,' Jayanti said. 'Now step with me to the window.'

The window overlooked a courtyard where a fountain tinkled, and tamarisk trees provided shade from the sun. Jayanti clapped her hands. 'Bring them in.'

Two lithe female warriors entered, followed by a tall, muscular man grotesquely dressed in what seemed like medieval armour, covered in metal spikes. He balanced a massive curved sword on his right shoulder.

'The man with the sword is my executioner,' Jayanti said casually.

Jack heard the rattle of chains, and then a procession of sixteen tattered men came in, all wearing the scarlet uniforms of British soldiers. He stiffened as more female warriors marched at the rear, pushing at the prisoners until they were all within the courtyard.

'Do you recognise them?' Jayanti asked.

Jack shook his head. 'I can see that they are British soldiers,' he said. 'I expect they are survivors of some garrison the mutineers overran.'

'Look closer, captain.'

Jack frowned, hoping that they weren't the men he'd led this far. He started when he saw the familiar yellow facings. 'They are from the 113th,' he said.

'These are the men from your missing Number One Company,' Jayanti confirmed. 'These are the proud British soldiers of the Queen. They are not proud now, are they? They are not proud after a few months' captivity. Not proud when they surrendered to the pandies that they despised so much.' Her bitterness was evident.

'The British are trying to bring peace to this land.' Even as Jack spoke, he knew it was a lie. He remembered Hook's words about money and power and saw the East India Company in another light, a place for faceless men in London to grow wealthy while British and Indians sweated and suffered and died fighting each other in wars that neither side understood.

'The British.' Jayanti injected scorn into the name. 'I will tell you what it means to live under British rule. It is to eat cows and drink wine. It is to bite greased cartridges and to mix pig's fat with sweetmeats. It is to destroy Hindu and Moslem temples on the pretence of making roads, to build churches and to send clergymen into the streets to preach the Christian religion. It is to institute English schools, and pay people a monthly stipend for learning the English sciences.' She stopped. 'These are not my words, but I believe them to be true.'

Jack nodded. 'I do not believe that the British plan to destroy the native religions of India.'

'Do you not?' Jayanti turned on him. 'And do you believe in British justice?' She nodded to the shackled British soldiers. 'Your generals hanged any prisoners they captured, or blew them from the muzzle of a cannon. As you see, we kept our prisoners alive. Who is the more civilised, Captain Windrush?'

Jack pursed his lips.

'You say nothing, I see.' Jayanti smiled. 'Then let us play, captain. She sat cross-legged at the table, and Jack copied her position.

The board sat between them, with the sun easing through the windows into the pleasant room, and the British prisoners standing in the baking heat of the courtyard, round-shouldered and bareheaded.

'I have not played for years,' Jack said.

'You may start,' Jayanti offered.

'Why are we playing chess?'

'Play,' Jayanti ordered.

Jack moved forward the pawn diagonally to the left of the queen, intending to free her to act as a mobile strike force, rather like the 113th.

Jayanti moved her queen's knight, taking a quick offensive. 'You are cautious, captain, like your commander-in-chief.'

'I hope I am as successful in defeating the enemy.' Jack moved the queen three spaces.

'Yet you are my prisoner, captain.' Jayanti moved her king's knight.

'Temporarily, in a war you have already lost.' Jack moved his king's pawn one space.

'The war is not over.' Jayanti moved her king's knight's pawn.

'Hugh Rose and Colin Campbell will finish it shortly.' Jack moved his king's pawn one space.

Jayanti's smile was as sincere as a hunting cat. She moved another pawn. 'Your British army sneers at General Colin Campbell, saying he is too slow, too cautious.'

Jack frowned. 'He has never lost a battle.' He moved his queen's knight.

'He allowed our men to escape from Lucknow and Bareilly.' Jayanti held Jack's eye and deftly captured a pawn. 'That is one pawn you have lost.' She held it up. 'The first casualty of our little campaign.' Standing up, Jayanti walked to the window. 'Join me, captain.'

Jack didn't see the two warrior-women move. One stood on his right, the other behind him, with a knife pressed against his spine.

The prisoners still stood in the broiling sun.

Jayanti leant out of the window. 'One pawn.'

The women in the courtyard shifted slightly. One lifted a hand in acknowledgement.

'Choose a private, captain,' Jayanti said and only then did Jack realise that the body of men below were divided into two halves. Eight were privates, and eight were NCOs and junior officers.

'Why?'

'You have lost a pawn,' Jayanti said patiently. 'Which private will you take out of the sun?'

'Oh.' Jack pointed to a man at random. 'That fair-haired fellow.'

Jayanti shouted something, and two of her warriors released the fair-haired private to a small space, away from the others. Without a word, they forced him to his knees.

'What the devil...' Jack said, as the executioner stepped forward with his sword still balanced on his shoulder. 'You murdering bitch, Jayanti!'

With a supreme effort, the private jerked to his feet. He saw the executioner approach with the gigantic sword, waited and spat straight in the man's face. Chained hand and foot, he could manage no other gesture of defiance. The executioner waited as two more female warriors helped drag the soldier down to a kneeling position. One woman grabbed the soldier's hair with both hands and pulled his head forward, and another tore back his uniform, exposing the neck.

Jack watched, feeling sick as the executioner rested the blade of his sword on the soldier's neck, swung the weapon back, braced himself and sliced down. The soldier's head sprung clear from his body and blood jetted from his neck.

'And you lose a pawn,' Jayanti said. 'Shall we return to the game?'

Shaken, Jack sat back down. 'Was that murder necessary?'

'We are both soldiers, as was that private. He knew that a soldier's life ends in death. What difference is it, if he dies in glorious battle or at the edge of an executioner's sword? All our decisions have consequences, Captain Windrush. If you play badly, then you lose a man.'

'And if I play well? Do I watch your chief murderer decapitate one of your warriors?'

Jayanti shook her head. 'No, Captain Windrush. If you capture one of my pieces, I free one of your men from today's possibility of death.'

Jack nodded. 'I see. And if I win the game?'

'If you defeat me, all your surviving men return to their cell for today. It is quite simple.' Jayanti's smile was calm. 'And tomorrow we start again, with the same rules.'

'You're a murdering, evil blackguard,' Jack said.

'Perhaps. Even so, I give your men a chance. Your army executes their prisoners, innocent or not. It is your move, I believe.'

After another three moves, it was evident that Jayanti was the better player. Jack sat in a fever of anxiety as he tried to block her attacks, watched her effortlessly blunt his offensives and hoped desperately to capture some of her pieces to save at least a few of the prisoners.

'Another pawn.' Jayanti lifted the piece in triumph. 'Would you like to accompany me, captain?'

'I would not,' Jack said.

'Then my soldiers will persuade you.'

Sword in hand, the two female warriors closed around Jack, and he rose and stepped to the window. The procedure was the same as before, except that the private seemed resigned to his death as the women forced him to kneel. The executioner used the same apparently casual swing, and the man's head rolled on the stone-flagged floor. The tinkling cheerfulness of the fountain was almost an insult to the men who remained.

Jack made two more trips to the window before he saw an opening and managed to capture one of Jayanti's pawns.

'Well played, captain.' Jayanti applauded with a soft handclap. 'Now choose which man will live for another day.'

It was as hard to select a man to live, as it was to point to a man for the executioner to kill. 'Oh, God forgive me,' Jack breathed as he chose a red-haired, snub-nosed youngster. 'That fellow there,' he said.

Thinking he was about to be executed, the man struggled desperately as two women grabbed him. Jack could not watch as the women dragged him away.

'Now, shall we continue?' Jayanti sounded nonchalant.

Knowing Jayanti outmatched him, Jack dispensed with caution and threw himself recklessly into the attack. By a minor miracle, he managed to capture Jayanti's queen's knight.

'You have my knight,' Jayanti said. 'That will save the life of a sergeant.'

Jack captured two more pawns and the king's rook before Jayanti put him into checkmate.

'I am sure you will try to improve by tomorrow.' When Jayanti clapped her hands, a servant tidied away the chess pieces. 'Or you will lose more of your men.' She looked up, her eyes gleaming. 'We will raise the stakes tomorrow, I think. Your Major Snodgrass will act as king.'

Jack said nothing. The thought of the slaughter in the courtyard sickened him. 'Now I can understand Hussaini Begum,' he said. 'Before I met you, I wondered how a woman could order the murder of innocents, could allow children to be dismembered and stuffed into a well. Now, having seen the cold-blooded manner in which you ordered the murder of these men, I understand. You are devoid of humanity.'

Jayanti salaamed. 'Thank you, captain. The insult of an enemy is a compliment indeed. If you give me your word of honour not to escape, I shall order guest apartments to be prepared for you, with all the comforts your heart and body could desire.'

'I will do no such thing, damn you,' Jack said.

'I rather thought you would say that.' Jayanti salaamed again. 'In that case, I am afraid we shall place you in the same rather more austere surroundings from which we fetched you.' She clapped her hands and spoke rapidly. Half a dozen of the female warriors filed in, grabbed hold of Jack and hustled him away. 'Until tomorrow, Captain Windrush,' Jayanti said. 'And let us hope your play is better, for the execution of a king or a major will be, shall we say, more colourful than that of a pawn?'

Back in his chains, Jack relived the executions in the courtyard, the sinister hiss of the sword, the clump of the head landing on stone slabs and the subdued gasp of the other prisoners. He wondered what horror Jayanti had in mind for Major Snodgrass. He remembered Jayanti's quiet, refined voice as she spoke to him and the click of ivory chess pieces on the board. He remembered the babble of voices and the chaos of colour in the bazaar. One image over-rode all others. He found himself reaching forward and mouthing "no" as he thought of the moment that hand snaked out and wrapped around Mary's mouth.

'Mary, where are you?' Jack rattled his chains in frustration. 'I wish to God that I could help you.'

He looked up as his cell door opened and two of the warrior-women entered. As one held up a torch, the other tossed a heavy bag toward him. The door closed with a bang.

'Is that my lunch?' Jack shouted. Only echoes replied.

As his eyes became accustomed to the dark, Jack realised that there was a tiny window, no larger than his hand, high up in the wall. The thin beam of light that entered showed nothing cheerful, only grim granite and rusty chains. Jack stretched forward, lifted the bag that his guards had left, opened the mouth and peered inside. The face of the fair-haired executed man stared at him; blue eyes open and tongue slightly protruding.

'Oh, dear God!' Jack pushed the bag away, and more heads rolled out, some to face the far wall and others to stare at him, as if accusing him of the sin of being a weak chess player.

Jack could not think of a worse time in his life. He had lost Mary. He had allowed the enemy to chain him inside a dungeon. He had watched helplessly as Jayanti's executioner murdered men of the 113th. Jack closed his eyes. *I'm a failure as an officer, and I have failed Mary, leading her into this terrible place.*

The scratching started again, and something ran over his legs. 'Get away!' He kicked out violently, hearing the chains rattle. For a moment he wondered who had been here before, wearing these rusted chains, and what had happened to them. He felt weary; he needed to sleep and closed his eyes. The scratching intensified and something bit at his leg.

'Get away!' He kicked out again. 'What foul things have these rats been feeding on? They're not going to eat me next.' At the same time, Jack knew that if he did not sleep, he would be stupid with weariness the following day and unable to concentrate on the chess game. He would be responsible for the death of more men. He closed his eyes, started as something with sharp claws crawled over his legs and swore softly.

Damn it all; I'm not thinking straight. I am Captain Jack Baird Windrush of the 113th Foot, I hold the Queen's Commission, and I am not going to die in some damned Indian dungeon. I'm going to get out of here, find Mary, get back to my men and raze this bloody fort to the ground.

Forcing himself upright, Jack inspected his chains. Although the metal was rusty, the links were still too strong to break, and the lock that held them required a key. He traced the chains back to the staple in the wall. Whoever had anchored it knew his business; it didn't budge when he yanked at it. He wouldn't give up though and began to shove the staple this way and that, trying to loosen it from the surrounding stone.

'Captain Windrush!'

The word echoed through his dungeon. Jack jerked his head from side to side. *What new torment is this?* 'Who's there?'

'Captain Windrush! Look up!'

Jack looked up. The sun had sunk so there was no light from the small window. 'Who's that?'

'Look up!'

Jack was wrong. There was a minuscule light flickering at the window. It hovered for a second and then slowly descended, swinging slowly back and forth. Jack watched and reached out when it came close. It was a small lantern on the end of a long rope.

'Got it?' The voice echoed in the granite chamber.

'I have it, thank you.' The echo distorted the sound. 'Who is that?'

'It's Batoor, Captain Windrush.'

'I thought you had deserted!' Jack felt a lift of pleasure. 'What are you doing here?'

'I'm trying to get you out of the dungeon,' Batoor said.

'I'm chained to the wall,' Jack said.

'Take the light and send back the rope.'

When Jack untied the lantern and put it on the ground, Batoor flicked the rope away. The lantern-light reflected on a dozen eyes as the rats withdrew. One gnawed on a soldier's head until Jack rattled the chains and frightened it away.

The rope returned a few moments later, with the end tied around a long knife. Jack held it gratefully. 'Thank you!' he said. There was no reply. 'Batoor? Batoor, have you seen anything of Mary?'

Only silence replied. Jack wished he'd asked about Mary first.

Perhaps Batoor considered his duty done by delivering the knife. Jack felt more like a soldier with a weapon in his hand. He tried the blade in the manacle lock, hoping it had a simple catch that the knife could spring. After a few minutes, he gave up in disgust. The blade was too broad to enter the keyhole. Instead, Jack returned to the staple in the wall. He scraped at the granite, pulling and twisting the iron until his hands were bleeding raw. With no method of judging the passing of time, except by glancing at the stars in the tiny square of sky through the window, Jack worked on, dislodging minuscule flakes of stone without making any headway.

He heard the rasp of the key in the door, pulled desperately at the staple and found it as secure as ever. Swearing silently, he snuffed the lantern, hid it in a corner and backed to the wall, trying to conceal his knife. When the door opened, three warrior women stepped in. Without a word, one drew her tulwar and held it to Jack's throat while the others released the chains and pushed him to the door. Jack slid the knife up his sleeve, wondering if he could fight all three at once.

No. That would be a quick and pointless suicide. Better to attack Jayanti instead. Jayanti was more valuable to the mutineers than he was to the British. Holding the blade of the knife in his folded fingers, Jack allowed the warriors to push him out of the dungeon and into the darkness.

Chapter Thirteen

'Get down, Captain Windrush!' The voice came from nowhere as Batoor erupted from the shadows. Jack barely heard the hiss of his tulwar, and the first of his guards crumpled, her throat slashed wide open. The second woman turned, and Batoor thrust his blade into her breast and twisted it. Her scream echoed as the third woman swung at Batoor with her sword.

Jack threw himself forward, knocking the woman sideways, so her blade missed Batoor by a handspan. Dropping the knife into his hand, Jack reversed it and stabbed, catching her at the side of the throat. Warm blood spurted as he ripped the blade sideways, ignoring the woman's gurgling screams.

'Glad to see you, Batoor,' he said as the Pathan wiped his blade clean on the clothes of his first victim.

'You were not hard to find,' Batoor said. 'The first person I asked knew all about the Windrush sahib prisoner.'

Jack thought it best not to ask about Batoor's methods of asking questions.

'Batoor,' Jack asked the question that had been uppermost in his mind for many hours. 'Do you know what happened to Mary?'

Batoor's smile was as broad as ever. 'Yes, I know, Captain Windrush.'

'Is she alive? Is she a prisoner in this fort?'

'Yes, she is alive, and no, she is not a prisoner in this fort.' Batoor's answers only created more questions. 'We'll have to get away now,

Captain Windrush. The Jayanti woman will soon miss her soldiers, and then they'll search for you.'

'How will we get out?'

'We walk out the front door,' Batoor said. Bending down, he tested each of the female warrior's tulwars and handed one to Jack. 'Strap that around your waist, Windrush, and swagger like a warrior.' He shoved a dozen betel nuts into Jack's hand. 'Chew these and say nothing.' He stepped back. 'You don't look much like a sahib.'

For the first time, Jack blessed his part-Indian heritage. 'Thank you.' He knew Batoor intended his words as a compliment.

'Follow me.' Batoor strode through the gloomy dungeons as though he owned the place. He kicked open a door, snarled to a man who tried to stop him and mounted a steep flight of steps two at a time.

'You were never an English public-school man, were you?' Jack asked.

'What is that?' Batoor asked.

'You have the same arrogance in your manner,' Jack said. 'As if the whole world belongs to you and damn anybody who tries to deny it.'

'I am an English sahib then.' Batoor increased his swagger.

Jack gripped the hilt of his tulwar as they passed the sentries at one of the minor gates and took a deep breath as they stepped outside. Freedom smelled good. 'Mary?'

'Come with me, Captain Windrush.' Batoor led Jack into the crowded, narrow streets until Jack found himself in a maze of small, flat-topped houses. 'In here.' He pushed open a surprisingly elaborate door.

The interior was much as Jack had expected, a bare, hot room with a minimum of furniture and an Indian woman sitting on a low stool, her head shrouded and her sari covering her from shoulder to ankles. The flame of a single *diya* lantern provided all the light there was.

'Good evening, Ma'am,' Jack said. '*Ram ram.*'

'Good evening, Captain Jack.' Mary threw back her head covering. 'I'm glad my teachings were effective, and you've finally learned a word of the language.'

Chapter Fourteen

'Dear God in heaven.' Jack stared at Mary for a long time, shaking his head. He was aware of Batoor in the room, or he would have folded her in his arms. 'You're safe,' he said.

'So are you.' Mary's eyes were huge.

'I'm glad.' Jack didn't know what to say.

'So am I.'

'I saw you grabbed,' Jack said. 'I saw somebody pull you into a building.'

'That was Batoor.' Mary looked at the Pathan. 'He saved me, and we have been trying to find you ever since.'

'There are other British prisoners.' Jack didn't know how to thank her, or Batoor. More used to the abrupt manners of soldiers and the code of gentlemen, he was unsure how to act with a woman such as Mary. He frowned as he realised what he was thinking. *A woman such as Mary? What do I mean by that? Is Mary different from any other woman he had known? Is she different from Myat, or Helen or that young barmaid back in Hereford? Yes, yes, she is.*

Why? Was it because she was Eurasian?

No.

Jack breathed out in relief. He didn't think differently about Mary because she was half-Indian. *There is quite another reason.*

'We know about the British prisoners.' Mary had been watching him, waiting until his mind had cleared. 'They are chained in a dungeon and guarded by Jayanti's warriors.'

'Can we get them out?'

Batoor and Mary exchanged glances. 'Batoor thinks not,' Mary said. 'They are too well guarded.'

'I'll come back with the 113th.' Jack didn't mention the chess game and the executions. He could feel Mary's eyes on him. 'I'll tear this place apart to rescue these men.'

'There may be another way,' Mary said. 'We could try to get the Rajah to help.'

'I don't understand.' Jack fought his tiredness. He had no idea what time, or even what day it was.

'The commander of the Rajah's army is British,' Mary said. 'If we approach him, he may help us.'

In this time of confusion and divided loyalties, Jack wasn't surprised to hear the nationality of the Rajah's commander. 'It was the Rajah who handed me to Nana Sahib,' he said. 'He's thrown in his lot with the rebels.'

'I'm not sure that he has,' Mary said. 'Nana Sahib and Jayanti are at one end of the fort, and the Rajah is at the other.' She sighed. 'Are you game to try him?'

Jack considered. His first inclination had been to return with his 113th, storm the fort and free the prisoners. On reflection, he knew that his handful of infantry, without artillery or cavalry, could never reduce the fort. His second thought was to take Riley, the cracksman, find the prisoners and release them, but Batoor had said that Jayanti's warriors guarded them too well, and he respected the Pathan's judgement.

'I'll have a look at this commander fellow first,' Jack said. 'And then I'll decide.'

'He drills his troops every day,' Batoor said. 'Left, right, left, right, attention, stand at ease.' He laughed. 'It provides the people with endless amusement.'

'Where does he drill them?' Jack had a sudden dread of returning to the fort.

'On the *maidan*, the parade ground, under the walls to the north of the fort, with trees all around for shade.' Mary explained. 'When I was young, we watched the army training.'

'What's this man's name?' Jack asked. 'I mean, who is he?'

'Commander-sahib,' Mary said. 'That's what everybody calls him.' She smiled. 'He's no youngster, Jack.'

'Show me,' Jack demanded.

If Mary had not told Jack that the Commander-sahib was British, Jack would never have known. He stood in front of his men dressed in the full uniform of a commander of native infantry, with a steel breastplate and a spiked helmet as he gave orders in fluent Hindi, while a dozen shrill-voiced rissaldars – officers – ensured their men obeyed.

'They're smart,' Jack approved, as the Gondabad Army marched and countermarched to the word of command. 'They could match up to any regular British line regiment for drill. It is as well that their weapons are outdated.'

The infantry carried the old Brown Bess India pattern musket, an excellent weapon in its day but outclassed by the British Army's modern Enfields.

'There must be three thousand men on parade,' Jack said. 'The Commander-sahib has drilled them well. Does he have any cavalry?'

'Over there.' Batoor pointed with his chin.

As the infantry marched into the fort in columns of four, ten squadrons of cavalry took their place on the maidan, each man dressed in a splendid blue and silver uniform and carrying a curved sabre.

'They look as impressive as the infantry.' Jack wondered if they had the discipline to advance into Russian guns, like the Light Brigade at Balaklava only four years previously. 'How good are they in battle?'

'The Rajah of Gondabad does not like battles,' Batoor said with a sneer. 'He keeps his army intact by ignoring everything that happens. His soldiers are children's toys, pretty to look at and nothing else. They would run at the sight of blood.'

Standing under the shade of the trees with a scattering of local men and women, Jack watched the Commander-sahib. He was undoubtedly elderly, with a neat white beard and grizzled face, yet he stood erect, and his commands dominated the parade ground. 'Yes, Mary. I will speak to that man.'

'He has the ear of the Rajah,' Mary agreed.

Batoor spat betel juice onto the ground. 'It will do no good, Captain Windrush. The Rajah will whine to the rebels, and they will ignore him. He is a man with no teeth and no courage.'

'Perhaps you are correct,' Jack said. 'I'll try anyway. Where can I find the Commander-sahib?'

'Over there.' Mary nodded to a walled enclosure beside the parade ground. 'He lives and works in the same building.'

'When he goes in, I shall follow him,' Jack said.

'I'll come as well,' Mary said at once.

'I want you to stay with Batoor,' Jack said. 'It might be dangerous.'

'Oh, Jack, will you stop singing that same old song?'

Sometimes even the bravest soldier has to admit defeat. 'If there's any trouble, Mary, turn and run. You can merge into the city far more easily than I can.'

'I know that, Jack.' Mary spoke as patiently as she would to a child.

'I will come too, Windrush,' Batoor said. 'In case the enemy chooses to fight.'

'You and Private Logan would get on well together,' Jack said sourly. 'He's also a bloodthirsty rascal.'

Two acres of gardens surrounded the Commander-sahib's house, created in a mixture of British and Indian styles, with flowerbeds wilting under the sun, small groves of trees and the ubiquitous fountains. The two sentries at the door looked efficient and bored.

'I'll talk,' Batoor said. 'I'll tell them we want an audience with the Commander-sahib.' He walked up to the sentries, speaking rapidly. They reacted at once, crossing their muskets in front of him to bar any entrance.

'I'll try,' Mary said and smiled as she addressed the sentries. One man laughed, and the other eyed Batoor with dislike before they stepped aside. 'I told them that I had two recruits for the Commander-sahib,' Mary explained.

One sentry shouted something over his shoulder, and a rissaldar appeared.

'He's demanding to know who we are.' Mary translated the officer's words.

'Use the same story,' Jack was aware of Batoor resting a hand on the hilt of his tulwar. *Can we fight our way clear of here?*

The rissaldar glared at Mary, evidently wondering why two stalwart men should have a woman with them. He jerked his head inside the building and shook a finger at Mary. They spoke for a while, and he grimaced and allowed her to enter.

'I told them you are dumb, Jack, and need somebody to speak for you.'

The interior of the house boasted a mixture of British and Indian styles, with beautiful carpets on the ground, and pointed and arched doorways. Hunting prints hung incongruously on the wall, together with a black and white etching of Robert Burns the poet, and a statue of Skanda, the Hindu god of war.

'The Commander-sahib is undoubtedly confused about his nation-ality,' Jack murmured.

The rissaldar brought them up a flight of stairs to a large room that overlooked the garden at the front. Nodding to the single sentry, he tapped on the door and thrust it open, closing it before Jack, and the others could follow. The sentry stood immobile, both hands on his musket. His eyes swivelled over them, disregarded Jack, lingered on Mary's breasts for a few seconds and settled on Batoor. His hands tightened on his musket, and Jack guessed he had no love for Pathans.

After a few moments, the door opened again, and the rissaldar beck-oned them inside.

The first thing Jack noticed was the mixture of European and Indian styles that made up the vast room. The next was the array of tulwars and Brown Bess muskets decorating the wall and the Commander-sahib sitting behind a teak bureau at the end of the room.

The Commander-sahib beckoned them closer and dismissed the rissaldar with a casual wave.

Mary salaamed politely, while Jack stood to attention, purely out of habit while in the company of a superior officer. Batoor was a few paces behind, right leg forward and his hand on the hilt of his tulwar. The Commander-sahib leaned back and contemplated them through narrow eyes, while the single ruby in the centre of his turban reflected the light that poured through the windows.

Mary spoke first, saying that she had brought two possible recruits for the Rajah's army.

'Enough of that nonsense,' the Commander-sahib interrupted her in gruff English. 'Don't perjure your soul with a lot of lies. You were taught better than that at the missionary school, Mary Lambert.'

It was the first time Jack had seen Mary truly astonished. 'Do you know me?' she asked at last.

'I do.' The Commander-sahib seemed pleased that he had caught her by surprise. 'And I knew your father, Major Lambert of the Bengal Fusiliers.'

'Oh!' Mary put a hand to her mouth. 'How did you know him?'

'The Fusiliers were based at Gondabad for a season or two,' the commandant-Sahib said. 'I don't know this Pathan fellow.'

'I am Batoor.'

'One name and no history,' the Commander-sahib said. 'There is a long untold story there, I wager. Whose throat have you cut, my man, or whose daughter have you ravaged to bring the wrath of the clan on you?'

The wrath of the clan? What Indian, however educated, would use that type of language? This man is indeed British.

Batoor smiled. 'It is better than I do not go back home for a while,' he said.

'And you.' The Commander-sahib eventually looked directly at Jack. 'I always wondered how you would turn out. I heard about your arrival with the 113th, although why you are with that bunch of blackguards and ne'er-do-weels, I can't imagine.'

'It's a long story.' Jack didn't wish to say too much until he knew more about this man. 'We have come to ask your advice, sir.' *"I always wondered how you would turn out." What the devil does that mean?*

'Have you now?' The Commander-sahib scratched his head under the turban. 'Well, I have a proposal for you, Captain Jack Baird Windrush, and as I considerably outrank you in both seniority and years, I will say my piece first.'

'Yes, sir.' Jack couldn't restrain his curiosity. 'How do you know who I am, sir?'

'You'll damn well listen to me first, boy!' the Commander-sahib snapped.

'Yes, sir.'

'I am in command of the Rajah's army,' the Commander-sahib said. 'As such, I train it, equip it and discipline it.'

Jack wondered if he should comment. 'Yes, sir.'

'My knowledge is thirty years out of date,' the Commander-sahib said. 'I need an officer with recent experience of British equipment and tactics. That could be you.'

Jack stared at him. 'I am an officer of the British Army, sir. I will not renounce my allegiance to Her Majesty.'

The Commander-sahib continued as if Jack hadn't spoken. 'I can offer you a position for life, taking over command from me after I die, with unlimited power and as many women as you desire.'

Jack knew that Mary was watching him. 'I have no desire for unlimited power, sir, and no desire for a harem of women.'

The Commander-sahib rested both hands on the top of his desk. 'I could have you killed,' he mused. 'I could have you trampled to death by elephants, thrown from the highest tower or blown from a cannon's mouth.'

'I am sure you could, sir.' Jack tried not to quail before the Commander-sahib's range of possible executions.

'I won't, of course,' the Commander-sahib mused. 'Damn it; one does not treat one's own family that way.'

Jack said nothing until he absorbed the full impact of the words. 'I am sorry, sir. I don't understand.'

'I think you do, Jack. Might I call you Jack? You are my grandson, after all.'

'Oh, dear God.' Jack stared at the Commander-sahib in disbelief. 'Who are you?'

'I am the Commander-sahib of his majesty, the Rajah of Gondabad. In a previous life, I was Major Jack Baird of the Bengal Fusiliers. I am your grandfather, Jack.'

'Oh, dear God.' Jack could only stand and stare at the old man. 'Oh, dear God in heaven.' He felt Mary's arm slide into his and was glad of her support. 'How did that happen?'

'The usual way,' Baird said. 'Man meets woman—'

'No, I mean, how did you become Commander of the Rajah's army? How long have you been here?'

'I was stationed here with the Fusiliers,' Baird said, 'and I loved the place and the people. The old Rajah, the present Rajah's father, offered me the position and I took it, about thirty years ago.'

Jack tried to work out the timeline. 'My grandmother? When did you meet her?'

'Long before that, Jack. I met her when I was in the Company's employ. We were together for years, it was no fly-by-night affair. We were legally married; such things between Briton and Indian were much more common then, than they are now.' Baird was smiling; his eyes warm as they probed Jack's. 'She was the reason I left the Company's employ, you see. The regiment was posted to Calcutta, and I wished to stay here, so when the old Rajah offered me the post, I took it.'

'My mother?'

'Your grandmother and I decided it would be better for her to grow up within the British sphere. The British star was on the ascendancy. It tore your grandmother's heart to hand her over.'

Jack nodded. Most British residents in India sent their children 'home' to be educated for much the same reason. Life was hard for British families in India.

My grandfather. This man is my grandfather. Jack's mind whirled with the new knowledge. *I have this man's name. Dear God, help me. I knew that I felt at home in India and now I have more family here.*

'We will talk about family matters later,' Baird said. 'You must know that I've been searching for you for some time. I gave out the word that nobody was to harm you.' His smile revealed perfect teeth. 'I even offered a reward if somebody could bring you to me, unharmed.'

Jack remembered the naik saving his life and the attempt to kidnap him, as well as Jayanti's surprising behaviour. 'I wondered what was happening,' he said. 'But other British prisoners have been murdered.'

Baird nodded. 'They are not my grandsons.'

'You are British,' Jack reminded. 'Don't you have any loyalty to Her Majesty?'

'My wife was Indian,' Baird said gently. 'My only daughter was half Indian. My grandson is part Indian. My employer is Indian. I have many more Indian than British friends. Am I more British or Indian? Who means more to me? Loyalty is not something to be assumed, taken for granted, or based on place of birth. Out here, whoever pays the most buys allegiance, while friendship has to be earned.' He glanced at Batoor. 'Our Pathan companion dances to a different tune with his loyalty to his clan.'

Jack remembered Colonel Hook saying something similar about money. 'I presume that the Rajah of Gondabad is in the pay of the rebels, then? Does Jayanti or Nana Sahib pay his wages?'

'The Rajah is neither for nor against Britain,' Baird said. 'Nana Sahib has little money. Oh, Nana taxes the lands he travels through, and his men rob the rich merchants, but he lost the loot of Lucknow, and when Campbell chased him out of Bareilly, he had no time to rob the treasury. My Rajah is waiting to see who is the stronger, and he will join that side. Like many out here, he is a pragmatist.'

'Jayanti and the rebels are sheltering in his fort,' Jack reminded.

'Yes,' Baird said, 'and if Sir Colin Campbell arrived, the Rajah would also give shelter to the British. You will notice that you're still alive, and the Rajah has confined the rebels – as you term them – to one area of the fort. My Rajah has not chosen yet, and although his army is small – well, three thousand well-trained men might turn a battle.'

'That is true,' Jack agreed. 'So the Rajah could be persuaded to join us?'

'He could,' Baird said. 'If the Company came up with a sizeable pension and could be trusted to keep its word.'

'I cannot promise a pension, but perhaps the British could muster up a single large payment,' Jack said, his mind working furiously. 'Perhaps the British could find payment enough to buy the Rajah and ransom the British prisoners from Jayanti.' He was aware of Mary staring curiously at him and continued, recklessly. 'Would that do the trick?'

Baird's smile was slow. 'It might. How would the British manage to find such a payment in the middle of a war?'

'I'm not certain that they could,' Jack said, 'but I think it might be worth trying.' He paused and held the old man's gaze. It had been a shock to meet his grandfather, and he hadn't yet analysed how he felt. 'The longer I take, the more chance there is that Jayanti will tire of the prisoners and kill them off.' He grunted. 'I'm surprised she has kept them so long.'

'Thank the Rajah for that,' Baird said. 'He was angry when Jayanti decapitated so many of the prisoners.'

Jack gave a slow nod. 'If I'd been a better chess player, more men would be alive today.' He knew that Mary was confused.

Baird nodded. 'Jayanti enjoys her little games.'

Now that the idea was in Jack's mind, he wished to get started. 'Commander-sahib... grandfather.' He paused. 'What should I call you?'

'Whatever you wish,' Baird said.

Jack avoided the issue. 'Thank you for your help, sir,' he said. 'I will leave at once, with your permission.'

'I've searched for you for years, Jack, and now you wish to run away?'

'Duty calls, sir,' Jack said.

'Wait!' Mary put a hand on Jack's arm. 'Commander-sahib. My father – could you tell me about him?'

'Next time, perhaps, Mary,' Baird said. 'Your man lacks his mother's patience. He is a soldier.'

Only when Jack left the room did he wonder if he would ever see the Commander-sahib again. He wished he'd spent more time with the old man. *No.* Jack pushed that thought aside. *I have my duty to do. I have to try to save as many of the 113th as I can and persuade the Rajah to support the British. My desires must take second place to my duty as an officer of the Queen.*

Chapter Fifteen

Elliot shook his head when he heard Jack's news. 'Your grandfather is the Rajah's military commander? We can surely use that.'

'Only if the Rajah decides to join us,' Jack said. 'If the Rajah is on our side, Jayanti and her warriors can't stay in the fort.'

'What's your plan, Jack?'

'Do you remember back at Lucknow, when Riley and Logan were absent for a while and Sergeant Greaves reported them?'

'I remember,' Elliot said. 'You caught them swimming, as I recall.'

'That was their story. Now, you and I know Riley better than that. He was after something more interesting than a face full of Indian river water.'

Elliot nodded. 'I thought it strange at the time.'

'Cast your mind back to when Campbell evacuated Lucknow, and there was a convoy of tumbrels and wagons carrying treasure and the crown jewels.'

Elliot glanced at Mary. 'I remember. We were a bit busy, what with escorting the civilians out of the city.' He didn't mention that Jack's mother had died during the evacuation.

'Riley and Logan disappeared for a while there, as well,' Jack said.

'I can't remember that.'

Jack saw that Mary was listening intently. She had been in a convoy of refugees, easing out of the besieged Residency while the outnumbered British tried to fend off the mutineers and rebels.

'At the same time, an entire treasure wagon went missing,' Jack said. 'Thirty-seven wagons left the city, and only thirty-six arrived safely. I had more important matters on my mind at the time.' Jack didn't refer directly to the death of his mother. That was still an intensely painful memory.

'Do you think Riley and Logan stole it?' Mary asked.

'I do,' Jack said. 'That's why they returned to the river a few weeks ago.'

'What are you planning, Captain Jack?' Mary narrowed her eyes.

'The Rajah of Gondabad might be bribed. The British prisoners, our men of the 113th, can be ransomed and we may know the location of a treasure wagon,' Jack said. 'Put them all together, and we can do a power of good.'

'There is a huge step from pure speculation to fact,' Mary cautioned.

'Would it not be better to ask Sir Colin first?' Elliot asked. 'Or even Colonel Hook? We're taking a lot of responsibility dabbling in such things.' He hesitated. 'If it comes out that we acted without authority from above, it won't do our careers much good.'

'Sir Colin is the best general in the army,' Jack agreed, 'but he's not renowned for his speed. He would as likely send a full expedition to find the wagon or rescue the prisoners, and by that time, it would be too late. As for Hooky – I beg your pardon, Colonel Hook – where is he? He jumps around so much.'

'With fifty of us, we'll make better time than Sir Colin.' Elliot looked worried.

'I'm not taking fifty men,' Jack said. 'This is a quick expedition. I will take ten men, mostly to act as porters, including Riley and Logan. You'll stay here in charge of the remainder.'

Mixed expressions of relief and disappointment crossed Elliot's face. 'If you don't mind me saying so, sir, this is not the best defensive site. The locals already know that we're here, so it won't be long before Jayanti and her women come probing, or maybe even Nana Sahib if he's still around.'

'That's true,' Jack said. 'The pandies would like nothing better than to snap up an isolated British garrison. It would hearten their supporters and increase their prestige. Do you have anywhere else in mind?'

'Yes, sir.' Elliot had evidently given his situation some thought. 'Do you remember that old Hindu temple we camped at last year, after the Gondabad massacre? It's a bit further away and much more defensible. I think we should move there.'

* * *

It was strange to return to the temple where they'd found refuge the previous year. It was strange to have the old Hindu gods watching over them and the exotic carvings staring at them through a green screen of vegetation. The war could have been on a different continent as child-sized monkeys capered and screeched, butterflies rose in clouds from the grass, and in the distance, a deer barked. Although the heat bounced from the stonework, the spring of bright water that bubbled in the centre of the temple was welcome, and the men relaxed in the shade, swatted flies and mosquitoes and set to work preparing defensive positions.

'This is familiar.' Mary looked around her, smiling. 'I'm going to explore and renew old memories.'

Jack nodded. 'Take care.' He called over Riley and Logan. 'You two, I want you.'

Logan came with his usual swagger while Riley was more cautious, suspecting trouble. Jack took them to a secluded area between two heavily carved pillars as Hanuman the Monkey God gazed down on them. 'Now, I want the truth, Riley.'

'Always, sir,' Riley lied.

'When we left Lucknow last year, you two hid some treasure.' Jack didn't try to be subtle. 'Don't deny it.'

'What makes you think that, sir?' Riley asked.

'Your behaviour, Riley, and your character,' Jack said.

'Could you explain, sir?' Riley asked.

That was sufficient fencing. 'When Sir Colin evacuated Lucknow last year,' Jack faced Riley directly, 'you two stole one of the treasure wagons. That wagon is the property of Her Majesty. You could be hanged.'

The silence confirmed what up until then had only been a strong suspicion.

'It is my duty to place you both under arrest,' Jack said.

'Yes, sir,' Riley said. 'What are you planning?'

'What do you mean, Riley?'

'We know each other, sir. You have something in mind that doesn't concern a noose.'

Jack hid his amusement. 'You're a clever man, Riley. Now listen.' He explained the situation as Riley and Logan nodded.

'So, you want us to go to Lucknow, retrieve this alleged treasure and hand it all over to some Indian Rajah,' Riley said.

'That's right,' Jack agreed.

'And if there's no treasure and we object?' Riley asked.

'There is a treasure, and you won't object.' Jack spoke softly. 'I know you, Riley, and I know Charlotte. You won't let her down.'

Jack knew that threats wouldn't work with Logan and appeals to patriotism would be a waste of breath. Men with the bitter-hard background that most of the 113th shared had little cause to love their homeland. However, while Pathans had *Pashtunwali,* loyalty to clan and family, British soldiers had loyalty to their regiment and Jack used that as a lever to persuade Logan to join him.

'I know you as well, Logan. You're not a thief.' That last part wasn't entirely accurate for like many British soldiers, Logan had the idea that anything not nailed down was fair game. 'That money will buy the lives of a score or more soldiers of the 113th.'

'Aye,' Logan said. 'We cannae let the pandies kill they lads, Riles.'

'We'll leave before dawn tomorrow.'

Logan grunted reluctant agreement and Riley could only nod.

'Very good. Get yourselves prepared.' Jack watched them walk away.

'Jack,' Mary touched his arm. 'Come with me.'

She led him through the temple building, past the statue to Hanuman and pushed past a tangle of creepers to an inner chamber that Jack had not noticed before. The sudden coolness surprised Jack.

'Where are you taking me?'

She put a finger to his lips. 'Shush Jack. Trust me.'

'I do,' he said.

A single shaft of sunlight permeated the chamber, highlighting strange carvings of copulating couples.

'A young man such as you should not look at these statues,' Mary linked her arm with that of Jack, 'unless he wishes to see.'

'I am always surprised how open Indian people are about such matters.' Jack felt a twinge of embarrassment at Mary's casual acceptance of the explicit images.

Mary smiled. 'Despite being brought up in a missionary school, I am always surprised how *closed* British people are about such matters.' She squeezed his arm. 'Come on Jack, you and I are both here because our parents made love, and the same goes for everybody else.'

'Yes, but there's no need to show such things,' Jack said.

'Why not?' Mary laughed again. 'Is it such a big secret that most of us need and desire love, physical as well as emotional?'

'No, of course not.' Jack watched as Mary lit a small *diya* lantern and placed it on a handy shelf. Yellow light pooled around them, illuminating the carvings, so they seemed almost alive.

'Are they not interesting?' Mary's fingertips traced the outline of a plump woman, following her curves with relish. 'Look at her, waiting to receive him, look at her anticipation, Jack. Is she not attractive?'

'Yes, she is, I suppose.' Jack agreed as Mary teased him, cupping a stone breast in her hand.

'And is this fellow here not impressively masculine?' Mary allowed her hand to drift to the woman's partner, a handsome young man evidently ready for the act of love. 'Don't they look happy there?'

'They do.' Jack couldn't hide his discomfort as Mary's hand stroked the man.

'Jack,' Mary said. 'Why are Englishmen such cold fish?'

'Are we?'

'Yes,' Mary said. 'I was taught, again and again, to hide my emotions, not to cry, to be phlegmatic like a true Englishwoman. You know that I am not a true Englishwoman, Jack. I am half-Indian. I am sure that English women share my passions and I think that Englishmen do as well, underneath that chilling exterior.'

'Do I have a chilling exterior?' Jack asked.

'Yes, sometimes,' Mary said. 'Not always. At present, you look embarrassed, bemused and lost. Here, let me help you.' Reaching over, she kissed him on the cheek. 'There, Captain Jack. Is that not better?'

'What are you doing?' Jack touched his cheek. 'I have a unit of men to command.'

'Lieutenant Elliot is more than capable of organising them, Captain Jack, and I am seducing you. Or did you believe I brought you here to admire the artwork?'

'Mary!' Jack said.

She stepped back. 'Jack Baird Windrush,' she said sternly. 'Are you rejecting me?'

'Heaven forbid,' he said.

'That is just as well for you, Captain Jack.' Mary stepped forward again, cupped his face in her hands and kissed him soundly. 'There now, that was a proper kiss for you.' Suddenly Jack allowed his growing desire to triumph. *Hang duty, Mary is right; Elliot and Bryce are more than capable of looking after the men, and O'Neill and Greaves are there if required. I am here, with Mary, we have survived a whole raft of dangers, and God only knows when we will get another chance to be alone together. Indeed, either of us might catch a fever and die tomorrow, or the rebels could kill us. India may be a place of death, but it's also a place of vivacious life and love.*

'Do you call that a proper kiss?' He looked into her brown eyes. 'Try this.'

Her lips parted beneath his, their tongues intertwined, and Jack eased his hands around her, caressing her back and smoothing downward to the plump swell of her bottom. He withdrew for breath, half expecting her to protest. Instead, she pressed against him, cupping his buttocks in both hands.

Before Jack realised what had happened, they were on the ground, using soft foliage as a bed as they slipped off their clothes.

'The men?' Mary asked once.

'They won't come in here.' Jack was no longer concerned about the men. Elliot would have them under control.

'Jack,' Mary whispered in his ear. 'I've only done this once before. Remember that time?'

Jack paused as the memories flooded back. 'I'll never forget. You're doing very well, again,' he said. 'Are you sure you wish—'

'Oh, Heavens, Jack! You know I do.'

The lantern cast their shadows across the carved couples, showing the living reality and a continuity of human desire in that chamber dedicated to love. There was no sound except their deep breathing and the soft tinkle of the spring outside. They could have been alone in the world, separate from the turmoil and horror of the war that still tore India apart. Nothing mattered but each other, and then nothing mattered at all. Jack rolled away and looked at Mary, as she lay naked and with her breasts softly undulating with each breath. 'You're beautiful,' he said.

She opened her eyes. 'We needed that,' she said.

'Did you do that because we needed it?' Jack asked.

There was a short pause before Mary replied. 'No.' She shook her head. 'No, I did *that*,' she emphasised the last word, 'because I wanted it.' She held his eyes for a long moment. 'I wanted you.'

'You got me,' Jack said.

'You're covered with scars.' Reaching forward, Mary touched the barely-healed white ridge that ran across his ribs. 'What was that?'

'That was in Lucknow,' Jack said. 'Bayonet or sword, I never knew which.'

'And that?' She touched the raised scar on his thigh.

'A pointed stake in Burma.'

'And this?' She touched a circular white mark on his arm.

'A Burmese decoit chewed me.' Jack didn't explain further.

'And this one?'

'Crimea.' Jack tired of the game and touched her face. 'Where do we go from here, Mary?'

'You go off to find some mythical treasure,' Mary said, 'and I either go with you or stay here with Elliot.'

Jack briefly wondered which would be safer for her. Should he take Mary on a long march through India, or leave her in this isolated garrison knowing that the enemy was only a few miles away? 'That's not what I meant.'

'What did you mean?' Mary's face was full of innocence.

'I mean, where do *we* go from here – you and I.' Jack hesitated for a moment. 'Us.'

Mary's head jerked up at the last word. 'Is there an *us*, Jack? Or are we just using each other because of this terrible war.'

Jack realised that although Mary was naked and lying within a few inches of him, he was concentrating on her face and her words rather than on her body. She meant more to him than merely a few moments pleasurable relief. Was there an *us*? Could there be an *us*? Did he wish an *us*? Alternatively, was Elliot correct and would any relationship with Mary, beyond the mere physical, wreck his military career?

'Would you like there to be an *us*?' Jack temporised by handing the question and the responsibility back to Mary.

'It's not my place to decide,' Mary replied at once. 'You know the difficulties that marrying a Eurasian would bring to you if it's marriage that you're thinking of. Or rather, if it is marriage of which you are thinking.' She smiled. 'There's my missionary school upbringing coming to the fore, Captain Jack.'

There had been no reason to ask the question. Mary lying there naked provided all the proof required that she cared for him. She was not the sort of woman to invite such intimacy with a mere acquaintance.

'No,' Jack said. 'You're right.' He looked around at the no-longer shocking carvings. 'I wonder how many people have come here to make love.'

'Hundreds probably, over the years,' Mary said. 'Perhaps even thousands.'

Jack had a sudden recollection of something his mother had said. 'My mother and father met in this temple,' he said. 'I wonder if they were in this chamber.' He had hardly known his true mother while his few memories of his father were of a loud, confident man. Yes, he could believe that they'd met in here, surrounded by images of long-gone lovers. It was something that would appeal to his mother's romantic side. His father? He would probably have found it quite amusing, perhaps even stimulating.

'Continuity,' Mary said. 'That's nice.' Reaching forward, she took hold of his hand. 'I'm not trying to put pressure on you, Jack. I know I am only a Eurasian, a *chee-chee*, a half-caste, a *teen pau* rather than a *pukka* British woman. I am country-born and country-bred. I didn't entice you here to force the issue, Jack.'

'The thought never entered my head,' Jack said truthfully. 'Anyway, I am country-born as well, not four miles from this temple.'

'Nor do I wish to be thought of as your bit of *khyfer*.'

'My bit of skirt?' Jack smiled. 'That's hardly the language an officer would use, Mary, or his lady.' He ran his hand down the length of her body, from her throat to her knees, enjoying the sensation.

'I'm yours, Jack,' Mary said simply. 'If you want me.' She took hold of his hand and pressed it into her groin. 'I want you, Captain Jack and I want to know you want me.'

For a brief, betraying moment, Jack wondered if Helen Maxwell, or other British women, would be as forward once they disposed of the outer veneer. He pushed the thought away. Helen had no place in his mind and certainly no place in this enchanted chamber. This place belonged to Mary and him, and no other, however many couples had been here before, and however many would be here in the future. They didn't matter. Only the present mattered, only what was happening between him and Mary at this moment.

'I want you,' Jack said.

Mary's smile was somehow wistful. She spread her arms. 'Then come and get me, Captain Jack.'

Chapter Sixteen

As Jack inspected his ten-man patrol, he wondered how many departures he'd endured. How often had he marched out of an encampment or cantonment with the knowledge that he might never return, that he could leave his bones in some foreign place, the cold uplands of Inkerman, the fever-jungles of Burma or the baking plains of India? Jack thought this time felt worse, perhaps because he was leaving behind somebody he knew cared for him. He patted his pocket, with the emergency medical bag that had been Mary's parting gift.

'You know how you always hurt yourself,' she had said and kissed him. 'Take care, Captain Jack.'

Do your duty. The stern words brought Jack back to the present.

'All set, O'Neill?' Jack had selected his men with care. As well as Riley and Logan, he was taking Batoor, Coleman and Thorpe, MacKinnon and Mahoney, Whitelam and Armstrong. Jack had chosen Coleman and Thorpe for their long experience, while Whitelam had a poacher's instincts, Mahoney was a quiet, steady Irishman and MacKinnon had some inner gifts that Jack didn't understand but guessed could be valuable. Armstrong was a thoroughly unpleasant man whom Jack personally disliked, yet he valued him as an efficient fighting man.

'All set, sir.' O'Neill threw a smart salute.

'*Shabash*, sergeant.' Jack glanced back at the temple. He would never forget this place with its special chamber and sweet memories. Mary was standing in the shade of Hanuman's pillar, trying to catch his eye. Jack lifted a hand in salute, still in an inner turmoil. Was their relationship only a brief episode in his life of campaigning and bloodletting?

He couldn't say.

Mary's gaze remained on him as he turned away. He knew she would watch as long as he was in sight, and probably a lot longer than that. He steeled himself. He had his duty to do, and Mary would have to wait.

He didn't want to leave her.

'We march fast and hard,' Jack said. 'We stop for nobody and nothing. We ignore trouble and don't get involved.'

The men looked at him, bitter eyes in hard sun-browned faces, Enfields held casually in calloused hands, uniforms a dozen shades of khaki and bayonets, buttons and all things metal browned to ensure they didn't reflect the sun.

'Bring double water bottles.' Jack had requisitioned a camel and loaded the panniers with *mussocks* – leather water bags – and ammunition. 'You look after the water,' he told the uncomprehending driver, 'and don't let me down.'

'Batoor,' Jack said, 'you watch this fellow. If he tries to run or does anything except what I tell him, you cut his throat.'

Batoor grinned and touched the Khyber knife with which he had replaced his tulwar. 'Yes, Captain Windrush.'

'We'll need transport on the return.' Riley sounded surly, unhappy to lose his prize.

I will have to watch him, and Logan. Logan lived by loyalty to the regiment and to his friends, of which Riley was the foremost. If Riley decided that Jack's throat should be cut, Logan would wield the blade – not out of any dislike of Jack, but through loyalty to Riley.

'We'll deal with that when we need it.' Jack decided he'd come too far to have scruples. If he needed more transport than one camel, he would find it, somehow.

When Jack had lived in his bungalow in the Gondabad cantonment, back in the far-off days of peace, there had been measures to cope with the hot season. The servants had placed hurdles of dried straw – *khas-khas tatties* – against the verandah and the open doors and had thrown water on the straw. This procedure cooled the air that entered the house, and incidentally, created a sickening smell of mildew. In common with other officers, Jack would sleep naked on his charpoy, with a mosquito net above and a table at his side complete with a brass bowl of water and a revolver. On some nights, he would sleep outdoors on the lawn, naked under his mosquito net.

Out here on the plains, he couldn't take such precautions, and from the moment the sun cracked over the horizon, the heat was intolerable and the glare so intense, it was impossible to move with eyes fully open.

'Keep moving!' Jack pushed the 113th on, following the road, with the heat rising from the ground beneath, burning the soles of their feet and coming up the legs of their trousers in unbelievable waves. The hot-weather birds were calling, with koels and brain fever birds, the latter with a rising call that ended in an irregular high pitch. 'I don't mind these birds so much,' Coleman said. 'It's the tin-pot bird that I hate. It goes hammer-hammer-hammer all the bloody time. Hammer-hammer-bloody-hammer.'

'We should shoot the bugger,' Thorpe said. 'It'll be working for the pandies.'

'If it was only one, I wouldn't mind,' Coleman said, 'but they're everywhere.'

'It's only a bird,' Armstrong said.

They marched on, avoiding settlements wherever possible, covering the ground twice as fast as Havelock's column had managed. Jack drove them hard, knowing their capabilities as well as their weaknesses. He posted sentries when they halted and ignored the terrifying howling of jackals. Twice they heard outbreaks of distant shooting, and each time Jack altered direction to avoid the trouble.

'We're British soldiers,' Logan said. 'We should go and see what's happening.'

'We've more important things to do,' Riley told him. 'Like giving away our treasure.'

Jack inched closer to the two men, trying to hear their conversation and gauge Riley's intentions. Logan saw him, grunted something to Riley and they marched in silence except for the monotonous drumbeat of boots on the pukka road.

'These jackals are like banshees,' Mahoney said. 'But quieter.'

'Have you ever heard a banshee?' MacKinnon asked. 'I mean a real one, back in Ireland?'

'No,' Mahoney said. 'I never have. I heard the old people talking about them though.'

MacKinnon nodded slowly. 'We don't have them in Skye,' he said. 'We have other things, especially up in the Cuillin Mountains.'

Mahoney looked over to MacKinnon. 'I've heard of Skye. It's a weird place for those with the power to understand.' He waited for a second as their boots hammered on the ground. 'You've got the power, haven't you?'

Jack moved fractionally closer, wondering what MacKinnon's answer might be until O'Neill interrupted the conversation.

'Sir!' O'Neill pointed north. They were on a track in a level plain, with small *topes* of trees and wide areas of grassland. 'Something is moving out there.'

Jack levelled his binoculars. 'The grass is certainly moving,' he said.

'Rebels? Dacoits?' O'Neill ran a hand along the barrel of his rifle.

'Something's coming this way,' Jack said. 'And it's coming fast.' He raised his voice. 'Form square lads! There's something or someone coming from the north.'

'There are only eleven of us,' Armstrong said. 'How can we form a square?'

'Follow orders, you grousing bastard!' O'Neill shoved him into place.

'Here it comes,' O'Neill said as the grass parted.

'It's only a dog!' Thorpe said. 'A little mangy dog.'

'Shoot it,' Jack ordered. 'Open fire!'

Veteran soldiers who had fought in a dozen battles and could un-caringly shoot at Burmese or mutineers or Russians, hesitated when ordered to fire at an animal. 'It's only a dog,' MacKinnon said.

As O'Neill lifted his Enfield to fire, Logan shifted sideways and nudged his elbow, sending the sergeant's shot wide.

'Oh, sorry, Sergeant!' Logan said.

'You bloody idiot!' Jack grabbed Logan's rifle, shoved him aside and aimed. The dog was running toward them, its mouth open and its course undeviating. Jack kept the dog in his sights, took a deep breath and let it out slowly. He measured the distance, waiting until he knew he could not miss. A bead of sweat formed on his right eyebrow, hov-ered for a second and dropped. Jack squeezed the trigger.

The dog jerked backwards as the bullet made contact. Its head ex-ploded in a shower of blood and bones.

'You've killed it!' Logan said.

Jack handed back the rifle. 'That dog could have killed at least one of us.'

'It was only a dog.' Logan automatically reloaded his rifle.

'Running like that, it was rabid,' Jack said. 'It only had to lick one of us to give us rabies. Have you ever thought about rabies, Logan?'

'No, sir.'

'You'll go mad, Logan, and froth at the mouth. You'll be scared of water, and you'll howl. You've heard the jackals howling at night. You'll sound the same, before you convulse and bend backwards until you break your spine and die.'

'Yes, sir.'

'And the next time you disobey my order or disrupt my sergeant when he's about to shoot, I won't save your life, Logan. I'll leave you for a rabid dog, or Sergeant O'Neill – whichever is most dangerous.'

'That would be me, Logan. That would be me,' O'Neill said quietly. 'When we get back to camp, I will deal with you.'

'Yes, sergeant. I thought—'

'You thought?' O'Neill shook his head. 'You're a soldier, Logan; you're paid to fight, not to think!'

They smelled the village an hour before dawn and came to it within fifteen minutes. The first body sprawled on the road, a woman lying on her back, legs and arms splayed out.

'Somebody's outraged that woman,' Riley said, as Logan used a more obscene expression and added what he would do to the men responsible.

The second body was a plump matron who must have been in her forties. She lay under a tree, naked and mutilated.

'Bastards,' Thorpe said. 'What had that woman ever done to hurt anybody? She's probably somebody's ma.'

'Maybe hers.' Coleman pointed to the body of a small child, who lay huddled beside a burned out hut.

'What're they killing babies for?' Thorpe asked. 'What harm can a little baby do to anybody? These rebels aren't human!'

'Sergeant,' MacKinnon said. 'Somebody's watching us.'

'Don't look in his direction, MacKinnon,' O'Neill said. 'Where is he?'

'I don't know,' MacKinnon said. 'I can feel it.'

'All right, son, keep moving and tell me as much as you can.' O'Neill slipped his finger onto the trigger of his rifle. He raised his voice slightly. 'Keep alert men; we're not alone here.'

'Probably another bloody dog,' Logan said.

'Probably another bloody dog,' Thorpe repeated. 'One with scabies.'

'Rabies,' Coleman corrected.

'Same thing,' Thorpe said. 'Except scabies is *worse* than rabies.'

They walked on, eyes mobile and the rear guard walking backwards, watching every ruined house in the village, checking every crumpled body to ensure it was dead and not waiting to pounce on them.

'Sergeant!' MacKinnon hissed. 'Something's wrong.'

'I can see that, MacKinnon. All the people are dead.'

'It's coming! Something's coming!' MacKinnon lifted his rifle.

'Halt!' Jack gave the order out of instinct a second before the house exploded. Flames and smoke rose ten yards in front of them, with pieces of blazing thatch and fragments of wood rising high, to fall on them in a burning shower. The patrol scattered, with some diving to the ground and others running for shelter. Batoor pulled the camel away from the danger.

'It's an ambush!' Jack said as a rush of people came from the abandoned houses. Deafened by the sound, Jack could hear nothing as a mob attacked them. Perhaps thirty men with swords, spears, sticks and unwieldy agricultural implements charged from all around, mouths open in yells that Jack couldn't hear. Drawing his revolver, he fired into the mass, shouting orders as his veterans met the attackers with bullet, bayonet and rifle butt.

Although the British were outnumbered, they were veterans of battle and brawls, trained soldiers, while the attackers were not. After just a few moments, it was evident that the fight was one-sided. The 113th hacked down all who opposed them and stood, panting, as the remainder of the enemy turned and fled, dropping their weapons in panic.

'What was that all about?' Logan cleaned his bayonet on the loincloth of a man he had killed. 'They lads were not even soldiers.'

'No, 'Jack agreed. 'They were villagers. They must have thought we were the men who killed their women and children.'

'Maybe so, sir,' O'Neill said. 'Either that, or they don't like the British. Anyway, they got that gunpowder from somewhere. Ordinary villagers don't have explosions. This country is a mess.'

They moved on, leaving the village behind them. 'That noise will have woken up half the countryside,' Jack said. 'We'll find a safe spot to hide up for a few hours and move through the night.'

'Is anywhere safe in this cursed country?' O'Neill asked.

'Some of the natives must think that we are the curse,' Jack said softly. That thought remained with him for the remainder of their journey. Perhaps if the British left India, peace would return.

Chapter Seventeen

The River Goomtee flowed turgid and brown between parched banks, with many of the surrounding buildings still in ruins from the previous year's siege. Women washed clothes and gossiped while children laughed and played in the water.

Jack shivered, remembering the terrible days of Havelock's relief and the evacuation. Not far from here, he had acknowledged his mother, and over there – he altered his angle of vision – she had died at the hands of a Pathan. He glanced at Batoor and wondered anew at his loyalty. He had so many memories of Lucknow, good and bad, for Mary was also here, in his mind.

'Are you all right, sir?' O'Neill asked.

'Yes, sergeant.' Jack concentrated on the task at hand. 'Well, Riley, this is where you lead the pack. You know where this treasure wagon is hidden.'

Riley glanced at Logan. 'I know where somebody hid a wagon last year, sir,' he said slowly. 'They may have returned for it since then.'

'Let's hope not,' Jack said and hummed the first few bars of Chopin's *Funeral March.*

'We'll look for it, sir,' Riley said.

'I'm sure you'll remember where to find it.' Jack glanced along the riverbank. 'Perhaps a good place to start would be where you chose to go swimming a few weeks ago.'

'Yes, sir.' Riley sounded frustrated. 'That might be a good place to start.'

'Sergeant O'Neill will make sure you don't get lost,' Jack said. 'And in case you're worried about Charlotte, she is very well.'

'Thank you, sir.' Riley saluted.

Jack posted four sentries along the banks of the river and sent all the others into the river with Riley.

'I believe that the wagon was submerged around here.' Riley looked around, searching for any familiar landmarks. 'It was a bit hectic at the time, what with the pandies attacking and General Campbell trying to get everybody out safely.'

'I remember,' Jack said.

'Over here.' Logan pointed to a tree that overhung the riverbank. 'I remember that crooked tree. Somebody had hanged a pandy from it, and he was swinging back and forward.'

'We'll work at night,' Jack decided. 'If we search through the day, we'll attract too much attention.' He was breaking every rule in the book. *By rights, I should contact my superior officer, Colonel Hook, wherever he may be, or Sir Colin Campbell.* By making this decision to search for and hand over a treasure wagon that by rights belonged to the East India Company, Jack knew he was far exceeding his authority. The Army could cashier him, or charge him with theft. On the other hand, if he waited for orders, Jayanti might execute her prisoners. It was a choice between his career and the life of an unknown number of soldiers of the 113th.

Most of the outskirts of that part of Lucknow were in ruins, with a gaggle of refugees huddling in whatever shelter they could find. Jack found a battered house within a walled garden, posted sentries at the only gate and settled his men in until dusk. Used to the tedium of army life, the men accepted their lot without demur, while Jack fought his frustration at the inactivity and led them back to the riverside as soon as the light faded.

'How did you come to find the treasure in the first place, Riley?'

'The last wagon in the column broke a wheel,' Riley said. 'The driver ran away, and a couple of men drove it into the river to hide it.'

'You and Logan would be the two men.' Jack smiled when Riley shrugged. 'It's all right, Riley. Carry on with your story.'

'The wagon was in a bad state, sir,' Riley said. 'It might have broken up in the river.'

'If that happened, the current would take the contents downstream,' Jack said. 'Whatever was inside could be anywhere, miles away.'

'Maybe, sir,' Riley knew more about treasure than Jack ever would. 'The river would take away the wood and any documents, any light stuff. It was last November, sir, after last year's rains, and this year's rains are not due for a couple of months yet.'

'I am aware of the seasons, Riley,' Jack said.

'Yes, sir. I mean that the current is not strong enough to shift anything heavy, or not far. If we look downstream from where these men – whoever they were – left the wagon, we should find at least some of the golden or silver items.'

Jack hid his smile. 'Can you remember where these mysterious men left the wagon?'

'Opposite that tree, sir,' Riley said. 'Logie and I were watching them and wondering what they were doing.'

'Yes, sir,' Logan added. 'We thought they looked a right pair of blackguards, sir, and wondered if we should tell you.'

'I'm sure you considered that, Logan.'

Jack spread the men downstream from the tree, with orders to scour the bed of the river and hand him anything they found. He sat on the bank and prepared to supervise. A lot had happened since he had been last in Lucknow. He had met his grandfather and played chess with Jayanti. He had also made love to Mary. Jack smiled at the memory. Now life had moved on again, and he was back in this city of palaces, watching his men wade in the river.

There was something surreal about this task, with eight men splashing about in an Indian river by the light of a sickle moon, dipping and cursing as they searched for a Rajah's treasure. Jack grunted; he hadn't expected to do this when he accepted the Queen's commission. The life of an officer in the British Army was full of variety and interest, although he could never tell his grandchildren about this particular experience.

'I've found something.' Mahoney held up a glittering object.

'Bring it here.' Jack stepped into the river.

It was a small golden cup with a single band of rubies. 'Well done, Mahoney.' That cup would be worth more money than Mahoney would pocket in ten years. Jack placed it in the canvas sack he'd brought. It was a start. 'Keep looking, lads, Mahoney's cup might be the first.' Alternatively, the Sikhs could have found everything months ago. Jack gave a rueful smile; the Sikhs were reputed to be the most expert looters in India.

As dawn lightened the horizon, he called in the men and checked what they had brought him. Among the assorted rubbish he collected was one human skull, a few miscellaneous bones and a silver coin with Arabic script.

'Well done lads,' Jack said when his men straggled ashore, dripping wet and slightly furtive. 'Now strip.'

They stared at him. 'What?'

'Strip,' Jack repeated. 'Why so shy, boys? I've seen you unclad before.' He raised his voice slightly. 'Shall I ask the sergeant to help you?'

Slowly, one-by-one, they began to take off their sodden uniforms, with Jack searching each piece of clothing and removing the items he found. Within minutes, he had a sizeable collection of golden artefacts, pieces of jewellery and coins.

'Good hunting, lads.' Jack bundled his treasure into a sack. 'We'll do the same tomorrow night and onward until we have sufficient treasure to free our colleagues.' He felt their eyes on him, the suspicious, predatory, bright eyes of some of the most desperate soldiers in the world. These were his men, yet he would not sleep easy until he had handed the treasure over. As Colonel Hook had said, the love of money, as well as power, was the root of all evil.

'Sergeant O'Neill,' Jack said. 'I want this treasure guarded. Its presence is a great temptation to some of the men. Batoor will help you.'

'The Pathan? They're the greatest thieves in the East!'

'Set a thief to catch a thief,' Jack said. 'Besides, he has eaten my salt.' He was aware that Batoor was listening and knew he need say no more.

Jack joined the men in the water on the second night, probing further down river and finding an elegant brass chest adorned with emeralds, and a jewelled knife scabbard that must have been worth a small fortune. On the third night, Riley handed over an ivory chess set.

'Thank you,' Jack said. The set with its exotic pieces brought back memories of his deadly game with Jayanti. It was a reminder why he was here.

'Keep working lads,' Jack encouraged. 'We have lives to save.' He drove them harder after that, starting earlier, keeping them longer in the water and taking more risks of discovery. He set Batoor as a permanent guard of their haul, with the Pathan sleeping on top of the treasure by night and remaining in their base house through the stupefying heat of the day.

When any locals came too close, Jack had Armstrong or Logan scare them away, and on the only occasion that a British picket looked curiously at these men in the river, Jack pulled rank on the sergeant in charge. With so many of the British garrison engaged in chasing after the remaining rebels in Oudh, the Central Provinces and Rohilkhand, there were insufficient soldiers to spare in Lucknow, to investigate his small party.

Twice MacKinnon reported that something was wrong. Each time Jack sent him out with Coleman and Thorpe to scout the surrounding area, and they returned without incident.

'It's just the general tension, MacKinnon,' Jack said. 'We'll only be one more day.'

The one more day stretched into two, and then three, and although Jack's store of Lucknow's royal wealth mounted, it was not sufficient to bribe a rajah. Every day at least one of the men would approach him with the suggestion that they could divide the loot between them and desert en masse. Each time Jack thanked the man for his idea and ordered him back to work. Such a reaction was inevitable when a collection of desperadoes such as the 113th collected treasure.

At the back of Jack's mind was the worry that the men might decide to slit his throat and run with the loot. Despite their valour in battle, the men of the 113th were still the dregs of the British Army. Jack slept with his revolver to hand and his sword loose in the scabbard.

'Sir!' Thorpe held up his hand as if he were a schoolboy. 'I've found something.'

'Well bring it over, Thorpe,' Jack kept his patience – Thorpe was doing his best.

'I can't, sir. It's too big.'

Jack splashed through the river. 'What do you have, Thorpe?' He grunted as he stubbed his toe on something hard and delved into the water. His hands encountered a wooden frame, and then something circular.

A wheel. Thorpe had found the remains of the wagon. He'd discovered the mother lode.

'They must have driven the wagon into a hole in the river bed, sir, and it's broke up.' Thorpe gave his opinion.

'Well done, Thorpe,' Jack said, raised his voice and gathered all the men together. 'Up here, men.'

Jack agreed with Thorpe's assessment. The thieves had driven the wagon into the river, aiming for the deep central area, but only quarter way across must have lurched into a hidden depth. *That was lucky for us.* After months in the river, the wooden body of the wagon had rotted, and it was the work of five minutes to tear a sizeable hole and reveal the contents. Jack organised the men, with the best swimmers diving under the surface to lift the booty and the others forming a human chain, handing the objects to one another until they reached the riverbank, where Jack took final delivery. The pile of golden objects and jewelled clothing, shining cups and strings of pearls and rubies grew by the minute.

Dawn was threatening before they finished, and the heap of treasure littered the bank.

'That will do,' Jack decided at last.

'There's more left, sir.' Thorpe had enjoyed looting the wagon.

'I'm sure there is, Thorpe. When you leave the Army, you can return here and take what remains.'

'No, sir,' Thorpe said. 'I would never do that. It's stealing sir.'

This was a new side to Thorpe. 'Well said, Thorpe.'

'You go to Hell for stealing, sir,' Thorpe informed him.

They carried the loot to their base in relays, with Jack leaving honest Private Thorpe in charge of the collection at the riverside. 'If anybody tries to take anything, Thorpe, shoot him. Whoever it is.'

'Yes, sir,' Thorpe said and happily pointed his rifle at Armstrong.

'Not one of us, Thorpey,' Coleman pushed the rifle barrel aside. 'Captain Windrush didn't mean that.'

'I was only jesting,' Thorpe said.

Jack wasn't sure. He should know by now to ensure his orders were explicit for men such as Thorpe. Armstrong didn't seem amused at the joke either.

'That's us,' Jack said when the last of the treasure was deposited inside their base house. 'Now we have to get this to Gondabad.'

'We have one camel,' Riley said. 'We'll need at least six, or a wagon.'

'No wagon,' Jack decided. 'They move too slowly, and we won't be on pukka roads most of the time. We'll use camels.'

'Where the hell will we find camels?'

'Batoor.' Jack tossed over half a dozen gold mohurs from the pile on the floor. 'You're the expert. Take our camel driver and find us half a dozen camels. Don't get caught, and if you cut anybody's throat, make sure he's not important.'

'Yes, Captain Windrush.' Batoor gave a mock salaam.

'Now we prepare and wait for Batoor,' Jack said. The fate of the British captives in Gondabad and the possible allegiance of the Rajah of that city depended on the loyalty of a Pathan who had lately fought against them. For some reason he couldn't understand, the thought made Jack smile.

Even inside the thick walls of the house, the heat was intense. The men of the 113th lay there, sweltering, aware that their future would be one of poverty and danger despite the king's ransom that lay at their feet. Jack leaned against the wall with his hand never far from the butt of his revolver. He hated himself for distrusting his men after all they'd been through together.

'Something's not right,' Mackinnon said. 'I feel it.'

'*You're* not bloody right,' O'Neill growled, 'and you'll feel my boot up your arse unless you shut your mouth.'

Flies buzzed around them, seeking sweat. The men swatted ineffectually.

'I hope Batoor isn't long,' Coleman said.

'He'll be as long as it takes,' O'Neill said. 'You go to the window and keep watch.'

'What am I watching for?'

'Anything that could be suspicious, Coleman. You heard MacKinnon; something's not right.'

'Why not send Mac, then?' Coleman asked.

'Because I sent you.'

'Get the loot into sections.' Jack gave the men work to reduce the tedium of waiting. 'We better be ready to load up when Batoor arrives.'

Jack let the day's routine continue, wondering if he was right to trust Batoor. It would be easy for the Pathan to whistle up a dozen unscrupulous rogues in Lucknow, descend on his small party at night and slaughter them for the treasure.

'Sir.' Coleman's voice awoke him from a heat-induced doze. 'Somebody's coming.'

'Stand to,' Jack said quietly. He'd convinced himself that Batoor would betray them and now expected nothing else. 'Load and cap, have your bayonets ready.'

'It's Batoor,' Coleman said.

Here we go. Jack unbuttoned his revolver.

'He's brought camels,' Coleman said, 'and some camel drivers.'

'Anybody else?' Jack asked.

'No, sir.'

Jack breathed out in relief and fastened the button of his holster. His initial faith in Batoor had been justified.

* * *

They moved out an hour after sunset, with flitting clouds reflecting the blossoming light of the moon.

'Sergeant.' Jack called O'Neill over. 'Keep alert.'

'Yes, sir.' O'Neill put just enough emphasis on the phrase to inform Jack he didn't need an officer to instruct him in the obvious.

'Watch Riley and Logan,' Jack kept his voice low. 'I wouldn't be surprised if they decided to slip away with a camel load of loot.'

'Aye, sir.' O'Neill nodded. 'I had thought that as well, although it's Armstrong that's been wandering recently.'

'Armstrong?'

'Yes, sir,' O'Neill said. 'Twice this week he's left the house to go into Lucknow.'

'I'm sure you can handle him, sergeant. In the meantime, take care of Logan and Riley.'

O'Neill raised his hand. 'Can you hear that tinkling? That's camel bells. I made sure each driver has them. It will make us more audible, but the locals know the sound anyway. If I hear bells from anywhere except in our convoy, I'll know somebody's running off with them.'

'Good man, sergeant.'

Leaving Lucknow behind, they headed into the darkness, with Jack watching for trouble from his men as much as from an enemy. The camels walked in single file, not hurrying but covering the ground at a steady pace and easing over the road with no apparent effort. The men marched alongside the camels; rifles slung over shoulders, hats pulled low and boots kicking up dust. Jack checked each man, trying to gauge his mood. Thorpe and Coleman marched side by side, not speaking much but as relaxed as veteran soldiers should be. MacKinnon and his rear rank man, Mahoney, were slouching a little, while Armstrong and Whitelam were a little apart. Jack turned his attention to Logan and Riley.

Riley remained very close to the rearmost camel, nearly touching the driver, while Logan looked wary, turning to look behind him every few steps. *What are you waiting for, Logan?*

The quarter moon revealed the road stretching ahead across the plains. Even in the night, sweat soaked through Jack's uniform tunic, forming beads on his eyebrows and easing down his face. He felt as if he had been journeying across India for years, marching through the hot darkness, worrying about his men, waiting for the sudden ambush, listening for the cry of "*Din, din!*" or "*Allah Akbar!*" or the crisp orders of the British-trained mutineers.

As they approached a grove of palm trees, something rustled above Jack's head, a night hunting bird or a bat perhaps. He quickened his pace. He must have passed a hundred such *topes* in the past few weeks, with each one a possible site for an ambush. Hurrying to the front of the convoy, he stepped beside MacKinnon.

'Is everything all right, here?'

'Yes, sir,' Mahoney answered at once.

'I'm not sure, sir.' MacKinnon was eyeing the palm trees. 'I've got that queer feeling again.'

'So have I, Mackinnon,' Jack said. 'Careful now, lads.'

The column speeded up, with Jack watching until the last camel passed the *tope*. Palm fronds hissed slightly in the oven-hot breeze, with a host of insects descending on the marching men and lizards watching them through stony eyes. There was no ambush, and Jack breathed his relief as they moved on over a featureless plain.

'My camel's lame, sir,' Armstrong shouted. 'The brute's limping.'

There is always something. Jack hurried over, shouting for Batoor to join him.

'Here, sir.' Armstrong pointed to the camel's front left leg. 'He must have injured it somehow.'

'Let me see,' Jack knelt beside the camel. 'I can't see anything.' He sensed movement and shifted sideways. Armstrong's blow crashed into his shoulder rather than the back of his head. Even so, the force was sufficient to knock him face-down into the dust as Armstrong fired his rifle.

That shot was a signal for a high-pitched yell as a mass of men rose from hiding in the surrounding grass and rushed onto the convoy.

'Fire!' O'Neill took command. 'Shoot the buggers flat!'

Jack tried to rise, staggered and fell again when Armstrong smashed him a second time with the butt of his rifle. He heard the irregular crackle of musketry as his men fired, then the patter of many feet on the ground and the calling of camels.

Logan's voice shouted, 'Would ye, you dirty bastard?' and then came the hammer of hooves.

'Fight them,' Jack shouted. He rose again, dazed, and pulled his revolver from its holster.

In the few moments that he'd been on the ground, the raid had finished. Only one camel remained, with Thorpe holding grimly onto the reins. Mahoney was thrashing on the ground, cursing as he clutched the gaping wound in his chest, and Riley lay still.

'Roll call!' Jack shouted. 'O'Neill, is everybody accounted for?' Still dizzy from the blow to his head, Jack peered around him.

'No, sir.' O'Neill was wiping blood from the blade of his bayonet. 'Mahoney is wounded, sir, Riley is down, and Logan and Armstrong are missing, as well as five camels and their drivers.'

'Armstrong was part of whatever happened,' Jack said. 'He knocked me down and fired a signal shot.' *You warned me, O'Neill. You told me that Armstrong was wandering in Lucknow and MacKinnon knew something was wrong. I'm to blame. I have to make amends. Has Logan joined Armstrong?*

Jack knelt beside Mahoney. 'Let me see that wound.'

Mahoney shook his head, pressing his hand against his chest. His eyes were huge. 'No, sir.'

'Let me see!' Jack eased Mahoney's hand away. Blood seeped from a long if shallow, gash across Mahoney's chest. 'It's not bad,' he said. 'We'll soon have that sorted out.'

'Logan!' O'Neill's yell split the night. 'Where are you, Logan, you Sawney dwarf!'

'I'm here!' Logan emerged from the dark. 'I couldnae catch the murdering, treasonous bastard. How's Riley?'

Logan wasn't part of it. Only Armstrong, then.

'Dead,' O'Neill said at once.

Jack felt a delayed thrill of horror. He was used to death, to losing men by bullet or disease but Riley was one of his old soldiers, a man who had survived the worst the Crimea had to offer as well as the battles for Cawnpore and Lucknow. Jack and he had shared hardships and adventures in and around Sebastopol.

'No, he isnae,' Logan said at once. 'There isnae a pandy born that could kill Riley.' He knelt beside the body. 'Come on, Riley man, up ye get.'

Unable to help Logan and Riley, Jack said, 'Bring me light.' He examined Mahoney's wound by the beam of a bulls-eye lantern. 'I'm going to have to stitch that, Mahoney.'

'It'll be all right, sir,' Mahoney said.

'If I don't, you'll bleed to death,' Jack said. *And if I do, the wound will probably become infected, and you will die anyway.*

Jack blessed Mary for giving him an emergency medical kit as they removed Mahoney's shirt and laid him face up on a doolie.

'Who has some alcohol?' Jack asked. 'Something to help this lad?'

'I have sir.'

'Good lad, MacKinnon. Help him drink it and then take hold of him. Make sure he lies still.'

'I'll be all right, sir,' Mahoney said.

'I know you will, Mahoney,' Jack said. 'But it's best to be sure.'

Taking a deep breath, Jack began to stitch the wound together. He had no skill in such procedures so relied on the number of times he had seen army surgeons working with the wounded. Mahoney flinched under the initial prick of the needle and then lay as still as he could under Jack's cumbersome attention.

'I'm sorry,' Jack said as he probed too deep with the needle.

'It's all right, sir.' Mahoney's eyes were huge.

'There,' Jack said. 'That will do you, Mahoney. A fine scar to impress your girl.'

'Yes, sir.' White under his tan, Mahoney managed to raise a smile. 'Thank you, sir. You will have to leave me behind, sir. I'll slow you down.'

'No, Mahoney. We'll take you with us.' Jack had no illusions what would happen to a lone, wounded British soldier left alone in this part of India.

O'Neill had organised the men into a defensive perimeter. 'What happened sir?'

'Armstrong knocked me down and fired a shot as a signal to whoever attacked us.'

'The dirty bastard. Do you know who it was, sir?'

'No.' Jack shook his head. He had never liked Armstrong, but hadn't expected anything like this. He'd lost his treasure, lost a good man in Riley, and had another wounded.

'See?' Logan's harsh voice sounded again. 'I telt ye that Riley wasnae deid. Come on, Riles, up on your feet.'

'What was that?' Jack looked over.

'It's Riley, sir. I'm telling you, he's no deid.'

Jack stepped over. Riley lay on his side with ants already exploring the blood that pooled under him.

'Who gave you permission to lie down, Riley?' Jack asked. 'Get up! We've a job to do!'

Riley opened his eyes, closed them again and groaned. 'I think I'm dead, sir.'

'Nonsense.' Jack could feel Logan's relief. 'It's an offence for a man of the 113th to die on the road. Get better at once, and that's an order.' Jack saw amusement on O'Neill's face. 'And when you report for duty, Riley, get a haircut.'

'Yes, sir.' Riley held up a hand, and Logan helped him up. The cut on his head was already congealing.

'Wash that scratch and get a bandage on it, Riley.' It was all Jack could say. 'Are you able to walk?'

'Yes, sir,' Riley said.

'We'll need a doolie for Mahoney,' Jack said.

'Are we heading back to Gondabad, sir?' O'Neill asked.

'No,' Jack said. 'We're going to chase whoever took our treasure. Whitelam! You're our best *shikari*. Follow the spoor.'

'Yes, sir.' Whitelam accepted the order as calmly as he did everything else. 'It won't be hard, sir. Half a dozen camels and God knows how many men will leave a deep trail.'

'MacKinnon, Batoor, you two have the first stint at carrying Mahoney. Whitelam, you take the lead. O'Neill, you're rear guard. Logan, look after Riley.' Jack gave rapid orders. 'I am damned if we'll allow some rebels to attack us and get away with it. They won't get the better of the 113th, and we need that gold.'

Chapter Eighteen

Whitelam was correct. Even in darkness, the trail was easy to follow, with the camels having churned up the dry ground and left plenty other evidence of their passing.

'Sir,' Mahoney said. 'We'll slow you down. Leave Riley and me behind. We'll look after each other.'

Logan glared at Jack. 'I'm not leaving Riley behind.'

'Nor am I,' Jack assured him. However, he agreed that Mahoney had a point. Carrying a doolie and helping the injured Riley was slowing them down. 'O'Neill!'

'Sir.'

'Take Batoor and run ahead. Find our camels, find out how many men we're up against and report back to me.'

'Yes, sir,' O'Neill said.

With O'Neill's dust receding in the distance, Jack pushed on with the remainder of his party.

Within an hour, they found a village, shuddering under the relentless onslaught of the sun. 'Maybe this is where the badmashes came from.' Coleman readied his rifle.

'No,' Jack said. 'These are poor people; farmers, not warriors. Even if they got gold and jewels, they wouldn't know what to do with them.'

They stopped at the well, with the men drinking all they could and filling their water bottles. Jack tried his meagre Urdu on the staring villagers.

'*Ram ram*,' he said and indicated Mahoney on his doolie. 'Medicine man? Doctor?' He asked hopefully. The villagers stared at him, and he wondered if they had ever seen a white man before, let alone a whole patrol complete with rifles.

'Hey, Johnnie!' Logan decided to take a hand. 'We need a doctor. A medical man, right?' He pointed to Riley's head. 'My mate's hurt, see? And so is Mahoney.' He lifted Mahoney's tunic, so the wound was visible.

The villagers gathered around and called to one old woman, who limped forward and poked painfully at Mahoney's chest. Lifting her finger, she gestured toward the nearest of the huts.

'She wants us to go in there,' MacKinnon said.

'It could be an ambush.' Coleman was sceptical.

'It's not,' MacKinnon said. 'Come on Mahoney, and the old biddy will sort you out.' One of the more active of the villagers took hold of the rear of the doolie and helped MacKinnon into the hut.

'You lads stay here,' Jack ordered, 'keep in the shade and be careful. Coleman, take over out here. Let me know if anything happens.'

The inside of the hut was dark and surprisingly cool. Noticing that Jack had his hand on the butt of his revolver, the old woman shook her head angrily at him, the caste marks between her eyes seeming to dance as she wrinkled her forehead. Chattering at Jack, she pointed to the ground.

'Put Mahoney down there.' Jack tried to appear as if he was in charge of the situation. 'And bring in Riley. The old witch may as well look at him as well.'

'She might kill him,' Logan said.

'No.' MacKinnon shook his head. 'She will help.' He salaamed to the woman. '*Jai ram,*' he said, and spoke to her in Gaelic.

'*Jai ram, sahib.*' Another voice spoke from a gloomy corner of the hut, and an old man appeared, nearly toothless and with silver-white hair.

'And who are you, grandfather?' MacKinnon salaamed again.

'Naik Abhi Basu.' The old man slammed to attention and threw an impressive salute. '31st Bengal Native Infantry Regiment! Bhurtpore!'

'He's a bloody pandy!' Logan lifted his rifle.

'No, he's not!' MacKinnon stepped between Logan and the naik. 'He's a veteran. Did you not hear him?'

Jack breathed out and returned the salute. He hadn't realised he was nervous. 'At ease, Naik. I am Captain Jack Windrush of the 113th Foot. These are Privates MacKinnon and Logan, and the wounded are Privates Mahoney and Riley.'

Naik Basu's smile could not have been more extensive. While Logan lowered his rifle, MacKinnon held out his hand and greeted the naik in Gaelic. Within seconds, the two were talking like old friends, both in their native tongue and neither understanding a word the other was saying.

'This naik was at Bhurtpore with Lake back in 1805,' MacKinnon said at length.

'How the devil do you know that?' Jack asked.

'He told me,' MacKinnon said.

'You don't speak Urdu or Hindustani.' Jack shook his head.

'He still told me.' MacKinnon looked puzzled as if astonished that Jack hadn't followed the drift of the naik's words.

Jack nodded. 'I believe you. Can the old woman help Mahoney and Riley?'

'Oh, yes,' MacKinnon answered at once. 'She's a wise woman; she'll know what herbs and plants to use. She knows the *Unani* treatment, sir, that's normally Islamic, but it's spread to the Hindu areas. We could not have come to a better house. We can leave them here, sir, and they'll be safe,' MacKinnon said.

'We won't.' Jack hardened his voice. 'I'm not leaving any of my men in the middle of India.' He watched as the old woman fussed over his wounded. She examined their wounds with surprisingly gentle hands and then gave sharp orders that had half a dozen younger women running around the village finding herbs while the old naik boiled a copper pot over a small fire.

'You lie still, Riley,' Logan said. 'The old besom will sort you out.'

When O'Neill returned from his solo patrol, he was hot, dusty and exhausted. 'They've stopped for the day, sir,' he reported. 'About a hundred and twenty men and some women, with a few looking as if they know what they're doing and the rest only to make up the numbers.'

'Is Armstrong among them?'

'Yes, sir.' O'Neill touched the lock of his Enfield. 'I had him in my sights. He's with the leaders.'

'Right, Sergeant. Keep them under observation and report back.'

'Yes, sir.' O'Neill immediately turned around.

With both wounded stripped to the waist, the old woman created poultices from the gathered herbs.

'You take care of them, granny,' Logan said as MacKinnon helped the woman to apply the poultices. The woman gave MacKinnon instructions in Hindi, and he obeyed with an instinctive grasp of what she needed.

'How long will this take?' Jack asked.

'Not long, sir.' MacKinnon looked up from Mahoney's chest. 'I've seen old witchy-women like this before. They leave the herbs on for a day or a night, and it sucks out all the poison.'

Jack glanced outside. Time was precious. He wanted to recover the stolen treasure and get back to Gondabad before Jayanti executed her prisoners. He could ill-afford even a day, yet if he left these men unattended, they might well die.

'We can spare one day,' he said, hoping that was sufficient time for his men to recover. He glanced at the sun, thought of Mary back at the temple and wondered if the burden of command was prematurely turning his hair grey.

Would I have it any other way? No. Jack gave a rueful smile and stepped across to Riley. These were his men, and he would care for them every way he could. *I will wait until these men are fit, and then I will regain our treasure.*

Chapter Nineteen

'Sir,' O'Neill panted. 'They're still moving.'

They waited on the crest of the ridge with the trees baking around them, looking down at the convoy. The five camels swayed as they walked, with the escort a straggling crowd carrying more sticks and spears than firearms.

Jack frowned, embarrassed that this rabble had bested his professional soldiers. Lifting his binoculars, he scanned the mob until he found Armstrong, riding a small horse near the head. 'I see you, you back-stabbing bastard.'

'Is that Armstrong, sir?' O'Neill asked.

'Yes.' Jack passed over the binoculars.

'He's talking to somebody,' O'Neill said. 'I can't see who for the dust.'

'Nor can I.' Jack glanced over his men. 'We'll find out tomorrow when we get our loot back.'

O'Neill's chuckle contained little humour. 'How shall we do it, sir?'

Jack watched as Armstrong leaned closer to the man at his side. 'We'll do it the old way, O'Neill. We'll hit them as we hit the Plastun Cossacks in Crimea. We are the 113th, and we'll fight like the 113th.'

'Eight of us and two sick against one hundred and twenty bad-mashes,' O'Neill said. 'It'll be a massacre.'

'It will,' Jack said softly. 'And I want Armstrong taken alive. I want to know why he turned traitor and I want to see him hang.'

'It's either because of a woman, sir, or money.' O'Neil said,

'You could be right, Sergeant.' Jack took back the binoculars and tried to focus through the heat-haze. The camels seemed distended, as if they had legs thirty feet in length and extra-long necks. 'We'll take them tomorrow.'

They moved through the night, jogging across the plain with the air clear and the jackals howling like damned souls. They stopped twice for water and overtook the convoy at half-a-mile distance as they searched for a suitable ambush spot. Nobody spoke. Nobody wasted breath, and nobody complained. They might be British soldiers, but they were also the 113th Foot, despised by everybody and with perverse pride that pushed them past the borders of endurance.

'Here.' Drenched with sweat and with his chest heaving to drag oxygen from the blistering air, Jack halted.

'There's nothing here.' O'Neill glanced around the featureless landscape. They stood on a bare plain that stretched as far as they could see, with only small copses of trees to break the monotony.

'That's the idea,' Jack said. 'When we march, we expect an ambush at every wood, village or bridge. We are more relaxed in this kind of country. Armstrong's badmashes will be the same.'

'Yes, sir.' O'Neill looked doubtful.

'Thorpe, I want you and Coleman to gather dry wood, grass, anything that can burn.'

'Are we making a fire, sir?' Thorpe looked eager. Before he joined the army, Thorpe's arsonist tendencies had brought him trouble with the law.

'You are, Thorpe. I want a broad stretch of dry wood, tinder, anything that burns, across the road and along that side, opposite us. Don't make it high, so the badmashes won't wonder what it is. I want it deep, tangled and hard to cross. In this climate, it shouldn't take you long.'

When Thorpe hurried away, giving instructions to Coleman how best to gather combustible material, Jack spoke to the remainder of his men.

'Right lads, dig rifle pits, deep enough to lie in, shallow enough so you can watch the road. Look out for snakes and scorpions and other creeping nasties.'

Tired and hot, the men struggled to make an impression on the sun-hard ground until Logan laughed. 'Come on, boys; remember digging on Inkerman Ridge when we shovelled frozen rocks and corpses under Russian artillery fire. This dirt is nothing compared to that.'

Jack hid his smile. It was unlike Logan to cheer anybody up.

Scraping out holes in the ground, they used some of the earth to form a slight ridge in front of them and the remainder they sprinkled over their prone bodies.

'Good.' Jack inspected them from a distance. 'I can't see you until I reach this point.' He thrust a stick into the ground. 'So as soon as the enemy reach this, we open fire. Who's the best with camels here?'

'Batoor,' O'Neill said at once.

'Batoor,' Jack called over the Pathan. 'I want you three hundred paces over there,' he pointed in the opposite direction to the dried kindling.

'Yes, Captain Windrush.' Batoor looked uncertain as he stepped the distance.

Jack nodded. 'Good. Now we wait.'

Lying prone proved a tougher ordeal than Jack had expected. The sun hammered their backs and legs, burning through the worn material of their uniforms. 'Stick it, men,' he said. 'We're the 113th.'

'Stick it, men,' Thorpe repeated. 'We're the 113th.'

As the sun rose, the heat increased, turning rifle-barrels to heated tubes and raising blisters on any exposed flesh.

'Bloody India,' Logan said. 'This is all Armstrong's fault.'

'Here they come,' Whitelam murmured at last, and Jack felt the tremble of the ground. He took a deep breath as the familiar sensations of fear and excitement danced somersaults in his stomach. He had heard that a man only had a certain amount of luck and when he had used that up, death was almost certain. So far, luck had been with him. He'd fought in battles where thousands had formed up on either side and in skirmishes of a few dozens and had escaped with only minor injuries. He knew that someday, perhaps today, he would finish his store of luck and a bullet or bomb would end his career and his life. Worse, he could be maimed, to exist as a crippled wreck for the remainder of his life. *Please God for a quick death, a soldier's death rather than that lingering hopelessness.*

The enemy convoy was thirty yards from the marking stick, a ragged mass surrounding the treasure camels. Jack searched for Armstrong.

'Ready, boys,' O'Neill's low voice carried along the British line.

Jack unfastened the flap of his holster. The steel of his revolver was hot enough to burn his hand. He wrapped his fingers around the butt, feeling the wood slippery with his sweat.

Twenty-five yards to the marking stick. The enemy straggled across both sides of the road rather than marching in military precision. Jack cursed; that made his job more difficult. He still couldn't see Armstrong among the mass.

Twenty yards now, with the mob seething toward the marking stick, talking, some singing and all pleased with themselves. Jack readied his revolver, feeling the excitement mount.

A group of the enemy surged forward, past the marking stick. One hauled it from the ground and waved it around his head, shouting.

'Sir?' O'Neill's whisper carried through the air.

'Now!' Jack yelled. 'Fire! 113th, Fire and keep firing!'

The rifles cracked out, seemingly few against the mass of enemy. At the first volley, there were screams and yells, and men began to fall, dead or wounded. A few ran toward the rifles, most cowered away or turned and fled. Jack watched the camels, guessing that Armstrong would be with his prize.

'Thorpe!' Jack yelled. 'Do your stuff!'

He saw Thorpe emerge from the cover of his trench and scrape a Lucifer.

'Come on Thorpe!'

'My matches are damp with sweat, sir!'

Swearing, Jack watched as some of the enemy ran past the kindling and into the plain beyond. Rising from his trench, he pulled a packet of Lucifers from his pocket and threw them over to Thorpe. 'Try these!'

'Thank you, sir!' Thorpe waved, struck a match and applied it to the kindling. A flame flickered, wavered nearly colourless and blossomed. 'That's it, sir.' Ignoring the enemy horde, Thorpe watched the flame spread until the kindling was ablaze in near smokeless fury. 'Isn't that beautiful?'

'Get down, you bloody fool!' Leaping forward, Jack dragged Thorpe down as enemy shots whistled around. They lay side by side on the hot ground, watching in horror as burning men screamed and writhed.

'Oh, dear God, what have I done?' Jack stared, unable to look away as man after man caught fire and ran, howling, in a blaze of flames. A woman screamed terribly as her hair exploded in a fiery ball.

Jack felt sick.

'The camels, sir!' O'Neill shouted.

Longer-legged than the men, the camels, had turned at the first whiff of smoke and loped in the opposite direction to the fire, bearing their helpless drivers with them.

'Leave them,' Jack trusted to Batoor to round up the fleeing animals. 'Concentrate on the enemy.'

With their retreat blocked by the flames, the surviving enemy re-alised they had no choice but to fight. They stood and fired, or gathered in small clumps preparing to charge, and the 113th shot them down like targets at a fairground.

'Keep firing!' Jack searched for Armstrong. 'Leave Armstrong alive!'

Jack flinched when something hissed past his head. Another bullet raised a fountain of dust at his feet. 'Somebody's aiming at me,' he said and rolled sideways for a better look. 'Is that you, Armstrong?'

A random gust of furnace-hot wind cleared the smoke, and Jack saw Armstrong with his Enfield in his hands, staring at him.

'Surrender, Armstrong, and I'll ensure you have a fair trial.'

Armstrong said nothing as he hurriedly reloaded his rifle, with his gaze never straying from Jack's face.

Somebody shouted, the sound high pitched and despite their losses and the hideous screams from the burning men, the enemy began to rally. Jack aimed his revolver at Armstrong, reluctant to shoot one of his 113th. 'Put the rifle down, Armstrong.'

'I have him covered, sir,' Logan said. 'Say the word, and I'll blow the bastard's heid right off.'

Jack shook his head. 'Not yet, Logan.'

As Armstrong lifted his rifle, the enemy charged. The mob covered the ground at an astonishing speed, screaming as they waved tulwars and spears, knives and iron-tipped staffs.

The 113th met them with a rolling volley that felled the leading half dozen and then it was down to the bayonet, boot and rifle butt. The enemy was brave, tough and hardy but they faced veteran professional soldiers whose business was fighting. Jack emptied his revolver, dropped it and drew his sword. The slither of steel from its scabbard thrilled him, perhaps with an inherited folk memory or some half-hidden desire to test himself blade-to-blade.

For a moment, the press of bodies concealed Armstrong. Jack stepped forward and thrust at the leading man, who dodged and ran on. Jack had a glimpse of the black turban and partial face-veil of one of Jayanti's warriors. As Jack hesitated, firelight flickered on the ruby ring on her left hand.

'You!' Jack shouted and rushed towards her. 'You murdering witch.' He slashed at a loin-clothed peasant who swung a staff at him, barged the man aside and squared up to the black-turbaned woman.

For a moment, they glared at each other until Batoor roared up behind Jack, slicing his Khyber knife into a luckless spearman. He shouted in Pushtu at the black-turbaned warrior and thrust with his blade. The warrior parried without seeming effort, and for a minute they fenced, slashing, thrusting and parrying with speed and skill that Jack could only admire. Only when the 113th rushed forward did Black-turban vanish, leaving Batoor panting.

'I ordered you to catch the camels, Batoor, not get mixed up in the fighting.'

'The camels are safe, Captain Windrush, and that woman would have killed you. Would you have me stand and watch when you die?' Batoor sounded amused.

'Where are the camels?'

'Knee haltered, sir,' O'Neill gasped. Sweat dripped down his face.

'I see.' Jack glanced over his shoulder to see six camels standing together. He swallowed his pride. 'Thank you, Batoor.'

'He's dead, sir,' O'Neill said.

'Who?' Jack's mind was on the warrior with the ruby ring.

'Armstrong, sir.'

Jack swore. 'A pity. I would have liked to question him.'

'That woman killed him,' O'Neill nodded to Armstrong's body, crumpled between two near-naked men on the plain with his face twisted in agony. Black-turban had emasculated him. 'There's something in his mouth.'

Jack prised open Armstrong's jaw and removed the crumpled sheet of paper.

British soldiers, why fight for a shilling a day when you can earn twenty times that amount fighting for a better cause? Why fight for the shareholders of the Honourable East India Company when you can fight for yourselves and have beautiful Indian woman as your companions?

All you have to do is walk away and join us. Welcome bhaiya! Welcome, brother!

'So much for brotherhood,' Jack said. 'Armstrong must have kept this note and contacted the enemy.'

'Yes, sir,' O'Neill said. 'I did report that he went missing a couple of times when we were in Lucknow.'

'Indeed you did,' Jack agreed. *And I did nothing about it.*

'These black-turbaned women use people and kill people, Captain Windrush,' Batoor said. 'Once Armstrong told them about the treasure he would not be of any further use.'

'Do you know the woman?' Jack cleaned blood from his sword. 'Do you know the woman who wears the ruby ring?'

Batoor looked away. 'We have met.' His voice was lower than normal, and Jack wondered if he was witnessing the real Batoor. 'And I also know Jayanti. Jayanti killed my wife and my son. I will hunt her.' He kissed the bloodied blade of his Khyber knife in a dramatic gesture. 'And I will kill her.'

'Why did she do that?' Jack was curious.

Batoor sheathed his knife. 'Who knows the workings of a woman's mind?'

He's not going to tell me anything more.

'The woman with the ring mutilated a young friend of mine,' Jack said. 'I want her dead.'

'Then we both follow *Pashtunwali*,' Batoor said. 'I thought you had Pathan blood.'

Perhaps I have.

'We have the camels under orders, sir.' O'Neill brought them back to the present. 'MacKinnon got himself slightly wounded. All the others are present and fit, sir.'

That was O'Neill's subtle method of asking for orders.

'The lads did well,' Jack said. 'We'll water at the last village; rest up until dark and head for Gondabad.'

We won the battle, and I learned something new. India gets more complicated by the day.

Chapter Twenty

Gondabad rose from the shimmering heat like a ship appearing over the horizon. For a while, the fort seemed to float by itself with the haze hiding the houses below, and then, one by one, minarets and temples appeared. The city itself was last, with the homes of the people barely seen and gold mohur trees eye-catching bright, as the coppersmith birds clattered relentlessly.

'There we are again,' O'Neill said as they halted. 'Gondabad.'

Jack nodded. 'I hope Elliot is safe.' He pushed aside the thought of Mary. He knew she was used to the company of soldiers, but he didn't like to think of her surrounded by the desperate men of the 113th.

'Lieutenant Elliot is a fine officer, sir,' O'Neill said. 'He'll take care of your men.' He hesitated for only a second. 'Miss Lambert will be safe as well sir. She's a brick, that one.'

'Thank you, sergeant,' Jack said. 'Yes, she is a brick. Now we have to find some way of getting this treasure to the Rajah. It's a shame Jayanti already knows about it.'

O'Neill relapsed into silence. He was a first-class sergeant, but nature had not blessed him with much imagination.

'We'll find somewhere safe to halt the convoy,' Jack decided, 'and I'll take Batoor into the fort and find the Commander-sahib.' *It will be more like Batoor taking me into the fort.*

'Yes, sir.'

They halted in a small *tope*, with the trees for shade and a sluggish stream for water. Jack sent Whitelam up the tallest tree to act as lookout and trusted O'Neill to post pickets.

'We'll be back soon, sergeant,' Jack said. 'Or we'll be dead.' He could speak quite cheerfully of his possible demise. In India, death was so prevalent and came in so many guises, that it was senseless to ignore it.

'Yes, sir.'

'If we're not back in three days, make your way to Lieutenant Elliot, give him my compliments and advise him that he is to act as he thinks best.'

'Very good sir.'

There was no need to advise O'Neill to watch the men. He would do that as a matter of course, and not one single *anna* of the treasure would be missing when Jack returned.

Jack and Batoor left an hour before dusk, sliding out of the *tope* and across the *maidan* to the city with the night sounds eerie and the crackle of distant musketry.

'Something's happening,' Jack said.

'Yes, Captain Windrush,' Batoor said. 'It could be Sir Colin Campbell, or perhaps something much closer. The land is very disturbed.'

'It is.' Jack hoped that Elliot and Mary were safe.

'Captain Windrush,' Batoor broke a long silence. 'How will you bribe this cow-worshipping Rajah to support the British?'

'Why, Batoor, with the treasure of course.'

'Yes, Captain Windrush, but what is to stop the Rajah from taking your treasure and then cutting all our throats?'

'I know the commander of his army,' Jack said.

'And I knew that devil with the ruby ring. We were lovers, she and I. It did not stop her from murdering my wife and son.'

'Do you have a plan, Batoor?' Jack thought it best not to comment on Batoor's ideas of morality, or on his angry disclosure. Batoor was gradually revealing himself as trust grew.

'I have a plan, Captain Windrush.'

'Let's hear it then, Batoor.' Jack nodded as Batoor explained.

The Rajput sentries at the fort entrance looked askance at Batoor, who pushed past them as if he belonged. Jack heard the words "Commander-sahib", and the Rajputs allowed them passage. Once more in the interior of the fort, Jack felt the claustrophobia clutch at him and tried to appear nonchalant.

'In the den of Shaitan.' Batoor tapped the hilt of his Khyber knife, looking a bit like the devil himself.

Jack forced a smile. 'Well, Batoor, let's show the devil what we can do.'

'God is great,' Batoor said, 'and all things are His will.'

'I hope His will coincides with our desires,' Jack said softly.

As Jack entered Baird's office, he saw a furtive figure slide behind a screen at the far side of the room and guessed that one of the Rajah's servants was listening to everything he said. *Well then*, Jack thought in a sudden devil-damn-you-all flash, *let's give him something worth reporting to his master.*

'Good evening, Commander-sahib.' Jack saluted his grandfather.

'Jack my boy, and Batoor.' Baird was all geniality as he stood up to greet them. 'Did your mission to Lucknow succeed? I know all about it, you see.'

'I thought you might,' Jack said.

'You don't look as if you've suddenly come into a fortune,' Baird said.

'I have hidden my fortune outside the walls of Gondabad, and there it will remain until I have assurances of its safety.'

'You're thinking like an Indian now, Jack,' Baird approved. 'What kind of assurances do you want? I can willingly give you my word.'

'It is not your word I doubt,' Jack said. 'It is the word of your Rajah.'

'Ah,' Baird nodded. 'He could not send out the army without asking me. I am their commander, after all.'

'Would you fight against the British if he ordered you?' Jack remained on the offensive.

'I hope it never comes to that,' Baird temporised.

'If it came to a choice, Commander-sahib, where would your loyalty lie?'

Baird didn't reply directly. 'How do you intend to encourage the Rajah to back the British, and keep his word?'

'With a hostage.' Jack saw Baird start. Batoor's suggestion had at least caught the Commander-sahib's attention. It might also work with the Rajah.

'Asking for a hostage will show your distrust of the Rajah.' Baird sat back down, with his fingers tapping on his bureau.

'I know,' Jack said.

'There is nothing to stop the Rajah from taking your fortune – if it exists – and then supporting the rebels.' Baird seemed to be thinking aloud.

'Yes, there is,' Jack said. 'I will arrange for the hostage to be sent to Calcutta. If the Rajah reneges on his word, then the hostage will be hanged.' Jack was lost in the murky waters of Indian and Imperial politics now, so far out of his depth that he felt as if he was drowning.

Baird lay back in his chair. 'The Rajah might not agree to that condition.'

'Then the treasure goes directly to John Company in Calcutta, less the cut that I will take to ransom the British prisoners from Jayanti.' He put an edge to his voice. 'I will take my men to Sir Colin Campbell and inform him that the Rajah of Gondabad has sided with the mutineers and has given shelter to Nana and Jayanti. I will say that Jayanti murdered British prisoners in this fort. Sir Colin will be incensed and will march here with his army.'

Jack stopped talking for a moment to emphasise his next words. 'Sir Colin will storm Gondabad and raze this fort to the ground. He will hang the Rajah and ensure his family lose any rights to British protection or British money. The Company will take over the lands, and that will be the end of the Rajah of Gondabad and his line.'

Although Jack had no authority to issue any of these threats, he had enjoyed acting the tyrant. Perhaps it was because of the strain of the last few months, or the abject poverty of so many people in India when compared to the gross luxury of the princes. He waited for a reaction.

Baird nodded slowly. 'I will pass on your message.'

'There is no need.' Jack felt more reckless than he had for months. 'The Rajah's spy is behind the screen in this room, so he will soon relate all that I said. Here is more for him. I wish the Rajah's sons as hostages. I know how important it is to Hindus to leave an heir, so I will promise the British will care for them, as long as the Rajah remains loyal. On the other hand, if we so much as sniff disloyalty, they will be hanged without mercy.'

That was a pure bluff, Jack knew. The British government and especially the Queen would never countenance such treatment. Once the Rajah's sons were in British custody, they would be as safe as any public schoolboy in England.

Baird breathed out slowly. Jack heard slight movement in the room and guessed that the spy had left, presumably by some hidden doorway. These old Indian forts were rumoured to be full of secret tunnels and entrances.

'The Rajah won't like the British threatening him,' Baird said.

'I'm not here to be nice to the Rajah,' Jack said. 'As somebody told me recently, I'm not a diplomat; I'm a soldier. How long will I have to wait here before I get an answer?'

'The Rajah might order you killed out of hand,' Baird said. 'I've never known anybody talk like that in this fort.'

'If the Rajah has me killed,' Jack said, 'then Sir Colin will undoubtedly destroy the place. My men know where I am and have orders to report to Sir Colin if I don't return within a specified time.'

'You're a brave man,' Baird said.

Jack shrugged. Nobody would ever know how untrue Baird's statement was. For all Jack's bluff, he was shaking inside, and the prospect of the Rajah killing him in some hideous manner was terrifying.

When the door opened a file of tall Rajputs in breastplates and helmets entered, each one carrying a tulwar.

'The Rajah's guard,' Baird said. 'Your fate is now out of my hands.'

Jack forced a smile. 'Well, grandfather, it has been interesting meeting you once more. I hope there is a third time, but if not,' he shrugged, 'look after yourself.'

As the guard pushed Batoor aside and formed around Jack, he wondered if the Rajah would call his bluff. *Think well of me, Mary. I tried to do my duty.*

The durbar room was much as before, with the Rajah and Rani sitting on their thrones as if they did nothing else. The Rajah still sported his jewels and finery while the Rani remained plainly dressed.

The escort pushed Jack inside.

'Good evening,' Jack said as he entered the room. He contemplated salaaming and decided not to. He was not here on a diplomatic mission. 'You will remember me – Captain Jack Windrush of the 113th Foot.'

'We remember you.' The Rani's voice was low.

'I believe that you are considering joining the rebels.' Jack thought it politic not to mention the rebel warriors already ensconced within the fort.

The Rajah looked at him as if he were some form of lower insect that he should squash underfoot, while the Rani raised a single finger.

'The wind blows this way and that,' the Rani said. 'If it blows from the north, it may blow the British into the sea. If it blows from the south, it may bring more British across the *Kala Pani.*'

'That is very cryptic,' Jack said. The Rajah looked away. The Rani lifted a small brass bell and rang it, once. A soft-footed servant appeared holding a silver tray on which stood a bottle and one glass.

'Have a drink, Captain Windrush.'

'Thank you.' Was the Rani offering him the last drink of a condemned man? It was impolite to refuse hospitality, so he poured himself a small glass of a milky white liquid and tasted it. 'Very nice.'

'I know how much British soldiers like to get drunk,' the Rani said.

'Some do,' Jack agreed.

'I hear that you have tribute for us.'

Tribute? That's one way of describing a bribe. 'I have some wealth that the British government may wish to exchange in return for the privilege of looking after your majesty's sons.' *That sounded good.*

'My sons are happy here,' the Rani said.

'If the war continues,' Jack spoke slowly, 'and Sir Colin Campbell or General Rose learn that Nana Sahib and Jayanti have taken refuge in Gondabad, they will believe that you are siding with the rebels. They will undoubtedly destroy this fort, and there will be no safe place for your sons. If I take them with me, they will be safe.'

'Will they?' Jack thought there was genuine concern in the Rani's face.

'You have my word as a British officer,' Jack said.

The Rani's smile was as cynical as anything Jack had ever seen. 'Even with that assurance from a captain in the 113th Regiment of Foot, will they be safe?'

'I believe so.'

Leaning across to the Rajah, the Rani whispered something, to which he replied. They spoke for a few moments, and the Rani returned her attention to Jack. 'How much tribute do you have for us?'

'I have five camel loads,' Jack said. 'I have not counted the value.'

'Will there be more tribute later?' The Rani held Jack's gaze.

'If you confirm your support to the British, I am sure that the Honourable East India Company will show its appreciation.'

The Rani leaned back in her throne as if exhausted by the conversation. She flicked her fingers as if in dismissal.

'There is one more thing, Your Majesty.' Jack didn't know the correct term of address for a Rani so used the same as he would for the queen. 'The outlaw Jayanti holds some British prisoners in another section of your fort. Perhaps they sneaked in without your knowledge.' He watched the Rani for some sign of emotion, either satisfaction or guilt. He saw neither. 'Could Your Majesty use her authority to free these prisoners?'

The Rani looked bored, if anything. She spoke quietly to her husband for some time while Jack waited for an answer. 'We know nothing of these matters,' she said at last and spoke to the guards.

As Jack opened his mouth to continue the conversation, he saw the guards approaching him. Without a word, they formed around him and marched out of the durbar room. It seemed that their majesties had no interest in helping the British prisoners.

Chapter Twenty-One

Batoor was waiting for Jack at the camp. 'I thought the Rajah would throw you to the elephants,' he said.

'So did I.' Jack forced a smile.

'What happens now, sir?' O'Neill asked.

'We try to ransom the prisoners.' Jack lifted his head. 'Can you hear firing?'

'Yes, sir. It's been going on half the night. Not constant, just every half hour or so and then it fades away again, maybe depends on the wind.'

'That might be our boys,' Jack said. 'I heard musketry earlier but thought nothing of it. As far as I'm aware, the only British unit near here is Elliot. Forget the prisoners for the present, O'Neill. We're heading to the temple.'

'Yes, sir. How about the camels?'

'We're taking them too; I'll be damned before I give the pandies a present of our loot.'

O'Neill grinned. 'Yes, sir. The pandies already know we're here, sir.'

'I thought they might,' Jack said. 'We're moving right away before the Rajah sends his army after our treasure.'

'There are about thirty men on that ridge to the south,' O'Neill said.

'As long as they remain on the ridge, they can number three hundred and thirty.' Jack patted the neck of the nearest camel. 'Come on, sergeant. We're on the road again.'

They headed north towards the jungle and the temple, keeping the camels in the centre of their small column and watching their surroundings.

'They're following us, sir,' MacKinnon reported.

Jack swore when he heard a spatter of firing ahead. Whoever was following him, he had no desire to lead them to the temple, yet his handful of men was too weak to fight off a determined attack.

'Go and find out what's happening, O'Neill. Don't get involved.'

'Yes, sir.'

Jack glanced around. 'We'll wait on that knoll there.' The small hillock would provide a decent all-round field of fire.

O'Neill slipped ahead, moving as silently as any jungle-dweller as he vanished into the trees. Jack led the others to the knoll, settled the camels down and formed a defensive perimeter. He sighed. None of his plans was working out in this campaign. He had made no progress with the Rajah, the enemy seemed to have discovered Elliot's position, and Jayanti still held the British prisoners. Colonel Hook had ordered him to find and destroy her, and she was as strong as ever.

'They're coming closer,' Whitelam warned.

'Good.' Logan hefted his rifle.

Jack scanned the now-nearby enemy. 'That's the same bunch that stole our camels.' He searched for the woman with the ruby ring.

The mob yelled at them, waving swords, spears and sticks.

'If shouting is the best they can do, we've nothing to worry about,' Coleman said. 'Bloody raggy-arsed blackguards, them.'

'They're bloody raggy-arsed blackguards,' Thorpe repeated. 'Aren't they, Logie, raggy-arsed blackguards?'

'Aye, that's right, Thorpey. A bit like you, eh?'

'They're nothing like me,' Thorpe objected. 'Eh, they're nothing like me, Coleman? I'm not a raggy-arsed blackguard; I'm a soldier.'

'Yes, you're a soldier Thorpe,' Jack said. 'Now act like one and have a decko around the perimeter. Take Coleman with you in case you get lost.'

A single shot ran out, and Jack flinched as the bullet thudded into the tree a few inches from his head. He ducked, swearing, and searched the surrounding forest. A betraying puff of smoke drifted high up and to his right.

'There's a sniper,' Riley reported.

'It'll be one of Jayanti's women,' Jack said. 'Do you remember Fort Ruhya?'

'How can I forget?' Riley scanned the treetops.

'There she is,' Whitelam aimed his rifle. 'She's in that palm, hidden behind a bunch of fronds. Can I fire, sir?'

'Yes, Whitelam.' Jack sighed. Sometimes he found it irritating working with men who needed an order for the simplest thing.

Whitelam's rifle cracked out. 'That's one less,' he said, as a body hurtled from the tree to swing upside down from the end of a rope. 'She was tied in.'

'There will be more.' Jack wondered if the markswoman wore a ruby ring. 'Keep your heads down and watch the tree tops.'

A figure appeared, weaving through the jungle. Hatless and dishevelled, O'Neill ducked as a musket roared out, jumped over something Jack couldn't see and threw himself into the 113th position.

'Trouble, sir,' he said. 'There must be fifty of the enemy around us, with these crazy women amongst them, and Lieutenant Elliot's under siege.'

Jack nodded, trying to assimilate the information. 'Thank you, sergeant. How is Elliot holding out?'

'He's doing all right, sir. I don't know how many men are besieging him, I couldn't get close enough to count.'

'A hundred? Two hundred? A thousand?' Jack asked. 'Take a guess, sergeant.'

'I can't tell sir. Maybe two hundred, maybe three.'

'We'll join Elliot,' Jack said. 'We're doing no good here.'

The temple was still a mile away through the forest, with narrow tracks perfect for ambush and overhanging trees on which sharpshooters could perch.

'Move fast,' Jack ordered. 'O'Neill, lead us, and I will be rear guard.' In situations such as this, the last man was in most danger, and Jack wished to ensure that all his men were safe. 'Drive those camels fast!'

Batoor grinned at Jack. 'We are now camel drivers as well as warriors.'

'I don't care what they call us, as long as we get through safely.'

The enemy was waiting, with men and women dodging through the trees, firing at them, throwing spears and shouting slogans that they may have been intended to intimidate.

'Push on!' Jack slapped the rump of a reluctant camel. 'Don't stop for anything!'

A half-naked man sprang from the trees in front of O'Neill, who barely broke stride as he thrust his bayonet into the man's stomach, ripped sideways and tossed him aside like a sack of meal. Somebody fired from the right, and another from the left, with Thorpe yelping as a shot grazed his leg.

'Hey! You dirty blackguards! Come and fight fair!'

'Never mind that scratch,' Jack yelled. 'Keep moving!'

Driving camels was never easy, and when the drivers were scared and the path narrow, the task was much more difficult. After another quarter of a mile, the enemy began to target the camels.

A black-turbaned woman emerged from a stand of bamboo, fired point-blank and ran away before Coleman could react. The leading camel spat blood, tried to recover and fell in a tangle of legs and tumbling panniers.

'Coleman, Thorpe! Lift these panniers; put them on the nearest two camels!' Jack fired his revolver in the direction the warrior woman had fled. He looked around. His convoy spread over twenty-five yards of the path, with the escort very thin to guard the five remaining camels. 'Close up!'

The enemy was getting bolder now, standing at the jungle edge to try to slash escort and camels with swords and spears. Jack saw Logan step sideways and thrust with his bayonet, and heard him curse as his attacker melted into the trees.

'Keep moving!' Jack said. 'We're nearly there.'

There was still a quarter of a mile to go, uphill and with the sun hammering down on them. 'One last push,' Jack yelled, and then a second camel fell.

Jack saw it happen. A red-turbaned man lunged from the jungle and pressed a long musket to the chest of the camel driver. MacKinnon, the nearest escort, was a second too late in swinging his rifle butt at the man's head. Red-turban fired the musket, the driver screamed and fell, and three more men burst from the trees at the opposite side of the track.

Lifting his revolver, Jack hesitated as the camel shifted, coming between him and his target. The men hacked at the animal with long knives before vanishing between the trees. MacKinnon began to follow until Jack grabbed hold of his arm. 'No, MacKinnon, they'll be waiting for you in there.' He fired a pointless shot after them and knelt by the camel. It was not dead but severely wounded, thrashing around on the ground beside its prone driver.

'Poor bugger,' MacKinnon said. 'Why do we have to bring animals to war?'

'Parker would agree,' Jack said. Placing his revolver against the animal's head, he pressed the trigger. 'Best to end its suffering.'

'Yes, sir,' MacKinnon said.

'Take the camel's gear and spread it around,' Jack said. 'Hurry man!' He could hear the rustlings in the forest and knew the enemy was gathering. If he had been their commander, he would launch an attack now, while part of the British force was struggling to unload the camel and they were still some distance from the temple.

'Come on, lads!' Jack helped MacKinnon carry the panniers to the next animal, which still walked with its characteristic slow lope along the jungle path.

'Not far now, sir!' O'Neill shouted.

As the remaining camels struggled with the increased loads, their speed dropped further. Jack sympathised with the animals, yet knew he had no alternative. He fired a shot when a face appeared in the jungle, swore as he tried another shot, and the hammer clicked on an empty chamber.

'Sir!' O'Neill's voice. 'We're at the temple!'

O'Neill's claim was slightly premature as the convoy emerged from the jungle to the hundred-yard-wide *maidan* that separated them from the temple, and intermittent firing on both sides. Mysterious small humps littered the *maidan*, and the acrid reek of gunpowder drifted among the trees.

'The lads won't know who we are,' Jack said. 'Tell them that we're the 113th!'

'Cry Havelock!' Coleman elongated the last vowel. 'Cry Havelock!'

'Cry Havelock!' The shout echoed from the temple.

'And let loose the dogs of war!'

Between the heat and the powder smoke, the outskirts of the temple were hazy. Although Jack knew that Mary, Elliot and the bulk of his men were there, he could see only the vague shapes of men darting among the ruins and the occasional orange flashes of muzzle-flares.

The small humps in the *maidan*, Jack realised, were the dead bodies of men, some recent and furred with flies, others older and already decomposing in the heat. The sweet smell of purification hit him.

'We'll have to run for it,' Jack said. 'A hundred yards with the pandies firing at us.'

'Yes, sir.' O'Neill showed no emotion.

'Right lads!' Jack shouted. 'There's the temple and the rest of our force. It's a little bit to cover, and then we're home. On the count of three, up on your hind legs and run.' He felt the tension and waited until Batoor translated his words to the camel drivers. 'Go!'

The men reacted at once, haring toward the temple ruins, yelling 'Havelock' as if the old general's name was a talisman that would protect them from enemy fire. The defenders of the temple responded in kind, shouting and laying down suppressing fire into the surrounding forest.

'Come on, Batoor!' Jack smacked the rump of the nearest camel. The animal gave him an imperious look and ambled forward, with the driver shouting encouraging sounds and ducking from the passing shots.

'Good man!' Jack said. Two of the three remaining camels were nearly across the *maidan* with only the last taking its time. Jack lingered to help any casualties to safety. He saw a bullet hit the camel in the neck, saw the spurt of blood and the animal twist its head. The second shot whistled past Jack and smashed into the body of the camel. The animal staggered, spraying blood.

'Make it move!' he shouted to the driver. The man stared at him, yelled something and ran for the shelter of the ruins.

'Run!' Elliot's voice was clear above the hammer of the guns. 'Run, Jack!'

'I'm damned if I'll run before a pack of bloody rebels,' Jack said to himself. He took hold of the camel's reins. 'Come on, boy,' he said. 'Try.'

Another bullet slammed into the animal, and it collapsed, kicking on the ground. Jack looked behind him, where the jungle fringe was about sixty yards away, dotted with little orange flares where the enemy was firing, and he looked forward the forty yards to the temple, where similar orange flashes showed the British response.

Without thinking, Jack began to unfasten the panniers. The buckles were stiff, the leather iron-hard and he struggled, trying to ignore the bullets that struck the camel and raised angry fountains of dust on either side of him.

'Run, Jack!'

Elliot was shouting again, with others joining in.

'Sir! We'll cover you!'

A bullet thudded into the pannier beside Jack's hand, numbing his fingers with the impact and ringing on the metal inside.

'Jack!' That was Mary's voice. *Thank God, she's still alive.* 'Run, you idiot!'

Jack looked up, suddenly realising that Mary was correct. He was acting like a complete fool offering himself as a target for every pandy and rebel gun in the jungle. And all for what? A few basket-loads of treasure that the Rajah had rejected, and John Company would take for its already bloated shareholders. *Is it worth dying to make other people rich?*

The rebel bullet had ripped open the pannier, exposing some of the contents. Grabbing what treasures he could reach, Jack huddled them close to his body and ran toward the temple. He heard the crackle of musketry behind him and the cheer of men in front.

Elliot shouted, 'Give him covering fire for Heaven's sake,' and then bullets whistled past his head.

Something slammed into the heel of his boot, spinning him around and throwing him to the ground. He lay there, dazed as the musketry continued. He heard somebody screaming – a woman – *please God, not Mary! Please, God, don't let her be hurt.*

Jack looked up. He was twenty yards from the British lines. Mary stood there, hands over her mouth with somebody – MacKinnon – holding her, preventing her from coming to his aid. Scrabbling to gather the items he'd dropped, Jack dashed forward, limping as the numbness in his heel spread to his foot and lower leg. There would be a beautiful bruise there tomorrow if he lived that long.

Then he was passing gaunt-faced Private Smith who grinned at him with a pipe at the side of his mouth. Elliot was giving brisk orders, O'Neill was raising a hand in salute and Mary was running toward him, arms outstretched.

Mary embraced him, held him close and then pushed him away. 'You could have been killed!'

Jack nodded. 'We could all be killed yet.'

'Sir!' Elliot's voice dragged him away from Mary. 'Glad you're back, sir.'

Jack nodded and tried to collect his senses. 'What's happening, Elliot?'

'We're surrounded, sir. I think it's a splinter of Nana Sahib's men.'

'How many?'

'I'm not sure, sir. I estimate three or four hundred.'

Jack grunted, trying to think. 'That's plenty. Do they have artillery?'

'No, sir.' Elliot shook his head. 'So far they've tried a couple of assaults and a lot of musketry. Their sharpshooters are accurate though.'

'They've no artillery, and they can't use cavalry in this terrain,' Jack looked around. 'We can hold out as long as the water and ammunition last, or we can break out and head for the nearest British garrison.'

'That's Bareilly, as far as we know,' Elliot said. 'Did you succeed in your mission, sir?'

Jack shook his head. 'No, Elliot. We recovered the treasure, but the Rajah won't play ball, and I didn't get a chance to try and ransom the prisoners.'

'At least you tried, sir, and you got the treasure. John Company will be pleased.'

'I'm sure they will,' Jack nodded to the dead camel lying in the open. 'That beast's loaded with gold trinkets, and I don't want to hand it to the enemy.'

'Yes, sir,' Elliot said. 'Parker, Hutton, watch that camel. Shoot any pandies that come close.'

'Yes, sir.'

Jack nodded. Elliot had matured in his few days of independent command. 'I want the treasure recovered. In rebel hands, it could buy hundreds of men.'

'Shall we send out a party after dark, sir?'

'I'll lead it,' Jack said.

Elliot shook his head. 'With respect, sir, you will be in command here. It's not the commander's place to take foolhardy risks.'

Elliot certainly had changed. Jack looked at him with increased respect. 'Whose place is it to take foolhardy risks, lieutenant?'

'The second in command sir, or a junior officer,' Elliot replied at once.

'That could mean Lieutenant Bryce,' Jack said. 'He'll be glad of the chance to have his name noticed.'

'Lieutenant Bryce is dead, sir. He died of fever three days ago.'

'How many other casualties, Elliot?' *I should have asked that first.*

'We have three dead, sir, including Lieutenant Bryce and Sergeant Greaves. We have two wounded and three down sick with heat exhaustion.'

'What's our strength now?'

'We're down to forty effectives, sir, including your men.' Elliot knew the numbers at once.

'Ammunition?'

'We've been conserving it. We still have fifty rounds a man.' Elliot pulled Jack aside. 'Excuse me, sir, the pandies like to wait until we stand still for a few minutes and then shoot.'

'Nasty little devils.' Jack glanced upward. 'It'll be dark soon. I want the treasure unloaded from the camels and put inside the temple, with a reliable guard. With Sergeant Greaves dead, that will be Ensign Wilden.'

'Wilden is sick with fever,' Elliot said at once.

Jack cursed. 'A pity. We'll have Ensign Peake then, and two privates.' *Soldiering to protect the Empire is like that. Men you knew and served with were hale and hearty one day and gone the next. India may be the jewel in Queen Victoria's crown, but she demanded a high price from the men who filled the ranks of the army and the woman and children who accompanied them. Even in a time of peace, cholera and fever, malaria and the heat can kill a little child or a strong man in a few hours.*

'I want you to take a party out to that camel as soon as the sun sinks,' Jack said. 'Bring back the panniers and all they contain.'

'I'll take three men,' Elliot decided at once.

'Be careful. I'd hate to write a letter to your father, lying about how good a soldier you were.'

Elliot lifted his hip flask. 'Here's to the next to die.' He took a swallow and handed the flask over.

'May his passage be swift and easy.' Jack sipped in turn.

'And may Saint Michael welcome him into his band of martial angels.' Elliot closed his eyes. 'That's what we are you know, Jack, guardian angels fighting the good fight against evil and ignorance. We are the sword and armour of the Lord.'

Jack said nothing. He wondered if the Lord agreed with mass hangings and destruction. Then he remembered that sack of soldier's heads in his dungeon and wondered if any side was right in this war, or in any war. Only a soldier could know the true obscenity of warfare, the mad game kings and governments played with the lives of men. Jayanti with her chess had been only a pawn in this ultimate sport.

'Let's hope that our swords are sharp and our armour strong,' Jack said. 'May the Lord protect you, Arthur.' He had never been more sincere.

'May the Lord protect us all,' Mary spoke from behind them.

Jack looked at her, unable to admit to his feelings. 'I hope He does,' he said. *Especially you.* For a moment, he was back in Herefordshire, with the blackbirds singing in a bright morning and a host of butterflies rising as he walked the gentle slopes of the Malvern Hills. The grass was soft underfoot, cattle were lowing softly in the fields, and the sky above was crystalline blue. He was walking toward a smiling woman in a long dress. He was home, far from India with its heat and diseases, ever-present flies and the threat from dangerous men.

That was only a dream. Without money, Jack knew he could never return home. He was destined to live out his life fighting for Queen and country. Only promotion could realistically bring him sufficient wealth to get back to Herefordshire. *Within fifty yards is a Rajah's ransom.*

For the first time in years, Jack was tempted. As a young, inexperienced ensign, he had looted two golden Buddhas from a Burmese temple. He'd intended then to buy his way back to Herefordshire until Myat, a Burmese woman, had persuaded him to return his loot. Since then he'd deliberately avoided temptation. Now it sprang to life, fully formed.

Why? What has altered?

'Are you all right, Jack?' Mary placed a hand on his sleeve.

'Thank you,' Jack said. 'I'm fine.'

'I'll leave in an hour, sir.' Elliot had been busy collecting men while Jack had been thinking.

'I'll arrange covering fire,' Jack said.

Mary patted Jack's arm and stepped back. She didn't say anything.

* * *

Clouds obscured the moon as Elliot led O'Neill, Williams and Parker beyond the thin British line and into the open ground beyond. Somewhere a leopard coughed, the sound sinister, and Jack wished he were in Elliot's place. It was hard to remain behind, hard to stand and wait while men, particularly friends, risked their life. Was a load of gold worth a soldier's life, or any life? Jack took a deep breath.

He knew the answer. He would pay a hundred Rajah's ransoms to keep Elliot alive, or Mary, or any of his men. He also knew that the world did not view a soldier's life as important compared to gold or silver or jewels. *We are expendable; we are Jayanti's pawns, that the nation can discard for the sake of wealth.*

Lifting his binoculars, Jack tried to penetrate the darkness. He could make out the dim shapes of Elliot's party as they crept forward, and he could hear the occasional crackle of dry grass.

'I can't see them,' Logan said.

'Good.' Riley had his Enfield at his shoulder. 'If we can't see them, then neither can the pandies.'

A bat flicked past them, hunting for insects, and somewhere a jackal howled.

'Bloody India.' Mahoney lay stiffly, favouring his still-raw wound.

'Sir!' Ensign Peake saluted. 'Permission to help Lieutenant Elliot.'

'Denied!' Jack hissed. 'You were ordered to guard the treasure. Get back to your post, Peake!'

'Sir, I want to help!'

'Your duty is to guard the treasure.' Jack knew he didn't have to explain. 'You eat, sleep and live there until relieved! Now move!'

'Yes, sir,' Peake turned away.

'Bloody Griffs,' Logan grunted.

'He's keen,' Riley said. 'You were like that once.' He considered. 'Maybe not.'

'Bad *cess* to you, Riley,' Logan said.

Musketry came from ahead, followed by a yell and then another shot.

'Elliot's hit trouble,' Jack said. 'Reserve party!' He called to the six men he had waiting. 'Over you go!'

Newly promoted Corporal Hutton led the other five forward, bayonets blackened to avoid reflecting any moonlight, boots thudding on the hard ground. Jack watched them go, cursing the responsibilities of command, praying that Elliot was all right.

'Dear God, look after that man.'

He had never actively prayed for another soldier, but it seemed natural to do so for Elliot. Jack desperately wanted to go out into the dark himself, yet knew that he could not. If the enemy killed him and Elliot, the command would devolve to Peake, who was too inexperienced. Jack knew that a few months ago he would not have hesitated to take the risk. What had changed?

Mary, of course.

There was a shout from the dark, more musketry and then an Indian voice, chanting something. Somebody was sobbing in pain.

'Sir!' Logan had his Enfield at his shoulder as he glared into the dark. 'I cannae see anything. Can I go out there?'

'Stand fast, Logan,' Jack said.

The silence lengthened, stretching Jack's nerves. He felt himself trembling. *Is it through fear or excitement? I don't know. Jesus, this is hard. Maybe Elliot and all his men are lying on the maidan, dead or wounded.*

'Somebody's moving out there, sir,' Riley said. 'I hear something.'

They listened, trying to ignore the natural night sounds and focus on Elliot's party. There was a definite sound, a shuffling, with the occasional clink. *Somebody is moving the treasure, but whom? Is it Elliot or the pandies?*

'Sir, I can go forward,' Logan said.

'Damn it, man!' Jack could take no more. 'I'm going myself.' Unbuckling his sword belt, he handed it to Riley. 'Look after that; it's too clumsy.' Drawing his revolver, he crawled forward.

There were shadowy shapes ahead, men coming toward him.

'Cry Havelock,' he whispered. 'Cry Havelock.'

'And let loose the dogs.' The welcome words returned to him.

'Evening, sir,' Elliot said calmly. 'The pandies thought the same as us. We have the treasure.'

'Any casualties.'

'Williams is slightly wounded, nothing serious.'

The musketry began then, a fusillade from the rebel lines.

'The pandies have woken up,' Elliot said.

They returned to the temple, keeping low as the enemy shots crackled and screamed above their heads. One bullet hit the ground an inch from Jack's arm, raising a furrow of dust. He watched it dispassionately. *I'm no longer scared.* The defenders fired back, with Jack's party between the opposing ranks of rifles.

'Come on, sir!' O'Neill shouted. 'We've left a gap for you.'

Jack waited until his men were safe before rolling over the defences and into the welcome shelter of the temple. *I'm shaking again. Is that just reaction?*

'You did well,' Jack said. 'Get that treasure to the storehouse and make sure Peake looks after it.'

'Yes, sir.'

Jack couldn't control his shaking. Waiting while others put themselves in danger was more of a strain than being in the field. He reached for a cheroot, remembered he had none left and swore, softly.

'They'll come tomorrow morning,' he said. 'I know these pandy lads, and I'm beginning to know Jayanti's women. They'll come for their wealth, and they'll want a victory to hearten the others. Well, I'm not Wheeler, and this is not Cawnpore. There will be no surrender and no negotiating.'

'Yes, sir.' Elliot dabbed at a scratch on his face. The blood was black in the darkness. 'They come most mornings, sir, a frontal charge with no finesse.'

Jack nodded. 'You've done well to hold out so long.'

Elliot shrugged.

'Post O'Neill and six men on the right flank, Elliot, and when we hold them in front, he can unsettle them. As long as they have no artillery, and our ammunition holds, we can last.'

'Aye, sir.' Elliot said. 'And we'll pray to the Lord for relief.'

'I hope He listens,' Jack said. He remembered Jayanti's executioner. 'I hope to God that He listens.'

Chapter Twenty-Two

The attack came an hour before dawn when the guards were tired and waited for their relief. There was little warning. One minute the sentries were staring into the darkness and the next the enemy was before them.

'Careful, lads!' Logan shouted. 'The bloody pandies are here!' He fired once and then backed off, bayonet busy.

'What's happening?' Jack ran toward the sudden noise, revolver in hand. A black mass of men emerged along the British front, screaming their war cry and swinging tulwars.

'Meet them!' Elliot led the counter-attack, firing his revolver as he ran, dropping it and drawing his sword. 'Cry Havelock!'

'O'Neill!' Jack shouted. 'Take them in the flank!' He slashed with his sword, feeling the blade slice through human flesh and bone, saw a screaming face before him, fired the revolver he held in his left hand and saw a man fall. He heard O'Neill's party fire a volley from his right and knew that the enemy would be taking casualties. There were more men in front, contorted faces and frantic swords, the flicker of baggy clothes and the crash of musketry.

And then silence.

As quickly as it had started, the attack ended. The enemy turned and ran, leaving their dead and dying in the *maidan* and the drift of white powder smoke across the temple ruins.

'As long as they don't learn new tactics,' Jack said, 'we can hold out here indefinitely.'

Privately, he wasn't so sure about the strength of their position. With a limited supply of ammunition and food, and with every day bringing casualties, the defenders were slowly weakening. Even a minor wound could put a man out of action, and the heat and strain were taking their toll. In India, every British army suffered more from disease and climate than from enemy shot and shell. The rebels wouldn't give up. They would know that this small party of the 113th was isolated, with no method of sending for help. The rebels seemed to have unlimited man and womanpower, so it was only a matter of time, of waiting and creating casualties among the defenders, before they weakened the British sufficiently to win.

'We normally hear them coming,' Elliot said. 'They must have crawled across the *maidan*.'

'They're using new tactics,' Jack said. 'Even so, that attack was not pressed home as hard as it could have been.'

'They're not the same quality as the men we faced on the march to Lucknow,' Elliot agreed.

Jack inspected the temple's defences, a range of rifle pits along the perimeter and lookout positions giving all-around visibility.

'You've done well here,' Jack said.

'Sir,' MacKinnon called down. 'There's movement in the jungle sir. I can hear lots of noises, like men dragging something heavy.'

Jack exchanged glances with Elliot. 'Artillery,' he said.

* * *

With enemy artillery advancing toward them, Jack knew that it was only a matter of time before the temple became untenable. He ordered the men to dig the rifle pits deeper, with sloping banks of earth in front to absorb the impact of the solid shot and loopholes through which the defenders could fire without exposing themselves. He altered the position of the strong points to enable interlocking fields of fire, ensuring that any advancing enemy would pass through a fearful fire-zone.

He had small parties go into the *maidan* and collect enemy weapons, firearms or swords so that even if his men ran out of ammunition, they would have something with which to fight.

'Make sure you lift any powder horns or wherever the pandies carry the powder,' Jack said.

'Yes, sir.' The inflexion of O'Neill's voice indicated that he didn't need an officer to tell him the obvious.

With the outer defences as formidable as they could make them, Jack created an inner ring, centred on the ornate ruins around the chamber where he had made love to Mary, and where the wounded and sick were presently under her care.

'This will be where we make our last stand,' he said.

'Aye.' Elliot pulled on a home-made cheroot. 'And then it's the end.'

'There is no surrender,' Jack said. 'I'm not handing my men to these people as hostages or worse.'

'And Mary?' Elliot asked.

That question had worried Jack ever since he had arrived at the temple. *What about Mary? What would happen to her once the enemy destroyed the 113th's position?*

'She might be able to merge into their army,' Elliot said. 'She is half Indian, so she could disguise herself without difficulty.'

'She might do that,' Jack said.

'Or...'

'Exactly.' Jack knew what was in Elliot's mind. 'Or.'

'If they capture her,' Elliot spoke slowly, 'God only knows what they will do. Remember Cawnpore.'

'I'll never forget Cawnpore as long as I live.'

'Who will perform the act?' Elliot asked.

'I'll have to,' Jack said. 'She's my woman. I have the responsibility.'

'Sweet Heavens,' Elliot whispered. 'How have we descended to such a thing?'

'It's this war,' Jack said. 'Crimea was bad. This mutiny is infinitely worse. We are fighting our own people. I know you see it as a war against superstition and evil, and you're right to an extent. I see it as a struggle against ourselves; we're reaping the whirlwind of our own bad decisions, fighting people who are our friends and our blood.'

Elliot sipped at his silver hip flask. 'It's beyond a nightmare, Jack. How will you do it?'

'I'll keep the last two bullets for Mary,' Jack said.

'Two?'

'In case of a misfire.'

Elliot nodded. 'You won't use one on yourself though.' He raised tired eyes to Jack's face. 'If they capture you and torture you, Jack, whatever they do, your soul is safe. You fought the good fight, and you'll die a Christian.'

Jack sighed. 'Aye, maybe. I hope so.'

'If you kill yourself, Jack, that's a mortal sin. You'll lose your soul.'

'I won't do that,' Jack said.

'Good man.' Elliot held out his hand. 'What if the pandies get you while Mary is still alive?'

'Would you do the necessary for me, Arthur?'

Elliot nodded, wordless.

'What are you two talking about so quietly?' Mary's eyes were red-rimmed with lack of sleep while stress had carved new lines around her mouth.

'Our future.' Jack told the truth as he mustered a smile.

'Well, we have another two sick men,' Mary said, 'and I could use a hand with the washing. There are many soiled clothes in here. My sick need clean linen.'

'I'll send one of the men.' Jack calculated who he could best spare from the defence. 'Corporal Hutton's a steady fellow, and Parker has a kind heart.'

Mary sighed and sat on a broken pillar at their side. 'I hardly see you, Jack. Here we are penned up in a few square yards, and it's like we're in different worlds.'

'There will be other times,' Jack said, as Elliot made polite excuses and walked away.

'Will there, Jack?' Mary leaned closer to him. 'How will we get away from here? Nobody knows where we are and the enemy is all around us.'

Jack tried to smile. 'We'll hold out,' he said. 'The pandies know that they're defeated. Sir Colin and Hugh Rose are smashing their armies and capturing their last strongholds. They will not last forever. The longer we hold out, the weaker they'll get.'

The deep boom of cannon fire and the passing howl of roundshot interrupted Jack's words.

'Sorry, Mary, I'll have to go. It seems that the enemy artillery is in range.'

'You be careful now, Jack.' Mary put a hand on his shoulder.

'You too, Mary,' Jack said. He kissed her quickly, felt her briefly press against him and then they parted. He watched her return to the hospital chamber and turned away.

Chapter Twenty-Three

'I think the pandies have only one cannon in position, sir,' Elliot said. 'I'll take a patrol and have a look.'

'No,' Jack shook his head. 'I'll take a patrol as soon as it's dark. You take over here.'

Elliot frowned. 'No, sir. I protest. The men need you here.'

He's right, damn it!

'All right, Elliot. Take who you think best.' Jack ducked as the cannon barked again and a large calibre shot crashed against a stone pillar. 'You'd think they'd have some respect for one of their own temples.'

Elliot chose O'Neill, Coleman and Thorpe, three Burmese veterans who had experience of fighting in the jungle. They slipped away as the sun set in an orange blaze.

'Arthur can look after himself,' Mary murmured.

'I know, but I worry so.' Jack admitted his fears.

'I know you do.' Mary touched his arm and withdrew to her patients.

It had been only a brief meeting, yet Jack felt better for it. He scanned the *maidan* for signs of Elliot and breathed his relief when the patrol returned.

'How close are the pandies?'

'They've set up firing positions about twenty yards inside the jungle perimeter,' Elliot reported. 'They've only two light guns in position so far, and they've cleared the trees in front to give themselves a field of fire. Heavier guns are still on their way, hacking and banging through the jungle.'

'We'll take them tomorrow night,' Jack decided.

'A raiding party?' Sweat dripped off Elliot's face as he looked back across the *maidan*.

'A strong one,' Jack said. 'If they get heavy artillery up, they can batter us to pieces, and we won't be able to do a thing about it.'

'How many men shall I have?'

'I'll lead this one,' Jack said.

About to protest, Elliot saw the determination in Jack's face. 'Yes, sir. How many men?'

'I'll take twenty,' Jack said. 'If we fail, we're lost. If we succeed, we'll buy ourselves another few days, or sting them into a massed attack we can deal with.'

Elliot didn't argue. 'What will you do?'

'Damage the guns and kill as many pandies as possible,' Jack said. 'It must be a decisive blow.' He shook away the image of Mary sitting in her chamber. *I can't think of her. I must concentrate on my duty.*

But he knew he needed to see her.

* * *

They sat side-by-side, leaning against a pillar while the sun eased downward. It was a moment of rare peace in the temple, with the monkeys chattering in the background and the jungle alive with nature's sounds.

'India can be incredibly beautiful,' Mary said. 'Sometimes I feel so blessed to live here, although I was brought up to think of Britain as home.'

Jack edged slightly closer. 'I don't know how I feel,' he said. 'Back in England, we thought we were the centre of the world and that all that is civilised rotated around London. Now,' he gestured to the surrounding temple, 'I find architecture that surpasses anything in Europe, a culture that predates us by a thousand years and people who have never heard of Great Britain. My little island seems so small and cold, somehow.'

Mary laughed. 'You're turning Indian, Jack!'

'Maybe I am,' Jack said. 'I still miss England. I miss the coolness and safety, without the constant threat of disease. I miss the long-drawn-out sunsets and the crisp winter frosts. I miss the old inns and fishing in the rivers.'

'I'd like to visit England sometime,' Mary said. 'I've always wanted to go Home.'

Putting an arm around Mary's shoulder, Jack pulled her close. 'You will do,' he said. 'You'll love the greenness of summer and the yellow fields of wheat in the autumn, the apple orchards of Herefordshire and Worcestershire and the soft slopes of the Malvern Hills.'

'I want to visit the libraries.' Mary snuggled closer. 'I want to see the great abbeys and the cathedrals, the River Thames and Wordsworth's Tintern Abbey, even although that's in Wales.' Her voice lowered. 'I don't only wish to see England, Jack. I grew up with the novels of Sir Walter Scott, so I want to see Scotland as well, the places Sir Walter wrote about; Edinburgh and the Eildon Hills, the Border Country, Loch Katrine and the Trossachs.'

'I've never been to Scotland,' Jack said. 'I've never been so far north.'

'You've read Walter Scott's novels though.' Mary pulled away slightly. 'Every educated person must have read Walter Scott's novels!'

'I've read some,' Jack said. 'His *Waverley*. The Jacobite one.'

'Scott wrote three Jacobite novels,' Mary corrected. 'Oh, Jack, we have so much to talk about and explore! I wish we could spend more time together.'

We have our whole lives. Jack bit off the words before they reached his lips. *Damn the woman. She is trying to trap me.* 'I'll have to read the others some time.'

Mary sensed his change of mood and pulled away. 'I'm sure you will, Jack, if you ever release yourself from your *duty*.' Tossing her hair, she stood up and walked away.

Jack watched the swing of her hips and swore repeatedly. *Damn, damn, damn, damn, damn! We never have sufficient time!*

* * *

Even in the dark, it wasn't hard to find the rebel convoy. There was no attempt to minimise the noise as busy labourers worked with axes and saws and scores of men hauled at the ropes.

'They have six pieces of artillery,' Jack noted. 'Two six-pounders in position, three eighteen-pounders pulled by bullocks and another eighteen-pounder pulled by hand. There must be four hundred men with the column, about two hundred of them warriors.'

'We have thirty-seven fit men,' O'Neill said. 'We're a bit out-matched.'

'We could delay them a bit, sir.' Coleman lifted his rifle. 'They won't expect it.'

Jack imagined the damage twenty rifles could do against such a large number of men. He would delay the advance by a few minutes or a few hours at best. What chance would all his men have of returning safely against so many? *Not much.*

My men are soldiers, Jack told himself. *They had known the dangers when they took the Queen's shilling. Soldiers?* He shook his head. *Thorpe was an arsonist, sent to the army as an alternative to jail. Coleman was an orphan and joined the army rather than shivering to death in the bitter winters of the 1840s. The potato blight forced O'Neill to take the Queen's shilling. Technically, they are volunteers, yet it was not for love of a queen about whom they knew nothing or a country that failed them, that enticed them into the scarlet uniform.*

They are soldiers. They have their duty to perform.

'Thorpe. I need your special expertise.'

'Yes, sir.' Thorpe paused. 'What does that mean, sir?'

'The two six-pounders in position must have ammunition,' Jack explained. 'They must have a powder store.'

'Yes, sir,' Thorpe said.

'Sergeant O'Neill will take you, Coleman and a two-man escort to blow it up. Do whatever you do, Thorpe, and make me a big bang and a huge fire.'

'Yes, sir!' Thorpe's enthusiasm was evident.

'Sergeant.' Jack didn't need to lower his voice with all the noise the enemy was making. 'Set fire to the powder and take the men back. Don't wait for us. Let Thorpe take charge where he can; he's the expert.'

'Yes, sir.' O'Neill nodded.

'I'll give you fifteen minutes to prepare, and then I'll have a crack at the column.' Jack watched as O'Neill led his men away.

Lying in the forest within a hundred yards of an enemy column was amongst the most nerve-wracking experiences Jack had ever had. He lay prone, ignoring the insects that investigated his body and hoping that his men retained their patience as the enemy crept ever closer to the temple. The hands of his watch seemed to crawl, with each minute a seeming eternity.

The enemy was working hard, widening the path they had already made for the small six-pounders to drag through the much larger eighteen-pounders. Jack watched them, admiring their energy even as he knew he must kill as many as he could. There was a swirl among the enemy, with men stepping aside to salaam as a disciplined unit arrived. *Please, God, that's not the Rajah's army.*

'Trouble.' Jack mouthed the word as he saw the black turbans and veiled faces, with every woman bearing a musket and tulwar. They marched in silence, purposeful and dangerous. 'That's Jayanti and her warriors. There must be sixty of them.'

And then the black turbans were past, sliding into the forest.

Forget them; concentrate on the artillery.

'Right lads.' The larger hand of his watch approached the fifteenth minute. 'Get ready. On my word, aim for the bullocks.' He knew that was an unpopular decision, but each bullock could do the work of ten men. 'If anybody misses, I'll put them on a charge.' He ignored the frowning looks, knowing that some of his men would deliberately miss rather than hurt an animal.

'Cap… On my word… Aim… Fire!'

They fired together, with the sharp crack of the rifles echoing in the jungle. Three of the bullocks fell at once while two others bellowed in pain. War was every bit as hard on animals as it was on men.

The effect was instantaneous with the bullock drivers running into the forest and the accompanying men staring around them or cowering on the ground.

'One more volley,' Jack said. 'Aim for the men on the leading gun this time. That tall fellow giving orders.' He pointed to a bearded man with an ornate turban.

The men loaded quickly, too experienced to panic, aimed with steady hands and fired on Jack's command. The officer staggered and fell, and two men nearby crumpled at once.

'That's enough, now. The pandies will have men after us in a second. Reload and back to the temple.'

They obeyed at once, sliding between the trees. Corporal Hutton led the way, and Jack was rear-marker, turning every few steps to see if the enemy was following. Behind him, he heard the noise from the enemy column increase as they assessed what had occurred.

After a hundred yards, Jack halted the rearmost five men. 'We'll hold them here and allow the others time to escape.'

Logan grunted, 'Aye, sir,' and slid behind a tree. The others followed, calm-eyed and controlled, levelling their Enfields and waiting.

'There, sir,' Whitelam gestured into the darkness. 'I saw movement.'

'Right, lads, give them a volley,' Jack said. A second later, the rifles crashed out. 'Load and withdraw.'

The 113th ran through the forest with scattered shots following them, bringing down leaves and pieces of branches. The men jinked and weaved to spoil the enemy's aim, with every step taking them closer to the relative safety of the temple.

The explosion was louder than anything Jack had heard since the siege of Sebastopol, an ear-pounding crash that blasted down trees and illuminated the night sky. Pieces of debris and fragments of men rose a hundred feet in the air, hovered for a moment amidst the white cloud of smoke and descended in a terrible rain that had the patrol diving for shelter.

'Dear God!' Jack lay prone and tried to burrow into the ground as pieces of burning wood and shattered men fell all around him.

After the explosion came the silence; a hush so intense it seemed unreal. Jack dragged himself up, winced as something stabbed in his leg and looked around at his men. Most were still lying, stunned by the noise, one or two were attempting to rise.

'Come on, lads!' Jack didn't hear his words and knew that the explosion had temporarily robbed him of his hearing. He shook Smith, the man nearest to him and gestured towards the temple. Hutton was swearing and patting at his trouser leg, which was ablaze from the falling debris. One man stood to stare at the flames and colossal tower of white smoke. That was Thorpe, of course, admiring his handiwork.

'I told you to get back to the temple, sergeant!' Jack shouted to O'Neill, whose words were lost in Jack's deafness. 'Seventeen, eighteen,' he counted his men. 'There are two missing.'

Dragging them up and pushing them towards the temple, Jack found his missing men. Both were dead; one lay crushed under the carriage of a gun that the explosion had lifted and dropped on top of him. Bromley, his name had been, a freckle-faced youngster from the London stews with a sharp wit and a foul tongue. He would never see the Thames again. A mass of burning powder had landed on the second man. Pinthorpe had been a drunken scoundrel, a wastrel although popular with his colleagues, now he was nearly unrecognisable, a blackened crisp. These men would join the tens of thousands of British dead in India, only remembered by their colleagues and possibly by their families, if they had any.

Staggering, each man holding his rifle, the surviving men crossed the *maidan* at a rush. Jack hurried the laggards, pushing them forward, roaring words he knew they couldn't hear. He saw the little fountain of dust by the reflected light of the fire, the mark of a bullet hitting the ground. The enemy had recovered far quicker than he had expected and were firing at the withdrawing British party.

'Move lads!'

The temple's outer defences were a few yards ahead, the earth banking dotted with men and Elliot standing tall, waving in the raiding party.

Corporal Hutton was lagging, limping and clutching his burned leg. 'Come on, Hutton,' Jack pushed him onward, 'get into the temple.'

Hutton stopped and put a hand to his ear. He mouthed something Jack couldn't hear.

'Come on!' Jack grabbed him at the same instant as the enemy fired. The bullet hit Hutton squarely in the back of the head, distorting it and exiting from the right temple. Hutton died immediately.

Elliot pulled Jack over the barrier. 'Are you all right, sir?'

Jack guessed at Elliot's words.

'We destroyed their powder store,' he began to shake with reaction, 'and we lost three men.'

'That's a success.' Jack's hearing eased. He could hear Elliot's voice as though through water, distorted and unclear.

'Jayanti has arrived,' Jack said. 'With scores of her women.'

Elliot lit one of his foul-smelling cheroots. 'Things are coming to a head.' His smile lacked any humour. 'With luck, we'll send Jayanti to Gehenna, where she belongs.'

Jack stared toward the jungle where the smoke was dissipating although orange flames still illuminated the sky. 'It looks as if she is already there.'

'If you wish, I'll take out a patrol and make sure.' Elliot sucked on his cheroot. 'Well, this is vile.' He walked away, leaving Jack to wonder if he meant that the war was vile or the cigar. *Probably both*, he decided.

I'll check on Mary and get back to duty. God, I'm tired.

The firing increased minutes later. *Are the pandies attacking again?* Jack raised his voice. 'Stand to!'

The 113th hurried to their positions, tired men with ragged uniforms and limited ammunition. They faced outward, bayonets loose in their scabbards.

'They'll come again,' Smith said, 'and again and again.'

'And we'll send them back, again and again,' Whitelam said.

'Each time they come we're a bit weaker,' Smith pointed out.

'And each time we repel them, we get their guns and powder to make us stronger,' Whitelam countered. 'Come on, lads, we've been in worse spots. Captain Windrush will see us through.'

As his hearing slowly returned, Jack heard the words and wondered. *Captain Windrush is nearing the end of his tether,* he said to himself. *He is running out of ideas.*

'Take positions,' Jack shouted. 'Peake, take the right flank, Elliot, the left, Wilden, I know you're just off your sick bed, but take charge of the rear.' He didn't wait for their response. 'Everyone get where he belongs!'

The men obeyed, sliding into rifle-pits or behind barriers, peering into the darkness for a sight of the enemy. Most of the defenders were in the front-line positions around the perimeter of the temple, with six waiting as a reserve. If the enemy broke through at any point, those six men were all Jack had to counter-attack.

'Ready, lads!' Jack roared. 'Here they come,' Jack saw the mass rushing across the *maidan*. 'Cap, lads, wait for my command... steady.'

He waited until the enemy was close, knowing the psychological effect of the first volley.

'Steady...'

The enemy was close now. The timing had to be right, wiping out the foremost men, disheartening the others yet still leaving sufficient time for his men to reload. Jack could make out the features on each attacker's face; he could see every detail of their clothing and weapons. *That is close enough, damn it.*

'Fire! Cap, ready, present, Fire!'

The front rank of the attacks disappeared as if swept by a scythe. The second rank wavered, until the men behind pushed them on, where the British Enfields felled them in turn.

'Keep coming and we'll keep shooting you,' Logan loaded and shouted at the same time.

'They never learn,' Riley said.

'Sir!' Peake called. 'They're over here, sir.'

'They've broken in, sir!' Elliot yelled. 'Jayanti's women!'

'Reserves! Bayonet men, throw them out!' Concentrating on the mob in front, Jack could only spare a second to glance behind him. He saw the six bayonet men rise from their position and charge Jayanti's women.

'Keep firing,' Jack ordered. 'I'll be back in a minute.'

The bayonet men were struggling. Already one was down, with a warrior woman hacking at his body. Swearing, Jack ran into the melee. He fired his revolver, hitting the closest woman, fired again to ensure she remained down and ran on. The fighting was desperate, with gasps and grunts, and the clatter of steel on steel as tulwar met bayonet. Jack saw another soldier fall as a woman sliced underhand into his belly, heard the man's despairing scream and fired at the woman, missing her.

The perimeter firing grew intense, and Jack knew that the enemy had launched another attack. They were pressing hard, slashing and thrusting with sword, bayonet and spear. The woman he had missed turned on him, her eyes gleaming above the veil, her tulwar slicked with soldier's blood.

For a second they faced each other, the British officer and the Indian warrior, a clash of cultures and beliefs in the midst of a ruined Hindu temple, and then Jack saw the ring on her left hand. 'You!' he said and fired his revolver at her. The hammer clicked uselessly.

'Misfire by God!' Jack threw the pistol, catching the woman on the side of her head and making her flinch. That half-second was all Jack needed to draw his sword. He parried as the woman slashed at his legs, swore at the force of the blow and hacked back, missing.

'You murdering witch.'

The woman said nothing, recovered her blade and aimed for his groin. Jack met her swing, followed through with a thrust at her throat and saw her block with almost casual skill. This woman was no ordinary cut-and-thrust soldier but a skilled warrior. For a minute, all Jack's world concentrated on the duel with this warrior woman. He could not think of the attack on the perimeter or the progress of the siege. The only thing that mattered was survival. If he relaxed for a fraction of a second, she would kill him. He feinted left, thrust to her face, felt her parry, and knew her retaliation would be swift and deadly. He saw her eyes, dark, unyielding and very familiar.

I know you!

'They've broken through!' Peake's voice was full of despair. 'Fight them, men! Push them out!'

Jack saw the flash of triumph in the woman's eyes. She shouted something in a voice that was high and clear despite her veil, and her warriors pushed on. Another of Jack's bayonet men fell, with two women chopping at him in a frenzy of blood and fury.

'To me!' Jack shouted. He could see seven of the warrior-women remaining, with others lying prone or thrashing on the ground. 'Cry Havelock!'

There was no answering roar from his men. The perimeter had collapsed, with soldiers in tattered khaki withdrawing, firing, fighting with bayonet and rifle butt against the attackers.

'Get to the inner defences!' Jack shouted. 'Withdraw, boys!'

The black-turbaned women had gone, leaving his surviving bayonet men gasping and bloodied, too exhausted even to swear. 'We'll hold them at the inner defences, lads,' Jack said.

Elliot was down, crawling through the temple with blood on his head and one hand clutching his left leg. Jack saw O'Neill lift a wiry attacker with his bare hands and throw him into a crowd of others. Logan was roaring, holding his rifle like a club as he fought. His bayonet lay at his side with the blade broken. Whitelam was writhing on the ground as a pandy thrust a bayonet into his belly, again and again, laughing with each blow.

'On me, the 113th!' Jack shouted. Grabbing Elliot by the collar of his tunic and ignoring his yells, he hauled him behind the second line of defence. '113th!'

The survivors were reeling back, wild-eyed or cursing, firing or stabbing at the mass of white-clad, scarlet-uniformed or bare-chested rebels that pursued them.

Jack thrust forward to where the mutineer continued to hack at the now-dead Whitelam. 'He's one of my men, you bastard!' Jack purposefully slid his sabre into the mutineer's belly, twisting the blade so there could be no hope of survival.

'113th!' That was Wilden's young voice.

'Good man, ensign,' Jack slashed at the back of a passing rebel, cutting the man wide open. 'Fight the bastards. Form a line, lads!'

Shocked, exhausted, reeling from the heat – the surviving men of the 113th took positions in the rifle pits and behind the shattered masonry.

'Cap!' Jack gave the familiar orders, relying on the discipline learned on the parade ground to bring his men back. They obeyed automatically, with hundreds of hours of drill having imprinted the words and movements into their minds.

'Aim!'

The rifles levelled. The sight of the menacing black muzzles gave pause to the attackers.

'Fire!'

The volley crashed out, felling half a dozen of the attackers.

'Number your ranks,' Jack ordered. 'One, two three!'

The men looked to left and right, shouting out numbers.

'Every odd number is the front rank, every even number is the rear rank,' Jack roared. 'Load!'

The attackers were recovering, rallying for another assault with Jayanti's warrior women adding steel in their midst. Jack saw Jayanti among them, talking to the woman with the ring. He frowned for a second; it seemed as if the ring-woman was giving Jayanti orders, rather than the other way around. *What's to do?*

'Both ranks cap and present!' Jack shouted. He could worry about the details of command among the enemy later, if he survived. *I wish I had kept my revolver and not thrown it away.* 'First rank, fire!'

The diminished volley crashed out. 'First rank load and cap. Second rank fire!'

The rifles crashed, the enemy reeled and withdrew a step, leaving casualties on the ground.

'Come on you bastards!' Logan yelled.

'First rank fire! Second rank, load and cap!'

Jack kept them firing. With a much smaller perimeter to defend, there were no gaps. The enemy couldn't approach without facing the muzzle of at least one rifle.

'Keep it up, boys!' That was Elliot's voice.

Jack glanced backwards. Elliot was leaning against a pillar with blood streaming down his face, using a branch for support and looking every inch a hero. His father would be proud of him.

'Second rank fire! First rank load and cap.'

They were using ammunition at a prodigious rate, with men scrabbling for caps and bullets.

'Second rank, load and cap. First rank fire!'

Some of the men had rags around their hands to protect them from the insufferable heat of the rifle barrels. Others held the weapons by the wooden stocks. What with the heat of the sun and the constant firing, the Enfields were becoming too hot to hold, the bores were foul and the accuracy impaired. How many rounds had the men fired? How long had they been fighting? Jack didn't know. It seemed his life consisted only of the crash of rifles and the screams of agonised men, the sight of yelling, distorted faces and the gleam of tulwars and bayonets, the acrid sting of powder smoke and the sick raw stench of human blood.

'First rank cap and load! Second rank fire!'

The volleys were less regular now as the some of the more fouled rifles fired before the men were ready. It would be bayonets and rifle butts soon, and then the end as the pandies swarmed over their dead bodies.

And what about Mary? Jack remembered his pledge to leave two cartridges to save her from the hellish fate of capture by the rebels. Unless he could recover his revolver, he had broken that promise. He could see his pistol lying on the ground between the bodies of a warrior woman and Private Gallacher.

'Second rank, cap and load! First rank, fire!'

'They're breaking, sir!' O'Neill said.

The sergeant was correct. The rebels were not pressing forward with anything like the same vigour. As long as the 113th had ammunition, the enemy could not penetrate their defences without taking unacceptable casualties. The enemy line was further back, beyond what had been the original British perimeter.

'Cover me, lads,' Jack said. Taking a deep breath, he stepped clear of the inner defences and walked forward. He didn't run, hoping to maintain his dignity as an officer. Ignoring the crack of musketry, Jack stooped to lift his revolver, turned and marched back to the 113th position.

'What were you thinking of, sir?' Pale-faced with pain and loss of blood, Elliot stared at him.

'Fetching my gun.'

'You could have been killed!'

Jack felt a mad desire to laugh. He indicated the surrounding carnage. 'We're in the middle of a battle, Elliot; the enemy could kill any of us at any time. Have you had Mary see to your leg?'

'Not yet,' Elliot admitted.

'Then do so,' Jack ordered. 'I'll need you when the pandies come again, and you're no good to me if you collapse. Sergeant O'Neill!'

'Sir!' O'Neill arrived at Jack's side.

'What are our casualties?'

'Five dead sir, six wounded, two seriously.' O'Neill listed the names. 'The less seriously wounded are fit to fight.'

Jack did a quick calculation. 'We're down to twenty-nine fit men then, plus four walking wounded. How about ammunition?'

O'Neill frowned. 'Not so good, sir. We've about fifteen rounds a man.'

'That will see off one major attack,' Jack said. With the reduced perimeter, he didn't have to raise his voice. 'Remember, men, no firing unless an officer or NCO orders it, and take the ammunition from the casualties.'

The men nodded silently, faces tired and lined. They knew the end was near.

'We have a smaller area to defend now,' Jack tried to encourage them. 'They can't get in.'

'Is there a relief column coming for us, sir?' Coleman asked.

'I don't think so, Coleman.' Jack had resolved not to lie to his men. 'We're on our own here. We stand here, and we may die here.'

The 113th nodded; they understood. Even the replacements were veterans now. They tried their best to emulate the old soldiers' nonchalance.

'I wish we had the Colours, sir,' Coleman said.

Jack agreed. It would be good to make a last stand under the yellow-buff regimental Colours, the same flag that had fluttered above them at Inkerman. However, the Colours remained with the regimental head-quarters wherever that may be. 'We're still the 113th, Coleman, with or without the Colours. There is no surrender.'

'Aye.' Logan spat on the ground. 'No surrender. Remember Cawnpore. They'll have to kill us first.'

'Cawnpore,' Thorpe repeated. 'Remember Cawnpore.'

Some of the men shouted the word as if it were a battle cry. 'Cawnpore! Cawnpore!'

'That's not our slogan,' MacKinnon said. 'Cry Havelock!'

Elliot was first to repeat the cry. 'Cry Havelock!'

The men shouted it, roaring defiance with all their remaining might. The reply came within a few minutes, Indian music sounding from all around the temple.

In between the music, another chant echoed that of the 113th '*Raja ram Chandra Ki Jai!*'

'What's that?' Elliot asked. 'Is that a threat?'

'That's the Karkha,' Batoor answered. 'It's the war cry of the Rajputs.'

'Fuck them.' Logan spat on the ground.

'The Rajputs are a warrior race,' Batoor said.

'So is the 113th.' Logan was cleaning his rifle. 'Let them come.'

'They will,' Batoor said. 'They will.'

'Water.' Mary walked from man to man, filling up their canteens. 'Drink your fill; water is one thing we have plenty of.'

'Thank you, Mary.' Jack touched her arm. 'We'll get out of this.'

'Yes, I know we will.' Mary spoke with such certainty that for a moment Jack wondered if she had information that he lacked. 'You always get us out.'

Jack tried to smile, thought of the two revolver rounds he was saving and turned away. *Maybe not this time, Mary.* On an impulse, he turned back and hugged her.

'What was that for?'

'Your faith,' Jack said. *I wish I could think of a way out.*

'We could send a man through the forest,' Elliot suggested as the sun swooped down and there were a few moments of lesser heat. 'We could send one of the Burma veterans who could vanish among the trees.'

Jack considered. 'There are only four Burma men left. There's me, O'Neill, Thorpe and Coleman. I won't leave, O'Neill is the best NCO we have, and I doubt if any officer of sufficient seniority would listen to Thorpe or Coleman.'

Elliot nodded. 'You've given this some thought, I see.'

'I have,' Jack said. 'I wondered if we could give the messenger a written message.'

'If the pandies caught them...'

'They'd know how desperate our position is.' Jack finished Elliot's sentence. 'We have no choice. We sit and wait and die together.'

They exchanged glances and looked away. Jack wished he could spirit Mary to safety.

Chapter Twenty-Four

'Something's happening.' Elliot looked up. 'It's all gone silent.'

Elliot was right, Jack realised. The music and the Rajput war cry had stopped. 'Jayanti is up to something. Come on Elliot.'

Dragging his wounded leg, Elliot followed Jack to the defensive positions. Only insects disturbed the oppressive silence, with all the bird sounds stilled. Heat rebounded from the stones of the temple, forcing sweat from suffering bodies, causing men to gasp for every breath.

'What's happening, sergeant?'

'Dunno, sir,' O'Neill stood behind one of the carved pillars, surveying the outworks and the *maidan* beyond. 'There's movement in the forest.'

'Keep your eyes open.' Jack spoke loudly enough for all the defenders to hear. 'Jayanti is a tricky devil.'

The men grunted, wiped sweat from their faces, swatted away insects and gripped their rifles.

'Sir,' O'Neill murmured. 'Over there.'

The woman who emerged from the jungle fringe carried a white flag and moved slowly.

'They're surrendering,' Thorpe said. 'The pandy buggers are surrendering to us.'

'Aye, that's right, Thorpey. They heard that you're here with your Victoria Cross and they're scared.' Coleman grunted. 'It's a flag of truce, you bloody moonraker. They want to talk.'

'Why?'

'How should I know? I'm not a bloody pandy.' Coleman shifted his rifle and settled the stock against his chin. 'Come closer, you murderous bitch, and I'll blow your bloody head off.'

'Hold your fire.' Jack knew the mood of his men. After so long on campaign, they would shoot anything that they even suspected of being an enemy. 'We'll hear what she has to say. Watch the rear and flanks. It could be a trick.'

'It could be a trick,' Thorpe repeated. 'Watch in case it's a trick, lads.' His laugh was unsettling, and Jack wondered if nervous strain had unhinged his mind even more.

'That's Jayanti.' Jack recognised the woman as she approached them. 'What devilish thing is she planning now?' He stepped out of cover. 'If they shoot me, you take charge, Elliot.' He handed over his revolver. 'You know what to do with that.'

'Yes, sir,' Elliot said. 'Take care.'

Feeling acutely vulnerable, Jack stepped beyond the defences and into the outer temple. He knew that the enemy would be aiming at him, as his men were aiming at Jayanti. Taking a deep breath that seemed to scorch his lungs, he straightened his shoulders and marched forward.

The dry grass crackled beneath his boots and a dozen insects buzzed around his head.

'Well, Jayanti?' Jack stepped twenty paces into the *maidan*. He could run that distance if the enemy tried to shoot or capture him.

'*Jai ram.*' Jayanti salaamed politely.

'What do you want?' Jack was as curt as possible.

'Here we are again, Captain Windrush.' Jayanti held her flag aloft. 'You and I, in the midst of my country.'

'Here we are again,' Jack kept his voice firm. 'You and I in British India. Do you wish to surrender to me now, or are you going to wait until General Rose or General Campbell arrives to smash your army?'

'General Rose is deep in the south, tied up before the walls of Jhansi,' Jayanti said. It was impossible to see Jayanti's expression behind her veil, yet Jack sensed some humour in her voice. If they had met as anything except enemies he could have liked, or at least admired, this woman. 'And as for Sir Colin, he is so slow that he would take months to reach you, even if he knew or cared about your existence. You and your men – how many? Forty? Thirty? You are all alone, Captain Windrush.'

Jack was not surprised at Jayanti's words. 'Do you wish to surrender to me, then, Jayanti?'

'We have a proposition, captain.'

Jack smiled. 'We? Who is commanding your army, Jayanti? Is it Nana Sahib, who Sir Colin Campbell and General Havelock have defeated so often? Or is it some other failed leader?'

'We have a proposition, captain.' Jayanti ignored Jack's probes. 'I advise you to listen and consider before you decide. We surround you, we outnumber you, and your men face defeat, disgrace and death.'

'We hold a strong position, we have plenty of food, water and ammunition and we have defeated every attack you have made,' Jack countered.

'Your wounded are suffering, your food and ammunition are running out, and you will not survive another three days,' Jayanti replied easily. 'Now listen, Captain Windrush. You have something we want, and we are prepared to be generous to obtain it.'

'Oh?' Jack placed a hand on the hilt of his sword. 'What do we have that you want?'

'You have the treasure of Lucknow,' Jayanti said, 'and you have the man Batoor.'

Jack couldn't hide his surprise. 'Batoor?' he repeated. 'Why the devil do you want a stray Pathan?' He recovered. 'As for the treasure, we only hold a small portion of it. The Honourable East India Company possesses the bulk.'

'Our reasons are our own,' Jayanti said. 'Hand over Batoor and the Lucknow treasure, and in return, we will allow you passage to the nearest British garrison. We will provide an escort to ensure your safety.'

Jack laughed openly. 'We have heard such promises before,' he said. 'General Wheeler at Cawnpore accepted such an offer. Where is he now? He's dead, with all his men and women. The word of a mutineer is not to be trusted.'

'Then I have another proposition.' Jayanti didn't seem surprised that Jack had rejected her offer. Her voice hardened. 'We hold some prisoners of your regiment. Hand over Batoor and our treasure, or we will execute them.'

Despite the heat, Jack felt a chill creep over him. Remembering the game of chess he'd played with her, he knew Jayanti was not bluffing.

'I will not hand over any of my men,' Jack said.

'Batoor is not one of your men,' Jayanti reminded. 'Batoor is a prisoner you recruited to find me. You have no further use for him.'

'I will not hand him over.' Jack was no longer surprised at the efficiency of the enemy's intelligence service.

'As you wish, Captain Windrush.' Jayanti took a single step back. 'My offer stands. If you choose to reconsider, come out under a flag of truce, or send out the brave Lieutenant Elliot. I hope he survives the wound in his leg. We will arrange an escort to take all your men to safety and even release our British prisoners in return for Batoor and our Lucknow treasure.' Her eyes were brown and sincere. 'It is a more generous offer than any British general would grant an Indian force in your position.'

Jack said nothing to that, he knew Jayanti was correct. 'If you wish to surrender to me,' he countered, 'I will speak to Sir Colin on your behalf.'

'Thank you, captain. That will not be necessary. You may return in peace to your men. Hostilities will restart in five minutes.'

Tempted to hurry back, Jack forced himself to stroll, pausing to light one of Elliot's disgusting cheroots to show his contempt for the enemy.

'What's happening?' Elliot's omission of the word "sir" proved his disquiet.

Jack explained what Jayanti had said.

'Bastards.' Elliot shook his head. 'Will they kill their prisoners?'

'Without a doubt,' Jack said.

'Is there anything we can do to stop them?'

'We could hand over the loot and Batoor.' Jack was glad when Elliot didn't even consider that option.

'We could use sharpshooters against them,' Elliot said. 'Our Crimea men were trained in shooting. I know they used the old Minié rifles, but they're still better shots than the average soldier.'

'Who are our best shots?'

'Whitelam, MacKinnon, Riley and Coleman,' Elliot said at once.

'Whitelam is dead,' Jack said. 'Tell the others to select a firing position, and we'll see what happens.' He drew on Elliot's cheroot. 'God, this is foul.'

'I know,' Elliot said with a grin. 'We might be poisoned to death even before the pandies get us.'

'Sir,' O'Neill called out. 'I see movement.'

First out were a group of men carrying muskets or rifles, followed by a dozen of Jayanti's women, and then three men in battered British uniforms.

'Oh, dear God,' Jack said.

'You were right.' Elliot tipped back his hip flask. 'Jayanti has kept her word.'

'That's our men!' Thorpe shouted. 'Look, that's Higginthwaite, Peter Defford and O'Malley from Number One Company. O'Malley still owes me a shilling.' He half rose from his rifle-pit until Logan shoved him back down.

'Keep your heid down, you stupid bastard! The pandies have got sharpshooters waiting for us.'

As if in confirmation, two rifles cracked out from the jungle and a bullet thudded into the earth a few inches from Thorpe's head.

'Missed!' Thorpe jeered. 'You couldn't hit a bull's arse with a broomstick!'

'Sir,' Coleman whispered. 'Can I fire? I can hit the sharpshooter or these devil women.'

'Not yet,' Jack said. 'Jayanti might only be bluffing.'

Behind Jayanti's women, a file of men trotted out with a selection of lengths of rough-hewn timber. As the 113th watched, the rebels built a triangular structure with three uprights connected at the uppermost point by three crosspieces.

'That's a gallows,' Jack said.

'It's a copy of the Tyburn Tree,' Elliot agreed.

'Ready your rifles, boys,' Jack ordered. 'Shoot any pandies that try to hang our men.'

'Yes, sir,' Riley answered.

The enemy sharpshooters took positions at the 113th's old front line.

Jack watched as a group of white-clad men threw ropes over the crossbars; each rope had a noose on its end.

'The pandies are going to strangle the prisoners.' Thorpe sounded interested in the proceedings. 'I thought they might break their necks.'

'That's too merciful,' Logan said. 'They pandy bastards will do things the cruellest way.'

Jayanti's women pushed forward the three British prisoners.

'Ready lads,' Jack said. 'Make sure you hit the executioners and not our men.'

The hush was so intense, Jack could almost taste it as the white-clad men placed the ropes around the necks of the prisoners.

'Get the bastards.' Logan fitted his bayonet with a metallic snick.

'Take that blade off, Logan,' Jack ordered. He knew that Logan was quite capable of launching a solo attack on the entire enemy army, getting himself killed in the process and losing Jack a valuable rifleman.

'Permission to fire, sir?' Coleman asked.

'Yes, if you can get a clear shot,' Jack said.

MacKinnon was first to fire, with the crack of the rifle startlingly loud and the echoes resounding around the temple. One of the white-clad men staggered backwards and fell, kicking on the ground. Coleman fired half a second later, with one of the executioners grabbing at his arm and spinning around.

'Winged the bastard,' Coleman said.

'I can't fire, sir,' Riley said. 'Our boys are in the way.'

The enemy reply came at once as their musket men began a rapid fire. Bullets pinged and whined from the stonework, spreading chips of masonry around the ducking defenders.

Jack slid behind a pillar, flinched as a bullet smacked against the stone and breathed out slowly. He inched back around the opposite side and swore as another bullet landed a few inches from his face. One of the rebels evidently had him in his sights. Dropping low, Jack rolled away and into the nearest rifle-pit. He crouched beside the occupant – a dapper man named Flynn – and peered through the embrasure.

'Murdering blackguards!'

The three British prisoners swung and kicked from the gallows, trying to grasp at the ropes that slowly tightened around their throats.

'Bastards!' Logan roared the word. 'Dirty pandy bastards!'

'If the pandies want us to surrender,' Flynn murmured, 'they don't know much about the 113th, do they, sir?'

'Give me your rifle.' Jack thrust the Enfield through the embrasure. He wanted to kill. He wanted to kill Jayanti and all her warriors. He wanted to kill everybody who murdered his men in such a foul manner.

Jayanti was not among the group of women at the base of the gallows. Jack selected a victim at random. He didn't sufficiently trust his marksmanship to hit her head so aimed for her belly, the widest part of her body. He grunted with satisfaction when she staggered and clutched her middle.

'Suffer, you witch,' he said and handed back the rifle. 'Load that, Flynn.'

'Can we fire back, sir?' Logan asked.

'No,' Jack said. 'Nobody fire, except the designated marksmen. Jayanti wants us to waste our ammunition.'

'You fired, sir.' Thorpe sounded indignant.

'I did,' Jack admitted.

Two of the prisoners had stopped struggling and were motionless at the end of their ropes, with the third still kicking. Even as Jack watched, the white-clad men dragged another three British soldiers forward.

'Sir!' Thorpe pleaded, 'can we fire now?'

'Fire be buggered,' Logan said. 'We should charge forward and free the poor buggers.'

Jayanti's strategy is working. My men are unsettled. 'You lads facing the gallows,' he said, 'fire, only if you have a clear target. Don't waste ammunition. The others sit still and face your front. The pandies could be using these murders as a distraction.'

Thorpe was first to fire, with Logan a moment afterwards. Jack nodded when he saw one of the white-clad men crumple. At least the executioners were paying a hefty price.

'Sir!' O'Neill called. 'Flag of truce!'

The enemy's firing ended as Jayanti stepped forward under the white flag.

'What does that woman want now?' Jack wondered. Again, he handed his revolver to Elliot, checked his sword was secure and walked forward onto the *maidan*.

'Well, captain,' Jayanti gestured to the gallows and the three dead men, 'you can see that we were not bluffing.'

'You are a murdering blackguard,' Jack told her.

'Your General Neil regularly hanged his prisoners.'

'The penalty for mutiny and treason is death.' Jack was in no mood for games.

'Fighting against foreign oppression is not treason,' Jayanti said.

'I am no foreigner.' Jack realised that Jayanti was drawing him into another discussion. 'Why do you walk under a flag of truce? Are you going to surrender?'

'Look.' Jayanti stepped aside to reveal the identity of the three British prisoners. Two were stony-faced privates that Jack didn't know. The third was Major Snodgrass, the commander of Number One Company.

For an instant, Jack met Snodgrass's gaze and then he looked away. As an officer, he should think that the life of Major Snodgrass was worth more than two anonymous privates. As a human being, and a man who had spent much of his career with the ordinary infantrymen of the 113th, he no longer believed that was true. Every single man of the regiment mattered as much as any other, no matter what the rank. *Besides, I don't like Snodgrass.*

'Windrush!' Major Snodgrass shouted. 'For God's sake, get us free!'

'Now will you agree on the exchange?' Jayanti asked. 'I guarantee you safe passage and the lives of these men. In return, all you have to do is surrender your Pathan and the treasure, which we will gain in time anyway.'

'Come and get them,' Jack said. 'If you dare.'

'Windrush!' Snodgrass shouted. 'I order you to free us! Hand over the damned Pathan and the gold.'

'We already are coming, and we already are daring,' Jayanti said and laughed when firing broke out at the temple. 'You see?'

Jack swivelled around. 'You treacherous hussy!' Jayanti had used the flag of truce to distract the defenders' attention and then launched an attack. Drawing his sword, Jack pounced forward, to see Jayanti withdrawing, with a dozen of her warriors running towards him. He hesitated for a moment, calculated the odds and ran back to the British positions.

The enemy had attacked three fronts at once, crawling through the long grass to the original British front line and then charging forward. Elliot must have been alert, for the defenders were firing regular volleys. Jack swore as a group of sepoys in the battered scarlet tunics of a Bengal Native Infantry regiment ran to cut him off. Jack glanced behind him, where Jayanti's warriors had spread out; there was no escape in that direction.

'Don't shoot the captain!' Jack heard O'Neill's roar through the clamour of battle.

'Fire away, lads!' Jack shouted. 'Shoot the bastards flat!'

The mutineers were closing, rifles levelled and bayonets glittering. Jack dodged right and left as if on the football field, slashed with his sword, missed, and ran on. A mutineer appeared in front of him, presented his bayonet and collapsed as a bullet crashed into his back. Jack ran on, jinking, and slashing with his sword whenever anybody came close.

He reached the old British outer perimeter, parried the wild swing of a tulwar, thrust his sword into the arm of a careless mutineer, withdrew, ducked a clumsy spear, dodged left and ran.

'Don't shoot! It's the captain!'

Jack leapt over the outer wall and landed inside a rifle-pit where Logan was firing and swearing with equal skill.

'Glad you could make it, sir,' Logan said.

'Thank you, Logan.' Jack looked around. The enemy was pressing the flanks harder than in front or rear. 'Number yourselves!' He waited until the men had intoned their numbers, one to twenty-four. *So few!* 'Every third man on the front move to the right flank, every third man on the rear move to the left flank.'

The reinforcements wouldn't add much firepower, but every bullet counted.

'Elliot! Revolver!' He caught it by the belt and buckled it around his waist.

'Here they come!' That was O'Neill's roar.

The attack came heaviest on the right flank, a mixed horde of men, some in near-mediaeval uniforms with steel helmets and chain breastplates, others wearing loin-cloths and carrying spears, a few with white clothes and wicked tulwars. They came at a rush and hesitated before the disciplined fire of the 113th.

'These are not soldiers,' O'Neill said. 'Most aren't even warriors. They don't know how to fight.' He shot a tall man with a red turban. 'Look at that poor fellow, he just stood there waving his spear.'

'Don't complain, sergeant,' Jack said. 'Shoot and keep shooting until they run.'

'Left flank!' Elliot shouted. 'They're on the left flank!'

Jack swivelled. While he'd been concentrating on the right flank, the real attack had developed on the left. The enemy came in two columns, one composed of Jayanti's women, trotting forward with musket and sword, and the other comprising a company of sepoys, still wearing their scarlet uniforms and fighting under their regimental colours.

'Another feint, by God,' Jack said. 'Jayanti's good, I'll grant her that. She's very good.'

'Fire!' Elliot ordered. The Enfields crashed out, knocking down half a dozen of the attackers, but they were Company-trained soldiers and dedicated warriors, rather than the unhappy peasants on the right flank. Ignoring their losses, they pushed on and clashed with the defenders, sword to rifle butt and bayonet to bayonet.

Jack saw Elliot shoot one of the sepoys; he saw two women hack down a private and neatly cut off his head, he saw a havildar heft his regimental colours and lead a section of three sepoys onto the parapet. By sheer force and pressure of numbers, the attackers drove the 113th back, fighting, swearing and stabbing.

'They've broken through!' Jack shouted. 'Form a square!'

It was the last line of defence, the solid British square that had withstood the test of time. The surviving men of the 113th formed around Jack; panting, bleeding, cursing but still fighting, still soldiers.

There is no retreat from here, and no hope of relief.

Jack looked around. Mary stood at the entrance to the carved chamber. He wanted her with him.

'Mary!' he roared. 'Come into the square!'

Mary shook her head. She replied, but Jack couldn't hear her words above the clamour of the battle.

'Damn you, woman, come here, it's safer inside the square!'

Mary shook her head slowly and lifted a hand in farewell before she returned to her patients. Jack swore. *Damn the woman and her sense of duty. Does she not know that the pandies will rape and kill her? Yes,* he told himself, *yes, she knows that only too well, just as she knows the wounded will feel better with her there.*

At that instant, Jack admitted what he had long known. *Damn you, Mary Lambert, I love you.*

Then there was no time to think of Mary. There was only the enemy, the crash of rifles and slash and thrust of bayonets and swords. The pressure of numbers forced back the right of the square until the 113th stood in a clump, fighting with all their strength.

'Well, Jack, it looks like this is it.' Elliot had a cheroot in his mouth. He dropped his revolver and drew his sword. 'It's been a pleasure to serve with you.'

'And with you, Arthur.' Jack spared him a smile. 'Your father will be proud of you.'

'Fucking kill the pandy bastards!' Logan interrupted their brief conversation.

'Logan has the rights of it,' Jack said. 'Come on, Elliot! Come on, 113th! One last effort!'

Perhaps the enemy heard Jack's words for they seemed to hesitate. The mob at the right flank pulled back, some dropped their weapons, and they began to drift away. The mutineers stepped back to straighten their ranks, with havildars and naiks shouting hoarse orders.

'What are they doing now?' Jack began. 'Never mind. Reform the square lads! Load and cap. Take any ammunition you can from the casualties. The rebels have given us a breathing space.' *We have a few more moments to live. Run, Mary, run and live your life.*

The ground was damp and slippery with blood, littered with dead and dying men and women. Jack crouched beside a young wounded private. 'Hold on, Preston. This battle will all be over soon, and we'll get you all sorted out.'

'Did we win, sir? Did we lick them?'

Jack looked at the odds against them. There were nineteen of his men still on their feet, and around fifty sepoys, plus forty or so of Jayanti's women warriors. Even without the armed rabble, the enemy still vastly outnumbered them. 'Not yet Preston, but we will.'

'That's good sir. We fought well, didn't we? The 113th fought well.'

'We fought like heroes, Preston. Now you lie quiet and let us finish this off. Close your eyes and think of home.'

'Sir! Look!' Bleeding from a gash across his face,' O'Neill pointed to the *maidan.*

'Oh, dear Lord!' Jack said.

A fresh army was marching toward the temple. Hundreds strong, there were scarlet-coated soldiers with Brown Bess muskets over their shoulders, led by men on horseback with yellow uniforms and ornate turbans. Their column stretched as far into the jungle as Jack could see, with a band carrying Indian musical instruments.

'That's the Rajah of Gondabad's army.' Jack recognised Baird at their head. 'The Rajah must have made his decision to join the rebels.' He balanced his sabre across his right shoulder. *I've failed. I failed to capture or kill Jayanti. I failed to save Snodgrass and his men, and I failed to turn the Rajah to support the British. Here I stand, Jack Baird Windrush, grandson of a traitor, bastard half-breed, rejected by my family and an officer who has led his men to defeat and massacre. It ends here at the ruined Hindu temple where my parents created me. I've travelled full circle.*

'We could surrender,' thin-faced Private Smith said.

'Bugger that.' Logan spat on the ground. 'We're the 113th, not some bloody Hyde Park Strollers.' He raised his voice. 'We're the 113th! Come and get us, you bastards!'

'Cry Havelock!' Coleman shouted.

'Let loose the dogs of war!' the 113th chorused.

Jack straightened his back. He may be a failure, but he led men. These were his men, and he would be proud to die alongside them. *How about Mary?*

'Sir!' O'Neill spoke softly. 'Look.'

The Rajah of Gondabad's army had formed into three long columns and was advancing toward the temple with slow, measured steps.

'Here they come, boys,' Jack said softly. 'Everybody take their position. How much ammunition do we have left?'

'Seven rounds a man, sir,' O'Neill said, 'and then it's bayonets and belt-buckles.'

'Don't waste ammunition.' Jack looked for Jayanti and the warrior with the ruby ring. He hoped he could kill them before he died himself. That was his final ambition. *Look after yourself Mary; please look after yourself.*

'Come on, you bastards!' Logan yelled. '113th!'

The Rajah's band began to play, with the music strange to Jack's ears. He frowned as the tune altered. 'What's that they're playing?'

'It's *Rule Britannia*,' Elliot said. 'Or it's meant to be.'

'The cheeky bastards!' O'Neill sounded more surprised than angry. 'Play your own tunes!'

'They are, sergeant,' MacKinnon said. 'They're not joining the pandies.'

'Sweet Lord,' Elliot pointed. 'Would you look at that?' The Rajah's army unfurled two flags. One was the Rajah's standard, and the other was the Union Flag.

'They've joined us,' Jack said. 'The Rajah of Gondabad has joined the British side.'

On sight of the British flag, the mutineers had begun an orderly, if rapid withdrawal. Jayanti's warriors lingered longer before they trotted away toward the jungle.

'After them!' Jack made rapid decisions. 'I want Jayanti dead! Elliot, try and find the prisoners, find our men!' In that few moments, the entire situation had altered. Jack led his 113th out of their positions to chase after the retreating enemy. Diplomacy dictated that he should wait to greet the Commander-sahib of the Rajah's army, but Jack had never considered himself a diplomat. Keeping his eye on Jayanti, he chased after her, leaping over dead bodies and ignoring everybody else in his pursuit.

'Jayanti!' he yelled. 'Stand and fight me, you murdering witch!'

When the warrior women reached the edge of the jungle, Jayanti paused, turned and raised her sword in salute.

'This battle is over, Captain Windrush. The war will continue.' Turning, she ran light-footed into the trees.

'Stand and fight!' Jack roared, knowing he wouldn't catch her in the jungle. *I've still failed. Jayanti will escape and return to cause more trouble and murder more British soldiers.* He saw the bullet catch Jayanti high in the thigh. She spun around, grabbing at her leg, and the second bullet smacked into her chest. Jayanti lifted her tulwar, glared at Jack and jerked backwards as a third bullet took off the top of her head.

Ensign Peake held his revolver in slack fingers and stared at the body. 'I killed her,' he said. 'I killed that woman.'

'You did,' Jack said. 'And you were right to kill her.'

'I killed a woman.' Peake dropped his revolver. 'Oh, what will happen to me?'

Jack stopped for a moment as the battle continued around them. 'It's all right, ensign. The first is always the worst.' He patted the boy's shoulder. 'You'll never forget it, but the memory will fade.'

As Peake began to cry, another voice sounded, educated, calm and feminine.

'I will fight you.'

'What?' Jack looked up. The woman stared at him with her black turban low over her forehead, and the veil pulled up until it touched her nose. Jack saw the gleam of the ruby ring.

'You!'

'Me.' The woman drew her tulwar. Sunlight glittered on the emerald in the pommel. No ordinary warrior could afford a weapon of that quality. *Who are you? I saw you give orders to Jayanti. Who are you?*

'If you surrender,' Jack said. 'I will guarantee you a fair trial.' *I hope you fight. I haven't forgotten Ensign Green.*

In response, the woman ran at him, swinging her tulwar like an amateur. Jack easily fended off the blow and cut backhanded, until the blade of his sabre tangled in the woman's loose clothing.

Unspeaking, the woman attacked again, her tulwar a blur of steel as she pressed Jack back.

'We may have lost this battle,' the woman said, 'but I will kill you, Captain Windrush.' She clashed her tulwar against Jack's sabre, scraped down the blade and twisted. Jack gasped as his blade snapped. Throwing the handle at her, he dodged backwards, reaching for his revolver. As he dragged it free, the woman thrust at him, with the point of her sword nicking the top of his thigh.

Jack swore at the pain and fired without aiming. He missed, and the woman advanced again.

'You will die slowly, captain, a screaming eunuch, like your ensign friend.'

Jack fired a second time, missed again and threw the revolver. The woman advanced, circling her blade, taunting as Jack backed away.

'Let me fight her, Captain Windrush.' Batoor stepped from between the trees. He was smiling as he drew his Khyber knife.

For a moment, the woman and Batoor spoke in Pushtu. Their voices rose and then they fought. Jack had never seen such fury or such skill. He knew that he wasn't a swordsman and watched as two experts traded blows, parrying, thrusting and swinging with a force that had both reeling.

Batoor parried one of the woman's swings and kicked her full in the stomach. She fell, shouted something and threw her sword. It missed Batoor by a yard and clattered uselessly on the ground. Jack lifted it and stepped forward.

'I promised this woman a fair trial,' he said.

'I made no such promise,' Batoor said, and thrust his Khyber knife into the woman's belly, slowly twisting as she writhed in pain.

'Batoor!' Jack tried to push the Pathan away.

'Leave us, Captain Windrush. This woman sent Jayanti to murder my wife and child.' Batoor twisted his blade, easing it slowly down her belly.

The woman died in front of Jack's eyes.

'That was murder,' Jack said.

'That was *Pashtunwali.*' Batoor flicked off the woman's veil. The Rani of Gondabad stared sightlessly upward. 'This is the Rani.'

Jack took a deep breath. 'I thought I saw her giving orders to Jayanti.' He looked up. 'Now tell me why you two hated each other?'

'We were lovers once,' Batoor said, 'when I was the captain of her bodyguard. Then she found out I was married and sent Jayanti and her warriors to kill my wife and my family.' He faced Jack. 'Did you think that the British are the only power in India? Many things happen without your knowledge, Captain Windrush.'

Jack looked at the twisted body of the Rani. 'The Rajah won't like you killing his wife.'

'The Rani has controlled the Rajah for years,' Batoor said. 'She supported the mutineers while the Rajah thought the British would win. Now she is dead; he is free to make up his own mind, so he will do the opposite of what she wanted.'

'I see,' Jack said. 'What a tangled country this is.'

Batoor smiled and wiped his blade on the Rani's clothes. 'Good-bye, Captain Windrush,' he said. 'We have completed our agreement.'

'We have not,' Jack said. 'I owe you a horse.'

'You can pay me if we meet again,' Batoor said, 'either as friends or enemies.'

'Hopefully in friendship,' Jack said. 'I would not like you as an enemy.' He picked up the Rani's tulwar and thrust it through his belt. When he looked up, Batoor was already walking into the jungle. *Now I'd better find the Commander-sahib.*

Baird was sitting on a gleaming brown horse, calmly directing his men to scour the jungle for Jayanti's black-turbans and the remnants of the mutineers. 'Ah, Jack, my boy.' Baird looked down at him. 'I believe we have something to pick up for the Rajah.'

'It's good to see you, commander,' Jack said, 'and I believe you are correct, in exchange for a couple of hostages.'

'Your Lieutenant Elliot rescued the British prisoners,' Baird spoke casually. 'And now that we're on the same side, you may wish to know that I know of another military position opening soon.'

'Is that right, sir?' Jack was still trying to recover from the strain of the battle.

'I'll come and talk to you when the dust settles,' Baird said. 'Now, where is the tribute for my Rajah?'

Chapter Twenty-Five

Gondabad, January 1859

The notes of the bugle faded as the 113th settled down for the night in their cantonments at Gondabad. Jack sat in a corner of the Officers' Mess, enjoying the noise and bustle of peace. Glancing out the window, Jack saw the tall bamboos casting shade over a patch of grass while half a dozen *ayas* looked after the regiment's children. Charlotte Riley was in the midst of the *ayas*, laughing as she lifted a small boy in a sailor suit.

God is in his Heaven; Queen Victoria is on her throne and peace, thank the Lord, has returned to India. Jack looked up when the door opened, and Elliot limped in, favouring his recently-healed leg and with a romantic scar on his left temple.

'Congratulations, Captain Elliot.' Jack held out his hand. 'Not that you deserve promotion, of course. Imagine you, gazetted captain for your services throughout the campaign! Well done.'

'There's more.' Elliot looked embarrassed. 'They're talking of giving me the Victoria Cross as well.'

Jack shook his head. 'They hand those out to anybody, nowadays.' He smiled. 'Nobody deserves it more, Arthur.'

'It's not right, Jack. You led us, you found Jayanti, and you convinced the Rajah to support the British.'

Jack asked a servant for a whisky and sank into one of the cane chairs. 'You held the temple, Arthur, and you rescued the prisoners.'

Elliot shook his head. 'I didn't *have* to rescue them; they were running loose. It's not right.'

Jack grinned. 'It *is* right. Besides, our new colonel doesn't like me much.'

'Our new colonel doesn't like you at all,' Elliot said. 'Here he is now. Mind your manners, Jack.'

Colonel Snodgrass stepped through the doorway and surveyed his kingdom. Still gaunt from his long captivity, he was greyer of hair and whiskers than he had been, and even shorter of temper. He snapped his fingers for brandy and stalked to his favourite seat, with the servants scurrying to avoid him and the officers stepping out of his way.

'I have to ask him,' Jack said. 'He won't like it.'

'Don't do it, Jack,' Elliot said quietly. 'You'll ruin your career. You'll never get your step, and you'll remain a captain forever.'

Jack sipped at his whisky. 'This Ferintosh is better than the kill-me-deadly you forced me to drink.'

'Don't do it, Jack,' Elliot repeated. 'You'll alienate yourself and lose all your friends in the regiment.'

'Did your Highland colleagues distil that stuff from dead elephants?' Jack took a final drink before rising. *Do I need Scotch courage? Or am I only putting off the evil moment?* Jack shrugged. He and Snodgrass had never been the best of friends.

'May I have a word please, colonel?'

'If you must.' Colonel Snodgrass gave a curt nod.

'I have a request to make.'

'What is it, Windrush?'

'I wish to get married.'

'Who is the woman?' Snodgrass didn't smile. 'Is she suitable?'

'Mary Lambert,' Jack said. 'Her father was an officer in the Company's service.'

'And her mother?'

'A native of India.'

'You may marry her if you wish,' Snodgrass said. 'And then you may leave my regiment. There is no place for half-castes in the 113th.'

Jack imagined his fist landing on Snodgrass's jaw. He could see the colonel rising from the chair and landing on the floor. He could also envisage the resulting court martial that would cashier him and leave him penniless and unemployed. He would be unable to provide for himself, let alone anybody else. Punching the colonel would grant instant satisfaction and long-term misery. It wouldn't help Mary in the slightest.

'No, sir. We only have a place for officers who surrender themselves and all their men.' Jack gave a little bow as a sudden hush descended on the mess. 'You will have my resignation in writing within the hour.' He could feel the tension and hear the shuffle as nearly every officer present moved further away from him. He'd expected such a reaction from men who were desperate to enhance the reputation of the regiment and advance up the career ladder.

'Captain Windrush,' Elliot's voice was loud in the subdued Mess. 'I hope I may have the honour of acting as your best man.'

Although Elliot had been at his side through a score of battles and skirmishes, Jack had never appreciated his friendship more than at that moment. 'The honour would be mine, Captain Elliot.'

Thank you, Arthur. I hope your loyalty has not damaged your career.

Jack paced to his bungalow and nodded to the bored watchman at the door. 'Do I have a visitor?'

'Yes, sahib.'

Pushing open the outer door, Jack walked into his front room. 'Good evening, Grandfather.' He poured them both a drink.

'How did the good colonel react?' Baird was lounging on Jack's chair.

'Predictably.' Jack balanced on the table. 'I hope I'm doing the right thing here.'

'You had a choice,' Baird said. 'You can remain in the 113th under Colonel Snodgrass and try and keep friendly with Mary Lambert as long as you are in India, or you can marry the blasted woman and leave the regiment.'

'I have chosen the latter course.'

'Women can do that to you.' Baird was smiling. 'That's how your mother came about.' His chuckle could have come from a man forty years younger. He held out his glass for a refill and smiled when Jack obliged. 'And I don't regret it in the slightest.'

'I'll miss the 113th,' Jack admitted. He liked his grandfather, although he recognised that he was a rogue. 'I'll miss the men.' He thought of Riley and Coleman, Thorpe and O'Neill, even the murderous Logan. Most of all he thought of Arthur Elliot.

'You could be too busy to even think of them,' Baird said. 'Our mutual friend can be very demanding.'

'How do you know him?'

'He contacted me,' Baird admitted. 'We discussed you.'

'Did you indeed?'

'We did,' the voice came from the outer door as Colonel Hook walked in. 'I am glad you chose to join me, Windrush. We have much work to do.'

'Yes, sir.' Jack knew that his world was about to change again. He smiled as Mary stepped into the room. Whatever happened, he knew he would never be alone, not with Mary beside him.

I have made my choice and have no regrets.

'Where are you sending me, sir?

'To the furthest side of the world, Windrush.' Hook said.

Dear reader,

We hope you enjoyed reading *Windrush: Jayanti's Pawns*. Please take a moment to leave a review, even if it's a short one. Your opinion is important to us.

Discover more books by Malcolm Archibald at

https://www.nextchapter.pub/authors/malcolm-archibald

Want to know when one of our books is free or discounted? Join the newsletter at http://eepurl.com/bqqB3H

Best regards,

Malcolm Archibald and the Next Chapter Team

Historical Note

The Indian Mutiny was arguably the most bitter of the British 19th-century colonial campaigns. Although the fighting spluttered on into 1859, the Mutiny effectively finished in 1858. The days of the Honourable East India Company ended, and those of the British Raj began as the Crown took control of India. The old Company armies merged into a new Indian Army, with the so-called 'martial races' as its backbone, with Sikhs and Gurkhas dominant and justly famed as fighting men.

The Mutiny left some British paranoid about the possibility of further outbreaks, with warnings to incoming officers to maintain their vigilance. The British never found Nana Sahib, although expeditions sought him and rumours and speculation abounded.

British rule survived another ninety years and two world wars, finally ending with the independence of India, Pakistan, Burma and Ceylon in 1947. Historians disagree about the events of 1857-58, and the real causes of the war. Nobody can disagree that all sides fought with incredible bravery.

In Britain, people have largely forgotten the generals and men who fought in that war and the battles of Lucknow, Cawnpore, Delhi and all the rest are barely known. Indian historians often brand the conflict as the First War of Independence and portray it as a national uprising against British rule. History rolls on; attitudes alter, what one generation accepts as a fact, the next will scorn. Jack Windrush, Arthur Elliot, Mary Lambert, Riley, Logan, Thorpe and all their colleagues lived within their own timeframe, with the attitudes and perceptions of the mid-nineteenth century. Their lives and adventures continued.

Malcolm Archibald

About the Author

Born and raised in Edinburgh, the sternly-romantic capital of Scotland, I grew up with a father and other male relatives imbued with the military, a Jacobite grandmother who collected books and ran her own business and a grandfather from the legend-crammed island of Arran. With such varied geographical and emotional influences, it was natural that I should write.

Educated in Edinburgh and Dundee, I began to write fiction and non-fiction. Now living in the north of Scotland, I still write.

Malcolm Archibald

he story continues in:

Windrush: Warriors of God

To read the first chapter for free, please head to:
https://www.nextchapter.pub/books/windrush-warriors-of-god

Windrush: Jayanti's Pawns
ISBN: 978-4-86745-648-4

Published by
Next Chapter
1-60-20 Minami-Otsuka
170-0005 Toshima-Ku, Tokyo
+818035793528
7th May 2021